ERA SINISTRA

SKYGLOW

ERA SINISTRA

SKYGLOW

BRAD MATHEWS

Unity Star Books

ISBN: 978-1-962577-02-1 (Softcover)

ISBM: 978-1-962577-03-8 (Ebook)

Re-release Second Edition 2023

In this era of division and censorship, may it be comforting to have an ally.
You do not stand alone.

"An eye for an eye will only make the whole world blind."

Mahatma Ghandi

1
Reflection

THE tiny city lights spread across the horizon in clusters like a galaxy—never uniform, but hardly random. The cross shimmered like a white, fluorescent halo, painting the sagebrush bluffs with a sort of luminescent illusion that somehow brimmed with color while still allowing everything to be viewed in steady shades of black and white. The lights bristled and beamed from their homes, combining their energy into a dome of orange haze over the city. It was ominous yet presented a stunning beauty that Taleah had rarely enjoyed.

It was only a short trip, she'd told Christine—a change of pace would do her well and charge those demons of seven years ago with a jolt of energy that could scarcely be contained. But for that to work, she had to be alone. No television, no movies, no technology. Just Taleah and her mind.

Seven years seemed a long time when viewed from the present going forward, yet it had flashed by with stunning impatience now that she looked back on it. Those days and nights in the cave and tied to a tree altered her perception of the present. Reliving the horror was something she avoided at all costs yet proved oddly necessary in order to corral the present.

The darkness in Art's eyes had produced charcoal and dark flame that seared into her heart. Fear became torture, and torture, in turn had morphed into a kind of resolve that Taleah could never understand. Even now, he taunted her from beyond the grave. She could still feel his grizzly beard against the back of her neck, the somber dissonance in his voice, and the utter emptiness where his soul should have rested.

Taleah allowed her eyes to roam the horizon from where the lake should have been to the stacks of organized white and yellow squares in the luminous downtown area. From Table Rock, it seemed peaceful, well-intentioned, and structured—just the way she liked it. But, as with personalities, perception from afar often starkly contrasted against the reality within.

Somewhere, behind one of those lighted windows sprawled her desk, where stacks of copies, both old and new had decorated her workspace as if she were a seasoned veteran. The job was hardly something she had dreamed about, but she had accepted it as a steppingstone. With enough hard work and determination, she could make the jump to copy writer and eventually to reporter, where instead of trying to deconstruct another woman's notes and mold them into a story, she could set the narrative herself by making the notes. But she had to be good, and for now she was only learning the ropes. Jalene set an example and showed her work. She was the kind of mentor one could trust, but also exuded a warning not to cross her. Jalene didn't actively pursue courtesy when doling out criticism; her rebukes were sharp and stung like the venom of a hornet. After all, critique always had purpose, and spinning that into her desire to advance did wonders.

In another building, just two miles away, another, softer light filtered out from the window. Behind it, a beautiful woman reclined on a comfortable sofa and buried her face in a book. A sudden twinge brought her to the realization that she needed to get home. After too long, Christine would grow worried, place the book face down and attempt to call her. "Maybe could you pick up a bag of lettuce on the way home?" she could hear her asking.

Still, some magnetic quality kept her glued to this one spot. Two cars had come and gone. A trio of drunken hikers threw rocks from the cliff and laughed. Taleah attempted to filter it all out. Men could be such asses. And they didn't know it, because no one ever told them, and even if they did, men's other intrinsic quality kicked in for the defense. The strategy was as old as Adam and Eve. She did it, too. *Everyone's an ass.*

Perhaps the shadow had taught her that debilitating lesson, but it could only cut off her progress if she refused to use it to empower herself. It was what her mother had told her and what her counselor had told her was true. It built an empire of emptiness within her in those days, before she had reached to climb out of the abyss. After Art, she never talked to Tommy again. She dated another boy, but it could never work, because something had risen in her heart to prevent it, something that chained her down until she was willing to see what was causing it. The realization had tumbled down on her like a thousand books, she'd thought, and the weight would surely suffocate her if she let it. But then she began to read one of the books, and then another. After all, the weight wasn't so bad when it came with another benefit.

For years, she assumed that this new thing inside her was awful and should be shunned. If you push it away, it will go away, eventually, she'd heard someone say. *Oh come on, honey! No you're not. You're not that. There will be...*

But she was. And denying it meant extinguishing a part of her soul that ignited her own heart. If life didn't divert into chaos with every step and the if her heart were composed of crystal rather than strings of yarn, then perhaps she could cling to some 'normalcy.' Her father had understood the concept well enough, but still protested.

Then there was Christine. Taleah's heart leapt at the thought of her. She gazed at the horizon, rested her head against the seat rest, and let a surge of agony course through her. The hikers cussed up a storm, cracked open more beers, and began hurling insults at one another. She closed her eyes briefly and attempted to drown them out before refocusing. Below, the city lights played a delicate symphony for her spirit. At once meek and submissive, it built into a coda of strength and power. Down there, darkness of a different kind dwelt with the lights and the people and the parties. Overlooking those flaws became easier from afar, where she could appreciate the beauty of the whole, and from this perspective, it glittered with passionate energy.

"Oh my God, you're such a moron!"

"Yeah, you're about to get alcohol poisoning," another hiker warned.

"No shit! Better than spending another night with that bitch. She's probably balling up her socks now, stuffing them in a goddamn pillowcase."

"What, Jim? Problems in your personal life? Or just blitzed out of your fucking mind?"

"Go to hell, bastard," Jim sneered. "Jump off a cliff."

"How are you going to get home?"

Jim paused and Taleah adjusted in her seat and clenched her thighs, attempting to tune out the banter. She'd better get going before the hikers caused trouble. She spun the keys in the ignition and listened to the old motor sputter to life. Not too long, probably, before it bit the dust and she'd have to pony up too much for another rusted chunk of metal on its last proverbial legs. But maybe this time Christine would help her through the purchasing process, thereby ensuring she could buy a car that would last a year or two.

"Just hitch a ride with that belle," Jim shouted. She couldn't see him, but she imagined his eyes digging into the back of her skull like dull mixer blades. Putting the car into reverse carefully, she craned her neck to check behind her and found that the drunk man was sitting ten feet behind her car with his legs crossed and his palms in the gravel. Taleah bit her lip and pumped the horn.

"Get off the ground, jackass!" called a woman from about twenty feet to Taleah's right.

"Come on, dude," one of the friends said, stepping toward him.

Taleah flung the car into park and cursed, as adrenaline began to stain her heart with a kind of iridescent stripe like oil on water.

"Yeah, little girl. Maybe you should call daddy like a little goodie two-shoes broad. Or your boyfriend, if you could get one desperate enough to—"

"Jim, shut the fuck up!"

"Yeah, daddy knows best. What's his name? I think I know him. Hangs out with that homo with the bumper stickers? Rupert?"

Taleah clenched her fist and pushed a tear off her cheek while her nerves began to flicker and tremble like infant candles in a chilly breeze. The adrenaline swamped her. She pushed the car into reverse once again, and without looking, began to inch backward toward him. If he didn't move, it would be his fault.

"Just call the cops," said a man sitting in the back of his pickup truck next to the girl who'd called Jim a jackass.

"Oh, I remember! Reggie."

Hearing a drunken idiot use her father's name so carelessly flooded her with the sort of venom that caused her foot to dig lower into the accelerator.

"Yeah, that son of a bitch went on a rampage in the woods and killed a guy. Saw it in the papers. And his precious little daughter. Oooh-whee, you know some like it hot. Come here, princess, I'll fix you up nice."

She released the accelerator and let the car coast to within inches of Jim's face. The scratchy roar of gravel suggested that she'd instinctively slammed the brakes while Jim's friends dragged him away, cursing.

Tears rolled down her cheeks as her heart raced.

"You better get home," the girl in the back of the pickup truck yelled.

Taleah nodded and pulled backward until she could swing her car out of the spot beneath the glow of the cross. Before she could catch her breath, she punched the gas. Spitting up a cloud of dust and rocks, the tires powered her toward the sharp bends leading down into the city.

The cross glistened behind her as she drove, pulsing like a heart in overdrive, as if to warn the masses below of impending disaster. Such ugliness in a place of such beauty, she thought, was either a sign of the times or a reminder of the wickedness many people had succumbed to. *It won't get to me,* she promised herself, but the sentiment was in vain, because Jim had already poisoned her heart. Forgetting that wouldn't be easy, but what if it meant more than just a hammered moron? What if Jim really did know her father? What if Jim...

"No, that's nonsense," she grated.

Memory flickered through the back of her mind like a black and white rerun from better times. Taleah had combed a hand through her sleek blonde hair and pushed the batter's helmet over her hat. A smile glided across her lips as she pointed toward the outfield fence. Behind her, her father cheered, while Willis attempted to remain neutral.

Come on, Taleah, knock this one out of the park!

It was her last softball game before life unraveled. Before the nightmare and the monster who called himself Art. Before the self-loathing and the unending bouts of post-traumatic stress gouged craters in what remained of her heart, and before she hastily reassembled the pieces into something resembling a whole. By the time she started college, she had cut her hair short, attempted to forget, and eventually fell hard for Christine.

She could picture her waiting there on the couch in her pajamas when she walked in, attempting to hide her tears. But Christine possessed a sort of sixth sense. She'd pull herself up off the couch, offer a warm embrace and gently stroke her fingers through Taleah's hair.

And then maybe tomorrow would be a different day and the anger and hatred could subside enough that she could spend another day editing print for next week's edition.

Still, the heat swarmed through her as she meandered through the foothills neighborhoods and stared as the city lights reappeared from behind trees and houses before vanishing once again. Still, their light remained. When she had descended from the hills to flat land, she glanced skyward back to Table Rock. The cross had hardly dimmed, it seemed, setting its symbol of light as a beacon for the weary travelers below. *Come to me, Taleah.*

Her father had told her every detail of his first encounter with Art, but she'd never listened enough to heed the story's implicit warning. Every time he'd uttered them, she knew of their significance to him, but to her they were only words.

A police cruiser flicked on its lights and began to ascend the hill, hopefully to escort Jim home safely, where with a sweet stroke of justice, his girlfriend, with her socks stuffed in a pillowcase, would storm out the door just one last time.

She grinned at the idea, which only wrought another wave of torment.

After rounding a turn in the street and joining into a broad boulevard, she dug her phone out of her pocket and dialed her father's number.

Three rings later, Rebekah answered. "Oh, hi Taleah! How's your job going?"

Rebekah always knew how to navigate difficult situations with grace. When she heard the stress in Taleah's voice, her tone dropped.

"Can I talk to my dad?"

"Yes, of course." As if she were cupping her palm over the phone, her voice became muffled as she called Reggie's name. "He'll be down in a minute. Is everything all right?"

"Yes," Taleah stammered. "Fine... well, really... I don't know."

"Girl troubles?"

Damnit! Why did people always jump to conclusions? Of course, Rebekah always meant well. She simply misunderstood her own compassion and how deep it could go. She'd never confronted Taleah with resentment or disapproval, but that didn't mean she could wield empathy for a lifestyle so foreign to her. Therefore, her attempts came out stale and loaded to the brim with false assumptions, which no amount of discussion could cure.

"What's up, sweetheart?" her father said.

"Nothing," she lied after swallowing.

"Taleah, it's after ten. You never call this late unless something is bothering you."

"Really," she said, allowing tears to once again spill onto her cheeks. She wiped them away and attempted to conceal her panic, which usually worked well enough over the phone. "It's just something stupid that happened tonight."

"Are you okay?"

"No, not really. I just had to get out and clear my head. You know I like to hike Table Rock, but I'm not about to do it at dark, so I drove. To get away and observe the city from a place of serenity and safety."

"I understand," he said.

"Do you?" She rolled her eyes and crossed into one of the straight lanes on the boulevard without looking over her shoulder. "It wasn't quiet. A group of hikers were swearing and drinking. One of them got so plastered he sort of harassed me."

"It was good of you to get out of there before the situation escalated. Were there other people around?"

"A few. His friend started to talk him down, but he tried to prevent me from backing out of my parking space. Which made me mad, so I started to back up anyway."

"Taleah. It's not easy to take abuse like that—"

"How can I turn the other cheek when he's taunting you?"

"Me?"

"He knows you. And Willis, I think. Or at least he thinks he does. It's just disgusting."

Her father hesitated, perhaps allowing himself time to gather his thoughts. "Did... did you catch his name?"

She bit her tongue and accelerated a little too hard after a car in front of her moved out of the way. "His friends called him Jim."

"I know a couple of Jims—actually, I'm sure everyone does—but neither of them are hikers and only one drinks. Maybe I shouldn't ask you what he said."

"He said... you went on a rampage in the mountains. He saw it in the paper. I know, that doesn't mean he knows you, but how would he remember your name, and Willis?"

"I'm sure there's nothing to worry about," he said. Taleah ruffled her hair and remembered Art's heavy fingers pulling her hair while he rasped about Reggie.

Almost as if he could sense what she was thinking, he smoothed and lowered his voice as he spoke. "He's dead, remember?"

"I know, but just the memories. God, I can't stand it." Her fingers began to tremble, and her voice wavered like wind chimes in a cold breeze.

"Listen, Taleah. You're stronger than you know. I don't know of many other people who, as teenagers, could go through what you did and still come out functioning, let alone sane."

"Right," she said, hardly believing her own words. "I came out all right. I came out *totally* all right. Cause and effect."

His breathing seemed to moderate, but his speech quickened, suggesting he knew how Taleah would react before she did. "Cause and effect doesn't have to mean your whole life is destroyed. Look how much you have to live for. And Christine? I know love, and that's it."

"Okay, dad. Now is a pretty good time, I guess, to pretend you're okay with it."

"It's not pretending."

She balled her fists and squinted in the glare of oncoming cars, adjusting her pressure on the gas pedal as her adrenaline started to return to normal. "Yeah, you're no good at that."

"Get some sleep," he said. "You have a busy day tomorrow and I can't wait to read the paper on Monday."

"You know I don't write the words."

"It's still a pleasure to see my daughter's work. That paper gets a bad rap sometimes, but I've yet to come across a typo since you've worked there."

"Come on, dad. I'm onto your tricks by now."

"Well, if they still work," he said, "then why quit?"

A weary smile flashed on her lips before being flushed away when a crazy driver tore past her in the wrong lane heading toward the freeway. "Good night, Dad. And tell Rebekah I said goodnight."

"Will do."

She hung up the phone and turned on the deserted street toward the apartment. Weariness struck her as she parked the car and peered up into the second-floor window, where the lamp bathed the beige walls in a yellow haze reminiscent of the city lights in the summer. At least Christine wasn't standing at the window waiting for her. Then again, maybe she'd fallen asleep reading like she sometimes did.

On a night like this, Taleah would tiptoe between the coffee table and the sofa and cover Christine's shoulder with a knitted blanket before traipsing off to bed, and that would make the scars heal better.

Taleah swallowed and got out of the car. Overhead, the light seemed to burn a hole in the sky, letting the cold sweep down out of the mountains. The stars were all invisible, drowned out by the pollution and the city lights and the clouds, but somehow, they winked at her as the sounds of the city faded.

2
Refraction

A towering plume of smoke and ash billowed over the miniscule town of New Meadows, about forty minutes by car from the slightly larger county seat of Council. High-altitude winds sheared the top of the column and stretched its contents westward over the Central Idaho wildlands.

Numerous fire-fighting vehicles clogged the nearest road access to the fire, which had already blackened thousands of acres of BLM and forest service land. Remote and helpless, the former Harrison ranch lay in the direct path of the flames. Having evacuated earlier in the morning, the family that ran the ranch benefitted from a day of light surface winds and high atmospheric pressure which slowed the advance of the conflagration. Bureau and volunteer fire crews had set up a base front along the road in an attempt to save the ranch, which occupied the windward slope of a gentle hill.

The smoke blocked out the sun in the immediate area, which had come to resemble a sort of hellscape. Stands of pine burst into towers of flame as the front approached. Helicopters whirled overhead, dropping large cargoes of orange fire retardant. The front line had moved steadily westward throughout the morning, but the wind suddenly picked up. The crew abandoned the line as the inferno raced toward them. The flames bulldozed through stands of timber, over a small earthen bunker, and entirely consumed the dwelling and the outbuilding in less than a half-hour. Undergrowth and canopy charred, the landscape would no longer resemble home to the family that operated the ranch.

With nature, however, new life always sprang forth from the ashes of destruction. The trees would take decades to grow back to maturity and the house could be reconstructed in under a year. But the memories could never be replaced, even if the halls were built precisely to the original plans.

Years before the family had moved in, an older couple ran the ranch, having inherited it from previous generations. The Harrisons put all they had into the land, before the monster invaded. Of course, Mr. Harrison had known Rassine, but Rassine had killed him and his wife, leaving the ranch to no one.

Its secrets had been revealed, but even finally disclosed, secrets often sprouted new mysteries. The FBI had collected all the evidence they needed—unearthed unspeakable tragedies of the human condition. But one large piece of the puzzle had remained. This early summer, the forces of nature reduced it to nothing but ash. With the destruction complete, the front moved on, leaving straggling flames to chew up the heavier, thicker timber.

A makeshift woodcarving shop, long forgotten and discarded, left behind a small pile of gemstones buried in the mud. One for each cardinal direction, the stones provided a vital clue into the inner workings of a deranged and isolated mind.

Rassine had truly never forgotten the ranch, even after death. After miscalculating the St. Clair family and Willis Ralston, Rassine suffered his final defeat, and the ranch could no longer be considered a crime scene. Now, the land itself had become a victim of an even greater crime, one that afflicted ranchers and backcountry farmers for decades and the severity of which increased every year.

The fire marched on, doubling its size. It left hillsides and ravines barren as its ravenous appetite annihilated hundreds of years' worth of growth, destroyed fences, and left families homeless. And even as Rassine had been considered part of nature, nature could not be stopped. The feeble attempts of man could only delay change.

THE tools of the trade were arranged in rows upon a felt blanket in the truck of the car, whose rear bore a hundred bumper stickers with clever slogans, hunting memorabilia, and souvenirs of adventures long past.

Reggie unfolded the tripod and marched to the origin point at the corner of the property. Willis followed, carrying a bag with other necessities and shouting something funny over the din of traffic.

"Never thought I'd be the one supporting big oil," he said.

"Well, the city," Reggie corrected. "They're the ones who signed on the dotted line, so maybe you should take it up with the mayor."

"No, it's okay," Willis said. "God, this dump is an eyesore. Neighbors are probably going to be thrilled with the prospect of tearing it all down."

Reggie chuckled and erected the tripod in a patch of weeds next to the uneven sidewalk. "You know what they say. Be careful what you wish for. In a few years, they're going to build a retail center on this site, you wait and see. What would you think of that?"

"Huh. Well, anything beats a run-down oil field, except maybe a junkyard." Willis counted his paces along the sidewalk until he reached an orange-painted piece of rebar that marked the start of a slight jog in the property line. After settling himself and setting the bag down, he gave Reggie a thumbs up and raised his voice. "And how in the hell do they plan on relocating this jungle without razing it?" That's gotta take a feat of engineering."

"Probably."

The city of Boise had called Reggie and Willis to privately survey the property before analyzing whether the eyesore could be relocated to a more industry-friendly area of the city, one not surrounded by hospitals, medical offices, and World-War-Two-era homes. This would theoretically open up the property for rezoning and construction of office and retail commercial, which would increase the tax base and prove more palatable for residents than a tank farm that was beginning to show its age.

With little fanfare, Reggie signed the contract and promised to have a complete surveying report to file within two weeks. The site contained dozens of giant oil and gas tanks, built at the terminus of Salk Lake's big oil pipelines, which supplied most of the gasoline to the valley. The tanks were built of stark white concrete and steel, some of which spanned more than a hundred feet in diameter and stood fifty feet tall. Down the block, the white towers of the Saint Margaret Hospital flourished in the sun, allowing the windows to shimmer.

At least today wouldn't be hot, Reggie surmised. Surveying was a mostly outdoors task and took hours of work to even get preliminary figures together.

Willis had unzipped the bag and withdrew a shorter tripod, atop which he affixed a laser beam receiver with a small LCD readout. Reggie watched him carefully while peering at his own screen, then motioned Willis to his left. "No, you're off. By at least a degree."

A single degree of error could result in shaving off hundreds of square feet of space, so precise measurements were critical. Willis offered a dry *humph* and moved his tripod about two feet to Reggie's right. "What about now?

"A little more, maybe six more inches... perfect."

Willis pressed a button and called out, "Shoot."

Reggie aimed the laser at Willis's tripod and shielded his eyes from the sun. "Got it?"

After shaking his head, Willis frowned and slumped his chin toward his chest, which most often indicated disgust and anger stemming from frustration. "Shoot."

"Shot," Reggie yelled.

"No, shoot. This piece of junk is malfunctioning again. I can have it repaired, but I'm afraid we won't get it back for more than a week. We want this thing done today, we'll have to get out the chains."

The chains were a relic of a bygone era in the surveying business. To Reggie's knowledge, no project had used chain-surveyed coordinates in at least twenty years. Lasers proved more efficient, more accurate, and required less time and budget for contractors. Surveying was one of those trades where technology had successfully reduced the cost of construction, even if labor costs were rising.

Reggie signaled for Willis to join him in walking back to the car and leave the tripod. Willis' trunk always sported a 'backup bag' filled with the old-school necessities of surveying, including chain and tape, a compass, and a level rod. The duffel was stocked with enough notepads and pencils to last a week in an elementary school, Reggie thought, which would be more than enough should it come in handy. Together, they examined the equipment to determine its usefulness.

"This isn't going to be as accurate as the EDM," Reggie said. "And the city is going to want precise measurements. I can use the GPS in my phone as a baseline, but everything will have to be adjusted when we get the original coordinates."

"How long have I been saying we need to spring for a Total Station?" Willis jabbed, referring to one of the most modern advancements in surveying technology, which was intended as a replacement for the EDM units.

Reggie chuckled. "If we can get regular contract work for the city and county, maybe we could afford it. But not without accuracy."

"Not my fault the readout kicked the bucket."

"Now that you mention it, I think I have an idea." Reggie suddenly changed course.

Willis issued a hearty laugh. "I think we both know how your ideas turn out. Last time you had a plan, you were getting your ass kicked and I bailed you out."

"Team effort," Reggie scoffed.

"Sure."

"My station works, but to get accurate measurements, we need to measure the light wave. So if we can set the level in my station and point it a mirror, it should be able to calibrate the distance."

"Don't think so," Willis said. "This system isn't set up like the old prism system. I think a mirror would just confuse it."

"Distance is a simple function. It should be accurate within a few millimeters over two hundred feet. We'll need to measure the angle, so if we point the laser at a flat surface, the surface will have to be small enough to cover any inaccuracies."

"And the altimeter doesn't need a second point," Willis said.

"Let's give it a try. Maybe we can start researching Total Stations soon."

The work took longer with each measurement, but the results proved satisfactory as far as Reggie was concerned. They made their way along the back of the property before deciding to call it a day. Reggie rested his foot on the bottom rung of a plank fence that marked the back end of the housing properties due east of the tank farm. The planks and posts had been painted red at least a decade ago and were beginning to show significant signs of weathering. The builder had made use of long slats of thin material to span the distance between three posts while bending around the center post. The result was surprisingly rigid, though the nails had begun to loosen over time. If and when the tank farm property was redeveloped, the contractor would likely replace the fence with a modern block wall at least ten feet high in order to block out excess light and noise for the neighbors.

Willis joined him in the moment of relaxation. "How's Taleah?"

"Well, she's..." Reggie considered the standard answer of 'she's fine, I'll tell her you said hi,' but a half-second delay caused him to change course mid-sentence. "Considering everything going on, adjusting well."

"Whoa," Willis said. "You haven't used a sentence that long to describe how someone is for a long time. Something's gotta be up."

Reggie sported a fake grin.

"Come on."

"You know, a funny thing happened last night. She's up at Table Rock alone and some drunk idiot starts taunting her, mentions you, and calls me a murderer, I assume over the debacle seven years ago."

"When I saved your ass," Willis finished for him. "That's hilarious."

"He mentioned you," Reggie repeated. "Some guy named Jim, do you know him?"

"I'll have to search my Rolodex," Willis joked. "Jim Jones, Jim Henson, Jim Varney...Jim Hendrix. There's a million Jims, and that's just in Idaho."

Reggie almost choked. "You don't have a Rolodex."

"Nobody does, but it makes you sound important when you say it."

"Last time you were into appearances around me was seven years ago at a softball game where you called Taleah out just to look unbiased."

Willis shook his head. "Lots of parents there that day. Parents are strange creatures when it comes to their kids when they compete. Suddenly they become interested in what's fair. You know what I'm talking about. I call too many balls on that pitcher, they could stuff my tailpipe with a potato or give me a dent."

"Not like either of them would actually hurt your car," Reggie said.

"So this Jim," Willis started, "Taleah know him?"

Reggie shook his head and stood up straight, eying a straight line between pairs of tanks that led to what appeared to be a central shut-off valve in the center of the property. If they could safely navigate that passage, they'd save time getting back to the car.

"Sounds like a real dude."

"You should know."

"Not anymore, my friend," Willis said, straightening his back and studying the passage between the tanks. "My wife would kill me if I acted that way."

Six years ago, the man who had made numerous jokes of innuendo related to marriage and the church, married a woman he met in church. Reggie found it humorous, if not ironic, but decided that everyone was due an opportunity for change. And it wasn't like Willis ever believed the jokes.

"How is ol' Melissa?"

"Oh, she's doing great," Willis said, cutting off his stare and sending a shard of seriousness his way. "Younger than you."

"Uh."

"And next time you say something like that, I'll punch you."

Reggie laughed and started walking toward the gap. "Taleah's pretty spooked, I guess. That drunk not-so subtly brought up memories of Art Rassine."

"Yeah," Willis said. "That son of a bitch." He followed Reggie a few steps and changed the subject. "By the way, did you see in the paper that there's a fire near New Meadows? Pretty close to the ranch."

"Not really. I only read the *Weekly* nowadays."

"I wonder why."

The hike between the tanks was unobstructed. A twinge of discomfort rose up in Reggie's stomach like a cobra's head poised to attack. Near the center of the property, a red, galvanized pipe penetrated above the ground and looped about ten feet before plunging below ground. The construction was fitted with a large bypass valve centered below a bigger valve between reducing fittings. The larger valve, attached to a flow sensing device with a massive electronic actuator to control the flow, had what appeared to be a nylon strap wrapped around it. Upon closer inspection, the strap belonged to a small duffel bag. The zipper, which had been undone a few inches, appeared to display a wire of some kind. Reggie swallowed and decided to steer clear of the valve.

"Maybe we should get out of here," Willis said.

"Yeah. Run."

They made it all of four steps before the concussion kicked in, accompanied by an ear-shattering boom. The pressure caused the flow control valve to burst and ignite. Flames shot upward fifty feet, creating an intense halo of heat, which baked the fresh wounds on their backs.

Willis rolled over in agony, moaning words that made no sense. Blood seeped through new wounds. With jolts of pain shredding both legs, Reggie struggled to his feet and helped Willis up.

"Gotta get to the car, before we burn," Reggie shouted.

Willis only moaned. Ambulances and fire trucks blared in the distance. Reggie limped hundreds of yards to the sidewalk, where Willis had parked the car in an unused driveway cut-out. Flames and smoke mushroomed higher overhead. The inferno cooked the valve, which was spraying what appeared to be liquid fire in every direction. If the fire reached the tanks, half of the neighborhood would lie in ruins within minutes. They could only wait for the real explosion, which stood a greater chance of killing them both than not, Reggie guessed.

The seconds seemed to stretch the moment to infinity. The fire trucks drove into the complex with ear-splitting sirens screaming. The ambulances wouldn't have to take them far, if they survived the blast. But through some miracle, the explosion never came. Numerous guesses as to why pumped through his mind. The flow control valve was situated between a pair of shut-off valves. That the entire assembly exploded meant that some gas flowed through the pipe. The actuator assembly might not have been independent and could have signaled other valves in the network to close, thereby restricting flow in and out of the tanks. Whoever had left the package had miscalculated two things, which had proved to be the difference between life and death.

Willis moaned in agony. Numerous pieces of shrapnel were embedded in his back and legs. Reggie seemed to have suffered less damage, just enough so that he could walk, while the crushing pain sent tears to his eyes. Survival meant more than the pain.

The paramedics aided them and quickly made for the hospital a few blocks away. A certainty of luck centered itself in Reggie's mind. The act was intentional, but Reggie doubted that there was a specific target. Boise had never coped with a terrorist attack. Reggie and Willis were simply in the wrong place at the wrong time.

3
Frequency

TALEAH'S eyelids sagged as she stared at the computer screen, working the afternoon into oblivion. Little had happened throughout the day, as two stories about human kindness and long-lasting relationships found their way into her inbox. When copy editing stories for which she could not summon interest, the subject matter blurred the lines between space and time, or between life and death, if she wished to exaggerate the dulling effect the stories had on her mind. At times like these, coffee would be the best medicine, but Christine had talked her into cutting back, as if to deny the existence of some forsaken monster deep inside her soul.

"How are Chen and Diane reacting to their time apart?" asked Jalene. Her voice sounded both cruel and hollow, as if devoid of nuance and meaning.

"Chen?"

"Yulan Chen, the immigrant and his wife of seventy years?"

Taleah tried not to roll her eyes. She leaned back in the chair and glanced up at her pallid face, wondering how long Jalene could distract her from monotony. "Didn't you write the story?"

Jalene straightened her back and turned her head slightly toward the screen, subtly prodding Taleah to share some of her concerns about the narrative. "I did. But I'm not perfect."

"Fooled me."

"Or have you tried to internalize that yet?"

"Well," Taleah said, arching her back and stretching her fingers across the keyboard. "I think we should emphasize his service in the war and the time leading up to those two years. Otherwise, it's just a happy story with little substance. I think it would be easier to invest in that way."

"That's a good point."

When her desk phone started to ring, she looked out the window into the small parking lot, which was shaded by a dense grove of cottonwoods along the river. Later in the summer, cotton would flutter down from the treetops onto the cars like fluffy snow, and if it rained or the sprinklers came on, the cotton would stick to the cars.

Jalene slinked away as Taleah picked up the phone and closed her eyes.

"Hi honey," the voice said.

"Mom? You never call me at work."

Anna let out a whisper that sounded like tempered anguish, but Taleah suppressed the desire to intervene. Instead, she rolled her chair away from the desk and stared out the window, where the leaves of the trees flickered and reflected sunlight in the breeze.

"I'm... I'm at the hospital."

"What's going on?"

"Your dad is hurt." Her mother's voice sounded as though it had been shoved through a grater—carefully reflexive, but unsettlingly calm. If her tone of voice didn't scare Taleah enough, her words would have a more profound effect.

"What?"

"Can you stop by?"

"Mom." Taleah's heart raced. She clenched her teeth and listened for more, but for the moment, her mother didn't expound. The time stretched before she summoned the will to reach for the information she needed. "What happened?"

"It was an accident. They think... well, they don't really know. You know where the big oil tanks are? Your dad and Willis were surveying that site and there was an explosion."

Her heart sank and her lip began to tremble. In response to the surge in adrenaline, she stood up and put her fingers to her lip in alarm. Nothing about that sentence seemed to make much sense. How? A million questions flashed through her mind. Her mother would perhaps have even fewer answers than she did, but she buried them in the back of her mind and would dig them up later.

Jalene was good at asking questions. It was her job, and whether or not her intent was to get Taleah thinking like a reporter, the tendency had begun to wear off. In order to get the whole picture, if indeed that were ever possible, one needed to ask the appropriate questions, and in such a quantity that left readers satisfied with answers.

"I don't understand, mom... Is dad all right?"

"I don't know. He's asleep now, but I think he would like to see you when he wakes up."

"Is Willis there? Can I talk to him?"

Her mother paused and let silence untie the emotion in her heart. "I think he's in worse shape than your dad. They said he's hanging on, but it doesn't look good."

"I'll be there in a few minutes," Taleah said, pushing her chair under her desk and glancing at Jalene, who busied herself fidgeting with the copy machine, which had malfunctioned so frequently that the publisher had finally begun debating about replacing it.

"Okay, we'll see you soon. Drive safe."

Taleah dropped the phone on the hook a little too loudly and then collected her headphones and her phone and deposited them in her purse before walking away.

Without turning around, Jalene seemed to scold her mildly. "Going somewhere?"

"My dad's in the hospital," Taleah said. "I'm going to go visit him, is that okay?"

"Of course. But the editor is going to need those stories by tomorrow morning. Are you going to be okay?"

"Fine," she said. "I made some notes in the margins and wrote down some stuff on my pad about changes to the Chen story. I think that's ready to be rewritten, if you want to get Laura to polish it up."

Laura was a junior copy writer, or a what she described as a 'glorified typist.' She didn't edit or provide any new content. In heavy workloads when the copy editors had stories that needed to be rewritten entirely, Laura would often step in.

"Works for me," Jalene said. "Sounds like I have a lead to go check out. Maybe if you are interested you can come with me tomorrow on the beat."

"Serious?"

Jalene nodded and Taleah smiled. Without saying anything else, she slung her purse over her arm and briskly walked toward her car. She pushed her hand through her hair as she started the motor. The drive lasted a little over ten minutes, as rush hour had not yet begun to clog the streets with slow cars and ill-timed traffic lights.

What had her father and Willis gotten into and how did it land them in the emergency room? The questions flowed freely, which allowed her precious seconds to explore each one and deposit it into a box to be examined more thoroughly later. Picturing what he looked like punished her heart with a thousand tiny daggers, each tipped with a corrosive strain of poison that, if left to burn, could consume her mind with torture.

She parked at the far end of the west lot, adjacent to the Connector freeway, which ushered relatively light traffic into the downtown area from the suburbs. The outbound side had begun to slow across from her, but still emitted the familiar chorus of thunder and wind. The journey to the emergency room allowed moments of pain to seep in. When the memory of last night prodded at her, it flavored this new event with a bitter taste that confronted her with waves of torment and shredded her.

"Dad." Only one word could escape her when she entered the room and took it all in. Her mother and Rebekah sat side by side with crossed legs, only glancing at one another long enough for a flash of emotion to bristle otherwise stoic faces.

Rebekah looked worse. Her makeup was smeared near her eyes, where mascara had run into dark streaks toward her cheek. Her hair was frazzled, as if she'd spent the last several hours brushing nervous fingers through it. Taleah didn't need to speak to her in order to feel the pang rip into her own heart. Instead, she glanced to her mother, who seemed momentarily more interested in the contents of her phone screen than the condition of her ex-husband. At least she was here, Taleah thought. Most ex-wives, she decided, wouldn't even bother with the trip and the man would receive a cursory 'get-well' card two weeks later via snail mail.

Paying for Boise State had been a mutual undertaking, which Taleah had promised to help with as much as she could. Still, money was tight, and her contributions had become irregular, which had in turn strained both her mother and her father with the added burden. Rather than complaining, they embraced her, though her mother patiently asked her when she could bring another check by.

Rebekah hardly cared whether Taleah paid up. She mostly handled the finances in the house, but involved Reggie when she decided that circumstances warranted, or big purchases demanded.

Taleah swallowed and stared at her father for almost a full minute before he started to wedge his eyes open.

"Dad? How are you?"

"Perfect, now. How's your day going?"

Taleah stepped forward and watched the tiny green chart on the screen cut a jagged line across black space, perfectly intermittent with a jarring beep that began to fade into nothing more than an annoyance. The pulse and the rhythm, she decided, were selectively chosen as a sort of soundtrack to injury, meant to placate, yet intensify the emotions of visitors. If all was well, the melody would blend into harmony, with each note producing a pleasant, aural accord. But if discord cut into harmony, the serrated storm would stir a crushing tide of agony.

The white lights spilled from numerous incandescent and fluorescent lamps overhead, plastering the room with an isolated, sterile ambiance that strictly reminded one how far from home he or she was. Instead of a different place, it seemed like another dimension, where time and memory provided a view of the past, but somehow replaced emotions of belonging with foreign illusions plucked from the deepest shadows of one's subconscious.

A tear formed at the corner of her eye as she grasped her father's hand, which he'd subtly extracted from beneath the pure white sheet. He glanced at the screen long enough to choke back a confused jumble of words that could only dizzy Taleah. "Isn't like that one was remarkable, or even such a thing as a miracle. At least, considering the given."

"No, dad. It's not a miracle."

"You sure? Whoever did it made a big mistake, but they were competent enough. If they didn't screw that up, both of us would have been pulverized."

"Does it hurt?"

"Eh... not as bad as it should. If you think I look bad, wait until you see Willis."

From behind a curtain came a groan that sounded like gravel scraping across a chalkboard. "Go to hell."

"Still a little mad at me, maybe."

"Why?" Taleah asked. "I guess I don't understand any of this. How did it happen?"

"Well, I can't remember all of it," Reggie insisted, but he plunged into the story nonetheless. Taleah clenched her palms together as he spoke, breaking eye contact when the nurse flitted in and out of the room.

"But, you know, maybe it isn't like I think at all. Seems like a terrorist attack to me, but not a perfectly conceived one, given that there were only two people there. Maybe the whole thing was going to go up and annihilate half the neighborhood."

"Why didn't it?"

"On that," Reggie said, reaching to scratch the front of his knee beneath the blanket, "I have a theory. If that valve was set up so that it served as a master switch that pneumatically alerted all the other valves to snap closed, the entire system could have shut down, and saved the neighborhood. But then again, I'm not an engineer."

"Why would someone do that?" Taleah mused. "That doesn't sound like a high-profile target, even if ISIS is making videos taking credit for it."

"Hell, I don't think we've even hit the national news," her father said. "Since the body count is low. But I'm sure the cops are on it. Maybe I'll even get a phone call from Special Agent Marks."

Taleah stifled the desire to laugh. "Oh, God."

Humor would have made a larger impact if Willis had been in the mood to offer the comedic insights, but it seemed that the pain was too strong. She paced backward and looked toward the curtain, behind which intermittent groans coarsened the air.

"Maybe if you dare," Reggie said, as if answering Taleah's desire to look.

"Please do," Willis rasped.

She pulled back the curtain and peeked in. A pair of nurses were dabbing at fresh wounds on Willis's back and preparing some sort of a solution to drip onto the reddened, bloody flesh. The debriding process would probably unleash new realms of pain.

"Hi, Ump."

"How's it going, slugger? Still... *shit!*... knocking them out of the park at the *Capital Weekly*?"

"I guess, if you can call it that. I just..."

"Your dad's so proud of you."

"I might go on assignment with a reporter tomorrow," Taleah said, though she clenched her teeth and forced thoughts of Chen's seventieth anniversary through her already crowded mind.

"Good deal. Can you tell these nurses to be careful?"

Taleah nodded and pulled away from the curtain. Her mother stood and offered her the chair while shuffling toward the door. She checked her phone again and said 'thank you' to a nurse that had just entered the room.

"You ready, Mr. St. Clair?" the nurse asked cheerfully.

"I don't think so, but I guess it has to be done."

She carefully folded the sheet up on his hip while helping him to roll partially onto his stomach, so that she could treat his wounds.

Taleah almost couldn't bear to watch, but passion and curiosity had a strange way of concocting a salaciously poisonous desire to look. She glanced at the small part of his back that she could see. The nurse unrolled some of the gauze, revealing reddened flesh, charred with stains of black around the wounds from which the shrapnel had been extracted. She dabbed at him with a clear liquid squeezed into a cotton swab. Her father emitted a low groan, which caused Rebekah to look away as if in shame.

Taleah peeled her eyes away from her father's back and sat down next to Rebekah. Offering her a hug seemed compulsory, and for a moment, her stepmother seemed to take comfort in it. Still, when the moment passed, she withdrew into a hazy subconscious stare at the floor while her bloodshot eyes scanned the tile at her feet. With a careful flick of her wrist, she grasped Rebekah's hand and squeezed it just hard enough to reinforce the notion that she was not alone with the emotional suffering.

Fifteen or twenty minutes passed when Rebekah shifted her weight away from Taleah, causing their hands to separate, Muted voices materialized in the corridor and lasted some thirty seconds before two police officers entered the room. Their blue uniforms were tidy and neat. The first officer, a Latino, introduced himself. His accent, once distinctive, Taleah guessed, had begun to show signs of weathering, as a natural response to speaking English for so long. "I am Officer Geraldo Ramirez, BPD."

The other officer seemed to address Rebekah directly. "Sergeant David Bones, Jr," he said, slowly shifting his gaze to Reggie. "I understand you were injured in the bombing this afternoon."

"What gave him away?" Willis sniped from behind the curtain.

"Yeah," Taleah's father said, purposefully delaying conversation with meaningless one-word answers like he often did when a difficult conversation was about to take place.

"Can you tell us what you were doing at the tank site today?"

Now staring at Reggie, Ramirez's eyebrow seemed to raise, indicating some hidden snarky attitude that Taleah wasn't in the mood for. She shook her head and glanced at the floor while sliding her feet closer together. Instead of exerting all her attention to the conversation, she allowed the symphony of beeps to fill her head. One after another, the sharp bits of siren marched onward, seemingly to infinity, suggesting stability. If the sensors were attached to her chest, she thought, the music would sound markedly different.

Reggie planted his gaze on Officer Ramirez for several seconds before he started to recount the tale once more. The officers traded questions between bouts of explanation, to which her father provided answers the best he could. Willis helped answer from time to time, but mostly stayed quiet. To Taleah, that alone built a dense haze of sorrow. Willis was usually the talkative one. He was the joker, so filled with a zest for life that his style of conversation was demonstrative. To get a feel for his personality, one had to watch his facial expressions and his body language more than listen to his words to gain a clearer understanding of who he was. But now that he was beaten, bruised and scarred to the very edge of that life he so clung to, almost nothing remained of his persona, at least until such time as he recovered from his injuries.

Rather than listen to the question-and-answer session, Taleah granted herself precious minutes to take in a more holistic understanding of the situation. The ebbs and flows of emotion, the constant, unchanging tune of the beeps in rhythm with the jagged line on the monitor, while the white lights showered them from overhead, overtook Taleah's mind. She leaned her head back and closed her eyes. Somewhere in her chest, her heartbeat joined in the lucid jingle, replete with the sounds of pens zipping across paper and shoes shuffling against the tile floor.

The power of it all hit her with a force from which she could scarcely recover. Memory filled in the cracks, and before she knew it, Rebekah was shaking her shoulder and staring at her with those warm, misty eyes.

The kindness therein leaked into her the way a draft from an open window might mix the air in a hot room. Taleah always loved that about Rebekah. How was it that she could show far greater affection than her mother even on Anna's best day?

"I can tell you that the chief has directed us to investigate this event as a terrorist incident, like you suggest," Sergeant Bones noted, "but until we can piece this thing together, we don't know what really happened."

"You're both very lucky it wasn't successful," Officer Ramirez said.

"Why don't you go home and get some rest?" Rebekah whispered.

Taleah clenched her teeth, and without realizing what she was doing, started to nod. Just a few minutes of sleep had successfully dulled her mind, morphing the pain with a sort of astounding realism that was a tad too much for her brain to immediately internalize. Instead of fighting the urge to stay, Taleah gave in.

"What are you and Christine up to tonight?"

"I don't know. Maybe just catch up on our TV show."

"The hospital one?"

Taleah scanned the room and almost rolled her eyes. Anything but that, she thought. Instead of speaking, she shook her head and glanced to the floor, again listening to the endless beeps fill the spaces in her head with a brand of surrealism that pushed at the boundaries of space and time.

"Well, you can come over if you like. I'm thinking of making teriyaki stir fry."

"Aren't you going to stay here with dad?"

She nodded. "For a while, I think. But he'll want me to go home and get some sleep. You know how stubborn he gets about doing things his way."

Again, Taleah answered with a nod. "Maybe we will. As long as you're okay with a little PDA."

"You know that never bothered me," she lied.

It was clear that Rebekah would resort to any tactic to not spend the evening alone, and Taleah allowed concern for Rebekah to wash over her.

"Sounds good. Drive safe."

The trip home this time of day promised to offer frustration in spades. There was no good route to take to get green lights and free-flowing traffic. As a result, the trip would take at least fifteen minutes, unless traffic was really bad, though by six o'clock, rush hour usually was winding down.

Taleah turned the music off when she started her car, so that only the sounds of thought clanging off the walls of her skull resonated. The sounds of beeps in the emergency room could last a lifetime, she thought, but already, the process of time was beginning to wear away at the memory, separating it into its own dimension. The minutes passed like a summer thunderstorm on a hot day.

Soon, Taleah would feel Christine's warm embrace, take in the serenity of her lips, and snuggle into what could be described as comfort. The thought allowed her to plaster her face with a complicated smile that somehow touched at discord. If Christine navigated the expression skillfully, she could begin to unravel it and to help Taleah reconstruct her perception so that it reflected both the passage of time and the singular sense of clarity.

4

Wavelength

BEAMS of white light darted through the wilderness, bouncing off tree trunks and scattering into the forest as a steady torrent of footsteps interrupted the sounds of nature. Sweat rolled off her brow and congealed into goop below her eyelids. Taleah's heart raced.

The trees had a way of localizing every sound, compressing the wilderness into a manageable circle, whose curve marked the limits of perceptible space. When howls and roars drifted in from the distance, the source of the noise was closer than anticipated. Still, the footsteps would never reach her.

"No!" she shrieked as a monstrous hand plunged from the darkness and clutched a fistful of her hair. She howled in pain as tears sparkled in the moonlight on her cheek. She felt herself kicking at him and attempting to bite his arm, but his strength allowed him to heft her around like a doll with one hand. He could throw her ten feet if he had the desire, but she would get away, somehow. And with the flashlights pulsing and scanning beyond the tree trunks, the intruders were close.

"Time to move on," he barked as his scent wafted into her nostrils. Almost as though he were caressing her neck as he hurried up a steep incline, his breathing seemed almost sublime, though erratic. The sting in her scalp spread and dulled as he slung her over his shoulder.

When Taleah squared her elbow, she struck at his back. The sharpness of the blow caught him off guard enough to change his trajectory, angling to a slower climb. The change of direction flung her neck sideways so violently that a surge of pain shot down her spine. Her head and elbow collided with a tree. Tears streamed down her face and her screams ignited the night.

If she could hear them amidst the confusion, the strangers could certainly hear her. Her heartbeat ticked up a pace as she intensified her screeching. The man called Art whipped her through the air like a limp katana, bounced her hip off of his shoulder and stifled her screams with his huge, dirty hand. Agony tore her nerves to fiber.

It didn't matter to him where he touched her. His hand could slither anywhere he wanted it to without recourse. As he scrambled, his free hand pounded against her chest as he roared in delight.

"Come get her, Reggie," he whispered. "Come on."

As a change of pace and to help him wield her like a weapon, his hand slid down her stomach and between her legs. She erupted with moans as her eyeballs flung themselves so wide open that they could gather light from distant galaxies. Pain bristled at her spine and her head. The beast laughed, shredding her with contempt as his evil lurched forth to scour the deepest, most private confines of her mind. With one fluid motion, Taleah was airborne. The motion ripped a hundred hairs from her scalp as she landed on her butt against the trunk of a tree that had been uprooted and leaned against a dense pocket of conifers.

Reggie and Willis's footsteps faded away, their lights died out, and inescapable darkness poured into her world to fill every corner of her conscience. Art caressed her and chuckled, breathed against her neck, and then the soft haze of green light flooded the room.

The breath on her neck sent warmth through her spine. She shifted and rolled away from Christine as agony pounded away at her skull. In response, Christine sat up and grasped Taleah's shoulders, pulling her gently toward her.

"Hey, are you all right?"

Tears dabbed at the corners of her eyes. "No. Not even a little bit."

"Talk to me." Her embrace sent shivers across her back that somehow cooled the fires of her sweat. Curtains of Christine's hair flapped against Taleah's shoulder and slid across her skin.

"It wasn't anything... just a nightmare."

"About?"

Tears flushed her eyes and Christine pulled her closer and pressed her lips against the back of her neck.

"Please don't," she said, wiggling away. "Not right now."

Christine sighed and scooted her body closer to the edge of the bed, so that they sat side by side facing the alarm clock.

"It was about him, wasn't it?"

Taleah had felt rewarded with the certainty that she could open up to someone who truly cared about her. The night she had opened up started with a glass of wine and perfect conversation. She had opened her pores that night, letting the pain condense into words. Christine had gasped at the revelation that Taleah was wounded. *Oh my God,* she'd breathed.

Instead of speaking, she could only nod.

"It's okay, honey. There is nothing to worry about. You're safe." She paused and drew in a deep breath, which she exhaled slowly as she spoke. "Remember what Rebekah said last night at dinner?"

She searched her mind but could grasp nothing of value.

"It's love that saves us, and it will always be there as a lifeline in dark times."

Taleah recalled the conversation and flinched. "Wasn't she talking about Jesus?"

Christine breathed deeply and rested her palm on Taleah's thigh while snaking her other arm around Taleah's waist. "Well, yeah. But I mean, doesn't that apply to other people as well? Look, your dad saved you and killed him because he loved you. He loves you, and so do I."

Taleah sniffed and turned her head away from her momentarily. "I know," she whispered. "I guess I should probably get in the shower. It's a busy day."

"Of course," Christine said. She grasped Taleah's chin and slowly turned her head to face her. "You know where I'll be."

"Yes."

The kiss was serene and gentle, encompassing a single heartbeat. Taleah wished she could stay and enjoy the moment, but her mind had suddenly kicked into overdrive, rendering comfort impossible.

She showered, dressed, styled her finger-length hair, and poured herself a small helping of cereal before Christine traipsed into the kitchen to grab breakfast and brew a pot of coffee. Taleah pecked her goodbye and shuffled out the door with her purse.

The light of the speeding traffic faded as the sun pushed above the mountains, signaling the mark of a new day. She breathed in the crisp air as she parked the car, trying to remember what Christine had told her.

Then again, it was only a dream. The last few days were an aberration—nothing more than a stark reminder of mortality and an assurance that life moved on, whether or not one was willing to keep up with the passage of time. Taleah was done with letting life race by. She was done watching it tear away, leaving her as a speck of dust in time's wake. Every moment was precious. This realization had gotten her moving again, in the right direction, toward whatever loomed as the ultimate goal.

When she arrived at work, she found nothing new in her inbox. She deposited her purse on the desk, flicked on the computer and searched the cubicles for another early riser. At this time of morning, she could usually find someone to talk to huddled over the coffeemaker while flipping through social media.

Taleah wandered the corridor until she strolled into the break room. Jalene had her hair pulled into a tight ponytail and wore a tan coat to match a tight, knee-length skirt. Instead of speaking, Taleah pulled out a chair, sat down, and sighed.

"Another morning," Jalene commented.

Taleah nodded. The morning raged like a memory clinging to the last thread of consciousness it could control. Until her heart settled and her mind cleared, she said nothing. "What's on the docket today?"

"You heard about that bombing yesterday, I presume?"

Her heart leaped. The isolated memory of the hospital accosted her. The beeps and the groans of scorching pain pulsed away into a muffled whine, as if doused in warm water. "We're already going to do a story on that?"

"Has to be an exclusive." Jalene chattered in excited, clipped sentences, which hit her like repeated punches to the gut. "It's already hit most of the news in the valley. But we're going to be the first paper to do an in-depth analysis. Mr. Miles has put all eight of us reporters on it, working a different angle. Since you have such an impeccable grasp of how to arrange a story to pique interest and incite emotion, I need you to help uncover the facts."

"Um... okay?"

"You're going to get promoted someday," she said, "soon. Because you're too good. And everyone around here knows it."

"Thanks."

Jalene shook her head and stared into Taleah's eyes. For a moment, she wavered, as though she could sense the storm of emotion that boiled within the confines of her brain. And then she spoke more slowly and calculated, the way a seasoned professional worked an angle of rationality rather than catharsis. "You know how I am with compliments."

True enough, Jalene didn't fling praise around at random. If she did something that truly warranted it, Jalene would be the first to offer praise, but she didn't run around saying "Good job, you nailed it" for simply doing her job. Only when Taleah went far above and beyond what the boss expected of her did she receive any verbal benefit.

"I guess so."

For almost two minutes, Jalene scribbled on a notepad and sipped coffee. Taleah scooted her chair away and straightened her back to stand before Jalene stopped her by speaking in a monotone that somehow communicated concern.

"You seem a little bit... despondent. Is your dad okay?"

Taleah let her shoulders slump and then placed her palms on her thighs. "Well, in that he isn't dead, yeah. He considers himself lucky. And I'm looking at him, asking how in the world he can even think that."

"What happened?"

She swallowed and glanced at Jalene's coffee and then into her eyes to witness a subtle thread of compassion. "Funny you should ask. You heard about the explosion yesterday, right?"

Jalene's eyes widened as if in horror. "Are you serious?"

Instead of verbally answering, Taleah shrugged and clasped her hands together.

"Oh my God. Well, then, let's get to work."

Jalene's boyfriend had to be either lucky or tormented, because she took the unconventional tack through life. She had a funny way of showing compassion, and always adapted her responses to better fit the personality of the person with whom she was speaking. Taleah couldn't decide whether she was improbably perceptive or aloof. But somehow, her tactics always worked. Her compassion spurred Taleah toward perfection, and when Taleah worked, the strains of life piled up in the dustbin of her mind instead of crowding her thoughts with deeper and deeper knots of desperation. Somewhere along the line, Jalene had witnessed this phenomenon and learned how to exploit it. In any other state of mind, Taleah might feel used, but Jalene somehow enforced the perception of importance through it all.

"You ready to be mentored?"

"Yes," she said.

Two other people slipped into the break room to use the toaster and the microwave. A younger man in a blue shirt and a sleek, skinny tie began to operate the coffeemaker as if Jalene and Taleah weren't even there.

And then Amber came in and pulled out a chair. She scanned Jalene's notepad from afar and nodded. "I think I'll be interviewing the neighbors," she said, combing strands of curly red hair behind her ear, revealing golden stud earrings.

"You're going that far? The police aren't even sure about that yet."

Jalene shook her head. "We're not going to make any assumptions. But since the chief of police mentioned it in his press conference last night, we are going to explore the big crimes of the past and how they might compare to terrorist incidents."

"There were two victims, from what they are saying," Amber noted. "I think Desret might try to talk to them today. You know who they are?"

"I'm aware of it," Jalene said. "What do you think, Taleah?"

"Well, my dad... I mean, the *victims,* are still in the hospital, I hear. One of them is not a big fan of the press but might make an exception for us. Maybe."

"But what do *you* feel about it?"

"I'm sorry," Amber said, putting a hand to her chest as if she'd just swallowed scalding coffee. "Do you know the victims?"

Please don't call them victims one more time, Taleah pleaded silently. Her father hated the connotation of the word. And words had meanings, he always said. The thought of being less or somehow vulnerable pushed him closer to anger than shame. If he had to be described as the recipient of wrongdoing, he'd prefer a different term, such as 'target.'

But then again, senseless violence such as what happened yesterday rarely targeted certain individuals.

Taleah nodded slowly and attempted to read Jalene's notes. Her scribbles were mostly legible, apart from the extra-bulbous loops. Taleah had a more mechanical approach to freehand writing, which had often been mistaken for boys' writing in school.

Flashing a smile at Amber and spinning her pen in her hand, Jalene invited Taleah to discuss the day's work at her desk, where she could look up pertinent facts and structure the day in order to maximize productivity.

Jalene's desk huddled in a corner of the open office away from the window against two plaster walls, which she used to pin up important notes, calendars, and pictures of family and friends. Rather than face the corner like most people did, Jalene had positioned her monitors on the left flank of the desk to get the most out of the sunlight from the windows. She often did her writing in the morning while using late mornings and afternoons to gather information and go on assignment. Everything was set up for certain standards of efficiency, which she'd claimed to have perfected over her seven-year career.

Whereas most workers angled their monitors away from each other in a wide V-shape, Jalene reduced glare from the overhead lights by aligning the screens slightly downward toward the chair and in a straight line. This setup, she claimed, made her feel like she had more screen space to navigate.

Taleah found an empty chair sitting against a cubicle wall and rolled it into Jalene's workspace. Jalene had affixed a small photograph of her boyfriend holding a giant fish in the lower corner of her right monitor, tucked between the plastic and the glass. Over time, the photo had curled away from the screen and its colors had faded, but to her it was priceless.

"I've done a little bit of digging already," Jalene said as Taleah leaned backward in the chair, which creaked as the wheels rolled across the plastic floor mat. "And you'd think that in a city like Boise, big story violent crimes are rare. Which is true, except for a few caveats. Our violent crime rate *is* low. But the BPD keeps diligent records of all major crimes, including cold cases. And it's all publicly accessible if you know where to look."

"You know," Taleah droned.

"Of course I do. You interview detectives to get the facts regarding open investigations, because they're not going to put their evidence online even with high transparency. But since I'm mostly gathering raw data, I can pull that from this site." She clicked on a link, which brought up a black screen with dozens of case numbers highlighted in blue hyperlinks. To the right of the numbers was a brief description of the case, which could be expanded without bringing up the case file.

"This is just in the last five years?" Taleah asked, staring at a set of dates near the top of the screen.

"You can narrow it down to certain timeframes," Jalene confirmed.

Taleah silently read some of the descriptions. *Double homicide and standoff, 1400 block of Euclid Avenue. Robbery and assault, 8600 block of West Fairview. Multiple stabbing, Fremont Street.*

Instead of the numbers on the screen, Jalene studied notes on her notebook, which she then displayed to Taleah.

"Can I look at that?"

"I was hoping you'd ask." Jalene dropped the notebook in front of Taleah and waited as Taleah carefully read each entry. Just as on the screen, Jalene had scribbled the case number in a neat column at the left side of the page and copied down the brief description of the crime in the open area of the sheet.

Suspicious package found at Boise State University on May 16, 2014. Suspect of Pakistani descent discarded package. No malicious intent found, suspect cleared of wrongdoing. Four shot at apartment complex in the Bench. Couple indicted on four counts of attempted murder and three counts of first-degree murder. Six stabbed in common area of apartment complex off Cole Road. Suspect had been wanted for illegal weapons charges in South Carolina and probation violation in Kansas. Eleven hurt in explosion near office complex, bombing suspect cleared after investigation ruled the incident an accident. Five injured, two killed in intentional hit and run when a large truck rammed a van... Jalene had written down details from more than a dozen cases.

Taleah closed her eyes and rolled the chair away as a knot of pain worked its way into her temple.

"Notice anything in common about all those?"

She shook her head. "Well, they all would have been big news."

"And they were," Jalene said. "Finding the press clippings should be easy, and that's going to be our first task, to curate a sort of media list detailing each event."

"But why just these ones?" Taleah asked.

"Does nothing jump out at you, other than them being big news?"

Taleah widened her eyes and stared into Jalene's face, which looked weathered, but dusted with the remnants of a smile. "If you're trying to get me on the Pakistani angle, it isn't going to work. And if all of these have a minority involved—"

"No," Jalene said. "Look closer."

"Not all of them are even violent," Taleah noted. "But maybe terrorism was suspected?"

Jalene folded her arms across her stomach and gave a pallid smile that worked the corners of her mouth into dimples in her cheeks. It was enough to make Taleah issue a silent half-chuckle, which would have sounded more like an interested *humph* to outside observers. When she looked at Taleah, her face changed. The smile drooped and her eyebrows leveled.

"Does this upset you?"

Taleah shook her head. "Nope."

"Suspected terrorism. Since 9/11 and the Boston Marathon attacks, suspicious packages are kind of a big deal, since almost anyone can make a bomb and you can probably find specs online for dozens of types of explosive devices. Of course, investigations revealed that none of them were actually terrorism, but speculation ran rampant. Our first job is to read all the articles and figure out what sparked the speculation of terrorism and whether the press first guessed. Then, we get to make a profile of all the suspects involved and what motivated them. After that, we get to dig into how the community reacted to each event."

"Big job," Taleah said.

"They don't call us the most in-depth journalism in the city for nothing," Jalene said, curling her finger around her pen and issuing a cool smile.

With a flick of her wrist, Taleah grasped a pen and started to scribble notes. She paused and tilted her head to the left, glancing up at Jalene, who looked pleased with herself. "I guess you want me to read all the articles."

"We'll split them, then compare notes. Let's get back together this afternoon."

Taleah shrugged and jotted down a paraphrased version of what Jalene had just finished describing. The pain in her forehead seemed to expand with every stroke of the pen. Now a distant memory, the lights and the beeps from the hospital room seemed to form a dense array of noise. Even brushing it aside could not completely dismiss the emotion that rode the crashing waves. As she wrote, she found herself beginning to frown, an expression that lingered longer than it should have and worked deeper into her face. The writing stemmed the sadness and exerting her mind eased the pain.

"Too quick?" Jalene asked.

"It's a lot of reading," Taleah said, allowing the frown to fade. "But I think I can do it, as long as I don't get interrupted."

"We'll do what it takes," Jalene said.

Taleah clicked the pen and stood up abruptly. Her shirt caught on some protrusion near the backrest of the chair. She scratched the resultant itch and briskly strode to her desk to start digging. Typing key words and phrases into the search engine saved valuable time and knowing how headlines were written proved advantageous in finding long-buried stories.

After reading each story, she copied down notes. In most cases, the article never mentioned terrorism, other than noting the intense scrutiny after major terror attacks. Instead, the speculation came from comments to the articles. Thinking that it might have been important, Taleah wrote down the names of the commenters in case Jalene decided she wanted to follow up with any of them on their opinion.

Most articles took ten to fifteen minutes to read, but one in-depth story in the Valley Times occupied the better part of an hour. Since most outlets reported on many of the incidents, Taleah found herself reading three or four articles per case. This kind of investigation could have sapped her of energy and dragged her into endless boredom but setting a criterion and searching for that brought energy into her work. She read article after article and jotted down notes, including the names of the reporters who had contributed to each story.

The Pakistani immigrant had been a student at the university when he'd mistakenly left a package of art supplies in a common gathering area in front of the arts building. He claimed to have been distracted by a phone conversation and was going to his apartment to check on something when he left the box. Two articles regarding this incident mentioned terrorism, but Taleah guessed that in this day and age, most bomb scares did.

When she read about the multiple stabbings, Taleah couldn't help but feel pangs of compassion for the victims of the attack. Since most of the victims were a minority group and totally innocent, the sadness tore away at the insides of her heart. The naturalized daughter of two Somali refugees, one of the victims was a child celebrating her fifth birthday. None of the press articles mentioned terror as a possible motive. Instead, the attack was deemed a domestic altercation in which a drunken neighbor had become irate over the noise as he tried to sleep and decided to take it out on several innocent bystanders. What really struck her about the stories was the comments. Some people had used the attack as justification for divisive political viewpoints, most decrying the influence of refugees, though others quickly called it a terrorist attack, citing the identities of the victims and the fact that the attacker didn't personally know any of them.

By the time she finished reading a story about the worst triple murder in the city's history, she had nearly succumbed to tears. She fought the emotion away by thinking about Christine, which often helped reduce the burden of sadness.

The murder started with a domestic dispute unlike any other. A husband came home one afternoon to find his wife, ex-wife, and daughter in some sort of game he misinterpreted. He began screaming at them and threatened to take his daughter away, when a neighbor burst into the house and shot all four of them. Only the husband managed to make it out alive. Again with this story, it didn't appear that terrorism had ever been mentioned. She made note of that and then moved on to the next case, which involved a retailer and a disgruntled homeless man, who hijacked a car and drove it into the store killing four people and injuring three others.

The papers had each mentioned terrorism, but the police had insisted that they were not going to investigate the incident as a terrorist attack. This story also appeared to have attracted national media coverage, which in turn incited politicians to stress the importance of national defense.

Reading about the last crime that Jalene had assigned, Taleah had already made some conclusions, which caused the next set of articles to drone into nothing more than a mess of jumbled words. She swallowed at her own predisposition, which would earn Jalene's ire if she found out. Reporters were not supposed to form an opinion, but Taleah couldn't help it. Instead of writing down anything that could have been construed as commentary, she reviewed the facts.

For lunch, Taleah elected to stay in the office and eat leftovers she had left in the break room's refrigerator. It almost made her gag, but it eased the irritation and discomfort from the morning just enough to make practical discussions relevant and bearable.

Jalene returned from a restaurant carrying two sodas and offered one to Taleah as a reward for her hard work.

They huddled at Jalene's desk and discussed their findings.

"What do you think?"

"I don't know," Taleah lied. "I don't see how any of this is relevant to the bombing yesterday and I think every time someone mentioned terrorism, it was a stretch at best."

"That's probably true," Jalene said. "But we're trying to gauge public reaction. Maybe we go downtown tomorrow and talk to some real people. These are stories almost everyone in the city has heard about."

"I don't know that you can assume people will react to these things as possible terrorist actions, especially after the cases have all been tried and settled. Knowing the facts tends to skew your judgment."

"We don't make any assumptions," Jalene chided her, flipping loose strands of hair over her shoulder. "We investigate leads."

"These aren't leads. I think our time is better spent looking at how this happened and why and I'm not sure people will be all that interested in reading about major crimes in the last five years."

"That's our starting point," Jalene said. "Unless you think I should get someone else to help me, I implore you to take the lead of an experienced reporter."

Jalene had been reporting news for seven years and prior to that had helped curate stories on local television newscasts. Her pedigree spoke for itself and Taleah found it difficult to argue with. She attempted to smile while writing neat checkmarks behind her notes as she went over them with Jalene.

Jalene scanned part of Taleah's notes and nodded, possibly at the copied social media comments. One paper in question had a history of erasing commentary they found to be unflattering or inflammatory and often reposted stories with the headline changed and didn't keep any of the comments from the original story.

"But you know, people will often say things in an anonymous social media thread that they wouldn't dare mention around real people."

"Very true," Jalene said. "It's still an exercise I think is important in the big picture. We're all collaborating here, not necessarily writing independent stories. And it's a big undertaking."

Taleah fidgeted with her pen and sipped her drink between bouts of notetaking. Jalene was in the middle of explaining something when Taleah cut her off and changed the subject. "Why aren't you at the *Valley Times*?"

"They don't have standards. They're so busy trying to water down controversial issues that they miss the mark. I understand why they do it, especially with the *Treasure Valley Register* eating up more of their market share. I realize that not everything is always going to be tidy and neat and not piss anyone off, and I've always prided myself in finding the real truth behind the stories. That's why I came here. We only publish weekly, but you're not getting stories where the truth has been scrubbed so as to not stir animosity. And I think our readers appreciate that."

"People will always accuse you of bias," Taleah countered.

"That's something you can't get away from in this business. If there are two sides—and there almost always are—and you balance your story, people will get upset because you didn't slant hard enough one way, which they see as slanting hard the other way."

Taleah nodded and veered back to the subject matter. "Maybe, then, we need to look deeper than random individuals downtown." She stared at the photograph of Jalene's boyfriend as the haze of emotional background lifted and clarity resumed. Without thinking about what she was doing, she clicked her pen and scribbled something on her notepad.

"What are you getting at?"

"It's just an idea," Taleah said, resuming her stare. "I can understand if you don't think it's a good idea. If we talk to people connected with the crimes in some way—"

"That's not ethical."

"I mean, not the victims' families, but maybe people in communities associated with people wrongly accused."

"What?"

"I know a guy," Taleah said. "He might have a relevant take on the university bomb scare."

"How so?"

"You're not going to like it."

Jalene bit her lip and tugged at her ponytail as if to verify that it wasn't coming undone. "I have to do a lot of things I don't like."

"Well, if I remember right," Taleah started, unaware that her voice was becoming firmer and more confident with every word, "people were going nuts over the nationality of the man who left the package. Not that they were right to, but people make assumptions."

"You're referring to him being Pakistani," Jalene said.

"I know a Jordanian guy who volunteers at the Islamic Center as an interpreter for refugees seeking jobs."

"I don't know," Jalene said. "I'll have to think about that one. It might cause bias."

Taleah shook her head and then gazed down at her notes. She clicked her pen and took another sip of her drink before listening to Jalene go off on a tangent only somewhat related to the case. Rather than focus on what she was saying, Taleah allowed her mind to wander. Talking to her father again would help repair what was left of her emotions and restore her faith in the best humanity had to offer. The conversation with Jalene got under her skin and reminded her that people were bigoted, angry, and flat-out mean, especially to those who didn't quite share the same viewpoints. The toxicity almost made her wish she hadn't chosen journalism in the first place. Indeed, she operated from a place of safety. No one ever accused copy editors of bias or reporting unconfirmed sources as fact, or even what she saw as the biggest complaint: editorializing the news.

Then again, failure to advance over some fear, whether unfounded or not, she decided, was the same as moving backwards. In that case, it would be just as good to settle on a career as a big-box store checker. Aspirations had guided her through the hardest times of her life. If she didn't have dreams, she didn't have anything. And nothing could be the most destructive substance of all time.

5

Spectrum

CLOUDS gathered overhead, beginning to converge into a storm that would pepper the cars with dust and kick up a fierce wind. This time of year, thunderstorms did little else, and they were rare. Taleah leaned back from the green picnic table, scanning the sky. A flock of birds drifted over a patch of blue flanked by stratus clouds. The scene reflected on the glass of the towers surrounding the Grove. Grove Plaza Inn rose up to seventeen floors, topped with full-wall penthouse windows. Adjacent to that building, a glass tower bathed in blue and silver hues followed the curve of the Grove. A tunnel beneath the buildings connected a foot path to the Basque block. She glanced down to the bricks before watching a couple emerge into the sunlight at the foot of the tower.

"You want to talk to them?" Jalene said without looking up from her notes.

The afternoon was wearing on. Most days, the late afternoon would inch along as if the clocks had come to a standstill and weariness would creep over her brain, which made thought pound inside her head. If she yawned, it only got worse. Today, the concept of getting out of the office seemed to light a fire within her. Suddenly, she became more aware of her surroundings.

The couple stood at the edge of the walking path, holding hands and staring down at the blue river pattern with lights embedded into the concrete. To her left, the fountain spattered irregularly as the intermittent pumps shot water to variable heights. The woman looked thirty-something and wore a patterned skirt composed of red and yellow triangles carved into a sea of black. A burnt maroon sweater draped beyond her waist. When she looked up, she flung a veil of golden hair over her shoulder and erupted in a smile that somehow painted the Grove with even more color.

For a moment, their eyes met. Taleah swallowed, stood, and planted a smile on her face. The pair followed the footpath into the giant circle of red bricks bounded by a ring of young trees straight toward the fountain. The woman laughed and gripped the man's hand tighter. To get their attention, Taleah raised her palm as if to wave. The woman didn't let confusion flash over her face and returned the gesture. Taleah stopped about five feet away and introduced herself as a representative of the *Capital Weekly*.

"Do you have time to share your insights on a topic we are doing a story on?"

"Well, actually," the young man started, looking at his watch as if suddenly realizing he was late for an important meeting.

"Of course," the woman said. She wrenched her hand free and shook Taleah's hand. "I'm Shantal and this is my boyfriend, Gabe."

"Count me out of this one," Gabe said, stepping backward and raising his palms in a defensive stance.

"Sorry, he doesn't trust the news. He's afraid of being misquoted and sounding like an idiot." She raised her voice slightly while grinning. "I tell him all the time how he doesn't need to be misquoted."

Taleah attempted to chuckle, but the glare from the glass tower shot a sort of film over her eyes, which seemed to glaze over the scene with a gray filter. Instead, she dropped the notion of laughter, lowered her eyes, and adjusted her gaze to level with Shantal's face.

"I completely understand," she lied. In fact, jabs against the press in general felt like a personal assault. It bit at the bottom of her heart where the deepest secrets dwelt. Instead of letting the comment visibly sour her attitude, she clicked her pen and wrote down Shantal's name.

"Is this about that horrible bombing attack? I never thought they'd do it to our city."

"Not exactly," Taleah said. "I'm working on an in-depth piece about major crimes and how the public relates them to the explosion."

"I'm game."

"Two years ago," Taleah started, "there was a knife attack, do you remember that?"

"The one where the little girl was killed and five others hurt?"

Taleah nodded.

"It was terrible. I felt so bad for the families to have to endure that, after they'd come to one of the safest cities for refuge. It isn't right, but at least the guy got what he deserved."

The perpetrator had been sentenced to death for the crime, which was exactly what the family had been hoping for. "Do you remember specifically what you thought of it the day the news broke?"

Shantal tilted her head, which allowed her sleek hair to drift away from her face like a wave. Her smile drooped as she attempted to recall the event. "I guess I don't normally make assumptions about the news until more facts come out, which I realize isn't exactly a popular response in this day and age."

"Did you ever consider it an act of terror?"

She gulped and glanced down to the bricks beneath her feet. "Well, the thought may have crossed my mind, but I mean it's sort of a state of shock, and you tend to assign it meaning for it to make much sense. Am I right?"

"That's a great point," Taleah said. She realized as she spoke that by commenting, she was breaking a fundamental rule of journalism. She drew back her smile and promised herself not to make the mistake again. "Do you remember hearing about other people assuming it was a terror attack?"

"Not verbally. But probably some people felt that way. Like I said, I usually wait for more facts. And come to think of it, I don't remember the victims or their families mentioning it, either."

Taleah took her time to write out Shantal's responses, being careful to note the stresses behind the words. If she could draw emotion from that, the story would be more relatable, she thought.

"Looking a little further back, do you remember an explosion near an office complex where a bunch of people were hurt?"

"Um, I don't... maybe vaguely. That far back is a blur. I'd just moved from Seattle and was just trying to readjust. You know how it is."

Taleah held the pen at the ready and looked up. "You don't remember how you reacted to that? Or those around you?"

"Not really. It sounds bad and you might have a point on the terrorism angle, but I thought I read somewhere that it was an accident."

"It was," Taleah said. "I understand you must be in a hurry. Do you have time for one more?"

"Yes. Maybe just one. I think my boyfriend is getting anxious."

Gabe had proceeded to loop around the fountain and study a metal sculpture of eagles on a dead tree from afar. Taleah noted his presence and attempted to frame her next question with the kind of simplicity that would engender a quick, but well-thought-out response.

"Also, in the spring of last year, a hit-and-run where the suspect fled on foot. Five people were injured and two killed. Do you remember that?"

"It was on my route home," she said. "Front Street was completely a mess that day. I thought it was an accident."

"Would it surprise you if I said it was intentional?"

"Maybe. But I might have read that later. It was a pretty busy week with my brother's wedding, cramming for a test at work, where we were gearing up to double our work force, and then having my car break down. Was it really on purpose?"

"It was presumed an accident at first," Taleah confirmed, "but the police later ruled it intentional. The suspect was identified after a traffic camera picked up the incident. During the last winter, they finally sentenced him. The prosecutors wanted a murder charge but felt they didn't have enough evidence to convict."

"That's awful. I felt bad for the people hurt. But then again, I don't know if I had much time to really process it. They didn't see it as terrorism?"

"It was never discussed. The investigators determined malicious intent with a solid motive, but it wasn't terrorism."

"Does that make this bombing the only terrorist attack in Boise history?"

"It very well may," Taleah said, "if they can determine that to be the case."

"I heard they were investigating it as one," Shantal said.

Taleah issued a sideways glance toward Gabe as the memory of the hospital tore into her mind once again. Over the mountains, beyond the brown brick bank tower, behind the blue and silver glass building, rain had begun streaking downward from the storm cell. It painted her mind with a chaotic sense of trauma. She bit her lip and decided to end the interview. Jalene would be watching her carefully about now, and making a mistake now would earn instant rebuke.

"I heard that, too."

"Just awful."

"I'll let you get back to your afternoon," she said, affixing a false smile to her face, though storm clouds gathered in her mind. "Thank you for taking the time to talk. Take care."

"No problem."

She watched Shantal walk away, adjusting her sweater as she reached out her arm to wrap it around Gabe's waist. Before she turned around, she let her gaze fall on a pair of kids riding skateboards into the square from beneath the skywalk that arced between the newer glass building and the old convention center.

Jalene scribbled something on her notepad and waited for Taleah to take a seat across from her to speak. "How was it? Maybe not so hot?"

"It was fine. She's pretty open-minded and doesn't rush to judgement on things. And she hasn't really lived here long enough to remember some of the crimes on my list."

"I see," Jalene said. "Look, if you don't think you can do this for any reason, I would understand."

"I have to," Taleah said, ripping her eyes from the skateboarders and instantly looking into Jalene's eyes.

They communicated a warm compassion, which eased Taleah's mind and soaked into her spirit. Understanding leaked forth rather than blame or dismay. Of course she didn't conduct the interview well, but for some reason, Jalene looked past the failure and witnessed Taleah's humanity.

"That's good to hear, I think." She set her pen down and fought against the breeze, which had whipped a loose strand of hair into her face, where it stuck to her lip. "Now, about your interview skills."

"I know," Taleah said, nodding at the tabletop. "Needs work, poor posture..."

"That's not what I was going to say at all, though 'needs work' does apply."

The comment dug deep. Taleah's heart seemed to burst into sudden decay, as if Jalene had set off a bomb that tore her away from reality.

"You're relaxed and confident, and that goes a long way in this business. If they don't feel comfortable talking to you, they're going to give you half-answers and probably misconstrue their own perceptions, too. What do you think you did wrong?"

"I let myself agree with her. I didn't stand up straight, and I didn't word my questions very well."

"See," Jalene said, "you're self-critical, which is a trait I find less and less common among reporters today. If you're not trying to improve your technique by acknowledging flaws, you're setting yourself up."

"Okay."

"It's like this," Jalene said, reaching across the table and gathering Taleah's hands into a cup beneath her face. "You hold the cards and you know what they are. But playing the game is as much about playing the cards as it is reading the other person's facial expressions. You were fine with that young woman because she was personable and relatable to you. But your questions were mechanical. When you interview someone different, that might come off bad."

"I understand," Taleah said.

"Now to improve on that, think of yourself as a lawyer or a prosecutor asking a defendant questions in court. You know what you ultimately want to get to, but you don't come right out and go for it. You have to build them up to it first. If you ask the main question immediately, the detail would be lost. Now imagine I am you, the interviewer, and you are the interviewee. How are you today?"

"Good," Taleah said. "No, that's mechanical—"

"Don't worry about it," Jalene said, smiling. "My name is Jalene Summers with the *Capital Weekly*. I'm wondering if I might ask you some questions regarding the vehicle registration bill being debated in the House of Representatives. Would you have a few minutes to spare?"

Taleah craned her neck and tried to watch an older woman struggling into the square with her cane. She saw it as a welcome distraction from what was to come, but she might as well pay attention. She squinted in the sun, keeping her eyes on the woman, and listened for her cue to speak. She had never taken part in a mock interview, but it seemed to induce less pressure than the real thing.

After Jalene finished asking her questions, she paused and smiled at Taleah for long enough to indicate the interview was over. "How do you feel?"

"Um... a bit inadequate." A smile creased her lips, but when her mind once again meandered to her father, the gloom seemed to return.

"Sometimes it isn't always clear how you should do it," Jalene conceded, "and every reporter has different tactics, but you know practice makes perfect. Do you think you are ready to give it a try?"

Taleah nodded slowly. The old woman seemed a little irritable from afar, but if she wanted a diverse background amongst interviewees, this woman would be as good as anyone. "I guess we have a little time."

"This time do you think you can do it unsupervised? I'm going to talk to that businessman."

"I can," she said.

"Then get on it, and good luck."

Taleah stood up and began to approach the woman. Trying to remember the mock interview with Jalene proved the easy part. Rather than confidence, the exercise left a vacuum of inadequacy. Then again, lack of confidence had rarely been a problem. Sheer determination always won out. In high school when she promised herself she wouldn't strike out, good things happened, be it a base hit, batting in another runner, or sacrificing to advance the runner on first. Strategy was more important than stats.

She hadn't survived the monster in the woods by giving up and living with the feeling she'd never make it out alive. She fought for survival, and even after her father and Willis arrived to save the day, she still had to fight like hell to avoid defeat.

Remembering that part of the past caused the tension in her head to skyrocket. Brutality and violence such as she could scarcely imagine had suddenly replaced harmony. Horrors that only took place in stories—whether fact or fiction—before now had injected panic and chaos into the threads of her life, poisoning it from within. It had taken years to rebuild and create something better, and perhaps she hadn't succeeded in all areas, but life was not a project that could be completed. If you stop building, you fail.

The memory hammered in her head until she started the conversation with a sheepish "Hi" that sounded like it should have been uttered in a sad made-for-television movie. Coaxing the force of action and work into pushing away the demons, at least temporarily, would be costly and difficult, but promised reward.

Art Rassine, she thought, had changed his name to evoke terror. Rampage... what was it that drunk idiot had said atop Table Rock? Her father had gone on a rampage?

Taleah's voice caught a snag, and she hurried through the interview without having scored one major admission from the woman, who seemed to ignore the news she found to be depressing on account of living life to the fullest and not letting negativity eat through the precious time she had left. Perhaps it was an admirable trait—even one she could, in a sense, apply to her own life—but with that attitude, her job would become more difficult.

Finally, it was time to head home for the day. Taleah noted that she'd talk Christine into going to visit the hospital with her, even though hospitals always gave Christine a queasy feeling. Jalene thanked her for coming and implored her to practice the art of interviewing on her own time. Tomorrow was Friday and the first deadline. Jalene would have to get something down to be debated on later and then they'd have all of next week to round up the last of what they needed and put the finishing touches on the story for publication the following Monday.

"What do you say about that thing I mentioned?" Taleah asked, hoping Jalene hadn't forgotten about it.

"I don't know if it's going to fit our narrative," she said, raising her eyebrows, but remaining relaxed. "But now that I think about it, your idea may have merit. If we have the time tomorrow afternoon, we can do a quick Q&A session. Though I can't promise that will make its way into the story."

"I know I have a lot to learn," Taleah said. "It's just been a rough couple days. I'll do better—"

Jalene cut her off. "You're doing great. Don't think like that. Admitting it is one thing, but letting it put a damper on your attitude is another. Never let that fear take hold, because it will show in your writing. People will hate you for it."

"Easier said than done," Taleah said.

"But still easier done than worried about."

The conversation turned to life in general on the way back to the office. Jalene seemed to keep it in the front of her mind that Taleah's father was one of two victims of the bombing and stepped lightly around topics that could darken Taleah's thoughts. If Jalene hadn't worked so hard, Taleah might think her a great person and an eternal friend.

The drunken man below the cross returned to her mind before long. Why did that have such a profound impact on her? By now, Art Rassine was little more than a footnote, even as the terror flooded numerous pages in an autobiography unwritten. The pain had been visceral, the trauma surreal, and the fear life-altering. Still, Taleah had to keep constructing. Additions, subtractions, renovations, and makeovers were the ever-changing structure of life. If she let history devour the present, construction would stop and life would grind to a halt.

The memory battered her mind for the entire drive home and its litter polluted her heart so thoroughly that Christine would of course notice and try to help. Perhaps that was her motive—self-induced pain for the sake of being rescued by the right person—but that didn't matter to her. Christine would do anything for her, even give herself to the unrelenting torture of being in a hospital, just to accompany the one she loved through the ordeal.

After she parked the car and climbed the stairs, she turned the key in the lock and surrendered herself to the nurture of love. Pushing the story and everything at work aside just for a few moments of solace would be the tonic that could once again ignite her soul.

6

Prism

PROBABLY as a gesture of politeness, Reggie carefully lifted the corners of his mouth until his face resembled a smile. To Taleah, the expression seemed mechanical and forced, an awkward portrayal of discomfort. She tried to smile in return but couldn't make her mouth communicate something she didn't feel. Rather than let the exchange ruin the visit, she gripped Christine's hand, took in her warmth, and felt her pulse.

This exchange passed as though contrived, but for Christine, it must have seemed natural. Either she was better at communicating, Taleah thought, or she and Reggie were strangers close enough to share a common bond without hidden deficiencies getting in the way. She relaxed and leaned against the back of the chair with one palm resting on her thigh.

"I guess you look better today," Taleah said, looking her father up and down as he reclined in the bed. The nurses had allowed him to adjust the angle of the bed so that he was sitting up.

"And I thought it would have been obvious," Reggie said. "They're going to make me go home tomorrow, but they're keeping Willis an extra day or more."

"You're in trouble," Willis deadpanned from the bed next door. Taleah and Christine had rearranged the chairs so that they were on the side of the bed nearest the door, staying out of the nurse's way. The curtain had been pulled back so that the friends could talk. The one who really seemed better was Willis. He was back to his old tricks, though he grimaced on occasion. "They're not going to let you get used to good food."

"Rebekah's an excellent cook," Christine chimed in without knowing who she was dealing with.

Taleah allowed a dry laugh, but Reggie faked a death stare that seemed to cut Willis down to size.

"I see," Christine said sinking deeper into the chair.

"How was work today?" Reggie asked, rearranging his face to make it resemble the deepest concern.

Taleah frowned. The question would invariably come up, she'd decided, yet she remained unprepared and without a reasonable answer. Instead of cooking up some simple 'great' response that her dad could see through, she scooted forward. Christine released her hand and rested it on her thigh. "Not a total loss, considering."

"What, this? It's just a scratch."

"No," Willis coughed. "The *Titanic*. That was just a scratch. You're sinking, you're on fire, and you're emitting so much radiation that Ukraine is considering letting people back into Chernobyl."

Taleah laughed, while Christine issued him a sideways glance that communicated how strange this situation felt to her. Perhaps it was just the surroundings of the hospital rendering her senses moot, or perhaps she simply didn't understand Willis.

"It worked," Willis said.

"What happened?"

Taleah dropped the smile and considered what happened at work. She grazed Christine's hand with her elbow and gulped, which seemed to cause Christine to stop touching her. "Jalene, one of the reporters I work with, was having me help her read some old stories about crime. And then she took me on assignment and let me interview a couple of people for a story we're doing. And I bombed miserably."

"What's the story about?"

Taleah glanced at Willis and once again attempted to smile. "Bad umpires in Japan's premier softball league."

"Local fare," Reggie said.

"I can't tell you that. Jalene would kill me."

"Whose definition of 'bad?'" Willis barked.

Taleah ignored him.

"Mister St. Clair," a voice sounded from the doorway. Everyone turned their heads to look at the visitor. He stepped into the room and cast a long shadow on the white tile floor. He wore a black tee shirt and blue jeans. His hair was rugged and his jaw punctuated with a stubbly salt-and-pepper beard that highlighted his features. Much of his hair was gray.

Reggie's expression made it obvious that he knew the intruder. "God, you look terrible."

"Look who's talking."

"I can't say I'm surprised to see you here."

"What, always fond of FBI agents showing up at your bedside in the hospital? Happens I'm here on assignment and heard you'd had some bad luck. How's the survey business treating you?"

Taleah nodded slowly when she realized who it was. She'd met him once, but she'd ushered out that part of history and tried to replace it with something less traumatic. He wouldn't simply show up unannounced for no reason. This realization hit her with the force of a freight train in overdrive. "Agent Torrance Marks?"

"Good to see you again, Taleah."

She could only concoct a lie, which anyone could recognize as a manufactured nicety which few people really meant. "Likewise."

"What's the assignment?" Reggie asked. He looked as though compassion had vacated his expression and skepticism had filled the void.

"Need to know," Marks said.

"Sounds about right," Reggie jabbed.

"All right. I'm here to question you."

Reggie grasped the sheet and pulled it up to his face. "Oh my God."

Agent Marks stepped further into the room and leaned against the sink. He made a fist on his midsection, rested his elbow on it, and stroked his chin with his free hand. "Something strange happened. Normally, this is something local police would handle. But they sent it my way because it started to resemble a cold case I've had sitting on my shelf for the better part of a decade."

"And they are," Reggie said, possibly referring to the local police.

"Funny. You know where the Army Navy store is?"

"Shoot," Reggie said. "It's not a place I frequent."

"I do," Willis said. "You know how my wife loves hunting. She thinks it's a sport, but I'm sure the animals disagree. She usually drags me in there kicking and screaming."

Marks nodded at him and grinned. "Willis Ralston? Married?"

"Agent Marks, not married?"

His smile drooped. Taleah suppressed a laugh and almost gagged. Christine leaned closer to her as if to whisper something but remained silent.

"It's in Garden City, actually," Marks said. "They don't do a lot of advertising, but they have a lot of stuff that could be useful—camping, hiking, anything nature. And they had a break-in recently."

"So?"

"Ada sheriffs responded to the call. Referred it to Garden City Police, which, it happens is run by the sheriff's office. So Garden City runs with it and starts to zero in on the thief. If you're trying to be anonymous, you don't break into a store and walk off with merchandise. Security cameras across the street caught the vehicle leaving. Registered to a James McAwan."

"Doesn't make any sense," Willis said. "If you're going to rip off camping and fishing gear, you'll get better, more expensive stuff at the sportsman stores."

"Unless you can only get it at an Army Navy store," Reggie guessed.

Taleah sat up straight and tried to remove a knot in her back. She grasped Christine's hand tightly while Christine snuggled closer. Her eyes sparkled like dew on an autumn morning.

"And James McAwan is acquainted with a family who owns a special ranch property that burned down just days ago. I don't need to give you three guesses who used to own that ranch."

"Of course," Reggie said. "Why not?"

"Are you kidding me? Taleah asked, incredulous. "The Crest Fire has been in the papers the last week or more, near New Meadows. I read the town has been mostly evacuated."

"You're aware of the property?" Agent Marks asked, staring at her. His gaze lingered a second too long and seemed befuddled, as if he'd never seen two women holding hands.

"Nope," Reggie said. "All the stories I told her, I didn't ever tell her about the Harrison family."

"The family that currently owns it, they are the Kleinman family. Husband, wife, two daughters. Kendall Kleinman knows Mr. McAwan on social media. Ada County arrested McAwan the other night after they got a tip. And now he says he's going to cooperate."

"Cooperate?" Reggie said. "You don't offer to cooperate unless you're not in on it alone."

"Of course not," Agent Marks said.

Reggie swore and groaned at the same time. The realization towered over Taleah like the victor of a bitter duel. Her heart raced as the memory of that night at Table Rock sped through her mind as though engulfed in flame. It eroded her consciousness and pummeled her with relentless agony. *He's dead,* she reminded herself.

"Wait a minute," Willis said. "You can't be telling us that he's come back from the dead. I'm an umpire and even creatures of the night know that's not possible."

"Creatures of the... what?" Christine's eyes seemed to skewer Taleah's disbelief. The comedic interjection offered a bit of relief, but the emotion must have still played out on her face.

"Nothing," Taleah whispered. "It's just a long-running joke. He thinks umpires are undead."

"I don't think that," Willis shot. "I know."

"See?"

"Really?" Christine smiled and refocused her attention on Marks.

"No," Marks said, letting his gaze rest on Taleah and Christine momentarily. "Not possible. I examined the body myself and it was Art Rassine, for sure. Face matched the photograph. You remember that picture, Reg."

Taleah stared toward the bed, where Reggie had turned to face Marks for the conversation. The white lights overhead cascaded into a sort of haze that seemed to prance over her father's head, making him appear divine.

"Ada County told you about all this?"

"Not exactly," Marks said, standing up straight again. "They told me it reminded them of a cold case from seven years ago, which I can't tell you about."

"But you are telling me about it," Reggie said. "You're telling me it doesn't have to do with Rassine."

"Well, now it does."

"So, that's it, huh? Case closed? And you still need to question me."

Marks appeared to ponder on something as he looked past Reggie toward the far wall, where two waiting chairs sat empty in front of the large window.

"Excuse me," a voice at the door said. "Am I interrupting?"

"Honey," Willis said.

She entered and flung a mane of curled hair behind her shoulder. She wore tight denim jeans and a plaid button-down shirt. The rustic yet refined style had become attached to her image. Taleah had only met her twice before, but she dressed almost the same way every time. She strolled past Taleah and Christine and took a seat next to her husband.

"Not yet," Marks said, lowering his voice. "I'm running down McAwan's relation to the Kleinman family. Something comes up linking him directly to the Harrisons, you'll be the first to know."

"Where's Special Agent Bill Coles?" Reggie asked.

Marks leaned back again and narrowed his eyes. "Retired. I work alone now."

"And here I thought you'd be the first to retire," Reggie said.

Reggie's eyes seemed to haze over suddenly, a sign that weariness was beginning to creep in. Taleah adjusted in her chair, crossed her legs, and scanned his face for a trace of justice. In her adult years, Taleah had learned that her father could scarcely hide emotions he felt too deep to reveal. Perhaps only familiarity could afford her the benefit of tacitly understanding those truths, but in matters regarding the heart, he couldn't lie because his eyes gave him away. The eeriness in his face stemmed from emptiness, when his heart should be battering him with thousands of questions that, if answered, could grind his expression to powder.

Then again, when her mother had fallen gravely ill five years ago, Reggie carried a jarringly serene face. When Taleah had attempted to unravel it, to make him explain to her why he wouldn't tell her, his expression had turned vacant, as if no emotion at all had swirled in his brain. That didn't turn out to be true, of course. Even more than a decade after the divorce, some connection remained.

"Well," Reggie said, struggling to look Agent Marks in the eye, "he was a good agent. I'm sure the Bureau is just a little bit worse off."

"It's service," Agent Marks droned, without so much as glancing at Taleah. "Sometimes it's time to go and let a younger agent step up. Seems like I've earned the right to work alone."

"Maybe that's not much of a benefit," Reggie surmised.

"They promoted Agent Clark and me to senior field agents," Marks said, glancing toward Willis, who had, over the last several minutes, grown bored with his intrusion. "You remember Clark."

"What? Who?"

Reggie glanced at Taleah while turning his head to face Willis, who wore a quizzical look that suddenly vanished when Reggie spoke. "Oh, please. You couldn't take your eyes off of her."

"Ah, *that* Agent Clark."

"Still partnered up with DeLaren," Agent Marks said. "When they both still reported to Bill, he got married back in France while he and Clark chased down a drug dealer in Southern Utah."

"I'm not sure I'm familiar with him," Reggie said, returning his gaze to Agent Marks.

Marks took it in stride and simply nodded before going on a rant about old age, and how deeply unfair turning fifty-five had been. Taleah allowed them to catch up and cozied with Christine. Marks's tone began to take on a muffled, underwater sound as she absorbed some of Christine's body heat.

"You seem comfortable," she said, gently closing her eyes. Normally, Christine would be fidgeting and wishing to leave, but she remained almost motionless. Her breathing was slow and inaudible.

"Do I?" Taleah whispered. "You seem tired."

"Nope. Just thinking."

"About what?"

She adjusted, pulled away, and stared at Agent Marks. "Nothing. I can't even imagine going through what you did. You're tough. I probably would never have survived."

Taleah straightened her back, causing Christine to release her hand, as if the moments of comfort could not last without some interruption of human thought muddying otherwise clear waters. Christine's intuition had always been an asset. To think otherwise was to abandon one of the sources of passion. But now, she needed convincing, and Taleah had no idea how to respond to it.

"You would."

"I know you don't want to talk about it," she said.

Biting her lip to keep from saying something terrible that must have been forming somewhere in her subconscious, Taleah turned toward the door, where pairs of footsteps shuffled by on the tile outside the room. Rebekah would surely walk through the door any second, she guessed. Every moment that passed by where she didn't, Taleah glanced at her watch.

Rebekah had fooled Taleah a time or two. She showed compassion in spades, even when Taleah's mother could not. Taleah didn't consider that to be a strike against Anna. Her mother ruled her own world, and every emotion and memory pointed inward for her. She loved Taleah ten times more than Rebekah did, but Rebekah was more fluent in expressing that care vocally, which Taleah sometimes needed more.

Before she could register that time was speeding away, more than an hour had passed. Friday was deadline day at the office and Jalene would grow impatient towards the end of the day. Her failures in the Grove glistened like distant memories wrapped in the delicate beams of starlight. The mock interview had only marginally improved her. Time, she promised herself, would provide ample experience if she could stomach the tides of unpleasant news.

But the nightmare from last night crashed on the shores. She'd been running. Running all her life. It became a horrifying metaphor before she even realized what it meant. Though she was no expert in discerning dreams, she sensed that running could represent the ugly truth attempting to confront her once again.

Years ago, the stress of Art Rassine had begun to fade away. But sleepless nights spent in darkness where her thoughts could not escape the interminable torture had consumed large portions of her soul. Her counselor taught her how to come to terms with it, and while the medication helped erase the depths, it was her counselor who had proved a more noticeable impact. The dreams had raged on for more than a year. The sounds of nature at night, the dripping of water, the groans of trees swaying in the wind, and the distant howls had caused the hairs on her arms to stand upright, and Art Rassine seemingly lurked somewhere behind every rock, ready to take her, to punish her. To crush her soul. And she could only run. Instead of leaving it behind, running fed energy into the shadow. The women he'd abused so many years earlier must have experienced similar trauma, Taleah guessed.

The only way to pacify the demon that carved up her spirit was to stop running and to confront it face-on. But bravery didn't come without its price.

Taleah witnessed in her father the kind of fear that could only trample him, she thought. The lack of expression was simply another testament to that fear. She didn't know what to say, but her heart beat on. She could stop running and he could defeat the fear if they worked together. Now that the rescue was up to her, planning would prove easier—if only she knew where to start.

7

Blueshift

A poster with a yellow motif adorned a wood-paneled wall with finishing strips turned sideways to resemble decorative slats. A half-dozen oblong tables sat perpendicular to the wall. Squares of sunshine spilled through the high windows in the walls. Taleah stared at the poster, which incorporated tiny, Arabic script below capital letters spelling out CAIR. After nearly a full minute, Jalene nudged her.

Having never dealt with the Council on American Islamic Relations, Taleah had not formed an opinion on the organization, but had heard negative rumors related to it. She scooted back against the plastic chair so that her spine straightened. Fidgeting with her pen to save the stress, she watched a pair of women wearing hijabs and scarves slowly walk to a table at the end of the row while conversing in Arabic. This atmosphere was new, which provided a sense of uncertainty that Taleah had come to expect.

Jalene jotted something down in her notebook using tiny writing, perhaps meant as a personal note for when she would write the article. This was not unusual; Taleah had seen Jalene writing notes down on sticky notes, the corners of napkins, and even on the backs of face cards, whenever a thematic idea or inspiration struck her. The writing looked sloppy, but she laid the pen down pointed toward the top of the page, where it rolled to the spiral binding.

The pair of women broke off their conversation as if in mid-sentence when Taleah glanced their way. Instead of appearing offended or secretive, the women nodded at one another and stabbed at their salads.

Two younger men, one sporting a full, wiry beard, pushed through a doorway, speaking quickly and approached Taleah and Jalene. Her college acquaintance Emmanuel removed his baseball cap, the bill of which he had molded into a perfect arch and carried it by the bill. He pushed his glasses up his nose and straddled the seat opposite to Taleah. She smiled at him politely and half-glanced at his friend. Beneath his beard, a worn-out plaid shirt highlighted seemingly frail features. His frown stretched momentarily, as if mistrust had guided his reaction. Taleah took this in stride and extended her hand.

Emmanuel rattled off a short sentence ending with her name, and then nodded at her. He grasped her hand and shook it lightly. The tradition was likely not firmly rooted in his home country, so his uncertainty could be forgiven.

"Taleah, meet Abal Salib. Abal is a refugee from Syria, here with his daughter. I am showing him around introducing him to people. Helping him make friends."

Abal didn't say anything. Instead, he regarded Jalene with an almost quizzical look. Taleah released Emmanuel's hand and waved it slowly toward Jalene. She attempted to smile. "Abal, this is my friend Jalene. We are with the *Capital Weekly* and we're gauging local interest in an in-depth story about the bombing the other day."

Emmanuel let go of his cap and offered a half-nod to Taleah before he began to translate. Abal frowned and responded quickly with what seemed to be an impassioned plea for understanding, almost to the point of anger. Taleah broke eye contact and waited for Emmanuel to translate his words.

"I know nothing about it. I seek only peace—goodwill. Why do you single me out?"

Taleah shook her head and glanced down at the table. The women at the end of the row laughed at something and got back to eating. "It's not that," she said meekly. "We were hoping to talk to both of you."

"If you talk as a friend," Emmanuel said, uncharacteristically breaking into a deep accent, "you will not find problem. Abal wants to be treated fairly."

"That's what we're after," Jalene said firmly, almost as an example to Taleah. She swallowed and let her gaze fall onto Abal's features. Finding empathy in his gesture, Taleah waited for Emmanuel to translate.

Abal relaxed his hands and placed them flat on the table in front of him.

"You must know, he wants privacy," Emmanuel stated. "Please don't use his name in your paper."

"It's purely confidential," Taleah said, squaring her jaw and flinging a wide-eyed smile to a point between Emmanuel and Abal.

"You look like yourself," Emmanuel said. "But so much has changed. What else have you done since university?"

Not wanting to get into specifics, Taleah clasped her hands together and glanced at the CAIR poster. "I mostly copy-edit now. Jalene here is a veteran reporter and my mentor."

"Investigative stuff, and lots of human-interest angles," Jalene said.

"And personally? Married? Children?"

Taleah shook her head and verbally responded seconds later, after she reasoned that non-verbal communication looked unprofessional. Jalene didn't give her any cues, so she let her words carry plainly. "Not yet. Maybe in a year or two. Who knows? You?"

Emmanuel smiled and shook his head simultaneously. The light reflected on his square-rimmed glasses, making him somehow look younger and more intellectual. "No. I meet some friends now and then, but nothing serious. And I spend most of my time here."

"Pay well?"

"I volunteer. And not just translating. Helping with job opportunities, training, understanding American culture. You do not know about leaving the only place you've ever known, moving halfway around the world, starting over. It is very difficult."

Taleah allowed herself to consider his use of English. Having lived in the city for five or six years, he had picked up on most American customs and his accent had waned. Still, many idioms seemed a foreign concept to him. Instead of attempting to assimilate into sayings he could scarcely understand, let alone translate, he elected to speak plainly, which might have made his speech a touch dry if not for the tone, texture, and cadence of his voice, which sounded uniquely American.

Emmanuel had migrated from Jordan before college. His parents and sibling had stayed behind, hoping to seek American citizenship in a few years. The Islamic community had adopted him, and his education had served him well.

"I am learning software. Part time. But the salary is good."

"That's good to hear," Taleah said.

"It is excellent seeing you again." He stroked his chin and tilted his face up, which allowed the light to form a soft reflection that highlighted his complexion. "I did hear about the bomb. The police did not mention Islam but said it might have been terrorist."

"I can't speak to the investigation," Taleah said, suddenly aware that her tone had changed. She shot a helpless glance at Jalene, hoping she'd interject and steer her back on course. Instead, Jalene listened without so much as touching her pen. Taleah continued. "But with some of that talk, there might be public interest in how our community deals with such tragedy. That is where we come in."

Possibly picking up on the word 'terrorist,' Abal clenched his fist and leaned toward the table. He stammered something that sounded either defensive or accusatory, but his expression seemed polite beyond words.

"I know nothing about it," Emmanuel translated. "It is senseless, and we weep for the people." He paused long enough to signal his own interpretation. "Abal has had to live through terrorism. Assad attacks the people often, including women and children. Too many times, and I can tell you that America is not helping by just bombing them. They know how to make it look deliberate against the Syrian people. They do not trust their government or ours at the moment. But America—this city—is a safe haven."

"How do you feel about the assumption that this was such an attack?" Taleah asked, injecting her speech with manufactured confidence.

"It is uncomfortable," Emmanuel admitted. "Most people here are happy to help and open-minded about the situation. But some people, since the 9/11, look upon people like us using stereotypes. Like they've been told it is the fault of Islam, even all Islamic people that some bad people do terrible things. But these are good people. What little rudeness they deal with, they do not want to play victim. Or get involved in politics."

"Would you mind asking Abal the same question?"

Emmanuel nodded swiftly, turned his head and uttered the question in Arabic. He translated as Abal spoke.

"Everyone here is good to me. They are kind and they understand what we go through before we get here. Terrorism affects us as much as American citizens, but it doesn't get reported much. If they say this is terrorism, then it probably is."

"Is it the religion aspect that gets touched on the most?" Taleah posed the question to both of them. Emmanuel translated.

"People are not comfortable with what they don't understand," Emmanuel responded. Abal attempted to speak over him which seemed to confuse Emmanuel. "He says the same. Cannot control what people think but respect them anyway."

"You've been around here long enough to read about some of the tragedies our city has had over the years," Taleah explained. "Do you remember the stabbing incident or the big hit-and-run? The shooting, or even the explosion at the office park a few years back?"

Emmanuel didn't alter his expression. He slowly nodded as she spoke. "Bad things."

"How has this city reacted towards the Islamic community? And these people? Can you describe the prevailing mood?"

"It was sadness and grief with the rest of the people in the city," Emmanuel said. "I remember a death threat once after the explosion. That was an accident, but it must have provoked certain people. The people in this city reach out with overwhelming support, especially after the stabbing attack. There was no anger over the press coverage in this center. We have a large support network with many charity and church organizations reaching out to help. The Islamic community here believes it is a blessing to live amongst these kind people."

Jalene had picked up her pen and started to scribble when Taleah found her rhythm. She didn't hesitate with the words or even attempt to modify any of the phrasing. Taleah would have approached this understanding with caution, but instead, she gave all her energy to Emmanuel.

"Has the Islamic community responded in kind when such crimes strike the majority?"

"It is the majority," Emmanuel said, offering a slow nod and eyeing a pair of women seated behind Taleah. "When such a large percentage of the people are white, we do not reach out to them like they are a minority, or even because they are different. We grieve with everyone else."

"Has the community lost any sense of safety after any of these attacks?"

"How do you not be afraid that the tranquility is fading lately?" Emmanuel said. "I think perspective can dictate reaction. And most of these people know they are safe. Even not trusting the government."

"Do you feel safe in this city, Abal?" Taleah eyed him curiously and injected a surreptitious smile that seemed to lighten his mood.

Abal stroked his beard and offered a warm expression when Emmanuel translated for him. As time went by, Taleah noticed that Emmanuel's voice drifted into the background, giving the impression that Taleah was successfully engaged in conversation despite the language barrier. When he spoke, he flourished with passion, which Emmanuel reflected flawlessly.

"It is safe. I chose here because there was a strong community. And as long as my daughter can play with the other children without being thought of as different or an outsider, I am happy. We are happy, but no place can be perfect. We try to make it so every day, for us, for our families. When violence happens, we grow together stronger."

A thought jumped into Taleah's mind, and she found herself piecing together a question before she even knew how to ask it. "If you could say one thing to the two victims—anything—what would you tell them?"

Emmanuel shifted his shoulders and translated the question before answering it himself. "I would tell them we are with them. Abal?"

Abal's eyes grew wider and his gaze softer. His jaw slackened, revealing the tender face of a man who had given up everything in the name of peace and freedom. The warmth in his expression radiated compassion and empathy.

"I would say," Emmanuel translated, "you are not alone. Don't fear. If they are terrorist, if you fear, they win. You cannot let them win. When they see they have succeeded, they will strike again."

Taleah's face flushed. Her hands twitched as Jalene furiously scribbled away at her notebook. Abal's sentences were choppy, but Taleah could not deny his words were true. They filled her heart with the kind of energy that could light a fire that could not be extinguished. She consciously stopped her lip from trembling, but her knee began to bounce up and down beneath the table, as if she were eager to get started on an engaging task. "Thank you," she said looking Abal in the eyes.

That two-word sentence didn't require translation. Instead of saying anything, Abal nodded slowly and offered a contemplative smile.

Taleah's eyes shifted to Emmanuel. His expression had changed while she studied Abal. As if searching for clues, he narrowed his eyes, leaned forward subtly, and exhaled. It was clear to Taleah that he didn't know what to say.

"My dad's one of the victims," Taleah blurted out.

Emmanuel seemed to have expected the revelation. His expression didn't change. He reached one hand across the table and grasped Taleah's left hand, which had begun shaking. On instinct, she attempted to pull away, which Emmanuel allowed. He rested his hand on the table and his eyebrow twitched.

Jalene dropped the pen, perhaps out of surprise and frustration, and let out a long sigh. She then whispered something to herself, which Taleah couldn't make out.

"You know already," she guessed, ignoring Jalene's unspoken pleas for professionalism. Whatever she had to say wouldn't matter, because she was speaking to Emmanuel not as a reporter, or reporter in training, but as a friend. That wouldn't stop Jalene from chiding her later, she understood, but she didn't care.

"I heard about it at the office. We are developing a new software for the city. Someone in the coffee room mentioned the name St. Clair while talking about the bombing. How is he?"

"He's..." Taleah stopped herself and attempted to swallow a lump that had suddenly materialized at the back of her throat. "They aren't letting reporters into his room. There shouldn't be anyone who knows."

"Someone does," Emmanuel confirmed.

"Taleah, we need to get back to the office," Jalene interrupted. "And I need to talk to you."

"I'm talking to a friend," Taleah snapped without so much as glancing at Jalene. With that sentence, her heart flipped in her chest and all at once, Emmanuel seemed closer and more real than he'd ever felt. Her voice dropped as she continued. "My dad is going to be okay. His friend got it worse and will be in the hospital for a week or so. But my dad is tough, and he's been through a lot."

"Tell him I wish him the best," Emmanuel said, at once retracting his hand and offering Taleah a sincere gesture.

A tear worked its way to Taleah's eye. She squinted to suppress it and then wrestled with her pen. "Thank you."

"Salaam," Abal said.

"Same to you," Taleah said politely.

Emmanuel stood up from the table while Jalene jotted down some thoughts in her notebook. When Taleah stood, she eyed the poster and tried to make out the smaller English printing at the bottom.

STAND FOR SOMETHING. CAIR FOR SOMEONE.

Jalene and Taleah gathered up their pens and their notebooks. Emotions battered Taleah with ease, but the sensation of resolution crept to the top. Whoever had caused the explosion, Taleah would help find him. When they got into the car, Taleah scrambled her face to hide her feelings, which Jalene would latch onto.

They didn't talk for several minutes until they rolled up to a stop light. Jalene sighed and tapped her fingers on the steering wheel.

"Look, I'm sorry," Taleah offered.

"You jeopardized the story. If you can't act like a professional, you can't make it in this business."

"He's a friend."

"I'm disappointed. You can have friends, that's fine. Do you know how many people were there watching us? If they told everyone they knew about this incident, we've got a big problem. I'm not going to protect you if it blows up in your face."

Taleah bit her lip. "Thanks for being a mentor."

"I'm going to let you copy-edit," Jalene said. Her words were like serrated blades that cut her deep, leaving excruciating wounds in their wake. "Never let your personal feelings interfere again."

Anger flushed through her, but she tried to restrain herself. What came out instead would have been easy to label as passive aggressive, but she exerted so much force with her voice that the tension revealed itself. "You're not my boss."

"You don't want to go there," Jalene warned. "Now, I'm going to write for the rest of the day. I want you to think about structure in the meantime, while you edit for Monday's back section stories."

Jalene's advice pummeled her with precise jabs that bludgeoned her with understanding. The last thing she wanted to do was edit. She wanted to talk to her father, spend the evening watching television with Christine, cuddled up under a warm blanket with a can of cola and a tub of popcorn. Anything to take the edge off of this nightmare. Snapping at Jalene wouldn't be helpful, but something in her had suddenly awakened and she could not hold it back. It provoked her into digging deeper.

Asking her to be professional on a story like this one was like asking a police officer to investigate the murder of his wife without acting out of emotion for even a millisecond. What she wanted to explain to Jalene would have to wait, but then again, Jalene would come to understand that on her own. It might take several hours, but she'd come around.

Instead of speaking, Taleah reviewed all the notes she'd taken in the last two days and tried to construct the story in her own way. Planning ahead seemed the right course of action, and it numbed her just enough to let her intellect shine through. Uncapping the pen and thinking fluidly, she underlined a section of her notes and drew a long, curved arrow to the top of the page.

Jalene parked the car and they hurried into the office. Taleah started writing in notes in the margins for the next story. Her phone rang twenty minutes later.

"This is Taleah," she said.

"Taleah, this is Casey," the girl said. Casey was one of the receptionists, thin and sleek with shiny hair that she kept in long, flat ponytails. "You have a call on line three."

"I'm a little busy. Did they say who is calling?"

"Sure did." She paused for long enough to write something down, and without altering her tone, continued. "His name is Art Rassine."

8

Infrared

PANIC flashed through Taleah's brain like wind-whipped flames tearing through old growth sagebrush. Its embers consumed her every thought as time froze into a single moment stretched to infinity. *I'm going to kill your father.*

Instead of retreating into darkness, she bit her lip, pushed the button to answer and swallowed. It couldn't be him. He was dead. If she recognized the voice as that of the drunken man from Table Rock, she'd hunt him down herself.

"*Capital Weekly*, this is Taleah."

The voice ground her sensibilities to powder. "St. Clair."

A half-formed thought rampaged somewhere in the central corridors of her brain, but she could not coax it out into the open. "Look, I don't know who you are, but this isn't funny."

Like a heaving beast, the caller roared. "You never did, sweetheart."

Taleah launched herself from her chair and shouted into the receiver, pouring every ounce of passion and disgust into her cobbled words. "Go to *hell,* you endless pile of... refuse!"

"That's not very lady-like. So much fire. So little time." His voice sparked memory that systematically destroyed every safeguard from the demons that had plagued her seven years ago. The tone and timbre of his voice seemed to mix course gravel with pine bark. It raked the agony over coals of tortured anguish as if to tear apart years of building with a single stroke.

"Taleah?" someone behind her said.

"You're dead. The FBI—"

Tempestuous laughter scorched the other end of the line but lingered only briefly. "The FBI. And your father. *That's* funny."

Anger rushed through her veins. She slammed the phone onto the hook, grabbed her purse and fled to her car, where she could unload the venom into heavy tears and spasms of rage. She raced toward the front door, despite the calls for her to stop. She could not stop. There was no choice but to run.

"Taleah, please wait."

"I'm not talking to you right now," Taleah said, her tone sour with a noticeable tremble. Jalene cared as much as anyone who didn't know about the monster she had dealt with years ago.

"You have to stop. Come with me to the alley. We can talk there."

"No, I'm going home."

Jalene tugged at the strings of her purse just enough to get her to turn around, and then gulped when faced with the destruction on Taleah's face. "I'm... I'm not going to let you drive like this."

"What do you care?"

"I was hoping we could be friends. Come with me and settle down."

Taleah's face flooded with tears. "You're not a friend. You don't know a single thing about me."

Jalene exerted more force and grasped Taleah's shoulder with her right hand, leading her out the front door. They turned the corner at the edge of the building and sat together on a circular, aggregate concrete planter facing the river. The grass flourished in the sunshine beneath the tall cottonwoods. The density of the trunks allowed interrupted views of the water, which still ran high and swift from the spring runoff. A pair of geese waddled into the rough grass bordering the trees a hundred feet away and a family of ducklings swam toward the far shore, beyond which stood the glass fronts of the River District office buildings.

"I know more than you think I do," Jalene started without warning.

Taleah forced her eyes from the ducks to her feet in the grass, which seemed ooze like some kind of primordial mud in a viscous concoction of saline tears and snot.

"For example..." Her voice seemed to wade in the shallows of some far-off body of water, uncertain as to the safety of the deep. "I know you played softball. And I know you are in a relationship with a woman."

"Don't even start," Taleah said, wiping away the tears.

"Is there something you want to tell me, then? So that I can understand you more?"

Reliving the memories would vanquish everything she thought she knew. She could get out only one sentence, which seemed to remedy the anger and the torture. "He's dead."

"What? Who is dead?"

Taleah placed her hands on her knees and lifted her eyes toward the shore. "*He* is. I watched Willis shoot him. They hauled away his body... but how could he..."

"Should we call the police?"

Taleah nodded quickly, and then amended her response by shaking her head violently enough to jar the miniscule thoughts that had been safely tucked away, undamaged by the barren, guttural voice of Art Rassine. "The FBI, I think."

Jalene fished for Taleah's phone in her purse and dialed someone in the office. The waiting was torture, like listening to the drip of water from cold, stone ceilings into pools on uneven clay and rock.

"Agent Marks... he is sort of friends with my dad. He showed up that night after Willis shot the monster. They said he was dead. I think my dad has his cell number."

Jalene handed the phone to Taleah and waited for her to finish the short conversation with him. When Taleah hung up, she immediately dialed Marks's number."

"Marks," he answered.

"Agent Marks, this is Taleah St. Clair. I just got a suspicious phone call. I need you at my office."

"Be there in under an hour," Marks said. "I know someone who can help with a trace."

"Taleah," Jalene said after she hung up. "can you tell me who *he* is?"

Taleah shook her head, raised her eyebrows, and let her shoulders slump. "He kidnapped... killed all these women. And got away with it. Until my dad and Willis caught up with him... seven years ago. Looking for me."

Jalene at once looked horrified, but the marks of fear vanished, replaced by a settling empathy.

"You... I don't understand. Maybe someday you could tell me the whole story, without evoking such heartache."

"I'll never tell that story again," Taleah said.

"Then who just called you?"

Taleah gripped her knee and dug her nails into the black cotton of her slacks. "It was... I don't know. He said he was him, he even sounded like him. A lot like him. But he's dead."

"Well," Jalene said, apparently trying to think clearly, "maybe we can get IT to see if they can find a recording, or the FBI can trace the origin of the call. If he's just some asshole trying to get you scared, that's one thing. If it's really some killer, they'll easily find him now. It's only a matter of time."

"Time," Taleah repeated. "Oh my God."

"What?"

"He's after my dad."

"It isn't him," Jalene said. "It can't be, right?"

Taleah wiped her eyes and then cupped both knees with open palms. Jalene pulled her into a half embrace just long enough to inject a measure of comfort. "No, of course not. It has to be a prankster."

"I'd advise you to go home and rest," Jalene said, leaning towards Taleah's right side, "after Agent Marks is finished." She pushed Taleah's phone back into her purse and then watched the ducks disappear behind a thicket of low-growing shrubs and wild trees.

Taleah nodded slowly. "About that thing with me being in a relationship. Think you can keep that to yourself?"

"I won't tell anyone," Jalene said, "but some people already know. I thought you were out already."

"I am," she said. "I just don't want it causing drama in the office."

"You know," Jalene said, lowering her voice a touch. "You're great at what you do. I was wrong to criticize you earlier. I'm sorry."

"No," Taleah said. "You were right, I messed up. I could have connected with Emmanuel on my off time."

"So you went to college together."

"Yes. We studied together sometimes. He was highly motivated, I guess the perfect example of what they are calling a Dreamer now. He worked harder than anyone I knew, graduated at the top of his class, and wants to be a software engineer at Lynx."

"Does he know?"

"That I'm seeing someone? No. And I don't really see any need to tell him."

"Are you going to contact him again?" Jalene was returning to her inquisitive nature and before long, Taleah thought, would be slamming her with how, where, when, and why.

"I don't know. We haven't talked since college."

"But it's nice to have friends you can count on."

Taleah looked up to witness the concern played out on Jalene's face. "Is that why you're doing this? Because you think I need a friend? As if I'm half a girl, shunned, looking for the light of someone I can trust?"

"That's not..."

"You see me as weak."

Jalene shifted her weight, at once looking uncomfortable. "Please don't turn this into something it's not. I'm not judging you for your choices."

Taleah leaned away and let her knees begin to bounce. "That you can even say that tells me you don't know anything about it. I didn't choose anything."

"I understand."

"You do not."

"Then teach me. Tell me everything I need to know." Her face changed as she slowly rose to her feet. Rather than confrontation, her expression revealed something resembling untold empathy, almost mirroring Abal's expression earlier. "I'm pretty open-minded, I think. There's nothing you can say that will offend me."

Taleah nodded and tried to paste a smile to her face, which only seemed to shroud her with an even thicker tapestry of misery, and rather than warm her spirit, it doused her in an inescapable cold. Time looked sharp on the horizon like a coming storm front on a cloudless day. If she didn't prepare for its arrival, the winds would shatter the structure of her soul. Time always lurked ahead, and when events defined it, dread prowled with it.

As the moments ticked away, she could only yearn to be at her father's side, to tell him what had happened. But something bigger was coming. The bombing wasn't an act of terrorism. That suggested too much coincidence. No, what had happened was a deliberate attempt to strike fear in only one person, who just happened to be the one person she knew who refused to succumb to it. One way or another she had to let him know before the day was out.

S unlight cascaded through horizontal oblong openings in the exterior cladding of the Eastland Central Garage, where hundreds of cars spent the day nestled side by side seven levels high. Though the sun had almost reached its zenith, its light produced acute parallelograms, distorted by the cars, on the concrete walls. A pair of stray people approached idle cars and went their way, but the garage this time of day was quiet more often than not.

A woman, distracted by her phone screen, flung open her car door and stood still, examining a text message.

Another woman ascended the incline about a hundred feet away from the elevator in a straight line, where her car waited. She ignited the engine, let it run for a few moments, and then cautiously backed out of her parking spot.

In the Eastland Garage in particular, levels three through six usually retained greater levels of silence, since people paid a monthly rate to park their vehicles, which always proved more economical than the regular hourly rate the city offered.

Three years earlier, the city had fully automated the garages so that a person hoping to park his or her car needed only push a button on a panel after stopping at the gate, retrieve the ticket, and then upon return, insert the ticket into a kiosk that would determine the amount owed and take payment. Though the system was not without its kinks, it allowed the city to reduce staff at nearly every public garage, saving millions of dollars every year. Even with the more efficient plan, however, the city still faced a shortage of parking spaces downtown. Tens of thousands of people commuted in from the suburbs every day and the city had no reliable means of transit.

The distracted woman looked over her shoulder to where the sun shone through a small window on a door that led into the elevator vestibule. Next to that, another door led to the stairwell. Both remained closed, but she thought she heard chatter and the echoing booms of feet on stairs.

The light spread inward from the openings on both ends of the buildings, angling inward as shadows overcame its rays. The woman in the car slowly descended the ramps and turned out of sight, while the distracted woman deposited her phone into the central console for long enough to start the car. Rather than pull out of her spot, she glanced at her phone and realized the text conversation was more important, and so allowed the car to idle.

Two opposite corners of the garage housed elevators and stairs. On the north side, the elevator opened into a vestibule facing an inlet in the sidewalk on Idaho Street. Most people, however, exited the garage from the Main Street side. Workers at City Hall only needed to walk a half a block and cross the always-packed Capital Boulevard at carefully controlled crosswalks. If one was lucky and wished to cross during the midafternoon or midmorning, the crosswalk would change the signal quickly. At busier times, several dozen people would come to wait.

A man with a thin leather briefcase stumbled out of the elevator vestibule without looking in front of him. The door swung closed faster than he anticipated, letting dark close in quickly on the temporary light. Silence reigned for a second, long enough for the man to take two steps.

He gulped when a firm hand clutched his shoulder. "You're here early," he said, his voice wavering.

"And you told. You're so stupid."

"Now wait a minute," the man named Saul said. "If this isn't done aboveboard, it will attract suspicion. I only filed the papers..."

The stranger gripped him harder and pulled Saul into a small alcove behind the door to the elevator vestibule, where the light from neither end of the building could reach.

"Who do you report to?"

"Well, I...you know, in financial matters, I often report to the city council." Saul's face flushed as he narrowed his shoulders, as if hoping to escape the stranger's grasp.

"They know?"

"I didn't include any irrelevant info. But, you know, you can't always control the rumor mill."

"Who did you tell?"

"Just my wife," Saul said.

"You just killed your wife."

Saul, at once struck with terror, slid backwards toward the nearest car, but the stranger didn't relinquish his grip.

"Come on now," Saul Stammered, "calm down. I'm sure we can come to a mutually beneficial agreement, contingent upon..."

The stranger listened for a few seconds, gently drawing in a breath as Saul hesitated. "We can make an agreement right here. Here's the first demand. You give me St. Clair or die."

"How do you know St. Clair? I didn't tell anyone about that."

"St. Clair," the stranger repeated, more firmly, yet quieter.

"You're a little bit obsessed..."

"No more stalling, you prick. Give him to me."

Saul pursed his lips and glanced toward the far end of the garage, where the taillights of a car filled the air with a surreal glow that could not quite illuminate this corner, as if they were invisible to the naked eye. "Well, I don't really know. You know, bureaucracy and all that. Red tape. And even then, you won't be able to talk to him. Rumor has it that he's surrounded with plenty of other people you don't want to know about our deal. It's too bad that..."

The stranger gripped his arm harder and flung him against the concrete wall with enough force to shoot jolts of pain through his shoulder. "Give me St. Clair!"

"Okay, okay! He's in the emergency ward at Saint Margaret's. Got hurt in the explosion the other day. God, you know the attacker!"

"Shut up!" The dark man pulled Saul away from the wall, pushed him onto the hood of the nearest car, and reared his fist for attack.

"Shit! What the hell?" On instinct, he kicked the man's legs, but he pretended not to notice. The fist collided with the sheet steel just as he managed to scoot himself away. In the interim, the man managed to clutch Saul's other arm.

Saul resisted and found an avenue of escape if he could wrestle himself free. Within seconds, he'd managed to get out of the stranger's grip. With a shout of victory, Saul began his sprint away, but made it less than a full step before his trailing foot collided with the concrete wheel stop. The momentum vaulted him forward. His hands broke his fall, but the stranger had already latched on to his jacket.

"God, no!"

The jacket would slide off easily, he decided. He wriggled on the ground, but the man had clutched the crook of Saul's elbows and lifted him to a standing position. Saul sent his foot toward the man's groin. In surprise, the stranger recoiled and momentarily loosened his grip, which allowed Saul a half second to get away.

It wasn't enough. The man's grip on his forearm intensified. In fury, he flung Saul against the concrete wall. Fresh pain bristled across Saul's spine. He got out one scream, before the stranger pulled him into an embrace, wrapping his arm around his neck and squeezing.

Saul's struggling abated as he blacked out, but the rage did not stop there. With even more force than before, the stranger lurched forth, swung Saul's head against the concrete, bared his teeth and bludgeoned his face with repeated blows.

"Damnit!" he screamed as he punched. The violence worked him into a sweat and then the garage momentarily fell silent. The brake lights brightened, filtering a faint red glow onto Saul's face.

The car backed out of the spot just as the stranger ran toward it. The woman slammed into a car parked behind her, shifted into drive and squealed her tires on the pavement just as the stranger arrived to confront her. In the distance, sirens spread chaos through the city. Saul was dead, and the witness had gotten away.

This location had confined him into a corner. He wouldn't make it to the street level before the emergency vehicles arrived. It would take them minutes to surround the garage and take him captive.

He thundered up the stairs to the fourth level, where openings on the west side of the garage allowed views of the adjacent retail building whose roof sat about eight feet below the fourth level deck.

The adjacent building featured an open-air lobby area housing an escalator. Hundreds of shoppers would occupy that space. Staring down to the white neoprene roof pad, he noticed what appeared to be an opening in the parapet just above the lobby area. The lights flashed and swirled on Main Street two blocks away.

The stranger climbed into the opening and allowed himself to drop to the roof. Running to the overhang of the lobby, he watched as a dozen police cars flooded the street. The opening in the parapet would allow him to drop into the lobby. This time of day, few shoppers occupied the concourse, but the impact would be painful. In a split second, he steadied himself, angled his body toward a bench below, and dropped.

The sirens whined and a shopper shrieked. At the foot of the escalator, a cab idled, waiting for its passenger to exit. The stranger descended the escalator and piled into the backseat of the cab.

"Help you?" driver asked.

"Head to Federal Way," he said quietly.

The police cruisers allowed the cab to depart as dozens of officers streamed into the adjacent garage, where they'd find Saul bloody and motionless against the wall.

9
Radiation

DELILAH Cottage combed through Taleah's phone records as the afternoon plowed toward completion. Convulsions of memory pressed her imagination into something like a fine paste. Art Rassine had a thing with his hair, which had been wiry and greasy from lack of hygiene. He hadn't ventured to a barbershop in ages, Taleah had guessed. The man she called "the shadow" pushed his hands through his hair on occasion and even fidgeted with its damaged ends when unencumbered with a dilemma.

His brutality was etched into her memory like a bad dream whose permanence often displaced rational thought with paranoia. Being tied against the tree and listening to him rage on in functionally simplistic, utilitarian sentences had induced in her a sense of morbid curiosity. How low could he go? She even questioned whether she could have considered him a man.

After seven years, her mind had already altered portions of the memories, she was sure. She wished they'd go away entirely. But his hair. What was it with his hair? It tangled and he battled it. He pushed water through it in effort to tame it, but wild had always been the perfect descriptor.

Delilah's dark hair fell in wavy sheets at the sides of her head, kept in place by a copious amount of hair spray. Its scent found its way into Taleah's nostrils and nearly caused a fit of coughing. She, too, combed a hand through it and fussed with it to an extent that Taleah picked up on it as a tic. Ms. Cottage allowed lopsided, curly bangs to dance on her brow before pushing them toward her ear while typing into Taleah's keyboard.

"I'm accessing the mainframe now," she said, sounding impressive. "If there's a bug, it will out itself eventually, especially if it's rudimentary."

"There wouldn't be a bug," Taleah surmised.

Though Ms. Cottage boasted a broad background of financial forensics, she operated her own consulting business as a technician and diagnostician with an expertise in computer science. Mostly, Agent Marks lurked in the background, answering and making calls, only some of which seemed to pertain to this case. She'd do in a pinch, Marks insisted while fretting over the logistics of getting an FBI agent up from Salt Lake on such short notice. If Delilah found something, she'd report it to Marks and Marks would have a forensic agent flown up from the Salt Lake City field office.

"You don't know that," Delilah insisted. "He could have software installed anywhere to track you. That thing in your purse that sometimes rings? That's a high-tech spy device. Hackers can and will use it against you."

"A hacker with a bad sense of humor is one thing," Taleah said. "But he knows my dad and me, somehow."

Once Delilah declared success, she rummaged through dozens of folders and determined the newspaper had installed ways to record phone conversations, but the capability had never been installed on Taleah's desk phone as far as she knew.

Ms. Cottage continued to dig for several more minutes before stopping on files inside an obscure folder. "Looks like there was a shakeup a few years ago. They must have swapped your phone out with an updated one."

"That's for reporters," Taleah said. "It's always confidential. But I think if a source agrees to it in the first place, the reporter can find value in it."

"I use it occasionally," Jalene noted from behind her. She migrated back and forth from her desk carrying her coffee mug, which bore some odd saying that must have carried significance for her. Using the trips as a cover for getting the latest was not really a useful skill, according to Taleah, and it seemed clumsy when stacked up to her other talents.

If it works, why abandon it? she could hear her father saying over dinner one night with Willis.

"But it is not accessible from your PC," Delilah said. "Even if the capability is there, it doesn't mean there could be a record, but you remember what he said, I take it?"

"I do," she said through gritted teeth as she offered a compulsory nod. Her body language often became disconnected from basic mental functions, even from a young age, which caused cascades of self-conscious doubt to wash over her in times of distress. Maybe it was a self-defense mechanism to mask what she was really thinking, but whatever the device, Taleah found it difficult to contend with.

"Forensics should allow for a trace. I'll patch it through to my laptop if you give me ten minutes."

Taleah glanced up at Jalene, who stared at Taleah's screen with narrow eyes and her forehead jutted forward as though she feigned interest.

Memories of Art flooded into her the longer she waited. They clawed at the backings of her mind like a persistent acid, intent to corrupt every thought with random sights and smells from the forest and the cave.

Ms. Cottage tapped a key. Its sound echoed in her ears like a distant drop of water into a tiny pool on a rocky surface. Taleah had inadvertently wedged her foot between a protruding chunk of granite and a large boulder. She kicked at her trapped foot with her other leg, scraping her shin with the edge of her shoe. That happened to be the leg with no sock, because in a moment of striking clarity, she'd tossed it out the back of the camper shell so it could possibly be used to help find her. Decisions though, were never without consequences and hours later, when attempting to run, she had mangled that ankle on the shattered tree stump, which had been charred by lightning before succumbing to wind and the jaws of animals. The pain had ripped through her like a tornado. Sometimes, the ache still lingered, like the foul aftertaste of a liquid drug that had the power to pulverize her soul.

Sweat had beaded on her forehead as she sat in front of the fire. The way the warmth radiated across her skin felt like a thousand needles raking her with pain. But the glow had turned out to a be a surprising tonic to what really ailed her. It allowed her to see the horror in a different light, make plans, and test reactions. Art was never adept at playing the games, but he'd enjoyed a huge advantage. His size and strength had rendered her mental skills practically useless. And he always caught her when she ran.

"Just about there," Delilah said, brushing her bangs toward her ear.

"Maybe you could use it on my boyfriend's call," Jalene suggested. A quizzical look spanned across her face, which indicated a joking demeanor in this instance. Still, the comment helped to humanize her. Bringing her to a level she could understand and connect with couldn't be a bad thing, but it prophesied certain perils as well.

"Almost anything nowadays," Ms. Cottage said.

"Indeed," Agent Marks said, leaning against the column near the copier. "If you want to hide, don't use the phone."

"Looks like the call came locally, from a cell phone."

"Track the phone," Marks urged.

Delilah pushed a slow, contemplative sigh between her lips and glanced up at Taleah, just as her heart fluttered. Was this really the first concrete evidence she'd get? She had a habit of tempering expectations, which in turn had helped to minimize the damage on her spirit when things didn't go exactly as planned. The habit came with unintended consequences, though. Christine had accused her of being aloof one night, which caused Taleah's emotions to coil up inside her heart in defense.

"It's triangulating," she said, waiting for a red bar to scoot across the bottom of her laptop screen. "Pinged downtown, near city hall in a garage. It's stationary for the time being."

She stared at the screen for what felt like minutes. Marks stood up straight and punched numbers into his phone like a wolf on the trail of fresh prey. Keep an eye on it."

"Downtown?" Taleah asked. Had it really been Art Rassine on the other end of the line, he would have considered the city an unwelcome adventure. The shadow feasted on nature, thrived on it, in fact, which constructed a persona of a recluse. Shunning city life and technology had hidden him away in the dark confines of nature, where no man-made invention could track him.

Marks must have read her expression as he waited for the phone to ring. "It's not him," he said.

"I know," Taleah argued, as guilt scoured the front of her mind. She shifted her feet and glanced up at the window. *I'm going to kill him,* Art had said. The calmness of his voice somehow shot even more terror into her. If patience were a virtue, the shadow would have been a virtuous criminal. His tone didn't suggest passion or arrogance, only a mechanical surety that had pecked away at Taleah's consciousness until it became an obsession.

"Marks, FBI," he started. "Yeah, Bones. Downtown, Main Street between... you don't say... Of course, I'm going to want to examine the scene. You tell your boys to keep it tidy. Got it."

"What?" Taleah said, her heart rate rising. Jalene flitted back to her desk and disappeared from view, though the sound of hurried and intense typing drifted through the office from her desk.

Marks slipped the phone back in his pocket. "BPD is already on the scene. They say your mystery caller had several cranial injuries from a fight. And there was a witness."

Taleah swore under her breath. "It can't be."

"Who would be interested in you in this way?" he shot. "Any strange occurrences lately? Maybe a lurker in the parking lot or something missing from your car?"

Taleah could only think of Table Rock, where the drunken idiot had verbally accosted her. "No. Well... something happened this week. I was trying to get fresh air by myself. You know, to ease tension and stress. Without Christine. A guy said some awful things, said I might give him a ride home. And...he sort of mentioned my father. And Willis."

"Name? Description?"

"No, it was dark. I could only see what looked like black stubble from my brake lights. His friends pulled him away. I thought he was just being an asshole. I think they called him Jim."

Marks stepped closer to her and bored his eyes into her expression, which she felt growing defensive again. She folded her arms gently and glanced at the ceiling before returning her gaze to Agent Marks. "Didn't get a last name?"

She shook her head.

"Nada. Wait a second." Once again, he withdrew his phone from his pocket and swiped past a couple of screens before he held up a photograph. "This him?"

Taleah shook her head again as she stared at the photograph of a young man with dark hair, a rounded chin, and eyes cut like shards of blue glass, jagged at the corners. His expression dimmed with some kind of hidden perception but seemed hardly angry. "Nope. I don't think so. He definitely had facial hair, maybe a bit taller, too. But like I said, it was dark."

"Well, it was worth a shot. I'd say if your memory were a little clearer, BPD could set you up with a sketch artist, but..."

"Why don't you ask the witness downtown?" Taleah asked, certain that she had found an angle Agent Marks hadn't yet explored.

"Because BPD already has this guy in custody for robbing—"

"The Army Navy store," Taleah finished for him.

"So now, we have to investigate the dead guy at the garage, try to piece together why he would call you at your office."

"Whoever it was," Taleah said, the fervor rising a notch in her throat, "he knows you're going to be on it. He's expecting you, and it doesn't sound like he considers you a legit threat. Like last time."

"We got to you, didn't we?"

Taleah frowned. She didn't blame Marks personally, or even the FBI as a whole. They did their jobs and followed every lead they had, but her father had beaten them to the punch. Only after her father and Willis had been beaten to within inches of their lives had the FBI settled on the wilderness like an invading force. "A little late."

"Do you think the guy has it out for your father?"

Taleah combed a hand through her hair and offered a dreary frown. "It's obvious, isn't it?"

"Let me handle that," Marks said. "But knowing Reggie, he's going to resist like hell. Being the renegade, independent and unapologetic, is his thing."

"You're not suggesting witness protection," Taleah said, raising her eyebrows and relaxing her arms.

"Not exactly. But he's still not going to like it."

"You're right. He doesn't seem to like many of your suggestions."

Agent Marks frowned and watched Ms. Cottage's computer screen. The phone had not moved, but she was busying herself with another task. She stopped and craned her neck toward Taleah as if an idea had just flashed before her eyes like a strobe light. "You don't use any voice recognition apps, do you?"

"Why?"

"A lot of times, they can be listening to you even when you don't think they are. And when that happens, sometimes they sort of have a mind of their own. They sometimes get turned into data, which can be mined and used to target you with advertisements, anything from face cream to a new Toyota. Maybe if you—"

"Not frequently enough for it to matter," Taleah said. "Not within the last week for sure."

"We're going to keep working it," Agent Marks said. "We'll keep in touch. Ms. Cottage, thank you for your services. You send us an invoice and the FBI will pick it up within the week."

She gathered up her equipment and stuffed it into an oversize laptop bag before nodding to Taleah and assuring her that all would be well.

But the pain had tethered itself to her mind already. She breathed deeply and sat down, pushed her face in her palm and felt the tears trickle between her fingers. Instead of letting them flow, she swallowed, considered Christine's warm words of advice, and stood up. She walked slowly back to Jalene's desk in the corner, flipped open a notebook and started jotting down notes, which would only lead nowhere. Though the story would change in due time, the mere act of writing and thinking distracted her enough that her mind could trick the memories and the fear into disappearing, if only temporarily.

Before she realized what she was doing, she was staring at the makings of a shoddy paragraph detailing the real thoughts on terrorism from a different perspective. Whether or not she wanted to admit it, she shared a camaraderie with Emmanuel and Abal more than ever. Marginalized and abused, they too had their own tales to tell, their own experiences to guide them. She clicked the pen closed and found herself staring at Emmanuel's name in bold, cursive writing. Before, she had imagined it in traditional typefaces or even some kind of Arabic script. Somehow, seeing it in her own writing, in strokes she had formed herself, painted a portrait of a real human being—of a real friend that Taleah could lean on to discover the truth.

R oom 334 overlooked a narrow slot of the hospital campus and offered partial views of the housing neighborhoods in close proximity to the tank farm site. It was situated in the old tower, which once dominated the skyline in the immediate area. The hospital staff had moved Reggie into this room early in the morning and had separated him and Willis into separate rooms.

Taleah had fought rush hour traffic for twenty minutes attempting to make the two-mile trip from the office, and when she arrived, stress choked her.

Her father looked improved, she thought. "How are you feeling?"

"Better and better," Reggie said. "I might go home tomorrow, but they said Willis is going to need another few days to recover. How was your day?"

Taleah shook her head, attempting to process everything that had happened into something resembling cogent thought that could be canned into easy-to-digest sentences. A frown sprawled across her face and her hands trembled.

"Well, it was… interesting."

Reggie raised his eyebrows and turned his neck for long enough to show empathy. "I take it not in a good way. What happened?"

"You remember the other night when I called? What we talked about?"

He nodded slowly.

"I ran into a friend from college this morning. We were gathering information for a story. Emmanuel is great, but we got to talking. He heard about what happened and he knew you were in the hospital."

"I don't know him," Reggie said. "I don't think you've ever mentioned him. Is he good-looking?"

Taleah flushed. "Dad, please."

"How would he know that? I haven't caught up on the press much, but it doesn't seem very prudent to release my name yet."

"You're right." Taleah said. "I checked up on it—after Jalene finished yelling at me for screwing up the interview—and not one news outlet has mentioned your name or Willis's. Emmanuel works part time in software development, and he said he heard it from someone at the office."

"Software engineers," Reggie mused. "Now that's an honorable profession. Wonder how one of them would figure out my name... Well I'm sure there's an app for that."

Taleah tried to smile but could not coax her muscles into the necessary moves. What she plastered on her face instead must have communicated pain and belligerence. "He might tell me more if I talk to him more. Maybe."

"Well, I think that could be a good move—"

"Don't start with me," she warned.

"Just saying."

"Don't."

He sighed and let it drop, signaling that he was ready to listen.

Taleah cracked her knuckle, scooted back into the chair, and closed her eyes to cool the stress, which rarely worked. "So then I got back and I got a call. They ran a trace and some guy called from downtown. And now he's dead."

"I don't understand." Reggie stared at her and started to move his lips to question more, but thought better of it and let the thought slip away. Taleah had witnessed this behavior from him numerous times. At first, she figured that it showed restraint and careful thought processes, but it had degenerated into nothing more than an annoying personality trait. Start to speak, then change your mind and leave the other person wondering what you were really thinking. Still, Taleah had never confronted him over it and never planned to. Rather than say anything, she sighed and glanced at the cabinets surrounding the sink.

After a few uncomfortable seconds, a knock came from the door. Taleah sprung to her feet to open it, expecting to see Rebekah—but then again, Rebekah wouldn't bother knocking.

One of the police officers from the other day offered a curt smile and stepped into the room, holding a yellow legal pad and a pen.

"Another round of questioning," Reggie grunted, wincing.

"Just a few things, as we're investigating," Officer Ramirez said slowly without looking down at his tablet.

Reggie nodded and offered him a chair, but Ramirez stood firm. "We're getting sworn testimony from a witness now. May have more questions from you later. Do you know a Saul Goodweather?"

"Got a picture?"

"A blow-up from his driver's license," Officer Ramirez said.

Taleah frowned and interrupted. "This wouldn't be the same guy that called me this afternoon would it?"

"Could be," Ramirez said, breaking eye contact with Reggie and studying Taleah. He looked as though he were ready to jot something down, lifting the notepad to level, and clicking the end of the pen. "Investigation is still ongoing." Instead of offering more, he stepped toward Reggie and withdrew a three by five picture on printer paper, which had been cut down to fit the photograph.

"Never seen him before," Reggie said. He coughed and turned toward a small tray on the table next to the IV stand. He picked up a cup with a straw and sipped some water before letting his gaze fall on Ramirez once again.

"It's curious. One of the first things our witness said was your name. Last name only."

Taleah swallowed and pressed her hand to her face as she let the adrenaline swarm her to release the imprisoned nightmares that had tortured her into therapy all those years ago. "He claimed to be Art Rassine."

Reggie rolled his eyes back, placed the drink on the table, and stared at her in shock for what seemed like five minutes. Taleah could, in essence, see the memories gathering in his head. His eyebrows twitched and his face became pale and ghostly. "You didn't tell me about that."

"Happened this afternoon. And Agent Marks for a minute seemed to think it was the man who robbed the Army Navy store. At least that's the way I interpreted it."

"You... *you* talked to Marks?"

"I had them call the FBI and ask for him."

"Taleah, he's dead. We've been over it, years ago. It's time to let it go."

"I'm sorry," Officer Ramirez said, raising his eyebrows and readying the pen and pad. "Is this *the* Art Rassine, who kidnapped and murdered several women eighteen years ago? The one who..."

His voice trailed away, but Taleah could hear the rest of the sentence clashing with reason inside her skull. *The one who kidnapped your daughter as revenge.* Her heart fluttered in her chest like the thunder from a hundred birds fleeing from an approaching car. When she closed her eyes, she was running again through dense pine on a game trail tracing the contour of the mountain before plunging into a wash, where a tiny, dried-up creek led to the Lochsa River. The birds fluttered when she ran as pain scraped through her wounded ankle. He was going to catch her, but she fell. Her screams battered her with agonizing memory as she swatted at him with a heavy stick.

"The same," Reggie said.

"I don't think the chief wants this going to the FBI," Ramirez said, his voice seeming to scatter in the brightened room, like rays from a single point.

"Now you have a situation where you have to work together," Reggie said, "instead of waging pointless turf wars they always show on TV."

Ramirez uttered what seemed like a nervous laugh. "That's made-for-TV drama. You know turf wars don't exist."

"I've seen them," Reggie said. "Adams County wanted to handle that kidnapping thing their own way, but then the FBI came in, took the whole thing over, much to the dismay of the late Deputy Jaminson. He didn't trust the FBI, and I now understand why."

"A small-town sheriff's office wanted to solve that thing all on their own? That's delusional."

"What can I say? They are independent out there."

Taleah stood up and stepped toward the door.

"Going already?"

Her voice trembling and her eyes darting in all directions, Taleah clenched the muscles in her hand to curl her fingers as if to claw at someone. "I can't take this anymore. I need someone I can count on."

"Ouch," Reggie said dryly.

"It's too much."

"You don't need to be coddled right now," Reggie said, raising his voice just enough to be noticeable.

"What do you know?"

Taleah shuffled out the door, pulled it closed and scurried toward the elevator as panic filled her veins. Her father had exacerbated the torture rather than successfully minimizing it. The resultant steam burned through her eyes and coalesced into tears. Emotion scraped at the scars of her past to open new wounds.

Why did he have to take it so lightly now? Years had passed, but did she somehow mean less to him now, after coming out, only to have him try to talk her into chasing men? The questions beat their way into her brain as she ran. The cars in the parking lot faded into emptiness, flushed away by the rays of late afternoon sun. The trees seemed to stand alone, like structures in the wild where the birds sang hymns of desperation. Running was the only escape.

Whoever had bombed the oil tanks wasn't a terrorist. Her father was a target and acting like he didn't care shoved a bolt of misery down Taleah's throat and twisted it. How could he not understand? He was the only reason she was even alive, yet he didn't have the instinct to acknowledge that he was in trouble now. Now that the pendulum had swung to her, she had no idea what to do. Only one person on the face of the earth could give her a clue on where to start.

She wiped the tears away, started the car, pushed it into reverse, and looked up into the mirror. A shadow stood behind her, hulking, waiting, punishing her with waves of torment that crashed against the walls in her brain. She slammed on the brakes and shrieked, scanning the lot in front of her for anyone who could intervene, but the shadow had moved on. An aging man plodded along the rows of cars with a cane. He nodded at her and continued. Taleah sat frozen to her seat as the adrenaline spiked within her. There was no preparing for what would come, but into the unknown she had to stray. It was the only way to avert the doom surrounding her father.

10
Diffusion

THE lamp on the end table cast parabolic shadows on the painted and textured wall opposite the front door. Christine stepped out of the bathroom just as Taleah entered the apartment. In any other setting, the smile on her face would have softened the glare of agony as if to make it seem tolerable, but today the mood carried the scent of desperation. Taleah looked ashen, though she exerted no effort to alter her expression. Christine could have seen the emotion from a mile away.

She dropped her purse on the table and frowned while Christine stepped in front of her and gently pulled Taleah's head into her shoulder. Christine stood several inches taller than Taleah, which had caused her to make some joke about the height differential and its advantages. "You stopped at the hospital, I take it."

Taleah only nodded. When Christine attempted to pull her closer, Taleah wrestled her shoulders free and tilted her head upward. Christine's natural resistance flashed more trauma though her mind. The hushed growl of Rassine's voice at once permeated the pitter-patter of rain on underbrush leaves as he gripped her shoulder with a cold ferocity meant to imitate warmth. She shuddered and escaped to the couch, but Christine grasped her hand and followed her.

"From what I gather, not good."

She shook her head and stared at the dark of the television screen before letting her shoulders push into the cushions. A grimace spanned her face, but she managed a pathetic smile that Christine could see through any day of the week.

"Is he doing okay?"

No answer came to her. The image of the shadow beyond her rear bumper scarred her thoughts into the kind of nightmarish oblivion often induced by fainting.

"Am I going to be answering my own questions all night?"

Taleah only glanced at her, clasped her hands together, and pulled her feet out of her shoes. Rather than annoyed, Christine appeared thoughtful and almost serene. The dichotomy between their demeanors was unnerving. Her voice wavered as she finally spoke. "I might need some time."

"Tell me what happened first."

Taleah attempted to tell the story of how the caller had claimed to be Art Rassine, and that Agent Marks insisted that the caller lay dead in a parking garage, but she omitted large chunks of the tale, which would leave Christine guessing.

"Maybe it's not that bad," she said, balling up her fist and positioning it in front of her lips as if to spread warmth into her fingers. But he doesn't seem to care."

"Your dad? I assumed he was doing his thing where he pretends to be thoughtful just so you can make note of his body language." Christine's expertise in nonverbal communication shouldn't have come as a surprise, but Taleah looked up and allowed her eyes to narrow and her brows to angle downward.

Christine majored in communication with a minor in sociology and wrote a fascinating term paper on the techniques of deception via nonverbal cues. She used what she'd learned with stunning regularity. Her job, she insisted, was not to analyze, but to listen. The rate with which she deciphered the clues at first made Taleah uneasy, but the longer it went on, the method seemed to offer more positive results than negative.

"No, not that," Taleah said. "I know he realizes the implications... shouldn't he be a little more worried?"

Christine straightened her back and scratched her foot. "Art Rassine is dead. He's not coming to get your father again."

Taleah trembled. She propped her elbow on the arm of the couch and let her face sink into her palm. "I. Know. That."

"And even at that, didn't you say the guy who called is also dead?"

"Why does everyone assume that?"

Christine narrowed her eyes, relaxed her shoulders, and gazed at the floor with a simplistic look of confusion dangling over her face. "I don't think of it as an assumption, just a fair observation."

A sigh pushed through Taleah's mouth as Christine attempted to scoot closer. She usually sat with her knee bent and her foot curled up under her, which allowed her to lean forward with minimal effort. Her knee pushed against Taleah's thigh like the force of a gigantic fist. "I don't know what to do."

"Maybe you just need time to think it over, sort of process the events of the day, and a different course of action will present itself."

Her words seemed to echo her father's most fervent advice but delivered in fewer syllables. "Let time take its course and solutions will become obvious."

"What did your dad do when he found out you'd...when you were gone?"

Taleah wiped a tear from her eye and kept her forearm in a defensive stance. "He came to find me."

Christine wrinkled her nose and then combed her left hand slowly through her hair. "That's what he did."

Taleah let her arms relax and let her mood sour further. Christine put forth more effort to console her, and though Taleah wanted some physical contact, she withdrew more and more into the dark, where her thoughts lay barren against stone walls to be devoured by creatures of the night. *Drip drip,* reverberated through her skull as the chill of terror worked its way into a knot somewhere below her stomach. If she was going to be forced to ride out the storm, she stood alone.

You don't need to be coddled.

With little effort, she placed a hand on Christine's thigh, pushed herself up and traipsed away to the sanctity of the bedroom. Christine would join her in the middle of the night when the dreams marched in front of her eyes in waves, if she ever succumbed to sleep.

The sound of a fist knocking on his door snapped Reggie from sleep. He'd just located his daughter and was plotting his rescue and planning on how to deal with Rassine's traps. For several seconds, he didn't speak. If it were a nurse, she'd have entered after a few seconds. The waiting lasted for the better part of thirty seconds before the rap repeated more forcefully.

"Come in," he rasped.

The door slowly opened as he wedged his eyes open.

"We'll get right on that, sir," someone said before two people entered the room.

A knot of discomfort pulsed at Reggie's midsection, and he scooted his body toward the middle of the bed, which sent icy waves of pain across the raw flesh on his back. "If this was good news, you wouldn't be sending people out on errands."

"Good news?" Agent Marks said. "When was the last time you heard good news? Maybe we have a little bit of both this time."

Reggie scanned his demeanor, which suggested an air of sophisticated grandeur. At times, Reggie had learned, the man could hardly contain his pomposity, and the more energized he was, the deeper his arrogance. He rolled his eyes and turned his head to Sergeant Bones, Jr., of the Boise Police Department, who hadn't yet emitted so much as a sigh.

"Mr. St. Clair," he said, offering a curt nod.

Reggie returned the gesture and grimaced as he attempted to adjust the slope of the bed to make conversation more effective. "Pull up a chair."

"We have an eyewitness," Bones said. "It sounds like the FBI already alerted you as to what happened."

"They did," Reggie said, staring at Marks. "They just didn't tell me what it has to do with me, other than the caller pretending to be Art Rassine to get at my daughter."

"Why do you think he'd do that?" Bones asked.

He snapped his attention back to the sergeant. He had changed his expression from anticipation to a more suitable juxtaposition of cunning and meekness. If he'd ever seen that look before, he couldn't remember it, and not remembering it now seemed impossible. "Beats me."

Marks sat down in the nearest chair, which had been pushed back against the window. The liquid in the IV bag bubbled and sloshed as Marks bumped the stand.

"If this guy really does know the whole story, you might be in danger," Marks said. "But our witness had a few thoughts on that last night when we questioned her. She's home now. Imaginably, pretty spooked about the whole ordeal. But she has a good memory. She'd left work early, got in the car, and was looking through text messages when it happened. Didn't hear everything since the car door was closed, but she says a name jumped out at her because the assailant repeated it loudly."

"My name?"

"Looking into that, but it seems to fit. The victim worked at City Hall under the Planning and Zoning Commission. She said he yelled 'Give me St. Clair,' which mildly suggests a motive for at least the phone call, if not the bombing."

"You told me the victim made the call."

"That was a guess," Bones said, shaking his head and standing up straight. "An incorrect one. Analysis found three sets of fingerprints on the phone. After isolating the victim's and his wife's prints, the third set didn't match anything."

"Fingerprint scanning software has come a long way," Marks interjected. "I can find a match within minutes if the person in question had ever been fingerprinted to begin with."

"And he hasn't," Bones noted.

"You pulled prints from Art Rassine," Reggie said as pain ripped across his spine. He curled his fingers into fists and let them relax. "I remember that pretty well."

"He's dead."

"Repeated *ad nauseam*," Reggie shot. "Which ironically, doesn't make you any closer to identifying the suspect. Instead of doing police work, you're here bothering me like I have all the answers. I got blown up, but no one knows why."

"It gives us reason to believe you are a target," Marks said, leaning forward and resting his elbows on the armrests.

"Not too many terror attacks are targeting," Reggie scoffed.

"P and Z gave us the rundown on the victim," Bones said, all at once appearing more comfortable. "His name is Saul Goodweather."

"What kind of name is that?" Reggie needled.

"Goodweather was involved in something fishy down there. He accessed archives he had no business getting into. The project in question is pretty much public knowledge, but the details of the contract aren't. And what do you know, the contract has your signature on it." Marks didn't attempt to smile. Instead, he leaned back again, as though victorious. It made Reggie want to jump out of the bed and punch him, but he practiced restraint.

"Damn it," Reggie said.

"So the assailant in the garage has to be the person targeting you," Bones said, stating the obvious.

"Question is," Marks said, "who is he?" He stared at Reggie for more than a half minute before anyone in the room spoke. Reggie let thoughts accost his mind but could only offer one name.

"Taleah said someone harassed her on Table Rock this week. She said his name was Jim. Could be the same guy."

"I guessed the same thing," Marks said. "It still could be, maybe, but there's still no evidence that he's involved. I wondered if this Jim character was the same guy Ada County arrested for robbing the Army Navy store, but Taleah says it's not."

"Taleah said someone must have called the police after that incident," Reggie said, turning his head to face Sergeant Bones. "Get into your log and check it out. Maybe that will give you a clue."

"Interesting speculation. You should be a cop."

"I practically am," Reggie said. "Eighteen years ago, Adams County and the FBI both failed to identify a killer. And then seven years ago, I beat the FBI to finding my daughter."

"Didn't you have illicit help?" Bones said. "I'm sure I recall something like that. Your wife?"

"She was never investigated, much less found guilty," Reggie said.

"Your ex works at City Hall in cyber security, which may indicate your wife had help."

"I hardly ever talk to Anna. She came by a few days ago to wish me well, and we talk maybe a couple of times a year around Taleah's birthday and Christmas."

"Back to our witness, though," Marks said, rubbing his chin and widening his eyes. "She didn't get a good look at the assailant because it was too dark, but he went after her when she drove away."

"If you just killed someone, you'd want to silence the witness," Reggie guessed.

"Funny thing is, killers don't just disappear out of thin air. BPD had the garage pretty well sealed off mere seconds after the witness left the garage. We feel pretty confident that he wouldn't have had time to leave on foot, so he probably had a car parked on that level and got away just in time."

"Don't garages have cameras?" Reggie asked.

"At the entrances and exits, they do," Bones confirmed. "And they're all automated. We're examining all passes issued for that level as we speak. Time stamps, arrival, departure, the works."

"Look at the tapes."

"Already have," Bones insisted. "Not one of the faces in any of the cars within that timeframe matched the eyewitness description remotely."

"Did you show her all the pictures to verify that?"

"Everything you can think of, we're already on it," Bones said. "We're professionals. I've been in this business for twenty hears and learned from my father, who spent forty years tracking down criminals. Technology has changed, but the process hasn't."

"So he didn't get there by car," Reggie said.

"He wouldn't have had time to escape on foot," Bones said.

"That's an assumption," Reggie argued, curling his lip and letting his anger show. "You'd think a sergeant would know better than that. I can't believe you lost him."

"Seems to me like he had a plan," Marks said. "But here's what I don't understand. A guy kills someone who knows about the contract you signed, then uses his phone to call your daughter and harass her? If he knows that much about your daughter, he no doubt knows how to find you anyway. Which means he wouldn't have had to kill someone trying to get to you. He could have just walked in here and finished the job."

"Not very likely," Reggie said. "He wouldn't make it past the nurse's station."

"Precisely," Agent Marks said, nodding slowly and resting his index finger and his thumb on his chin. "Which would seem to indicate that he has a plan for when you get out of here. It's a game of chess now."

"What are you suggesting?"

"Taleah said you're not going to like it," Marks said. "But we're going to catch this guy. It's only a matter of time. I'm putting you under surveillance."

"Oh, *hell* no," Reggie said. "I've proven I can take care of myself."

Marks sighed. "I agree you have. You get comfortable in your life. You know the routes you take every day, you know your surroundings so well you don't even have to pay attention to them anymore. But that person across the street, that passerby in the van with the tinted windows, he's got everything mapped out, and he's making plans."

"I'm pretty aware of my own neighborhood," Reggie shot. "And it's safe."

"Safer with law enforcement personnel in front of your house," Marks said.

"What I object to is invasion of privacy. You don't have the right to watch my home or keep tabs on my wife and me."

"I'm not asking permission," Marks said.

"Then I'm going to get rid of them," Reggie said, fuming. "I'll cook up some kind of diversion."

"This attacker is going to relish that," Marks said. "But thanks for showing your hand."

Reggie lifted his hand and pointed at him, his arm bent at the elbow and his index finger shaking. "You son of a bitch."

"Oh, and while we're at it, don't think of asking your next-door neighbor to help you out, because he's under surveillance too."

"The Hudsons or Mr. Sanders?"

"Mr. Ralston, Reggie. I meant the guy in the next room."

"I'm pretty sure you have to have permission to do that."

"Wrong again," Marks said, looking pleased with himself. "You can sue to stop it, but that's not going to accomplish anything within the next few days, by which time, we're likely to have this guy in our grasp and we can ask him why he's harassing Taleah."

"You going to follow her, too?"

Marks glanced at the lights on the computer screen and fidgeted. "There's no reason to believe she's in any danger. She says he was threatening you."

"She's having a rough time right now," Reggie said. It's better to not make her relive the trauma, so maybe don't talk to her anymore."

"Can't say she won't have more evidence to offer up at some point," Marks said. "At any rate, I'm not going to ignore her calls."

Reggie rested his head on the pillow, closed his eyes and let his thoughts tug at the image of her face when she left his room last night. He'd seen her in that much pain a few times in her life, and though he realized he had something to do with her expression, he understood that Taleah was about to make a choice. The fear punctured a hole in his heart, allowing emotion to leak out more fervently. He shifted his legs, parted his lips, and remembered her screams. A frown brandished itself on his face and his lip began to tremble. Of everything he could have said, only one simple sentence could form as he spoke. "She's going to run."

11

Aurora

CHRISTINE'S lips pressed against Taleah's with a tender under-tow. A single kiss would spark the day like ions crashing into the earth's magnetic field. She opened her eyes, let the moment pass, and then turned away. Christine slipped her arm around Taleah's waist just as dawn began to tread above the mountains to the east.

"Good morning," she mumbled.

"Feeling better?"

The headache had started to pulse intermittently before she fell asleep the previous night, but her eyelids grew heavy and her breath stretched. Like most recent nights, dreams plagued her, but didn't wake her. She gripped the pillow and stared at the alarm clock as the pain darted across her skull. The first thoughts dwelt on her father's dismissal of the notion that he was in danger, but the memories quickly flashed through the darkness in the trees where the glow of flame licked at the stars above. The shadow occupied a blunt tree trunk with fresh saw marks ending in course ridges of splintered wood. It looked as though a lumberjack had started to harvest the great tree and decided against it, only to have a bear finish the job a few days later. The shadow lurked like a bear. He pressed his hand against his midsection while clutching the blade with his teeth. Beyond the hem of his clothes, the wound would look gruesome. Dad had called it a lucky shot, but Taleah found herself disagreeing. A lucky shot would have killed him. And even though Willis had ended the conflict seven years later, bitter memories slashed through her mind like a katana.

"Don't... I'm not sure."

"What are we doing today?"

That was Christine's favorite Saturday morning question, one Taleah grew to expect and even planned on with predetermined answers from time to time. She said 'we' as though she understood Taleah's thoughts before they even formed in her mind.

Ultimately, Christine would not be able to help much. If she was expecting a relaxing weekend at home, Taleah guessed, Christine would close the day with disappointment.

"Did you tell me your brother had a case of guns?"

Christine withdrew her arm, sat up straight and stared at her. Though Taleah couldn't see her expression, she could feel it glowering like a cattle prod in a furnace, pressing into the back of her skull. "What are you getting at?"

"I need protection," she said, blinking at the alarm clock and without changing her tone. Christine would balk at the notion, of course. To her, firearms represented stark danger no matter what the circumstances, and society would have been better off had they never been invented in the first place. Her brother, however, was an avid hunter and outdoorsman. Asking him to venture into the wild without a gun would be suggesting someone swim amongst the coral without a snorkel. "Just in case we cross paths," Taleah said after an uncomfortable pause drove a wedge between them.

"Guns aren't very good at protection," Christine said. "They were made for one purpose and that isn't self-defense. Besides, you've never even held one."

"Maybe he'll have to teach me the basics of how to handle it."

"Oh my God," Christine said, inching across the sheets to the other side of the bed. "You're really thinking about this."

Taleah slid the blanket from her shoulder and struggled to sit up as the first rays of blue light filtered through the window. "You reminded me of what my dad did seven years ago. I remember it now. He was armed. And that's the only reason either of us survived."

"He's not coming for you now," Christine said, referring to the shadow. "You are one hundred percent safe. You know David? He's not going to let anything happen to you."

David resided across the hall and lived alone, though he took up the noble mantle of protecting every woman he ever met from harm, as though he was some sort of rogue fighter and defender of all that was good. Taleah rolled her eyes at the notion. Of course, she'd pretended to be friendly, but David was a classic misogynist and let it show without apology. While true that he had no idea what he was doing, he meant well.

"That usually makes you laugh," Christine said, scanning Taleah's glum expression.

"Not today."

"So then what's your plan?"

"We'll go target shooting with your brother," Taleah started. "He knows where the range is, I take it? Then, maybe I'll call my mom. She might have some info."

"Just because she works for the city doesn't mean—"

"She can find anything," Taleah said.

"She makes me uncomfortable," Christine said, as if finally deciding that honesty was the best policy. The last time they were in the same room, Anna had said something off-color about how same-sex relationships always followed clichés. Never the joker, Anna meant what she said. Christine had bit her lip and attempted to pass it off, but exploded later on the drive home. *Who does she think she is?*

"Really? Maybe you can go to the dollar store then. You don't have to talk to her."

"Gary isn't going to let you handle one of his guns without twisting your arms to teach you what recoil feels like. He isn't stupid."

"Yes he is," Taleah said. "You said so yourself."

That conversation felt as though it had taken place on another plane entirely removed from the world at large. She had intimated when they first started dating that Gary was going hunting again, shooting at defenseless animals. *God, he's so stupid.*

"Okay," Christine said, strutting around the foot of the bed while avoiding the landmine of Taleah's belt buckle, which she'd stepped on numerous times. "Maybe he is, but are you?"

"Of course," Taleah said, stretching her arms and beginning to yawn. "What would you expect?"

"Not to be crazy?"

"Crazy's my thing," Taleah said. "It's why you fell in love with me."

"That we're even having this discussion suggests you're neither stupid nor crazy," Christine said, sitting at the edge of the bed next to her and sliding her hand across the knees of Taleah's pajamas. "But I guess if you insist, I can't stop you. Just try not to shoot me, okay?"

She nodded and stood up as if to race Christine to the shower. After they first moved in together, Christine had developed a strange tendency to want to shower first because the water would be perfect.

The day passed away quickly. After catching up with Gary, they had lunch and made their way to his house in the historic East End neighborhood. Taleah and Christine followed his black truck to the shooting range, which lay amid arid sagebrush and shallow bluffs about two miles south of the airport control tower. When they arrived, he hurried over broken glass and shredded aluminum cans and affixed a paper target to the earth and railroad tie wall.

The shooting range resided in a makeshift bunker, cut out from the surrounding hills and sagebrush in a narrow U-shape. The walls of this little cove tapered to grade closer to the starting line and swooped around the target wall in a fifteen-foot-high arc.

Gary glanced at Taleah and then skyward before visually assessing the situation. Taleah got the impression that he had trained people to shoot before, but seemed somewhat hesitant and unnatural about it. He stared at the target for several seconds and then took one step toward her.

"Now, the first thing is to get your stance ready. You set your feet because that back foot steadies your body." He demonstrated by holding his arms up and pointing his finger like a gun. He bent his knee slightly and aimed. "So when you feel that kick, your body is gonna want to go backwards. That foot stops you and keeps you from slinging the gun toward the sky. Try it out."

Taleah pointed her finger and rested her foot behind her like a sprinter getting ready from a standing position.

"You'll want that knee joint firmer," he said.

Christine shook her head, put her hands up, and hurried toward the car, whose windows were down. She didn't want to damage her hearing.

"Now it's gonna be loud. Consider hearing protection. Let me get some plugs out of my truck while you practice."

Taleah felt silly, but reminded herself for whom she was doing this. Remembering Willis firing the gun, she attempted to mimic his posture, but her stance felt all wrong. Instead, she parted her legs and planted both heels firmly in the dirt while pointing her pretend gun at the target.

Gary gave her a set of foam ear plugs and watched her jam them into her ears. Surprisingly, she could still hear everything he said.

"Now let's work with those arms. The recoil on these puppies is pretty fierce. You want your shoulder to absorb the blow... no that's not right. Let me help you." He grabbed her hands, clasped them together, and then bent her elbows properly. With one swift motion, he swiped upward at her hands and Taleah's arms failed.

"Steady," he said. "Got it. Now, do you want to simulate the kick?"

She nodded and eyed the target. He turned to face her, squared his hips, and slugged her in the shoulder. Taleah's arms buckled. "Ow!"

"Yep, still not ready. You gotta let your back and your shoulder relax, but keep them steady."

This went on for at least ten minutes before he let her hold the gun, which was a jet-black semi-automatic handgun with a clip that could load fifteen bullets. After ten more minutes, she loaded the clip, snapped it into place and aimed at the target.

"The sighting on handguns can be tricky," Gary said. "Safety on? Now, if you'll raise it to eye level and look straight down the barrel, you'll see that little V-shape. That's where your slug's gonna go. Nope, don't squint, it messes up your sight. Line it up with the center of that target, steady your hands, and fire."

She did as she was told, but did not squeeze the trigger.

"Now do it with the safety off. Give it a try."

The boom resonated through the cove and echoed in her eardrums, which resulted in a soft *ring* that gradually faded away.

"You blinked."

"Did I hit it?"

"No, I think you hit a school bus in Nevada. Look, it's a natural reflex to blink. Keep the gun steadier. Don't blink. Now try again."

Taleah unleashed another shot and relaxed her arms.

"Well, that looked a little better, but you're still letting the kick-back tilt your hands up at the end."

Before long, Taleah had unloaded the clip, Every shot had missed the target, but on the last three, powdery dust rose up from the back wall of the cove and flitted away in the breeze.

On the second clip, all but one of her shots hit the back wall, and one even punctured the corner of the paper.

Taleah relaxed her arm and sighed. "I'm no good."

"No, you're doing good," Gary insisted. "Try one more clip."

More confident in her mechanics, Taleah gripped the pistol and unloaded the entire clip in less than one minute.

"Hey, this time, three of them hit, and look, one went through the stripe. Maybe we can practice again next week?"

Taleah shrugged as she relinquished her grip and let Gary take the weapon from her. He carefully jogged to the wall, pinned up another target and returned.

"Watch me. I'm going to put every one of them through the bulls-eye."

"You have to let him show off," Christine yelled from the car.

He positioned his feet, raised the gun and fired bullets until the blasts became a continuous roar. Within thirty seconds, he emptied the clip. "See, that's how you do it."

Gary brought the target back and showed it to Taleah. "You keep practicing and this is what you'll get," he boasted. "Pretty much just one big hole that fifteen slugs went through."

Taleah shrugged, closed her eyes, and let her voice drop an octave. "Think you can let me borrow one?"

"No can do," Gary said. "Safety first."

"Just so I can practice aiming on my own time. You don't have to give me any ammo."

He sighed and stared at the skyline towards the air tower. "Well, I suppose you're not going to go on a rampage. But I can't be held accountable for accidents."

"What accidents can happen without bullets?"

He grabbed her shoulder and stared into her eyes. "Always treat a gun like it is loaded. Always. Keep the safety on at all times, and for God's sakes don't actually pull the trigger."

She nodded and followed Gary to his truck. He opened a black plastic case he had bolted to the bed and dug for a revolver. "This one is going to be pretty reliable and safe. It's old, but easy to handle. Make sure you bring it back on one piece."

"Of course I will."

With a sour look on her face, Christine swung open the car door and approached her brother, who busied himself with repacking his gun in the chest behind the cab. "What?" he said.

"Are you out of your mind?" Christine asked.

Taleah shook her head and slowly made her way to the passenger door of Christine's car. The dust dirtied her shoes as she walked and drifted into a haze that dimmed the sun.

"Oh? You sanctioned this from the get-go. And you hate guns. I'm thinking there's a pretty good reason for your support. If I didn't know you better, I'd have hesitated."

"You're not helping."

Taleah's frustration grew as she settled into the seat and closed the door. Christine walked quickly, looking down and shielding her eyes from the wind-blown dust. When she got in the car, she said something under her breath, strapped on her seatbelt, and started the car.

"Why did you confront him?"

"I don't confront anyone," Christine said. "Besides, I'm trying to protect you."

"Oh, thanks."

"You need all the support you can get—"

"I need you to let me be me," Taleah said, shifting her weight against the door as Christine gently angled the car into the road that headed southward through empty sagebrush toward the Snake River. The Snake must have meandered out there through desolate rangeland and canyons, but Taleah had never seen the section from Glenn's Ferry to Marsing. All she knew is that it had to exist because it was on the map and major rivers didn't just disappear.

"I am," Christine said, lowering her voice and peering through her mirror. Her brother was accelerating behind her and making his way home.

The remainder of the drive went by almost silently. Christine said something about music, tuned the radio and sang along for a few seconds, only to grunt at another driver, bite her lip, and pass a dozen stopped cars. Before either of them spoke again, Christine was pulling into the driveway. She stopped the car, got out, and climbed the stairs to the front door. Instead of opening her door, Taleah removed her phone from her purse and dialed her mother.

After four rings, Anna answered. "How are you this afternoon?"

"Are you busy? I need some help."

"I can put the gardening aside," she said after a sigh. Taleah imagined her sitting on her knees in front of the flower garden with a tiny spade and clumps of uprooted weeds littering the grass beside her. She would be wiping the sweat from her brow and removing the rubber gloves right about now. "What's up?"

"I don't know if you've heard from dad," Taleah said, suddenly aware that someone was watching her from a behind a bush across the parking lot.

She sat up straight, peered at the stranger, and let her gaze linger until he flitted away into a parked car, started the engine, and drove away. A lump formed at the back of her throat. Was that the creep from Table Rock?

"Not since the other day. I'm sure he's doing okay or he would have called, knowing him."

"I don't know what I'm... I have a weird feeling right now. Someone is trying to kill him, I think. Pretending to be Art."

The other end of the line remained bathed in murky silence for at least thirty seconds. Her mother was notoriously slow at processing information dumps like that and reacted a bit differently each time. When Taleah had come out, she had frowned, furrowed her eyebrows, sipped her drink and visibly swallowed before managing a reply, which had sounded something like a garbled, "Are you sure?" And when Taleah had nodded, she shook her head, folded her arms on her lap, almost as if in prayer, and softly mouthed the words "I see."

The event had shaken, but not unnerved, Taleah. She'd expected disapproval and even disappointment.

"Well, I don't…"

"What I really want to know is, do you know about the guy who was murdered yesterday?"

"No."

"Well, apparently a witness heard the killer shouting dad's name. The FBI is going to have dad followed for precaution."

Anna swallowed and summoned a comment about the weather before letting herself sigh. "Well, if that's all true, I think he'll be safe."

"I don't know," Taleah said, gazing into nooks between cars, entrance-ways, and void spaces behind shrubs as she sat there. The heat inside the car was beginning to rise and sweat had started to condense at her underarms. "You know him. He's what they used to call a maverick."

"Watching a few Westerns?" Anna chuckled.

"It's not funny," Taleah argued. "Why don't you take this with just a little more—"

"We should trust them—"

"You didn't," she barked. "You helped Rebekah hack the FBI's communications and she managed to do it undetected."

"Not quite," Anna said.

"But that's the point. I know you don't care about dad, but I still do and knowing what he's going to do is killing me." Taleah felt a frustrated tear form at the corner of her eye, but she gently brushed it away and attempted to settle her nerves.

"Fine," Anna relented. "Maybe you should come over so we can go over plans."

"I'll be right there," Taleah said. She swung open the car door and looked up to the second-floor balcony, where Christine had just emerged to watch.

"I'm going to my mom's," she said. "I'll be back."

"Don't let her straighten you out," Christine said just loudly enough for Taleah to hear.

Taleah nodded, made her way to her car, and checked her surroundings. She pulled the shifter into reverse, checked her rearview mirror, and slowly proceeded to back out of her spot. When she turned to face forward, she shrieked as terror flashed through her veins. He was standing there, next to the window, all grizzled and gray, the emptiness soaking through him like an eerie vein of trauma. His hair was mangled and damp, his eyes wide and menacing.

She let out a gasp when she realized she was staring at the face of a homeless person she'd seen strolling the sidewalks nearby with a cardboard sign.

"I think you dropped something?" he said.

"No, um..." She looked at something the man was pointing at that appeared to be a card. "Not mine. But thanks."

The drive lasted for long enough to cool her nerves. When she arrived, Anna sat at the edge of the couch and typed on her laptop, which she'd positioned on the coffee table with the screen angled upward.

As always, Taleah didn't bother to knock before she entered. Anna looked up from the computer to greet her, motioned her to the couch, and sat next to her, resting her shoulder on the cushioned backrest.

"You're saying you want me to hack the FBI? I think they installed a new patch after your stepmom's last foray though their servers. I won't be able to get in."

"Not the FBI this time," Taleah said. "Police. I imagine they are a little less sensitive in their approach."

"Well, I can probably do it, at least if I remember Rebekah's methods well enough. Just about any frequency scanner can pick up chatter. There are people who actually make a living doing that, from vendetta-seekers to clients of unscrupulous lawyers."

"They have evidence on the attack in the garage and the tank yard," Taleah said. "I want it."

"Can't be done," Anna said. "Police keep physical evidence well-guarded."

"So?"

Anna lowered her voice and looked to the table. "I haven't been in a police station in a long time."

"But you have city clearance. Tell them you're taking over for the city on the tank site proposal and maybe they'll let you look at some of it."

One blink from Anna said it all. Taleah wasn't going to get anywhere, but she pushed anyway because it felt like work and work massaged the demons out of her skull, albeit temporarily. "Unlikely. Plus, they'll check credentials. When they figure that I'm not under that department, they'll ask me to leave."

"Maybe you can pose as one of those dirty lawyers."

"Fake an ID?" She shifted and glanced at the computer screen. "I don't have the software."

"I know someone," Taleah heard herself saying it before the thought finished forming in her mind. "He might be able to download something for you."

"Taleah, what are you into that I don't know about? You've never sneaked around like this before. Whatever it is, I can't pretend I don't see it."

"I'm going to help dad," she shot, flinging herself upright. "If you refuse to help me, then that's fine. But I thought I could count on you. This is just like when I told you I was—"

"It's *nothing* like that," Anna defended herself.

"You resisted."

Her mother frowned and furrowed her eyebrows. "Because I knew you were something better, and you still are."

"Better?"

"Fine, I'll—"

"Yeah, right."

"I'll help, just settle down. But if your friend is so talented, why doesn't she make her own fake ID?"

"It's a he," Taleah said. "And he could never pass as a lawyer because there are too many people around here who pass judgment on appearances. And the police probably know who he is anyway."

"He has a record?"

"No," Taleah said. "He's offered translation services."

"Is this young man a good person? Do you really trust him?"

Taleah clenched her jaw and flashed a look of anger at her mother. Perhaps her questions weren't misplaced, but the tone in which she asked them sparked uncertainty. She gulped when she thought of him, sitting across from her at the Islamic center and speaking plainly. She knew then that he was more than an acquaintance. Her lip quivered momentarily as she spoke crisply. "More than anyone right now, except maybe Christine and dad."

"The police probably don't have much right now," Anna guessed.

The change of pace was jarring enough for Taleah to abandon the mood of fear and replace it with rationality. She swallowed, bit her lip, and listened.

"If they did, they would probably already have a suspect and would be looking for him. That would mean there would be a warrant out, and they'd be printing wanted posters. I doubt they are there yet."

"They're watching dad," Taleah said. "It seems like a stupid idea to go for him while they're all over the place, so I'd count on a distraction—something big—just for long enough to create confusion."

"Maybe," Anna said. "But you might be assuming too much about this killer. Who says he's that smart?"

"I have to take every precaution," Taleah said. "If you can think one step ahead, you'll almost always win. You remember how I used to do that at the plate. I would work the pitcher until she threw me the perfect pitch, and I'd smash it into the outfield. Softball is a game of strategy, a lot like other endeavors. Whoever he is, he's going to give me the perfect pitch, and I'll be ready for it. I have to be."

Anna frowned and let her eyes wander to the couch. A tear sparkled near the bridge of her nose. "When did my little girl grow up?"

Taleah felt a pang of compassion at the back of her heart. She cast a warm stare at her mother, relaxed, and allowed thought to lurch forward once again. Perhaps sensing the change of pace, Anna backed away and spoke more slowly and with more rigidity in her voice. The morning plodded along until her mother invited her to lunch, after which Taleah would head home for a couple of hours with Christine.

Now that she was thinking clearly, the strategy seemed simple. Art had managed to overpower strategy with brute strength, so if she was dealing with anyone half as intelligent or strong, precision could be the difference between failure and success.

She left her mother with a show of good faith and a hug before promising that Emmanuel would be in touch. That was, if he would agree to help in that way. She tried to remember the look in his eyes when she interviewed him. The sincerity flickered like a flame that could not be doused. It drew her in and pulsed through the darkness of her soul. If trusting him turned out a mistake, she would suffer the consequences, but not reaching for it would leave her wandering through a frozen void where hope straddled the line between life and certain defeat.

12

Halo

THE glass tower and its skywalk to the convention center curved around the Grove in a cool embrace as the sun bounced white light off the windows. The resultant effect seemed to dance above their heads as they walked toward the restaurant at the ground floor of the tower facing the Grove.

Emmanuel dodged a flock of young girls ogling the fountain, each trying to goad her neighbor into running through the streams. The fountain consisted of twenty-five jets arranged in a perfect square formation. They reached variable heights and were capable of alternating flow rate. During special performances, engineers could program the pumps to synchronize with music while an LED light display on the walls of the convention center flickered in tune. On normal Saturdays, no special events were planned.

The public market had already wound down and vendors had packed their tents as most of the crowds dispersed, yet on Saturdays, one could normally find hundreds of people dining, picnicking, or walking through the plaza.

Taleah read the names etched into the paving bricks as she walked and almost collided with a tall, athletic young man who looked like he could jump over her head without even trying.

Emmanuel stopped and glanced toward the top floors of the glass tower. "That is my building," he said. "I work with some students at the university. They lease space on the sixth floor. The engineers I collaborate with stay on the seventh to ninth floors. It is an open plan. They say it encourages teamwork."

"And then some weekend warrior has plans for a big trip and has to tell everyone all about it in detail and there are no walls to stop you from joining in," Taleah noted.

"The benefits mostly outweigh the drawbacks," Emmanuel said, taking off his ball cap and scratching the back of his head. He looked flummoxed for a moment. I can show you if they kept the elevator unlocked."

"It will be a quiet place," Taleah said. "Fewer people to overhear us."

"What is the purpose of our meeting?" Emmanuel asked. He was smarter than she thought, perhaps a product of tacit stereotyping stemming from years of not having to interact with Middle-Eastern immigrants. "You would not call me if you did not have reason. And being with a friend does not count."

"It's about my father," Taleah said, after they had approached the front entrance of the restaurant, safely out of earshot from at least twenty people strolling through. Ahead, along the northern spoke of the Grove, soothing street music faded with traffic and reasserted its melody, which at this distance was distorted from the traffic, the buildings, and the breeze.

"They have not found a suspect," Emmanuel commented, edging along the fence separating the restaurant's patio seating. Six people linking arms and wearing funny, colorful hairdos marched in from the northern spoke, almost prancing to the upbeat music. Two of them engaged in laughter, while a third provided somewhat vulgar lyrics. "They say on the news."

"Now it's more complicated than that," she said.

"How is that?"

She waited until they reached the street at the northern end of the tower and turned the corner into the entryway of the City Center Plaza. The main entrance was a broad inlet in the north-facing wall after the sidewalk had passed the windows of the adjacent coffee shop. Emmanuel held the door as she slipped into the lobby. "Did you hear about the murder yesterday?"

"It happened right over there," Emmanuel said, turning around and pointing to the garage across the street. The entrance was no longer barricaded, and two cars were turning in and stopping at the ticket kiosk.

"The police say there was a witness who said the killer was yelling out my last name."

Emmanuel turned his head and stared at her. Beyond the security desk and a narrow, dimly lit corridor, the elevators faced a broad, tiled wall decorated with well-placed paintings and sculptures. His expression ran the gamut from surprised to concerned. He pressed the elevator button and waited as if he didn't know what to say.

"And then there was the call. The killer called me at work and threatened my dad."

"That is not good."

"You know, with my history and all..." Taleah had never told Emmanuel about how Art had kidnapped her, tied her up, and drove for several hours into the deep Bitterroot wilderness to bludgeon and torture her, just waiting for her father to show up so he could kill him. Still, she was more than certain Emmanuel understood that some dark event stalked her past and he more often than not tiptoed around that, at least in college.

"I do not know all of it," Emmanuel noted. The soul leaked into his voice, even though the structure of his words didn't flourish with passion. Instead, they were marked with a still, quiet precision that carried only certain wisps of emotion when he accentuated certain syllables. His English was flawless and scholarly, therefore scant on innuendo, American idioms, and slang. "Do not tell me unless you want to."

She bit her tongue and tried to erase the memory of the homeless man spooking her earlier.

"Are you better now?"

"Mostly," she said. "I just talked to my mom, and she agreed to help me. And that's part of why I wanted to talk to you."

"I never met your mother. Is she kind?"

"Well," Taleah hesitated. "She has her opinions, and let's just say they don't necessarily agree with mine.

Emmanuel waited for the elevator door to slide shut as the feeling of motion set in before he spoke. "Back in Jordan, we had a name for those kinds of people. It means they are ignorant without understanding what makes them so. I understand a passage in your Christian Bible mimics that."

"They know not what they do," Taleah said, her voice flat and devoid of emotion.

Emmanuel nodded. "I think if most people understood that we are more similar than different, there would not be so much judgment in the world today."

"You seem philosophical today," she commented, letting her voice rise again. After a few seconds the elevator stopped and beeped, and the doors slid open, revealing a corridor lined with windows and paintings with glass doors that led into the offices.

She read the lettering affixed to the wall adjacent to the elevators. *Riverside Analytics—Software Reimagined.*

"Crafty slogan," Taleah said.

"Let me show you to my workstation." Together, they navigated a maze of desks littered with dozens of pairing computer screens, paperwork, and wires that fished through openings in the floor, which was made of some kind of heavy, meshed tile where flashes of light and reflection fed through the tiny slots into the room above.

They stopped at an ordinary workstation and pulled out two chairs. Emmanuel motioned her to sit and she did, while running a hand through her finger-length hair. A programmed pause drifted between them. Taleah didn't know what to say next, or at least how to begin her sentence.

"I told my mom about it... about you. And she'll be expecting you to drop by her house and show her how to do it."

Emmanuel flashed a quizzical look and then glanced at the darkened computer screens. A young man walked past them in a hurry and fled through the corridor away from the elevators without looking at them. "How do I take that?"

"Well... here's the thing." Taleah frowned and glanced at a rug covering the tiles. "My mom works at City Hall, and she's pretty good with computers. She said she'd help me in any way she could, and I told her I needed her to get some evidence of the crimes for me. She can't do that without an ID, but she doesn't have the software to make one."

"Are you asking me to commit a crime with you? I would have to decline. They would make me go back to Jordan, which I cannot do."

Taleah shook her head and squinted in the sun diving through the full-wall windows. "No, of course not. I was just hoping you could make her a program."

"I could," Emmanuel said after a long exhale. He relaxed into a chair and then stood up just as fast. "But there are probably quite a few apps available for download already."

"But how good are they? My mom needs one that doesn't scream 'fake' the second you look at it. Something a cop could glance at and decide it's legit."

"Making the card is easy," Emmanuel said. "But it will not stand up to deep scrutiny well, so if they really verify it, they will know she is a fraud."

"I know," Taleah said. "I'm willing to take that risk."

"I do not see how this is going to be good for you," Emmanuel said slowly, with little emphasis on words. I do not want to see you in trouble."

Taleah glanced to the slots in the floor and let out an exasperated sigh. "It's just that I already am. And at this point, I'll do anything to save my dad. Even if it means risking my life."

"Family is the most important thing," Emmanuel said. He took two steps toward the glass exterior wall and nodded for her to join him. They meandered through rows of desks and to the end of a partition wall that separated the open floor work area from a drinking fountain and an open door.

Emmanuel led her through the door and reached for the light switch, even though the adjacent room was well lit. "These are not our main servers. There is a farm on the next floor down. This is our backup room. Two complete systems prevent the spread of unintentional viruses, malware, or computing errors from infecting the most vital thing we do. This floor is for the software team. Data analytics and consultation make up the bigger part of the company."

"Impressive," Taleah noted, taking in the rows of tall computer machines, each flickering with an array of green lights that seemed to dance above the dull hum. It all blended together into a lucid trance, like strobes firing over the vacant landscapes of ambient music.

"What kind of system does she run?" Emmanuel asked, flipping the lights off and closing the door behind him.

"I don't know for sure. It's a Windows-based laptop, I know that. But you can ask her when you get there."

"It is better to be prepared and have the hardware and patches I need," Emmanuel said, "than to not ask and have to go find something else."

"I understand."

"But Windows is standard. Do you happen to know the processor and flash card?"

Taleah grunted and stared at a motivational poster above the drinking fountain. It depicted a woman standing atop a rock overlooking one of the most famous fjords in Norway. Only the woman's backside was visible amidst the scenery, but Taleah would have guessed at her mood: reflective and full of wonder. The all-caps lettering in the black border read "PERSE-VERANCE: The work is worth the reward."

She attempted to smile at the poster, but before her muscles could fully make the adjustment, a loud smashing noise tore through the room, followed by a throat-ripping male scream.

"God, don't do this! SHIT!"

Silence creased the commotion, but lasted only seconds, followed by a disheartening thump.

She started to sprint toward the door leading to the corridor, but Emmanuel stopped her, shushed her, and pulled her to kneel down so that neither of them were visible from the corridor. He put his index finger to his lips as beads of sweat began to condense on his forehead.

"What is going on?" Taleah whispered.

Emmanuel shook his head.

The shouting resumed, but a gruffer voice replaced the higher-pitched screams of the first man. "You shouldn't have told him."

A muffled smattering of footsteps followed, and then ceased.

"He's dead!"

Silence settled over them. The footsteps thundered down the corridor, past the elevators and toward a stairwell before either of them made a move. "There is a security camera pointing at the elevator," Emmanuel said. "But none in the kitchen or the stairs. The lobby and main entrance have several. They will catch him."

Taleah breathed hard and stood up, her knees shaking with the pressure. They carefully trod into the corridor and followed it around a corner into a small kitchen with a laminate-topped dining table and six chairs. The man lay face down in his own blood, his hands tied behind his back and his breathing erratic. Emmanuel sprinted back into the office area to call for an ambulance, but Taleah remained glued to the spot as her entire body began to convulse with shock and sickness.

"Oh my God," she whimpered through the sting of tears. She backed out of the kitchen and slumped against a wall. The blood, the scattering last breaths, and the vacant eyes poured worlds of emotion into her own wounds, dabbing them with a viscous brine.

The forest roared to life as she darted between trees along a narrow game trail that led to a narrow slot ravine feeding the Lochsa River. Footsteps thundered behind her like heavy boots on mesh-panel floor tiles. Her own breathing had become erratic. She changed directions, attempted to hurdle a fallen tree, and tumbled down the slope as Art closed in.

"Taleah!" Her father's screams ripped into her eardrums as she rested against the granite-faced wall and stared through the glass partition wall into the open office area. Emmanuel sprinted to her side, gripped her underarms and pulled her into a solid embrace.

"God," she croaked.

"He won't get away," Emmanuel said. "They are going to barricade the entrance."

A smothering sense of terror slipped into her bloodstream. She shook against his shoulder as she slowly regained her strength and then began to push him away.

"I'm sorry," she said.

He stood there motionless, his expression rapt with rigid understanding, yet reserved sorrow. Instead of saying anything to attempt to comfort her, he allowed himself to step backward. His gaze narrowed and his eyes seemed to gloss over as if intimate reflection were pouring into his soul. They waited for the paramedics to step out of the elevator before they slipped back into the office and took seats. The cops would want to question them.

Taleah's eyes drooped. If only she'd run after him, she thought, but the truth caught up with her as surely as Art had all those years ago. She wasn't ready for the confrontation and having the gun at her hip wouldn't have saved the man's life.

"I knew him," Emmanuel rattled. "A little. And I know what he told. I want it to come from me."

"You?" She searched his eyes for a warm expression of remorse but found little other than a stark realization that somehow, he was as tied into this as she was. They were both eyewitnesses to murder.

"When you asked about the bombing. I told you I heard your father was hurt. That man is David Yerring. He's who told me Reggie St. Clair was one of the victims. I thought about you."

She covered her mouth and altered her breathing as she looked away from him toward the windows to the outside, where the sun beat down on the Grove relentlessly. If the killer managed to escape the stairwell, he wouldn't make it a block without the police apprehending him, even if an underground bus depot would prove to be a good spot to hide out. Taleah thought of the possibilities, but where a sense of relief should have prevailed, only discord and dread won the day.

She shuddered as a dozen cops poured out of the elevator. Emmanuel stood and waited for them to enter.

Fear torched the corners of Taleah's mind. The anger faded when she thought about her father, lying there in the hospital bed seemingly without a care, even as chaos unfolded around him. How did he cope? What must have raged in his mind when he thought about the past and about how he nearly succumbed to death in an effort to save his only daughter? No answers stepped into the light. The only light in her mind seemed to lurk beyond the silhouette of a man's head, dimmed by his grizzled beard.

Her father would be the next target. She had less than forty-eight hours to prepare.

13

Scattering

TALEAH scooted to the edge of the rocking swivel work chair that faced dual computer screens, bounced her knees, and glanced at the clock on the wall. The elevator opened, letting out two paramedics and four cops. There were no signs of either Sergeant Bones or Officer Ramirez, but she assumed it wouldn't be long until they showed up.

One of the investigators slid through the plate glass door, pulled out her own chair, and studied Taleah first before scanning Emmanuel's body language. At first glance, this officer appeared thorough and professional. Her blonde hair was pulled in a tight bun at the back of her head. Neither decorated nor particularly plain, her uniform had been neatly pressed. She wore the gun on her hip as a symbol of pride. Taleah barely glanced at her nametag before she introduced herself.

"I'm Officer Landerman," she said, straightening her back and peering into Taleah's eyes with an air of careful introspection.

Taleah barely waited for her to finish speaking before starting, biting her tongue, and then continuing. "Taleah St. Clair, and this is Emmanuel Al-Rajhi."

Officer Landerman looked into Emmanuel's eyes as he peered back with a sort of placid defeat striking a chord in his own expression.

He didn't speak for several seconds until the officer made a sideways glance at Taleah. "Can I ask why you are here of all places on a Saturday afternoon? It's not a business day, is it?"

"I was showing her my workspace," Emmanuel said deliberately, so as to not allow any accent to be heard. "I work here part time, studying with university students to build software solutions. We met at university."

"We're friends," Taleah clarified, spinning her chair toward him and attempting to force a smile. Her reaction would have looked fabricated from afar, but maybe Emmanuel would see beyond that and understand the fire in her words. Subconsciously, the notion seemed to overcompensate for some deficiency, and once she recognized the shortcoming, living up to the idea would become less a fallacy and more of an opportunity.

"And the office happened to be open today?" Officer Landerman led with her question but didn't assume the answer.

"Usually, some colleagues work on weekends. Did not know David would be here." Emmanuel placed both of his hands on his knees, glanced to Taleah, and then refocused his attention on Officer Landerman.

"What did he say to you when you arrived? David, I take it, is the victim?" She scribbled something on a notepad balanced on her knee and then nodded subtly toward the door. The paramedics scrambled at the end of the hallway, talking in quick, clipped sentences, one of them even addressing David by name.

"Nothing."

"He barely acknowledged us," Taleah said.

"Did you see the perpetrator?" The officer barely looked up from her notepad, but the way she accentuated the word 'see' provided comfort.

Taleah shook her head. "There was commotion and shouting. We stayed out of sight."

"He is on the security video," Emmanuel noted without missing a beat. He offered a quick smile to Taleah and fidgeted with his fingers as though intentionally looking impatient. This was a different look for Emmanuel. She'd never seen him make such obvious signs of any emotion, let alone frustration or impatience. If the act were manufactured, then why would he be so conspicuous? Then again, opacity, Christine had told her once, was often a technique used to deceive and distract from some feeling one wished to hide. What, then, was he hiding?

"Martin and San Pablo are examining them now," Officer Landerman said. "Did you hear David or the suspect say anything of importance to each other?"

As if he'd been expecting the question, Emmanuel carefully constructed a sentence as if it were aimed at Taleah instead. The shift of perception, Taleah guessed, offered him a chance to settle whatever nerves had built up. He likely felt more comfortable addressing her rather than the officer. "He shouted at David, only 'you should not have told him,' and 'he is dead.'"

"Who?"

"I don't know."

"He had to be talking about the man who was beaten to death in the garage across the street the other day," Taleah surmised. "It's the only thing that makes sense."

Officer Landerman looked amused initially, but changed her expression when she witnessed the certainty in Taleah's eyes. "What makes you so sure of that?"

"You know who's handling that case," Taleah said, leaning forward and tucking one foot under the chair. "Sergeant Bones, and he's working with the FBI now, because the person who did it tried to kill my dad. And he's taunting me."

"I'm aware of that case," she said slowly. But how do you know the suspect was talking about that? You may be reaching."

"Don't you have a responsibility to follow the evidence?"

"And when the evidence leads us to that case, we will."

Emmanuel piped up to defend her. "I think it is a valid guess."

Taleah bit her lip and narrowed her eyes while letting her knee bounce. "It isn't a guess. The voice sounded the same as when he called me. Talk to Bones or Marks."

"Bones doesn't have a suspect either," she said, as if attempting to sound impressive. "But it won't be long."

An uncomfortable silence stretched between them. Taleah turned her head slightly as the sun began to change hues as it cascaded through the windows. Instead of pulsing with a blinding white light, a softer orange glow slid into the window as the sun began to dive toward the western horizon. It was as if the rays were bleeding color and emotion into a dark blue canvas that served as the backdrop to its powerful display.

"What was David supposed to have told the other victim?" Landerman asked.

Emmanuel shook his head, but Taleah had already connected the dots. "Obviously, he told him about the explosion at the tank site."

"But how would he know that?"

"He told me about it, too," Emmanuel said. "He was having coffee, I was sipping water at my desk and talking with a client on the phone. He asked me if I heard about that, told me Reggie St. Clair was in the hospital."

The officer's face momentarily became pale, but she made no indication that she was convinced. "When was this?"

"Day after," Emmanuel said.

"As in, before the press started publishing his name?"

"That *is* right," Taleah said, eying Emmanuel. "How did he know? What aren't you telling me?"

He lowered his voice and let his expression droop. "I have told you everything. I want you to trust me like I trust you. If he finds out I know... based on the pattern... he will come for me."

"But," Landerman said, wrinkling her nose and readying her pen, "how would David know? And why would he have told him?" Her questions hit like a hammer that chipped away at Taleah's notions and left them in a heap of gray powder. She shook her head and stared at her knees, which had suddenly stopped bouncing. The memory of David's eyes, powerfully shocked and driven with specks of fear, pummeled her senses. Her heart beat faster and seemed to plunge from her chest toward her stomach, invoking a heavy pain that pressed down on her emotion like an iron sheet. Blood had pooled beneath his body. The man had stabbed him perhaps a half dozen times.

Art had wielded several weapons, among them small, uprooted trees, heavy sticks, and large rocks, but the knife was the most precise. The way he had caressed the cool steel of its blade in the firelight shrouded her memory with further despair. She bit her lip, leaned forward, and battered Officer Landerman with a defiant answer. "If I knew that, we wouldn't be having this discussion."

"What would you be—"

"Trying to protect my dad," she said, her voice raised.

"You're getting awfully emotional about this."

"Am I? Such solid insight. No wonder you're a cop."

The insult seemed to hit home. Landerman recoiled, slackened her shoulders, and scribbled more notes onto her pad. "I think that will about do it. You can leave the premises now. If we need anything else, we'll be in touch."

Her radio crackled. She pressed the button and barked into the radio. "What, San Pablo?"

"Building locked down. Suspect gone."

"Did the security cameras pick him up?"

"Affirmative. But we won't get facial rec."

"Officer San Pablo," she started, "this is a big building. Lots of places to hide. I want your people checking service rooms, janitors' closets, duct shafts, ceilings, on every level, stat."

"Already being done," San Pablo said.

"He couldn't have gotten out of the building," she shouted.

Taleah's chin sunk lower, and her eyes widened. "He did," she said softly. "He's gone."

Fear darkened the corners of her eyes, yet she stood with the fire of determination casting her dancing shadow into the darkness. The anticipation began to build in her veins. She clutched her fist and stared at the slots in the floor, wondering whether it was possible to access the area where the cables ran beneath the tiles.

She swallowed and stood, staring at Emmanuel for a split second. Concern showered his expression with an unexpected wave of uncertainty. He stood up slowly and glanced toward Officer Landerman, who was already rushing toward the elevator. More cops would be arriving shortly to turn the whole building upside down only to come up empty.

If the perpetrator had escaped, it would be a feat becoming of whom her father had called the shadow—Art Rassine himself. Letting that thought free in her skull shredded her emotions like a thousand daggers clawing into raw flesh. Escape seemed impossible, but it was the only way the entire scenario made any sense. It couldn't end like this, because nothing this severe ever vanished without a final confrontation, and this wasn't it.

They rode the elevator down in silence, passing by several guards in the lobby and at the entrance. The tallest of the three, an aging man with a stubbly gray goatee, nodded at Taleah subtly as if he knew her. Rather than returning the gesture or otherwise signaling she'd received his greeting, she kept her head down and emerged with Emmanuel at her hip on the busy, shaded sidewalk of Main Street. The sun had begun its slow descent toward the horizon, casting shadows eastward into the street. The garage loomed across the street. Two cars pulled in, while at least a half dozen were waiting at the gate to insert their tickets before driving away.

While passing the coffee shop, Emmanuel raised his eyes toward the oddly shaped peak of the adjacent triangular building, a large-footprint marble structure that shielded the Grove from the traffic and lights on Main Street. He let his gaze shrink gradually down its ten floors before Taleah reached the corner. She studied his expression, wondering at first whether the events in the office had soured him on the idea of helping her.

"It will be a difficult journey from here, I think," Emmanuel said, a trail of stark desperation meandering through his voice.

"Yes," Taleah said. "But it's one I have to take."

"I understand. What are you planning to do?"

Taleah let her eyes wander through the crowds in the Grove. Saturday night often meant packed bars and restaurants along Restaurant Row, a block of Eighth Street fronted by a dozen or so bars and restaurants, each with ample sidewalk dining flanking the pedestrian-only street. The plaza enjoyed a somewhat quieter presence most evenings, unless hockey games or concerts rocked the arena. At least a hundred people gawked at the foot of the building from which they'd just emerged. Law enforcement officers barricaded each possible entry point, some with weapons drawn while police vehicles idled with flashing lights.

Discomfort spread through her as several glances landed on her. Instead of shrinking from the attention, she attempted to front a smile, though the blood and the eyes of David lingered in her mind like the ashes of a gruesome nightmare.

"I don't know yet," Taleah answered. "My dad's getting out of the hospital in the morning he thinks, so I'll probably spend some of the day at his house. I'm going to have to get used to the cops."

"Is your father armed?"

"I don't think so," Taleah said casually. "But I don't see how it matters." Her father, though scrappy, had been outmatched on both encounters with the shadow but did manage to wound Art. She instantly pictured Rassine dabbing at the remnant of his wound, almost in admiration. It had served as a reminder and a point of vengeance for years, he'd told her, and it would be worthwhile when he finally killed Reggie St. Clair.

The ensuing match, when her father found her in the woods saw Reggie similarly overmatched. Art beat him to the edge of his life after he had easily dispatched Willis. But Willis, undetected, had grasped the gun from a pool of mud and fired the shots that killed Art.

The aftermath brought the kind of dread Taleah had only flirted with in her worst illusions. The therapist worked the demons out of her for more than a year.

"Be careful. And call if you need anything."

Taleah watched him wander through the crowd of spectators and for a moment, they were separated. She searched the plaza for him for at least thirty seconds before he emerged at the foot of the fountain, which splattered water seemingly in tune with the drama in the air. He didn't say anything, but looked as though he were about to open his mouth. She waited for words that never came.

"I will. Do you think you can still help me? I know that wasn't the best of motivators, but I'm desperate."

"I know," he whispered. The water almost drowned out his voice, causing her to tilt her head sideways. "I will help you. Is your mother busy this evening?"

Taleah sighed. "Knowing her, yes. But she's already expecting you to drop by."

He waited and turned toward the skywalk at the south spoke of the Grove approaching Front Street through a wide, brick-paved walkway between the two buildings. They kept outside the parallel rows of trees and strolled past the windows of a tourist-themed gift shop and a fancy art gallery without looking inside.

To amend her statement, Taleah cleared her throat, as a pair of taller boys in denim jackets and colorful, spiked hair smiled at her. "Tonication, Saturday Night!" One of them shouted at her.

"I don't know what that means," she said, trying to appear interested.

"Punk rock at The Factory, man!"

The Factory stood two blocks south in a historical building that had been extensively remodeled as part of a large construction project a decade earlier. Its main entrance fronted the alley between Eighth and Ninth Streets and accommodated about three hundred fans of typically noisy music.

"I'll hook you up," the guy with the green Mohawk said.

"No thanks," she said casually, allowing her elbows to slacken.

Emmanuel frowned. "What were you going to say?"

"My mom can be a little prejudiced sometimes," she explained. "Try to smile at her and be nice, though, and she will warm up to you."

"Prejudice has never bothered me," Emmanuel said. "But I will do whatever I can. I only hope I have the right equipment in my apartment."

She smiled as he tiptoed past a young couple who were laughing at something. The girl bent at the waist and nearly collided with Emmanuel.

"Drunk," he whispered when their paths merged.

Taleah watched dozens of cars speed by on Front Street as they approached the crosswalk at the corner of the garage where Taleah had parked. She thanked him again as he settled against the corner of the convention center building as though waiting for a ride to pull into the narrow loading zone, which buses often occupied.

"You don't need a ride?" Taleah asked.

"No. I have the app. I will talk with you tomorrow sometime between shifts at the center. Will that be good?"

Taleah nodded and waited for the light to turn green. Dozens of people had approached the crosswalk in the time it took to say goodbye. She fished the ticket out of her pocket as she crossed the street, then rounded the corner into the shelter of the green-glassed condo tower that overhung the sidewalk. She waited patiently in line at the kiosk and swiped her card to pay before riding the elevator to the fourth level, which overlooked the urban park, business center, and gathering place across the busy Ninth Street.

The drive home lasted only a few minutes. Christine would probably still be at home, perhaps reading. As hard as she tried to think up something interesting to discuss, she knew Christine would want to hear about what had happened inside Emmanuel's office and how her mother had reacted to her request for help. They'd order in Chinese or something else unhealthy and share a card game to break up the tension, though Christine hated to lose so much that inconsequential arguments sometimes broke out.

A frown lingered on her face, even as she tried to smile it away. She looked in every direction as she parked the car, ready for fright if the homeless man reappeared at her door. The credit card on the ground had been picked up. A dog barked in a nearby building as she ascended the stairs.

Christine flipped through channels on the television with an annoyed expression spanning her face. "What a jerk," she said, pushing the power button before firmly setting it down on the coffee table.

"Took a little longer than I thought," Taleah said. "I'm sorry."

"It's okay," she said. "I was just letting that moron on the singing show get a little too up close and personal, if you know what I mean."

"Creep," she commented slyly.

"What happened?"

Taleah sighed and deposited her purse on the kitchen table, which Christine had earlier used as a mail sorting station. One pile was designated as junk, while one larger stack held her bills. Taleah's mail was spread like a poker hand next to Christine's bills. "What didn't?"

After another sigh, this one somehow less painful, she dove into the story of the disagreement with her mother and the murder in the office building. Every detail appeared to disturb Christine. Her brows furrowed and she sank backward into the couch almost with each word. "God, I'm so sorry."

"And I'm going to my dad's tomorrow, if you want to come. We'll watch golf and let Rebekah make cookies."

"Exciting," Christine said sharply, her eyebrows still pulled together in a look of disgust.

"Always."

Christine pushed away from the couch and approached the kitchen before unplugging her phone from the charger and flipping through a dozen advertisements. She showed Taleah a silly meme to lighten the mood and then suggested a card game.

"This time I'm going to win," Christine taunted.

Taleah swallowed a swig of water, coughed, and pulled out a chair. "Sure."

The evening whittled away quickly. When Taleah yawned and stretched, Christine grasped her hand loosely and led her to the bedroom early. She didn't know what tomorrow might bring, but for the first time in the last week, she felt ready for it. Dreams or none, she would face the day with enthusiasm, even if the events piled up into mountains of dread. Something had to go right for once. An unspoken optimism filled her spirit as she rolled over and drifted off to sleep.

14

Mirage

REBEKAH sat cross-legged on the couch, her phone perched on her knee at the hem of her black and pink floral-pattern skirt. She lightened the room with continuous smiles, which helped to lift Taleah's spirits. Her father rolled his wheelchair into the room halfway into Taleah's story about the murder downtown and her discussion with Emmanuel on what he knew. Concern grew on Rebekah's face with every sentence as the lines dug deeper into her face and her complexion grew paler.

"This was one of your college classmates?" Reggie asked, affixing a look of surprise to his face.

Taleah nodded and sipped off her glass of water, holding the rim to her lips an extra second and furrowing her brows.

"Sounds like a wonderful young man," he said.

"Really, dad? Mom tried this crap yesterday and it didn't work then, either."

"What crap?"

"He didn't mean it like that, sweetheart," Rebekah said, pushing herself back into the cushions.

"But now you're acting defensive."

"Am not," Reggie said. He cast a warm expression across the room before lifting himself out of the wheelchair and gingerly planting himself on the recliner facing the television set. Taleah watched him grimace in pain as he settled in the chair, but didn't let her body language communicate deep concern or sympathy.

She shook her head. "Okay. He is a good friend."

"And?"

"And nothing," Taleah bit. "This guy David... do you know him?"

Reggie shook his head. "Again with the vanilla names. Am I supposed to remember every David I ever crossed paths with?"

"He's the link," Taleah said, "between you and the killer."

Reggie rubbed his chin and let his eyelids droop. "Let's see, there was a David Leonard in church a few years back. He and his wife Nancy moved into the city and started a family. And a Dave Clapp, who organized that fun-run for cancer awareness, overate the night before, and had to be rushed to the ER. Didn't Emmanuel mention his last name?"

Taleah sighed and rocked her knee back and forth before wiping a tiny piece of lint from her blue jeans. "I don't remember. Maybe something starting with a Y? He would have told the cop about it. He's only part time and not that familiar with him."

"That info is going to make it to the press, anyway," Reggie said, glancing out the window. Taleah's car was parked across the street in front of the worrisome neighbor's house. They were an older couple who kept their lawns and gardens so well-manicured that they could have put them on the cover of a landscaping magazine without having to edit the image whatsoever. They'd keep a copy of the magazine laying around the house to impress visitors, ostensibly as a conversation starter. 'How'd you get your lawn so green, Bob?' 'Well, Jackie, I apply Tony's Evergreen every week and it keeps my lawn healthy and vibrant.'

On the close curb, the Meridian Police Department watched from inside the car. Taleah guessed that would be a spectacularly boring way to spend a Sunday, but at least officers would take it in shifts. Reggie had worked out an agreement with them, he said, where if they stayed out of his hair, he'd pretend they weren't even there. Absent that, he had planned on being as big a nuisance as possible.

"And speaking of that," her father grumbled. He cleared his throat and rested his hands on the armrests of the chair. "How's that gig going?"

"Well, our story is running for Monday's edition, but I don't see how it really matters anymore since I think most people realize it wasn't terror-related."

"Of course it matters," Reggie said.

She smiled and changed the subject. While she spoke, she tilted her head. "How's Willis?"

"He'll be back to calling strikes in a week or two," her dad guessed. "But they're going to keep him in the hospital the next couple of days to advance the healing process. He got it worse than I did."

"Is Melissa at least helping him out?"

"I haven't seen her," Reggie said. "But that doesn't mean she hasn't been there. You know since we were put in separate rooms, we didn't exactly have much time to talk. On that note, how is everything working out with Christine?"

Taleah blushed and held back a smile. She could only nod and turn her eyes into cartoonish half-crescents that must have looked so inane on an actual human that they alone would elicit laughter.

"Can't complain?" Rebekah scooted toward the edge of the couch and glared out the front window. Bob's dog was about to cross the street to bother the cops and start a bark-off with every other dog in the neighborhood. "I'll bet she's worried about you."

"Of course," Taleah said. The small talk felt like murder at this moment, especially when so much remained to play out. The anticipation worked its way into her bones after pulverizing her muscles so consistently that after a while, they began to numb. As an old song put it, the waiting was the difficult part.

Overly concerned about the dog, Rebekah stood from the couch and hurried to the front door. She swung it open and shouted, "Get out of here, Rup!". The dog emitted a bark so forceful that it caused him to jump off the street nearly a foot, and then stared her down. She stepped menacingly onto the porch, which spooked the dog just enough to get him to scurry back onto his own property. Bob stormed out the front door and called the dog into the house.

"I can see how that might be hard," she said after closing the door and making her way back to the sofa. "But she seems pretty insightful. Even if you don't tell her everything immediately, she's going to figure it out on her own."

"That's part of it," Taleah said. "But even she doesn't really know what Art did to me psychologically." Her voice sunk lower with the next few sentences and her face gradually grew paler. "I've been seeing his face lately. And I'm scared."

Reggie cleared his throat. "You are not..." he started, but then relaxed his tone and attempted to smooth the delivery as his jaw slackened. "I mean, it's going to be tough right now. But you're not in danger."

"You're the one I'm worried about," she said dryly as though weariness had crept into her voice.

"I'm not either, thanks to the boys in blue."

"Are you saying you trust the cops now? A few years ago, you openly defied them to come find me."

"That was different," Reggie defended himself.

"Was it?"

He nodded and grimaced as he shifted his weight in the recliner. Taleah broke off the conversation and sat silently in the couch, folding her knees under her, and staring out the window. The image of her car blurred and folded into a viscous wash of color that seemed to undulate like tides of hot air turned glassy in the distance with the sun's rays. She allowed a tear to trickle down her face, wiped it away, and continued to stare.

Rebekah scooted closer and patted her thigh gently. She offered an emotive gesture that somehow pulled more tears out of Taleah's eyes. She'd promised herself she wasn't going to cry. Not today, but the pain blasted her in waves driven by the changing winds of uncertainty.

Rebekah offered her a tissue and sat still. For several minutes, no one spoke.

Taleah broke the silence, her lip quivering as the tears ceased. "I'm going to do it. Whoever the imposter is, I'm going to stop him before he gets to you."

"You don't have to act like a hero, Taleah."

"No. Just a loved one. I don't care if they are listening right now," she said, glancing up at the cop car. The two officers inside were busy snacking on some doughnuts and filling the car with small talk, probably. "Mom is helping me find out who planted the package. And I have a gun."

Reggie coughed and doubled over in shock.

"Yeah. It took Christine's brother a little while to show me how to shoot. I'm not a good shot yet, but—"

"And what, he just let you have it?"

"Borrowed," she corrected him. "With no ammo. I don't even know what kind of bullets it takes, but I can find out."

"Taleah—"

"This guy isn't getting to you," she said, biting her lip. "I'm making sure of that. That's why I was downtown yesterday with Emmanuel."

"Don't do anything stupid," he warned.

"What do you mean?" she said, allowing her voice to exert more force at the end of her question. "Like I did in college when I started dating girls?"

"You don't have to be so sensitive," he said.

"No, Taleah's right," Rebekah said. "You crossed the line."

"There are lines all over the place," Reggie said. "Can you just print me a nice little spiral-bound manual about what is appropriate and what isn't under every possible scenario? I don't want to walk on eggshells around you. But I don't want conditions in our relationship, either."

"Maybe I'll just go. Christine was going to come over, but I'll tell her to stay home and we'll order a pizza."

"Isn't your golf game on?" Rebekah nodded, glancing at the clock and subtly inching away from Taleah.

"Yeah," Reggie said. "It's boring as hell, but I guess it beats this."

"If it's so boring, why do you watch it?"

"Hunter Madison's in the lead," he said as if the name had some sort of special relevance to either of them. When their expressions didn't change, he raised his palms. "Come on, the guy who won four majors in a row and single-handedly turned the sport into something exciting to watch."

Taleah could only listen. In essence, she agreed that it was boring to watch. It was probably more fun to play, but Taleah had never held a golf club before and the concept of how to swing it was lost on her. The professionals made it look so easy. And the advertisements for the championships were full of enticing camera angles, zippy panning and zooming, raucous crowds, and animated expressions as the players celebrated great putts. So exciting! And then, an Englishman who'd consumed too many muffins and not enough tea carried the narrative straight into mind-numbing territory capable of putting the Energizer Bunny down for the count while the crowds politely clapped when a player sank a putt, then gracefully tipped his hat to the crowd, rather than pumping his fist and shouting with glee. The gimmick was, of course, as old as time. But golf games came with a lot of sponsors, and sponsorships sold products. The new top-flight ball with the newest in aerodynamic technology was guaranteed to get the most out of every drive or your money back. And that was a lot of money, too, especially if you were foolish enough to buy your supplies from the pro-shop because you lost all your balls on the front nine.

"Sure, honey," Rebekah said, laughing.

"I guess I'm sorry," Reggie said. "Damn, I'm becoming such a fuddy-duddy in my old age."

Taleah chuckled and relaxed her shoulders. "Go ahead and turn it on."

"You want to help me with the hydrangeas?" Rebekah asked, raising one eyebrow in a curious twist. Taleah scooted to the edge of the couch and rose to her feet.

"Come on," Reggie protested. "It's not *that* boring."

Taleah and Rebekah laughed as they made their way through the kitchen. She had devoted almost their entire backyard to beautiful gardens stocked with flowers, native grasses, and a floor of bark amongst the trees, which had started to grow up over the last few years. The neighborhood was somewhat new still, so most of the trees would not fully reach maturity for another decade or so.

The backyard was small enough to be less than a nuisance where maintenance was concerned, but just large enough for young families to engage in fun games that didn't involve hard balls. Rebekah turned on the hose, started to fill a small watering can, and spoke over the hydraulic sound of running water.

"He loves you, you know. Half the time, he's a little past the times, but he usually gets it. Are you going to be all right?"

"Of course I am," she said, picking up a hefty pair of scissors from the railing around the back porch.

"Do you really expect this man to come after your father? I realize the cops aren't perfect, but they really do their best to protect us every day." Taleah had the impression that she was subtly pointing to recent national controversies where police officers had mistakenly shot innocent, unarmed men. With that, Taleah agreed, but Rebekah's words had another layer. Taleah could only ask one question to get to the bottom of it at last.

"Do you really think it's okay to put his life in their hands when there is still so much nobody knows?"

"Seems a little inappropriate," she said. "But he can handle himself. He wants you to enjoy your life and stop worrying about him so much."

"I guess I can do that," Taleah lied.

"They're going to find the bad guy soon. You don't kill people in broad daylight and get away with it in this day and age. There's too much evidence."

This killer, however, didn't seem to operate with a desire to get away with it. He wanted to cause as much chaos as possible. Some people thrived on chaos. It was as essential to them as food or water. Taleah cracked her knuckles and knelt down beside the flower bed where the hydrangeas soaked up a triangular patch of sun between a pair of trees and the eaves of the house. Small talk would do until Christine arrived, she thought. Every thought between bouts of speaking and listening was tainted with memories of the body, the impending confrontation, and the nightmares where the shadow swallowed up all life, leaving only scarred wastelands, charred by the ashes of history. It was real enough to invoke panic and potent enough to bring tears, but she bit her lip and pressed onward. She was staring down an oh-and-two pitch in the sixth inning and she could either swing or retreat to the dugout.

Rebekah turned off the water and gently drizzled water on the plants individually as she started into some small talk about the weather this time of year. In another week or so, it would turn so hot that hydrangeas would wilt in an afternoon. Rebekah would have to resort to setting the sprinklers every afternoon to counter it, Taleah guessed. For now, the watering can would do.

This sparked some odd discussion on why the *Capital Weekly* never ran weather forecasts. Truly, a weekly newspaper could never hope to keep up with the changing weather, but the real reason was because readers viewed it as inconsequential filler material not worth the print space unless it was a large weather event that caused heavy damage and loss of life.

Taleah grabbed at a weed that had penetrated the layer of bark and yanked it out of the ground. Weeds, if left unchecked, could suffocate flower plants relatively quickly. Rebekah spent hours in the yard tending the flowers and Taleah guessed having someone to share in the experience would offer greater pleasure.

Her phone in her back pocket began to ring. She dropped the weed and the scissors and reached for it. Recognizing the number as Emmanuel's, she swallowed, pressed the button, and spoke.

Horror spit venom into her ears as the rocky crunch of static ripped through the line. The voice on the other end prodded with a slow, guttural, roar, "I know you were there."

15
Focus

S HARDS of pain ripped through Taleah's head as she shouted into the phone. "Who is this? What do you want from me? You son of a *bitch!*"

It was no use because the caller had already hung up. She dropped the phone into the grass between her crossed legs, cupped her hands over her eyes and issued a deep, tearless sob. Rebekah deposited the watering can on the brick pavers that separated the garden from the grass, crawled toward her, and wrapped one arm around her shoulder. She didn't speak, only attempted to calm her by squeezing tighter and slowly rocking her side to side.

"Goddammit!" Taleah shook. She removed her hands from her eyes after a few minutes, leaned back and picked up the phone from the grass.

Jolted by Taleah's profanity, Rebekah leaned her head back in recoil and wore a half-hearted stare of empathy tainted with disgust. "Who was that?"

"I. Don't. Know."

Rebekah loosened her grasp on Taleah's shoulder and eyed the phone as Taleah rose it to eye level and began punching numbers. "Maybe call him back."

After three rings, which seemed to pulse longer and longer with every fraction of a second, spreading waves of chaos through her mind, Emmanuel answered.

"Emmanuel," she gasped. "I don't know how, but your phone has been compromised."

"Compromised? I installed security apps." His voice sounded flustered, but patient. Without speaking further, he breathed deeper, which seemed to soothe Taleah's nerves just enough for rational thought to flow back into her brain. Did you hear anything from the police?"

"No, did you?"

"No. You sound... like you have a bad day. Can I help?"

Taleah flipped her shoulders back, allowed them to slump and then spoke in a high-pitched, sheepish voice that sounded like the murmurings of a child scolded. "No, you don't... you don't have to do anything. Maybe I'm talking to the wrong person. But it was your phone number. He knows we were there, Emmanuel."

Emmanuel emitted an edgy whisper that seemed oddly like an Arabic curse word. Did they have swearwords in Jordan? "He knows? I do not understand."

"I'm going to call the FBI," Taleah said, worry springing up in her nerves once again. The thought of calling in Agent Marks with another phone-related crisis caused her to feel worthy of pity, as if some sort of force field separated her from the rational world, where reason prevailed, rather than the destructive tendrils of spiritual demise.

"Call me back," Emmanuel said. "I'm leaving the center now."

Taleah shook as she slid her ankles beneath her, pushed at the ground, and struggled to her feet. Rebekah supported her weight as she got up, then held out her hand for Taleah to return the favor.

She flung open the French door with perhaps too much force and waited for Rebekah to enter the dining room behind her. Forcefully punching the buttons, though frustratingly random, offered a foreign concept of catharsis, which temporarily calmed her jittery fingers. When the ringing tone commenced, Taleah collapsed onto the sofa and then pushed herself forward.

"Keep it quick, Taleah," Agent Marks said. "In a meeting."

"It happened again," Taleah said. "Call Ms. Cottage. He called my cellphone."

Agent Marks managed to let a pause linger several seconds while still sounding rushed. "Looks like we may be getting a break. But I'll call her right now. Did your phone indicate the number?"

"It was my friend Emmanuel's number," Taleah said. "Like he stole his phone number?"

"A clone?" Taleah assumed Marks was furiously sliding the tip of his pen across the paper in rigid, yet manic handwriting. "That's unusual. Where are you at, your father's house?"

"Yes."

"Stay there. I will make sure Delilah gets to you within the hour. We'll talk more." Marks hung up the phone, yet Taleah still held it to her ear. Bitterness swarmed in her heart as her breathing intensified. The room seemed to grow dark under a cloud of fury, behind which Reggie's soulful eyes sparkled with shimmering dismay.

Her father turned off the television, relaxed his head, and attempted to cool the tension with steady speech. "You were talking to Agent Marks. I could recognize his voice anywhere. What's up?"

Taleah stammered, rocked back and forth on the balls of her feet, and then relaxed her shoulders. "Remember how the person pretending to be Art called me at the office the other day? He just called my... well, at least it sounded a lot like him, but it was Emmanuel's number. Ms. Cottage is going to come over and trace the call."

"Ms. Cottage? What an unusual name."

"Dad, this is serious."

"I know that. But for a guy who supposedly wants to get at me, he sure seems fixated on you. Maybe those clowns should be tailing you." He glanced out the window during his last sentence. The cruiser hadn't moved, and its occupants now seemed somewhat bored. One of them nodded subtly at Reggie and then spun his gaze to the neighbor's house. "And what do you suppose his break is about?"

Taleah shifted her weight again, rested her phone on the armrest, and let her thoughts spin out of control, surrendering them to the arms of chaos that wrapped them asunder to explore darker territory. The shadow's face flashed against the sky, illuminated by a distant lightning bolt, just quick enough to poison her soul with shattered memory. With the knife clutched between his fingers and a pine stick propped against his knee, his breath scratched at the silence before succumbing to the gurgle of thunder. When silence resumed, the heavy scratching of steel on wood resumed. He said nothing, only stared at Taleah's silhouette pressed against the tree where the glow of the coals could barely reach her. The mood drifted from terror to wonder and then back to planning her next escape attempt.

"Not a good sign, anyway," Reggie said. "Marks is a thorough guy. If he's getting breaks by now, the crap is really going to hit the proverbial fan."

Taleah snapped her mind back to the present, witnessed her trembling fingers and attempted to downplay what agonized her. Her father, no doubt could sense it. Only one other person in the world understood the way emotion and fantasy collided within her brain and could use an array of verbal tools to defuse the tension. Christine's car would be pulling into the driveway soon, she guessed. If the city offered any safe respite, this was it.

"When did you start talking like that?" Taleah asked.

"Like what?"

Taleah raised one eyebrow and then leveled her gaze at his forehead, which seemed to teeter back and forth as if on a ledge. "You once chided me for using slang. I remember it vividly." She imitated Reggie's voice in an exaggerated monotone. "We speak English in this house."

"Well..."

"And clichés, Dad? The last time I heard you use one of those, I was having my wisdom teeth pulled and you were joking about hammering my thumb."

"Yeah..."

"It was like you were the one on nitrous."

The back and forth raged on for several minutes before a knock on the door. Escorted by one of the policemen, Ms. Cottage stood there with her laptop bag slung over her shoulder. She smiled at Taleah and entered the room.

After getting her laptop set up and her equipment ready, she punched some codes on the keyboard, waited for her program to respond, and then spoke quickly. "Okay, let's see your phone."

Taleah set it down on the coffee table next to her and then knelt down on the carpet to watch.

"Seems like risky business to call, even from a cloned device these days," she said, draping her bangs toward her ear. "People assume it offers you some security and anonymity, which couldn't be further from the truth."

She nodded and waited.

After connecting Taleah's phone to her laptop, Delilah typed something quickly and waited. "Doesn't look like the call lasted very long. What did he say?"

"He said he knew I was there. Which I assume refers to the crime scene downtown yesterday."

"It doesn't mean he does know," Ms. Cottage said. "Maybe he was just trying to... what's that saying? Get your goat?"

Taleah recoiled and shrugged sheepishly. Of course, she could have been right. Probably, even. But that still didn't explain how he was calling from Emmanuel's number, which would only lead to a million other questions. He must have had access at some time or another to his phone. When did he take it? How did he get past Emmanuel's security? How long ago? And why?

"Another incorrect guess people make is that you can't trace a call that doesn't last thirty seconds. You can trace any call. In fact, in some cases you don't actually need to make the connection at all. If someone is smart enough, they can intercept it and kill it before the recipient even answers the phone. High tech world."

"Scary," Reggie said, sounding unsurprised.

Ms. Cottage waited and then a dot came up on the screen. "He's travelling east on Fairview. We can get the BPD on him."

"There's got to be thousands of cars in that area," Reggie said. "Have you ever attempted to get through there at rush hour? It's like trying to stuff a caterpillar into a tube of toothpaste."

Taleah smirked.

"As long as the signal is on," Delilah explained, I can track it and the cops can follow my directions. Once it's isolated or stopped, they can make their moves, apprehend the suspect, and everyone goes home."

"That's the way it's supposed to work," Taleah guessed. "If he even still has the phone."

"If it is a clone," Ms. Cottage said, "It doesn't seem likely he'd use it just to make a prank call and then ditch it. Has to have an end game."

"He's trying to corral me and Emmanuel," she said. "It doesn't make sense."

"Excuse me," Reggie grunted. He gritted his teeth and glared at Ms. Cottage. "I'm supposed to be the victim here. Why isn't he pranking me?"

"I'm afraid I can't answer that, Mr. St. Clair," she said firmly. Her hair dragged across her sweater and curled at the end. Ms. Cottage stared at the dot on the screen for a second or two and then glanced out the window to summon one of the officers.

The officer jogged to the front door and waited for Rebekah to answer. Delilah didn't waste time. "I'm gonna need you to radio for a squad on Fairview approaching Cole immediately. Suspect is possibly in the area."

"Copy," he said, and hurried back to the car.

"That's that," she said. "I'll wait here and watch the signal for a few minutes if you don't mind."

Reggie sighed. "Why would I mind?"

Rebekah sat down on the couch quietly, as if with careful, measured steps. She said nothing and picked up her phone from the end table to scan through her social media in search of something interesting.

Taleah nodded her way and then refocused on Delilah's computer screen. Hope hadn't the faintest glimmer in her heart. This wasn't going to work. Subconsciously, she never even questioned that assumption, and nothing suggested that the criminal was smart enough to clone a cell phone and get away with murder not once, but twice. Would he be brazen enough to use that phone to prank call the daughter of the man he'd tried to blow up?

"We're going to get him," Delilah said, glancing up to meet Taleah's eyes.

"He's gone," Taleah said. *He has to be.*

Delilah nodded and turned back to the screen. "Let's see if we can narrow down where our mysterious caller was when you answered the phone. Time stamp on the call works out... ETA time matches up close."

"What?" Taleah jumped to her feet when the dot on the screen suddenly relocated to a point closer on the map, less than two blocks away from her father's house. She swore and sprinted toward the front door as adrenaline shot through her veins.

"What on earth are you doing?" Reggie asked. "Settle down."

"He's going to... I have to find Emmanuel. Tell Christine."

"What's going on?" Reggie yelled.

Taleah never thought about answering the question. She fled to her car, watching the police talk on the radio as she went, running to anywhere but here. If he was two blocks away, he knew Taleah was at her father's house, he knew where Reggie lived, and he was going to find Emmanuel and do whatever he wanted to do, because Emmanuel was defenseless. The gun would be waiting at home. She floored the accelerator and started the thirty-minute trip with floods of superheated adrenaline cascading through her veins. Danger was only the beginning.

Reggie scooted painfully toward the edge of the chair when one of the officers knocked on the door. The officer didn't wait for Rebekah to jump up before pushing the door open and announcing himself as Detective Strata. He stood next to the woman watching the little dot on the screen and waited for instructions that he could radio to the BPD officer in charge of following the signal.

"Suspect is merging onto the Connector," Ms. Cottage noted. "Eastbound."

"Inbound Connector," Strata barked.

Reggie attempted to look impressed but frowned instead. He tried to wipe it away when Rebekah glanced at him, but the damage was already done. Worry spanned her face and settled like a monolith of granite. Rather than saying anything, he refocused his gaze on the dot, which had settled into a stationary pulse.

"Must be at a light," Detective Strata noted. "Moving again."

Seconds passed. Ms. Cottage held her breath as the dot moved slowly along the Midtown portion of Fairview Avenue, which could only be accessed by merging onto Interstate 184 and then taking the Fairview exit toward downtown. Reggie swallowed and, wondering where Taleah was going, clutched his phone tightly in his fist so that he could call at a moment's notice.

"Left on Garden Street," she said.

Garden Street was a short, backway access to Chinden Boulevard that darted across Main Street and meandered along the sprawling River-lion Hotel property. The better access to Garden City from Fairview would have required turning left from Fairview onto a less-traveled route and descending the bluff to reach Chinden. Reggie already knew where the suspect was headed but watched the dot for what felt like forever.

The dot pulsed in one spot, waiting for the light at Main Street before speeding forward and rounding the bends along the hotel. The dot slowed just before it reached Chinden Boulevard and turned down a narrow side street along the far western edge of the hotel property, where three or so buildings formed a right angle abutting the greenbelt.

Ms. Cottage held up two fingers and waited for the vehicle to stop.

"East Thirty-Second Street," Detective Strata said. "Via the hotel parking lot. Suspect is stationary. Deploy with caution."

The static from his radio crackled as the answering officer's voice seemed to materialize mid-sentence. "Taxicab pulling away. Twenty on the suspect."

"Stationary," Strata said. He looked at Ms. Cottage and squinted. "Can it get more precise?"

She zoomed in and waited for the screen to sharpen. The dot lingered there, mid-block between Osage and Clay Streets on the side opposite the hotel.

"That's a residential area," Reggie said, which the detective ignored.

"North side of Thirty-Second," Detective Strata said. "Target remains near Import Motor shop. Move in at discretion."

"Copy," the voice radioed back.

Reggie winced at Rebekah, who had inched toward the front of the couch as the seconds ticked away. Reggie's heart pounded as he waited for the voice to radio the status back. The wait dragged onward as impatience flooded his senses with every second. He swallowed and widened his eyes when he realized how close Taleah and Christine lived to the hotel. Their apartment complex was nestled on the Boise side of the river, less than a half-mile away from the hotel property.

Rebekah eyed him and let her gaze soften as a way to soothe his nerves. The expression worked on him sometimes, but when tension reached such a pitch, his nerves remained impervious to her influence. "It's okay," she whispered. "They've got him."

"Give me status," the detective commanded.

"Ten-four," the voice replied. "Suspect in custody."

Detective Strata cautiously looked at Reggie and tilted his head subtly to his left. "He'll report to the Ada County Jail where BPD will question him. I will let you know when they give us more info."

Unsatisfied, Reggie let his muscles relax. Something about this didn't feel right, but he couldn't identify what was out of place. Instead, the situation resembled a famous painting but with one tiny detail missing, mirrored, or colored wrongly, the piece ended up looking almost foreign, even though a casual observer could not find the mistake. Reggie studied every aspect he knew of the investigation while Ms. Cottage packed her equipment into its carrying bag and Detective Strata made for the front door and exited.

Whatever it could have been, Taleah could possibly have a better feel for what the investigation had entailed, but he didn't want to worry her by saying that the suspect had been apprehended so close to her house. And what if the suspect wasn't really the suspect at all, but a random passerby who just happened to cross cellphone signals with the real caller? The loose strands were too numerous to count, and while the arrest tasted like the sweetness of victory, it was but one tiny battle in a wider conflict. What would happen next Reggie could scarcely guess at, but his instinct had served him well over the years, especially on matters relating to Taleah.

He clutched the phone, squared his jaw, and dialed Taleah's number. The confusion torpedoed him as he waited for Taleah to answer. Two rings, three rings, and then utter silence. Something was wrong. Horror doused his insides as he reached for the handle of the wheelchair.

16
Blur

THE gun was positioned toward the wall in the top drawer of her nightstand with a bottle of lotion, a package of perfumes she'd never opened, a paperback book, and a pair of delicates. She flung the drawer shut after she grasped the pistol and shoved it into her purse so that the handle stuck out. The weapon could not look more conspicuous, she thought, so she quickly rearranged the contents of her purse to create a neat pocket that would allow her to withdraw it in a second.

She didn't know if the sporting goods store would allow her to bring it in, but that store sold a lot of guns and ammunition, so it seemed likely that people would pack firearms into the store from time to time.

The drive to the store lasted just under ten minutes. Traffic, as usual for a Sunday afternoon, was light and the signals were timed so that they would change faster than at peak hours, when they had to be programmed to let hundreds of cars go through in a single cycle. From her apartment, she simply cruised westward in the fourth lane of Main Street, which turned into an on ramp to the Connector. That freeway terminated at a large interchange called "the Wye" and its last off-ramp led to a major shopping hub anchored by the mall and a half-dozen other strip malls, one of which housed the chain sporting goods store she chose. Just as she parked the car in the lot, her father's number appeared on her phone. She inadvertently pressed the button to answer it and pressed it again to hang up. She'd call back when she was done shopping, which she hoped would take little time.

She darted through the rows of parked cars and through the main entry way. The guns and ammunition were stocked in an impressive area of the store marked by a glass display case and manned by several helpful salesmen. A separate room jutted off to the left of the main aisle in the section, which another salesperson guarded. She didn't care what they guarded. She started browsing the rows of boxes with different styles of ammunition before making eye contact with an older gentleman who appeared weathered and ready for a hunting trip. He limped toward her, shook her hand, and offered assistance.

"I don't really know what I'm looking for. It's my brother's, and I decided to get him some bullets for his birthday so he can go target shooting." Her motivation for lying escaped her, but inviting suspicion seemed like a poor opportunity, especially on a time crunch. It was easier to come up with a fraudulent excuse than to blow her entire story for someone who, thinking he would be helping, would likely call the police.

"That's understandable," he said. "What caliber are you looking at?"

She shrugged. "Um. Forty-four? I have it here in my purse."

He watched as she pulled the gun out and set it in the gentleman's hands. He did a quick inspection and handed it back to her. "That's a fine weapon. One of the best ever made. You're after nine-millimeter ammunition, and we have lots of that.

With a subtle wave of his hand, he motioned her to follow him past two racks of guns and into the ammunition section. Before saying anything else, he glanced at her sideways, perhaps to understand her real motive.

"Our nine-millimeter is all here on the left. Please browse at your leisure and don't hesitate to ask questions."

The polished steel of the barrel reflected the overhead light as she slipped the weapon back into her purse. At least a half-dozen brands offered at least three different bullets for nine millimeters. She spied a box of preloaded clips, but it didn't seem likely they'd fit the weapon she'd borrowed from Christine's brother. Another box looked more promising. It offered twenty-four rounds for what seemed like a decent price, at least when compared with other brands. Another box with eighteen rounds was priced even lower, but she determined that she'd save money by going with the twenty-four-round box. Deciding it was better to be over-prepared than under, she scooped up three boxes and carried them to the registers at the front of the store.

They set her back a healthy sum, but she didn't let it bother her. After paying for the bullets, she made her way back to her car, passing three or four bearded men during the walk. One of them hulked in the sun like the nimbus clouds that were beginning to tower over the mountains. She attempted to smile at him, but recoiled when he met his eyes, which shimmered like opals. Though she pegged him to be an avid hunter or fisherman, his overall demeanor brought a sudden chill to her spine. He glanced back at her, nodded politely, and sped toward the front door. Peeking back at him twice seemed a little paranoid, but by now instinct seemed to have a mind of its own.

Her next destination would be to track down Emmanuel. He would probably be hanging out at the Islamic Center most of the day volunteering and translating. She dialed his number after she started the car and waited for him to answer.

"How are you?" he asked.

She didn't mean to sound impatient, but her words bit down like a frosty breeze as her muscles tensed. "How did he clone your phone?"

"He could not have," he said.

"Well, he must have figured out how to bypass your security. Have you left your phone unattended for more than fifteen minutes at a time? It can't be that difficult to clone a device."

"Have you ever tried it?" He seemed somewhat amused, but his tone hardly changed, which suggested either opaque sincerity or a flatly humorless approach. Whatever his method, the question didn't seem like anything Emmanuel would ever say. Hearing the humanity in his words sparked another dimension for him, far deeper than she'd viewed him before.

"Okay," Taleah relented. "What are you doing? Are you busy? I could use a—"

"I am always busy," he said, "but I can take time out for you. I can get Rashid to help with the applications."

"I don't want do inconvenience you," she lied, attempting to smooth over her voice into something resembling politeness.

"You should not worry about that. We are friends?"

She stammered, unsure of whether he'd meant that as a question. Friendship, in this case, seemed more than implied. Why would he ask if he knew it as well as she did? His voice belonged to him, but it seemed like he was reading the words off of a teleprompter. "Of... of course we are. I'll stop by then. Are you talking with Abal today?"

"He has been here. We ate lunch together one hour ago and talked about a job he was applying for. His skills are better than most, but I still have to convince him that he is qualified. Abal is still a little timid here. I told him that what he's hoping to do isn't much different in America than Syria."

"I liked him," Taleah said. "Do you—"

"I have to go," he interrupted. He waited for her to say goodbye before he hung up the phone.

Taleah tapped her fingers on the steering wheel as she merged back onto the freeway toward downtown. She decided on the easiest route to the Islamic Center relatively quickly and selected her father from the contacts list. He answered immediately, sounding relieved.

"I tried to call you, but..."

"I was a little occupied," she said a few seconds later.

"Where did you run off to? I had to escort the... what was she, a phone-lady? Rebekah and I offered her a few bucks, but she refused. But the way you tore out of here..."

"I'm scared, dad," she said. Her voice wavered as she spoke, and before she knew it, a tear had dripped in front of her eyes, shrouding the world around her in a watery abyss that darkened shadows, softened edges, and clouded the scenery. She wiped the tear away and her perception seemed to streak like glass cleaner.

"I understand that, but don't worry. The cops got him."

"That somehow doesn't help," she said. Her father wouldn't understand, since his own view of the events was so sharp that layers didn't exist. He'd almost been blown up, but the story didn't burrow deep into his psyche, both because he refused to let it and because he'd seen trauma before. Age had done a number on him but had not inflicted as much damage as her own kidnapping had. She swallowed hard and tried to summon the words to explain herself, but when her lips failed to move, her father spoke for her.

"It seems too easy," he admitted. "I don't really know why. But you're okay?"

"It's... I'm fine, dad." She sharpened her voice and narrowed her eyes as she drove. "I'm going to talk to Emmanuel. Has Christine dropped by?"

Reggie paused just long enough to glance out the window, and by her estimation, glare at the officers so that they knew how uneasy their presence made him feel. "Looks like she's pulling up right now. She doesn't look happy."

"What did the cops say?"

"Not much," Reggie said. "They followed him to some auto body shop or something by that hotel off the Connector in Garden City... it's real close to where you live. They arrested him and took him, presumably, to Barrister for questioning. They said they'd be in touch."

"Why was he in your neighborhood? He knows where you live."

Reggie's voice seemed to hollow out as he emitted a dry chuckle. "Well as long as the MPD is swarming around here like flies on... a cheeseburger... I'm perfectly safe. And if that really was the killer they just arrested, then we can get back to normal life again."

Taleah rolled her eyes at her father's sense of humor. When he did joke around, his voice was stale and rigid, the inflections that more indicated grave seriousness, which led him to sometimes complain that his humor was unappreciated. In contrast to Willis, who leaked sarcasm so fluently and frequently that he'd learned how to incite laughter. Reggie didn't have the chops for humor. He could tell the funniest joke in the world in a comedy club and not get even a smile because he could never master the delivery.

"What would that be like?" Taleah asked.

"I don't know," he said. "I might have to get on the phone with old Richard Kerrin on that one."

"With careful meditation and... what is it?"

"An eye single to the glory of God," Reggie repeated. "Always the same prescription for different ailments. Good thing he's a helicopter pilot instead of a doctor."

"Yeah," Taleah said, wishing she could laugh. The emotion instead hit her with more weight than she thought she could fathom. Its burden soaked her soul with the oppression of a mountain of rags absorbing rain. She sparred with him until she reached the small parking lot of the Islamic Center, which was nestled into an older neighborhood and separated from the tiny yards by an aged wooden fence, which had been spray painted dozens of times over the years. The center never used anything more than muted earth tones to cover up the graffiti, but Taleah was able to guess why.

After saying goodbye, she hung up the phone, got out of the car, and entered the building. Emmanuel waited in a small foyer scanning through something on his phone when she walked in the door. He subtly bowed to her and then waited for her to speak.

"I don't really know what to do right now," Taleah admitted.

"I was looking at my phone while I waited. I found a software I do not recall installing, but it was deleted and uninstalled about a month ago. It must have happened when I was in the office."

"He was in your office?" she said. "No wonder he knew how to get in. And out."

"What?"

"Do you know where we can get floor plans of the building? I might have an idea."

"They probably keep them at City Hall," he said, without so much as flinching. "But I doubt they would be anywhere in the analytics building."

"It might explain how he got out undetected," Taleah said.

"How does it matter?" He looked confused momentarily, and then balanced his phone on his knee and rubbed his eyebrows. He reached for his baseball cap, sighed, and slid it onto his head.

"He's after my dad," she shot. "You'd do anything for your parents, wouldn't you?"

"I know. But right now..."

"Then again," Taleah said, shifting gears, "I really hate asking my mom for so much help, but she works at City Hall. She can get me in there to see the plans. Can you come with me this afternoon?"

"I think it is closed on Sunday."

"It is," Taleah said, "But she can get in."

Emmanuel pulled his cap down tighter, brushed his ear like a baseball manager making signals to the pitcher from the dugout, and then slipped his phone into his pocket.

"And I have to call Agent Torrance Marks of the FBI," Taleah said. "He said he was about to break the case and he was going to tell me about it. You don't mind, right?"

"No," he said.

"We can take my car," she said.

Taleah swallowed and dialed her mother while Emmanuel explained something to her. She attempted to listen to the ringing and his words, but lost track of him when Anna answered her phone.

"She was looking at something. It looked like a document or something…"

"Taleah," Anna said. "I've been meaning to call you."

"Sure you did," she sighed. "I don't have a lot of time. Do you have anything?"

"Why are you so busy on a Sunday? It can't be that bad, can it?"

Taleah cleared her throat impatiently and started the car after she and Emmanuel closed the doors. The clouds had been building over the mountains and had begun to crowd out the sun, bathing the city below in a bleak aura that wrought a sense of doom sprinkled with a dusting of hope. She frowned and swallowed when her mother shifted gears.

"Well, actually I have quite a lot. I managed to dig up the archives on your father's contract and looked at the details, including who negotiated it and who had viewed it recently. It seems it's been through a few hands, but I can figure out who has opened the file through the computer. It's been checked out twice since just after it was signed. Both by the same person, or at least the same terminal. One of them is Saul Goodweather, who worked under the Planning and Zoning Commission, until recently."

"The first victim," Taleah said.

"Unless you count your father and Willis," Anna corrected.

"Yeah."

"And the police department isn't great at covering their tracks. I managed to sneak into one of their accounts by a Sergeant Bones, who just happened to be one of the contacts on a housing project proposal running through City Hall. Bones apparently lives in the area and asked to be kept in the loop. But he runs with a pretty unsecured email connection, which is how he keeps up to date with the chief." Anna's voice seemed to dance like candlelight over a piano.

Taleah listened as she continued.

"Sergeant Bones is a busy man. Currently, he has the lead on some embezzling case as well, but the bombing and its aftermath is the big one. He tells the chief that the prints on Saul Goodweather's telephone match the ones taken from the scene of the crime across the street. And Goodweather has been in contact with someone who worked at the software firm your friend works at."

"David?"

Emmanuel perked up when he heard the name. He dropped his phone in his lap and stared at her as she continued to listen to her mother.

"I'm still digging today," Anna said. "I'm going to try to get into real evidence by tomorrow after the start of the day. I can work on it from my desk. Anyway, Bones has been digging through contacts both of the victims made and looking for irregularities. And one name in particular came up that has me worried.

"You know that person," Taleah guessed. "Oh my God."

"I don't think I should tell you."

Taleah's heart ached as she frowned. Emmanuel looked out the window at a pair of older refugees walking slowly to the front door of the center. They glanced at him, and he waved back before focusing on the fence in front of him. "Please tell me," she said.

"You're not going to like it," Anna said.

"I know," she whispered. "There isn't much that I do like."

"Goodweather has eight calls over the last four months that suddenly stopped one month ago, which is usually indicative of a relationship."

"You're stalling, mom. Tell me who it is."

The name rocked her spine and plunged her heart into chaos. Agony ricocheted through her brain like bullet, nearly bringing tears to her eyes.

"It's Mindy Caldwell."

"Shit!" Taleah said. "Shit! You have to tell her—"

"I'm afraid she already knows," Anna said softly. "Sergeant Bones has already made contact with her."

"Dammit."

"I know how you feel," Anna said.

Taleah unloaded on her mother with such a fury that her muscles seemed to vibrate out of control. She shook as she spoke, her biting words digging deeper and deeper until they cut to the heart, where Anna's deepest emotions lay.

"You don't have a single clue. You don't even love dad and I'm supposed to believe you care about Mindy? You even pretended to be friends with her. For years. Until she became unimportant, and she got over everything that happened to her. And you don't even know why all of this is happening."

Anna's voice grew sheepish. "When he took you, I almost lost everything. But she was there. She'd been there."

"And then I came out and you started treating me like you do dad. It makes me sick!"

"Taleah."

She hung up the phone and, biting her lip, felt a warm tear trickle down her cheek. Emmanuel had given up looking out the windows and stared up into her eyes without speaking. A fascinating flicker seemed to linger there, only to be extinguished by a tide of morose understanding, which washed across Taleah's face, seeming to warm her from within. Emmanuel issued a frown and then straightened his gaze. He didn't know Mindy Caldwell, but he managed to express concern for her anyway.

After the events of seven years ago, Taleah had maintained infrequent contact with Mindy. She had aided in the rescue attempt all those years ago. Taleah never added her to her friends on social media but spoke with her from time to time over the phone and in person. They weren't close friends, but their commonality sealed a bond between them that could not so easily be broken. And Mindy had in turn helped her through some dark times. She was there for her when Taleah discovered she had a crush on another woman. Arguably, she was part of the reason Taleah announced it to her family. Her mother had never understood any of that, and her dad hadn't talked to Mindy in more than six years.

Taleah swore and dialed her mother again. Her voice indicated that she'd given in to tears. "What is it now?"

Taleah spoke slowly and softly. "I'm sorry. I didn't mean to... I just need to ask you a favor. Can you do something for us today, Emmanuel and me?"

"Anything," Her voice sounded like a whisper strained with the agony of crying. "I thought you were at your dad's house today."

"I was," she said. "Can you get into work this afternoon? I want to take a look at the plans for Emmanuel's office building. I think the killer has been in there before and knew how to escape without getting caught. Maybe if I can figure out how, I can guess where he went next."

"They keep those in archives, she said. "Sometimes you can view PDFs online, sometimes not. That building may actually have printouts. We can get in and take a look."

"Thanks," Taleah said. Her phone beeped, indicating another call. That would be either her father or Agent Marks, she guessed. She frowned, hung up the phone, and answered it.

Where her mother's voice had edged into the cold waters of defeat, Agent Marks's swam with pride. "I have something you're going to want to hear about," he said. "And it's good news, too, I think."

"Good news?" Taleah said. "I haven't had much of that today."

"Yes, I heard they caught the person who called you, but I have something even better. Our friends down at ATF did some analysis of the bomb and its residue and determined that ammonium nitrate was used. The bomb was rudimentary in construction, but powerful, to say the least. And one corner of a receipt was all we needed to match up with a hardware store up in Grangeville. The materials had to have been purchased with cash, but there was another interesting connection. You know about the family who now owns that ranch, the Kleinman family? They were on a camping trip to Montana a little more than a month ago, and they happened to have stopped in that store for some gear. The family's credit card was run. And now we know who harassed you up at Table Rock last week."

"How?" she asked.

"The woman who called the police that night thought she recognized him from somewhere, and the police already had a warrant out for a man driving a vehicle that matched the description of a car used to rob the Army Navy store. You said it wasn't him when I showed you his picture, do you remember that?"

"Yes," she said, scratching her scalp.

"He changed his appearance, but it's the same guy. And you'll never guess how she knew him." Agent Marks didn't allow her to respond. "We checked on her family tree. She is related to the Kleinmans by marriage. Her husband's brother is the cousin of Mr. Kleinman. And James McAwan? Just happens to be the name of a former landscape worker who was helping out at the ranch when the family did a remodel. They were both at the ranch at the same time. Amazing coincidence, isn't it?"

Taleah flashed a quizzical look as she slowly pulled out of the parking lot onto the street. The cars streamed by unusually fast for a Sunday, but a break allowed her just enough room to maneuver into the lanes of traffic and accelerate up to the speed limit. "So James McAwan is Jim? And he has been to the ranch where Art Rassine held the women he kidnapped?"

"That's right," he said. "Case is pretty much closed now."

"No it isn't," she said. "How do you know what else the bomber bought? Does the store have security cameras?"

"Way ahead of you," Agent Marks said. "We checked all that. There doesn't appear to be any connection between the Kleinman family and whoever purchased the materials for the device. That, we're still looking into, but we're cooperating with the BPD on a couple of murder cases that seem to revolve around you. I'm starting to think I put the wrong person under surveillance."

"Yeah," Taleah said. "My dad does, too."

"I'm going to give him a call if he's ready for it. What does he normally do on Sunday afternoons?"

"He was pretty excited about watching golf for some reason," Taleah said, massaging a knot at the base of her neck. "I'm sure he'll be happy to hear from you."

"We'll keep in touch," Agent Marks said. "Good luck with—"

Taleah hung up the phone when she noticed Emmanuel pointing at the mirror. The shadow's eyes, devoid of color and humanity, burrowed into her with agonizing memory. He sneered at her, accelerated, and mouthed her name.

17
Rays

HER heart hammering in her chest, Taleah gasped, dropped the phone in her lap and stomped on the accelerator. The motor hesitated before emitting a thundering rattle that vibrated the windows and the interior of the car. Cold chipped away at her spine as she sped away, but her pursuer easily kept pace. Without looking behind her, Taleah merged hard into the left lane, tore ahead, and then lurched between thickets of oncoming vehicles into a residential area.

The follower roared past the intersection and flung himself into a squealing U-turn before veering hard-right into the neighborhood behind her. Taleah gripped the steering wheel tighter and attempted to plot an escape course that would leave the chaser behind. In a neighborhood like this, traffic was frequent, but offered enough space to maneuver. She roared along a narrow, tree-lined street flanked by rows of historic houses. Occasionally, the speedometer registered speeds of nearly fifty miles per hour. Children played on a grass strip between sidewalk and curb. Cars parked on both sides of the street hindered views, making the drive even more treacherous, but the stranger nosed closer and closer to her rear bumper.

A last-minute change of course led Taleah onto a different street. She nearly took out the chrome-plated mirror of a classic pickup truck before correcting and speeding up again. Tires squealed behind her. She glanced into the mirror and floored it. Ahead, a young woman on a jog with her dog jutted out into the street. Panicking, Taleah laid on the horn and allowed the motor to slacken. The man behind her pushed at her bumper close enough to smash a bird.

Taleah screamed when she sped past the runner so fast that her hair fluttered in the wake. In the rearview mirror, the jogger raised her middle finger and gazed down at her watch before bending at the waist for a breather.

"Careful!" Emmanuel shouted over the commotion.

Taleah spun the steering wheel so that she faced oncoming traffic on a two-lane street that led through the triangular Near North End neighborhood wedged between downtown and the North End. Her heartbeat quickened as oncoming cars honked and slowed to a crawl. If she did it just right, she could jump the grassy median between huge cottonwoods and flush herself out of the neighborhood, but such a maneuver carried the risk of a violent crash.

Emmanuel ducked as she angled toward the cars along the grassy strip and then corrected. The car slammed into the median curb and leapt into the air. The bounce induced neck-cracking whiplash at the moment of impact. Pain spiked at the base of Taleah's head when she corrected the car into the proper lane. The line of oncoming cars had nearly stopped to watch. The man following her pounced on the horn, zipped into the southbound lane and again pushed dangerously close. Emmanuel fumbled with his phone, attempting to dial a number, and then released it when Taleah sped toward a stop light.

A black and white police cruiser sat idle at the crossroads. Hoping the car was occupied, Taleah swallowed, sped toward the light and flashed through the intersection between cars.

Seeing the cop car, the pursuer suddenly slowed and came to a stop.

Taleah looked into the mirror and gasped as the blue and red lights swirled behind her. Slowing down and looking for a driveway or parking lot to pull into, she gathered her thoughts. Her heart pounded away inside her chest for several minutes as the officer settled into park behind her.

"Who was it?" Emmanuel asked.

Taleah closed her eyes, intentionally bringing up images of grizzled, greasy hair. The man who followed her somehow looked younger and more human. She winced as the memory of pain itched at her ankle. "I don't know."

"Do you think it was the killer?"

"Could be," Taleah said, keeping her hands on the steering wheel.

Almost as if he'd been trained how to act in a situation like this, Emmanuel remained calm and stared straight ahead with his hands perched on his knees. He mouthed something to himself and tilted his head.

"I ran the light on purpose," she explained.

"I would have done the same," Emmanuel said, lowering his head into a slow nod. His expression, while remarkably calm, bristled with remnants of fear. She considered asking him about it and then let the silence slice between them. She breathed deeply when she glanced into the mirror and watched the stocky officer climb out of the cruiser with a ticket book.

She rolled down the window and issued a sigh as her heartbeat pummeled her and her hands shook.

"Good afternoon, ma'am," the officer said. He couldn't have meant to be so pleasant, she told herself, but his eyes looked more concerned than agitated. "You know why I stopped you?"

"I ran a red light," she said.

"And you were speeding. I clocked you at forty-six. This is a safe neighborhood. Who were you trying to get away from?"

"He was chasing me," Taleah said, her voice sounding shrill. She relaxed her hands on the wheel and attempted to breath normally.

"I'm going to need your license and registration," he said.

He stood back as she dug into her purse for her wallet and then reached for the compartment above Emmanuel's knees. In her peripheral vision, she thought she could see the officer position his hand over the grip of his revolver as he peered through the window.

"Who is your friend?" he asked.

"It's Emmanuel," she said, thumbing through papers in the glove compartment.

"Where are you and Emmanuel headed?"

She grasped her registration paper and glanced at it before searching for her insurance card, which normally lay with the registration. When she gathered them into one hand, the officer stepped toward the window and looked down at her picture. "Downtown," she answered. "We were going to meet up with my mom."

"Miss St. Clair," he said. "Please wait here while I run this."

He stalked back to his car as Taleah waited. She looked back to where she'd run the light at the wrong time. The green pickup truck remained stalled at the light, as if he were waiting for the cop to be done with her. She gulped when she realized she was staring at an empty cab. He had abandoned the car at the curb right before the light.

She looked every direction and detected no sign of him.

Emmanuel was already onto her before her breathing could quicken. "They have a traffic camera," he said. "He cannot run for long."

"He's been running for seven years," Taleah droned, without thinking of where she was going or what she was allowing herself to insinuate. She swallowed hard, glanced to her shaky hands, and then burrowed her eyes into Emmanuel's sympathetic gaze. Of course it wasn't Art, but everything indicated he was somehow involved. Mindy's name couldn't have just come up at random.

"This is the one?" His accent thickened and then corrected itself midsentence as realization dawned on his face. "Do you mind telling me more?"

She shook her head and softened her tone to a frightened whisper. "I can't."

Emmanuel slowly nodded and glanced toward the green pickup truck. His chest rose and fell with the sort of serenity that seemed oddly mesmerizing if not out of place. She tried to relax, but her eyes darted back and forth from the apartment buildings to the offices, to the cars, and then back to the neighborhood she'd been chased through.

He remained silent for several minutes, during which the officer swung open his car door and carefully approached.

He studied her for nearly two seconds before he spoke. "I'm only going to issue you a ticket for speeding today. You'll need to get it paid at the address listed or online by this date," he said, pointing at a line on the ticket. "Running the red light can pass this once. Please be more careful."

"What about him?" Taleah asked, her hands shaking again. She grasped the ticket, her license, and registration, while glancing toward the green truck.

"We'll find him," he reassured her. "Another officer is headed that way."

She swallowed, suddenly becoming aware of the dryness of her lips. She bit at them and deposited the papers in the glove compartment.

"If he's involved in the murders, they'll throw the death penalty at him. Stay safe, Miss St. Clair."

The officer walked away slowly as Taleah faced forward. She closed her eyes and waited for Emmanuel to speak.

"He knows who you are," he said matter-of-factly.

"Of course he does," Taleah whispered. "The biggest case in the city right now. And I'm somehow in the middle of it."

He relaxed his hands, lowered his eyes, and waited for her to turn around and find her way back to the street before bludgeoning her with questions.

"I'm going to need to know why he is after you now, and why I am in danger… if I will help you."

She nodded slowly and frowned at a car that raced through a red light as she pulled into the street. Of course now that she'd just gotten a ticket, the officer was gone. Why did life always work out like that?

"Please, you have to tell me."

Taleah swallowed, let her gaze stretch for several blocks, and then pulsed onward in an emotionless drone that could have ripped her apart if she let her heart feel her own words. The agony would come one way or another, but for now, she suppressed it.

"Mindy Caldwell is a friend of mine, and she helped my father. And the killer, or whoever is doing all this, knows my father, and maybe even about Mindy. If what my mom says is right."

"And…"

"That's all I can say," she said, biting her lip.

"Is it because I am helping you now, or I am a witness?"

"Sounds plausible," she said, pulling to a stop in the far-left lane, once again aware that her speech was shaky.

She peered toward the nearest street corner. A half-dozen young girls waited at the crosswalk while giggling at something and one of them glanced at Taleah. The light turned green, and she waited for the girls to cross before turning. She advanced several blocks through a series of green lights that changed in sequence as she approached. Without speaking, she bypassed the garage where Saul Goodweather was murdered and eyed an empty parking stall across the street from the red brick City Hall building.

Several people lingered on the wide sidewalks, glancing up at the towers, and watching the traffic pulse by on Capital Boulevard.

Taleah reached for her phone and dialed her mother. The conversation only lasted a few seconds. Anna would be there shortly.

The two of them waited several minutes before Taleah swung open her door and stepped onto the sidewalk. After checking to make sure traffic was clear, Emmanuel exited the car and approached the meter, digging for change in his pocket.

"Sundays used to be free," Taleah said.

Emmanuel shoved six quarters into the slot and pushed the button to accept the allotted time, which began to count down on the screen.

"I usually park in the garage," she said. "I hate parallel parking. I tipped over a barrel during that part of the test, and the instructor immediately marked an 'F' next to my name."

"Is that the only thing you have ever failed?"

"It's the story of my life," she said, standing tall and slowly stepping toward the intersection, where two young couples had stopped on the wheelchair ramp with the bumpy yellow plate embedded in the concrete. "Mostly good grades, though. I spared my mom the heartache when I brought my report cards home. And my dad only asked about my grades when I visited him."

"Your parents did not live together, they divorced?"

Taleah nodded and stood behind a short, slender woman with black hair, who clutched her boyfriend's hand and nuzzled closer to him as they waited for the crosswalk. "When I was six. Right before my dad met Mindy."

"It was hard, not being with both? I do not see my mother and father. They write sometimes from Jordan. They would like to come visit."

"They should," Taleah said. "I could show them around." Taleah became aware of what she said and how Emmanuel might have interpreted it a split second after she ended her sentence. Indicating promise and intent to see him again seemed like a taboo. The last time she'd done that, she'd been interested in a girl whose friends called her Swan because she was pale and an amazing singer. Recalling that had once bordered on torture, but now that Christine occupied her every dream, the pain no longer stabbed at her.

Swan had sat across from her at the deli, biting into a sandwich. Taleah had smiled and stared at her. "Maybe I'll take you to a game next month," she said. Swan almost gagged on her sandwich, looked up, and frowned. She didn't say the words Taleah knew she was thinking. It wasn't like she was proposing exclusivity, but casually suggesting another date seemed awkward. In hindsight, Swan was right. It would have never worked out. And, as luck would have it, she ended up 'batting for both teams.'

The crosswalk changed and the couples proceeded toward City Hall. When they reached the broad, plaza-like sidewalk, Emmanuel stared up at several twenty-five-foot-tall iron structures with irregular, strategically placed holes. The sculptures were, at first glance, hideous, but taking in the spectacle more carefully, led Taleah to an interesting discovery. The beauty of the sculptures wasn't their monolithic, rusted appeal that stuck out of the sidewalk like wasted columns from a defunct construction project. On sunny days, the sculptures cast their shadows on the pale sidewalk below, scattering into an array of tiny spots like sunshine poking through a wooded canopy. Immediately, the plaza felt like home in the City of Trees, a fabulous moniker that the city intended to live by every day.

They strode up the steps together and waited for Anna to approach from across the street. Anna frowned and looked to her feet as she approached them. She carried something in her purse that looked like a folded sheet of paper, but Taleah couldn't make it out.

"Emmanuel, nice to see you again," she said as she planted a stale expression on her face, aimed at Taleah.

"And you... what was your name again?" Taleah's voice oozed with sarcasm. Anna only stared at her, as if coldly. Her greeting wasn't exactly warm, but Taleah understood why. A pang of regret swatted at her.

"Let's go inside," she said.

Taleah and Emmanuel waited for her to unlock the door. The darkness behind the glass seemed to lurch forward, extinguishing every bright thought that darted into Taleah's brain. It brandished a harrowing discord tinged with sour monotony and foreboding atmosphere. Turning to stare into the unknown felt like ice water on her bones. The face scarred her mind with contempt careening through vacuous eyes that stared back at her like tiny slits through a mane of oily, curly hair. Taleah groaned and leaned toward Emmanuel, who bore the weight of her shoulders and spent the next seconds searching her for clues and answers. Her heart leapt as Anna swung the door open. She, too, looked as though she'd seen a ghost.

18

Beams

ANNA stepped into the lobby first and flashed a confrontational look at the face behind the glass, but she altered her expression in a split second. Taleah regained her balance and followed her mother into the dimly lit lobby. Behind the window, a dark-haired woman stood with a mop bucket and a cart, which was tucked against a column adjacent to the window. A badge was draped around her neck.

Taleah greeted her with a sheepish 'hello' while Emmanuel followed by simply smiling at the custodian. When Anna flicked on the lights, Taleah took it all in. A large aerial rug covered a portion of the tile floor, whose white, gray, and brown hues offered a vintage sense of charm. The overall décor, which Taleah described as utilitarian, effused vibes of 1980s office buildings. The room was a broad T-shape as one wing housed a reception desk, a large potted plant, and a row of metal chairs clad in thin, brown upholstery. The other legs of the room led to stairs, offices, and elevators to the upper floors. The light seemed to miss those corners of the lobby, locking them in warm shadow. Anna entered a narrow corridor off the lobby next to the reception desk, passed a pair of doors marked with only room numbers, and then swung open a door to a large storage room.

The archive room stretched beyond several columns. Thousands of documents must have been stuffed into this room, tucked away in crannies, slots, filing cabinets, and even what looked to be a large bin.

"They have a system to the madness," Anna said. She nodded toward a computer terminal at the far wall. "Electronic archives are stored and backed up on that server. I was able to remote in and found some approval and permit drawings, but no real construction documents."

"How could you find anything in here?" Taleah asked. "This is worse than my dorm in college."

Anna smiled at the memory, which caused Taleah to shrink in shame. She hunched her shoulders, leaned backward against the door frame, and let Emmanuel cautiously enter the room.

"Files relating to construction change orders and permitting are periodically purged from the server. When that happens, the files are sorted by project and date. These filing cabinets store most of those." Anna pointed to a wall stacked from floor to ceiling with narrow, vertical slots, where thick reams of bound paper leaned against divider panels.

"The plan sets are stored here. After a certain amount of time, the archives are brought current, and the oldest plans are documented and stored on discs. As for 2015, when Riverside Analytics offices were built, we have a full set of construction plans." She scanned labels on the dividers and reached for a slot near eye level. Straining with the weight, Anna pulled down a thick packet of paper. The plans were printed on large sheets at least six times the area of an ordinary sheet of paper. She hefted the plans onto a table, upon which rested an array of current plans and flipped past the first few pages.

"There are that many plans?" Taleah asked.

"And details, schedules, elevations, everything a construction team could possibly need to erect a modern building. The civil section won't be of much use." The first dozen or so pages used an alphanumeric numbering sequence to differentiate the drawings. Each page number started with the letter C until Anna flipped the last civil page and an A fronted the architectural sheet numbers.

The first page consisted of dozens of notes and legends. Anna flipped through the pages until she started glancing at elevations and sections. She flipped back to the beginning of the section. "What floor were you looking at?"

"The office is on six, seven, and eight," Emmanuel said. "Where it happened was the kitchen on seven."

"Let's take a look." Anna flipped past several pages before she landed on a view labeled as LEVEL 7 FLOOR PLAN-OVERALL. She tapped the page and allowed Taleah and Emmanuel to study it.

"I have no idea what I'm looking at," Taleah said, furrowing her eyebrows.

Emmanuel pointed to a rectangle with an X drawn through it. Inside the box the room was labeled ELEVATOR. "That is the elevator. And this..." He ran his index finger along a narrow hallway that led to the kitchen area. "This goes into the office and kitchen."

Taleah pointed at a circle with a number in it. The attached arrow pointed to what appeared to be a lightly printed grid inside the office next to a cluster of dimensional notations. "What does this mean?"

"I'm no expert at reading plans," Anna said, "But I assume the notes at the top corner of the drawing have something to do with it."

The number she pointed at corresponded to a note number in the list. She read it to herself. "Raised floor grid. Reference drawing A307 for raised floor plan."

Anna flipped through dozens of pages before finding A307. The same grid appeared, this time darker. A small dot marked each grid intersection. As on the first page, a column of notes pointed to other drawings. Drawing A613 carried a series of details on the design of pedestals.

Emmanuel explained it to her. "They can lift up floor tiles so they can access the cables. The whole structure consists of metal beams and pedestals."

"And it's three feet high?" Taleah said, eying one of the details. "Does every floor have it?"

Emmanuel shrugged. Anna flipped back and found that no such grid was shown on floors one through five or nine and ten. She flipped back to sheet A307 and studied it. A small opening appeared to lead into another unmarked chamber between walls next to the elevator. She stared at the open area and wondered what it indicated. "You know what this is?"

Rather than answer, Emmanuel read the notes at the top of the page. After giving up, he breathed deeply. "I know there is an electrical communication room where all the cables go, next to the server room. Maybe all floors have it."

"So why is there an opening into this room?" Taleah asked.

Anna stared at it. "It's next to the elevator, so it might be some sort of chase where the pipes go up and down?"

"So if he were able to crawl though this opening," Taleah imagined, "he could climb all the way down to the first floor. Mom, go back to the first-floor plan."

After Anna flipped to that page, Taleah studied it for a few minutes. The same area was used for an unidentified room, with an X drawn through it, though it didn't appear to have an opening.

"Then he would be trapped?" Anna scratched her head and leaned closer to the plans.

"He had to get out somehow," Taleah guessed. The room adjacent to the chase was labeled as a mechanical room and faint, thin lines indicated equipment. "Do the pipes just cut through the wall?"

"Probably," Anna said.

"But if he were able to get in this room, he would probably be able to get out. This door leads into the garage, which they didn't search. He might have parked his car in there."

"That door would have to be locked," Emmanuel said. "Only if he had the keys could he get in."

"But he entered through the lobby," Taleah finished for him.

"I'm on it," Anna said. "Capital City Development Corporation runs all the garages. I may be able to... *borrow* access to look at camera files, maybe."

"He also had to know David was going to be in the office," Emmanuel said slowly. "Did he follow him?"

"He knew Goodweather," Taleah said. "And Art... um... the killer knew that."

Anna swallowed and then protested. "You have to forget about that monster. He's *dead.*"

Taleah swallowed painfully and stood up straight. No amount of studying the plans would confirm what she already suspected, but it was a good start. If her mother could find video of the perpetrator coming or going, it would be easy enough to identify him. The police would want to know about this. Whatever the scenario, she guessed the cops would have him within twenty-four hours. But twenty-four hours left a huge window for the killer to strike again. His next target could be Mindy. Taleah groaned at the thought of it and her heart felt as though it sunk so low in her chest that it began to compress and leak blood. "Yeah," she said. "I'm fine."

"I've seen you this 'fine' only once in your life, Taleah. I'm trying to help, and the cops are going to catch this guy before he can hurt anyone else."

Clenching her fists and gently tapping them together seemed to release more tension than anticipated, though the gesture meant nothing and must have looked disturbingly awkward to Anna and Emmanuel. She summoned the courage to at least mumble her next line. "It won't be worth it if—"

"Mindy is going to be *fine.*"

She retreated one step toward the door and searched Emmanuel's eyes for some clue she could use to steady herself. His eyes looked like gemstones on which light revealed flaws. Only one emotion persisted, but it only spread more darkness into her veins.

"Why didn't he run me into a tree?" The ferocity of her voice surprised her, but she didn't attempt to suppress it. "Every opportunity, and he didn't take it. Why?"

"What are you talking about?" Anna asked.

Taleah didn't bother to answer. She stared into Emmanuel's eyes and waited for him to mumble something half-heartedly. "I was thinking about that. I think probably a fear and intimidation tactic like some of the gangs use. Back in Amman, they would threaten your family, get you so nervous you have to join, and then they can expect you to do terrible things."

"He wasn't trying to recruit me."

Emmanuel breathed slowly, carefully closed his eyes, and then spoke clearly, letting his accent nearly vanish in the process. "It is not the end, but the means. He can still control you."

"The hell he can," Taleah snapped.

"He already is."

She swore under her breath, removed her gaze from Emmanuel, and gently set it upon her mother. Anna stood with her hand clutching her waist and used it as a prop to hold her other arm vertically so that she rested her chin on her fingers.

Speaking quickly felt like rage unleashed, but Taleah managed to keep her composure. "You can hack into the building's security. How many times has he been in this building? Match faces leaving the garage with those on the security cameras at the entrance. To pull off that kind of escape, he had to have a pretty extensive knowledge of the architecture."

"Is that really important?" Anna asked. "We already know he's at large and he's already going to be plotting his next move by the time we're finished figuring out how he escaped not one, but two crime scenes. It seems like a waste of time."

"The cops think they already have him," Taleah said, her fingertips fluttering with hidden venom. She lowered her eyebrows into an expression of contempt and let them slacken. "They tracked the phone and made the arrest."

"It's really—"

"I don't think it's a coincidence at all." Rather than regulating as she relaxed her muscles, her breathing became erratic and quietly labored as if she were forcing the wind through her pipes rather than welcoming it into her lungs. The sensation flooded her with a sense of violence and a sudden desire to throw something against a wall.

"Taleah."

"I don't know what to do. All I can think is to do something."

Her mother raised her eyebrows, slid her feet together and straightened her shoulders, suggesting a finality to the conversation that could only linger like coals from a fire robbed of fuel. Taleah's fingers vibrated and her breathing slackened.

Emmanuel watched curiously as waves of adrenaline smothered her eyes and pulsed through her veins. The agony scorched her insides until it condensed into a rage she could scarcely understand. As if the ground below her feet were shaking and the clouds overhead were gathering into a single abusive storm, the tide of emotions roared. Yet, even through the darkest clouds in the direst night, a single hole no bigger than a fist could set forth a beacon to guide her through the turmoil, if only she could cling to it.

When she closed her eyes, the darkness folded like the interior of the cave. The opening stood starkly against the night, where the silhouettes of pines filtered the moonlight into a crescent glow that had enticed her. It drew her out and forced her to confront the shadow. If the killer were controlling her, he'd made a grave miscalculation.

19

Rising

THE light on the alarm clock flashed midnight so persistently that Taleah's head began to ache with every strobe. There was nothing like sleeping in and having to lay the blame on a faulty power connection. The sun belted through the windows as dawn swelled over the mountains to the east, which cast long shadows over the valley and bathed the city in a cleansing blue light. Where that blue sunrise wrought peace, the flashing green numbers brandished a sense of panic and discord.

Taleah lay on her back and shifted her knees. Feeling the movement, Christine rolled over slipped one hand over Taleah's waist and kissed her gently on the cheek. Without saying anything, she slipped out of the bed, neatened the covers and quickly got dressed.

The previous night, so much had happened that she could hardly remember all of it, though Christine's sweet embrace had at one time or another, warmed her heart. When she recounted yesterday's events, she had left out a few details so disturbing that she couldn't possibly wrap her head around them. What was it with the madman just letting her escape? And why was he going out of his way to mimic the shadow?

After the story, Taleah and Christine had become disinterested in a television show and then resorted to a card game that Christine seemed to lose on purpose. And then, kissing. Had she had a drink at some point? Christine was known to keep a bottle of wine for special occasions, and though Taleah mostly opposed the notion of drinking, she'd given in once or twice and enjoyed a few sips.

Being without Christine the whole day seemed like being stranded in her own thoughts, which decayed before her eyes. If she were present, Christine would massage the pain out of her mind and to shove the commotion to a darkened back corner of her brain, where it could rummage through her consciousness and produce the ultimate demons at a later date.

When she was dressed and ready to go, Christine rolled toward her and pushed the covers away, revealing bare shoulders and a mat of hair. Taleah gulped and considered calling in sick, but decided she needed to get going anyway.

"You're beautiful," Christine said.

Taleah attempted to smile but could only nod. She departed to the bathroom, combed her hair and set out the door. In another hour, Christine would be leaving. And they'd spend the whole day apart once again.

The drive into work lasted longer than normal, as the thick swells of traffic snarled the major boulevards. She often grew frustrated with the red lights, long lines, and people stopping unnecessarily, but this time, she merely grimaced with every minute that ticked away. Jalene had never once chided her on tardiness, but Taleah's misery grew every time she walked through the door after eight o-clock.

A half-dozen eyes fell on her when she strolled to her desk and logged in, but no one spoke, until Jalene appeared behind her. Taleah spun. Jalene's hair was pulled into a sleek ponytail, her trademark Monday morning look, adorned by a colorful but mundane hair elastic. She relaxed, with one hand wrapped around her midsection, which she used as a support for her coffee-carrying hand.

After another failed attempt at smiling, Taleah raised one shoulder, opened her email, and then turned back to her.

"Didn't know if I'd see you here today."

"Well, who's going to edit the articles for next Monday's edition?" Taleah knew she wasn't the only copy editor, but she strived for being the best, and Jalene trusted her.

"I guess they caught the bad guy," Jalene said. "Must have been a crazy weekend for you."

Crazy? Just who is she trying to kid? "That's probably not the right word," she said, relaxing her eyebrows and letting them stretch into a somber, tired expression.

"Chaotic?"

She nodded.

Jalene straightened her back and slackened her expression. "Want to talk in private?"

Taleah stood up and followed her out the front door and approached a bench that faced the parking area. Jalene eyed a pair of geese that casually stepped toward the greenbelt path and looked both ways before crossing. She straightened her skirt and sat down. Before she said a word, she crossed her legs and reached out her arms as Taleah gingerly sat next to her.

"I have to tell you, this morning's paper was a blockbuster. The advertisers are going to be lining up because the *Capital Weekly* is no longer a gimmick weekly newspaper. We might have to take some space from the clowns and strippers for actual, legitimate businesses."

Jalene's sarcasm was biting. The newspaper had already begun to attract advertising interest from a number of high-quality local business-es and readership growth had consistently outpaced the more traditional newspapers in the city, though there was no real way to gauge subscriptions, due to the no-holds-barred, always-free business approach. In the traditional sense, the *Capital Weekly* didn't even offer subscriptions. They didn't have to pay teenagers to deliver it or bother with credit card transactions. Many readers did frequent the website and offer donations, but the business model remained strong.

"Thanks, I guess?" Taleah said, pushing backward in the bench.

Jalene rested her hands on her lap and rocked her foot back and forth momentarily. "Who was he?"

"They didn't catch him," Taleah said. "Any report saying otherwise is... what do they call it now? 'Fake news?'"

Jalene almost choked. Her laughter subsided quickly, and she straight-ened her lips into a businesslike frown. Her posture remained impeccable, though her expression exuded concern rather than rapt interest. "Good one."

"It wasn't the guy. I don't know how it all happened." Taleah quickly found that the second telling lacked composure and common sense. When she finished telling Jalene everything she knew, Jalene let her hands do the talking.

She laced her fingers together, pressed her arms forward, and then clenched her fists before she started to speak. "This is where you let intuition fill in the holes. You, of course, have to present facts, and you can fact-check later. But actually telling the story, where you don't quite have the details you need—"

"He called, from Emmanuel's phone number. I don't know how. The police followed his signal and arrested him, but a couple of hours later, someone is chasing me through the streets."

"What's your guess?"

"More than one person is in on it," Taleah said.

Jalene smiled. "Right. You're going to be good. I'm sure of it. Which is why I've convinced the board to let you write your own story for next Monday's edition, about how the recent crime wave has impacted your life. I know you can write from the heart, because I see it in your eyes every day. Don't hold back. Let the keyboard and the words heal you. They are better at it than any psychiatrist could ever dream of being. I know."

It wasn't like Jalene to so willingly heap praise upon Taleah. Taleah greeted the news with a sheepish smile and a shrug. "I don't think I can—"

"Did I ever tell you the story of when my dad died?"

Taleah shook her head and blinked, not wanting to let any more pain invade her skull.

"Four years ago—you were in college—my dad had a heart attack. The doctors blamed it on overstressing and too much cholesterol, and from the complications, he... well let's just say that I assumed nothing would be the same again. Just like that, everything was falling apart. I was alone, I was dismal. But I had to write. Because it was the only thing I knew how to do. The hours and hours spent behind the keyboard, almost a whole day straight. Pouring the words into empty space as they came to me, as my heart nearly burst. Hungry, thirsty, scared, and I could barely see from rubbing my eyes. And then I printed it off, stuffed it into a drawer, saved the file into an archive folder, which I would never dig into on purpose. Let it marinate, almost forget about it. It offers real perspective when you read it all a few years later, when you're not so vulnerable to the emotions. And you know what? Yes, there were grammatical mistakes and typos, but it was the best writing I've ever done. Because it came from here." She curled her fingers and placed her palm on her chest.

"I... I don't know what to say."

"I know you can do it."

"What if I miss work this week?" Taleah said sadly. "I don't see this situation letting me off that easy."

"Bring your laptop with you. A notebook. Everywhere you go, always be ready to write, because you never really know when inspiration will strike."

"You sound like a novelist," Taleah noted.

Jalene shrugged. "When you come to work and you're paid to do it, it is difficult to muster the inspiration. But a couple of cups of coffee, always keeping your eyes open to the complexities and beauty of the world, and you start to train yourself to find those words every day."

"I'm not as observant as you," Taleah said, glancing to her feet, where a glistening droplet of dew was rolling down a single blade of grass.

"Yes, you are," Jalene said.

Taleah found herself nodding. "I guess I could give it a try."

Jalene wrapped her arm around Taleah's shoulder. The thought sent shivers down her spine. Their relationship sometimes seemed strained, but mostly cordial, though it had never resulted in anything more than a polite handshake. Backing down proved easy, she discovered. It was a gut reaction to slink away into a comfortable space, to pass it off as something unimportant. But that she could suddenly consider Jalene a real friend struck her with a sense of compassion. Her nerves scattered as Jalene pulled away.

"Have you talked to the cops since yesterday?"

Taleah pushed her feet under the bench behind her, clasped her hands in her lap, and watched a squirrel scamper up a tree. "No, but they'll probably be calling me today. They said they'd find the guy who chased me."

"I see."

"I don't think they see me so much as a witness anymore," she said, "but a target. I wouldn't be surprised if they have undercover people watching me right now."

Jalene straightened her back and chuckled. "There's no such thing as an undercover cop."

Taleah winced and waited for Jalene to stand up. They walked back into the building and separated for their tasks. For the first time in ages, Taleah opened a new document and considered her keyboard. The dust had worked its way into the cracks between keys. The letters on home row had been worn off. It had taken a beating over the years, but it rested there, serene and inviting. *Use me,* it seemed to say. *I'm yours. And I'll never reveal your true secrets.*

She fumbled with a headline, erased it, and typed exactly one line before her cell phone started to ring. Instantly recognizing the number, she answered it.

"Agent Marks," she started.

Marks issued a chilling, frustrated sigh, and then slammed forward into a punishing monologue. "Taleah, I'm wondering if you can meet with me and some of the investigating team at the BPD precinct this morning. I know you have a busy schedule, but we have some things we need to discuss. Something is troubling, and it keeps catching us off guard."

"Are you getting close?"

"Maybe, maybe not. But we need your help."

"I'm on my way," Taleah said.

She slid the phone back into her purse, stood, up and pushed her chair in before making the trek to Jalene's workstation.

Jalene glanced up at her while typing away. She rested her fingers when Taleah spoke.

"That was Agent Marks. I need to run down to the police station and answer some questions."

Jalene nodded. "Why doesn't he just come here?"

Taleah shrugged. The prospect of having several police investigators and an FBI agent discussing sensitive information and evidence in front of a room full of journalists seemed like comedy in the making, but Taleah let the impression pass. She gulped and clutched her purse at her side.

"Then go," she said. "Take care of it. Then get back here and get to work."

Taleah nodded and fled the building. Worry crept up in her heart as she strode toward her car. Her fingers twitched as she drove. Careful not to let the traffic get the better of her, she navigated to the police precinct as wave after wave of torment pulsed through her veins. All she could do to stem the tide, it seemed, was to think about Christine, her smile, her embrace, and her kiss.

She turned the car off after parking in the back lot and steadied herself before getting out of the car. The concern in Marks's voice had reached out like a dagger in the darkness. What did it mean? And why did it so suddenly manifest itself? The questions shot through her mind in rapid succession, each blast more potent than the one before. Taleah closed her eyes, tried to remember Jalene's advice, and then let it slide away.

The sun seemed to bore a hole in her skin as she sat there contemplating. She breathed in and clutched the door handle before making the walk to the front door. Her muscles grew weaker with every step, and with every thought plowing craters into the surface of her mind, she gave into the darkness, that sweet, enticing realm where truth lay naked, exposed, and forgotten in a corner. Cowering from the world at large, the gulfs and valleys of fear tore away at the fabric of reflection. Giving in felt like treason, like wielding some debilitating weapon against everything she loved. The last thing she wanted to do was hurt her dad, Christine, Emmanuel, or Mindy, but stepping forward meant taking risks.

It was always the unknown that brandished fear. "All you have to do," her father had once told her, "is take one step into the dark."

The memory blinded her and soaked up the tatters of agony.

Agent Marks awaited with a glum expression in the lobby. He shook her hand and hurriedly escorted her past rows of desks and into a conference room that was littered with folders of evidence that were spread across the entire surface of the table. Four policemen surrounded the table examining the evidence piece by piece. Sergeant Bones looked up when she entered the room while Marks invited her to take a seat.

She glanced at a folder marked as evidence from McAwan's residence. The memory of that night on Table Rock folded into her expression as she let the warmth fade.

"This is it," Marks said.

Bones stared at him, and in turn, Officers Ramirez, Landerman, and (she guessed) San Pablo stood at attention.

"This is everything we have. It's an unusual amount. And we can't quite figure out why everything links together. But it does, because of you, Taleah. Because of what you and your father and Willis endured.

"We have everything from James McAwan's residence, to the arrest over the Army Navy store robbery and everything McAwan knew about the Kleinman family, which is pretty disturbing to say the least. McAwan had sought them out, and we think he did so for a reason. And we have determined that not only did McAwan care for the old Harrison Ranch, he also took residence on a hunting trip in a cabin near the mouth of the Canyon where the Little Salmon River confluences with the Salmon. We know that because we found his fingerprints at the scene."

"And now we have Jesse Alvarez," Officer Landerman said, turning her eyes upward and gesturing toward the table with an open palm.

Taleah swallowed at the mention of his name.

"He's the man who called you the other day. And he's given testimony and agreed to cooperate. Alvarez, it seems, also knew McAwan. He went hiking with him from time to time. I wonder if you might be able to identify him, but I don't have to ask."

"What?" Taleah almost choked on her words. "Jesse Alvarez? He was in one of my math classes, and he offered to study with me once."

"Alvarez didn't remember that detail, of course, but they were friends for a long time. Since before you and he were in college together."

Marks swallowed and took the lead. "But neither of them is saying the name of their co-conspirator. I've got a bad suspicion about this one. The reason neither of them will give us his name is because they don't know it. Cross-examining both of them didn't reveal anything, and their stories were not even well-coordinated.

"Alvarez says he got the phone from someone else, but you'll never guess who."

"Oh my God," Taleah said. "David from Emmanuel's office?"

He nodded. "The same."

"David Yerring was apparently covert about it, and must have known how to bypass Emmanuel's security," Landerman explained. "But the story checks out, because Yerring's fingerprints were also on the device. This lets us theorize that Yerring had cloned the device and handed it off to Alvarez. But why would Yerring clone your friend's phone?"

"There are too many people in on this," Taleah said, swallowing. "It's all wrong."

Marks picked up where Landerman left off. "Which leads us to believe that if we are dealing with a copycat, it has to be the worst copycat of all time. But studied nonetheless."

"We don't have any evidence to suggest that either Alvarez or Yerring had visited the cabin. But we do know one thing." Landerman waited for Agent Marks to return the volley.

"The link is that we have documented proof on the sordid history of that cabin. Once owned by a recluse outdoorsman, the cabin traces to a man better known as Art Rassine. It can't be a coincidence. But the man who was Art Rassine is buried in an unmarked grave near Kooskia, up in North Idaho. Whoever we are dealing with knew everything about that case."

"Kooskia," Taleah repeated. "Isn't that close to where he... in the Lochsa Gorge?"

"On the Clearwater," Marks corrected her. "But yes, Highway 12 does lead up there from Kooskia. When we were done with the cadaver, we decided against donating it to science After all, most of it was unusable because years in the wild had led to a series of untreated diseases."

"Kooskia also happens to be near Grangeville, where the Kleinman family made a purchase at a store, as did McAwan," Sergeant Bones noted.

"I know that," Taleah said.

Bones continued. "And then there's the matter of Saul Goodweather. Goodweather knew Yerring too, but we're seeing his involvement to be divergent from the others' for a variety of reasons. You already know this I'm sure, but Goodweather is the only one who has had any contact with the only surviving victim of Art Rassine."

"Mindy Caldwell," Taleah said, her voice wavering.

"You mother's a smart one," Bones said. "But tell her to back off or she could be indicted."

"I'm sure she'll take that threat very seriously," Taleah said, lowering her voice and staring across the table at an open folder with Mindy's face on the front page. She stared at it for a long time before her mind finally made the connection. It made a pang of sickness punch at her stomach and defeat puncture her heart. They could have a file on her for only one reason.

"We're planning to make a very big arrest—"

"Where is she?" Taleah said, raising her voice. "Tell me."

Agent Marks sighed and let his shoulders slump. "She disappeared a day or two ago. No one has seen her."

Blindsided by this, Taleah forced venom into her veins. "Goddammit! Fuck you people!"

"Taleah—"

"You don't know her," Taleah said. "She'd never knowingly date a man who happened to be a co-conspirator in a plot to—to do what, exactly? She thought she was done with this Art Rassine after she helped my dad and Willis kill him."

"I know all that."

"You can go to hell," Taleah shouted. "We have to get her back."

"We're looking."

"Look harder, you son of a bitch!"

Taleah was letting curse words fly at record pace. In normal conversation, uttering even one littered her words with a contemptible reputation, where her meaning and delivery were muddied. She'd heard people utter the F-word ten times in one sentence during a conversation about the weather in Paris, but even years later she remembered only the (F-word) humidity and how the (F-word) pastries smelled, and the (F-word) birds liked it, too.

"Sit down and relax," Sergeant Bones warned. "I don't know what you and your friend Emmanuel are up to, but I'm going to have to put a stop to it to protect both of you."

"You can't control me."

"How does protective custody sound? As a trade-off for not getting killed?"

"I don't care," Taleah shot. "I'm not going to let Mindy or my dad die due to negligence. I'm going to have to do this myself."

"Taleah," Agent Marks said, lowering his tone, "I know the last thing you want to do is sit back and let this whole thing play out. I know how this feels. Can't put yourself in harm's way. We're experts on this sort of thing. We're going to find this guy and put him in jail the rest of his life, probably look for the death penalty. You want to help. So help by staying safe."

"You wanted to know what I know about Mindy," Taleah said, lowering her voice and leaning forward in the chair. "I know she's tough. And she doesn't trust men."

"You and she share that in common."

"Too much," Taleah said. "And I hate it."

"We're still watching your father's residence," Bones said, clearing his throat. "No one is going to get at him while we're there. You can get back to work now, if you just answer one more question."

Taleah waited for it.

"Do you know why Mindy Caldwell frequents the Spectrum Club? It's where we suspect she met Goodweather. He paid for everything in cash."

"I didn't know," Taleah said. In truth, she'd only heard rumors about the club and its clientele, but most of that was third-party conjecture and likely didn't reflect reality. She and Christine had never mentioned it to one another, even though word spread that it was a gay club.

"Maybe you can ask her that when you find her naked and tied to a tree, screaming for her life."

"That's not helpful."

"None of this meeting was," Taleah said. Though her words were lies, they had the desired effect. Agent Marks leaned back in his chair, stroked his graying stubble, and took a moment to look forlorn, if not distraught. His frown seemed to soak up the light in the room, whose light-gray, unadorned walls installed impending agony, in order to elicit the unabashed, unvarnished truth from those being questioned. The colors of psychology presented themselves everywhere she looked when she realized what they meant. There was no escape. Of course, the meeting was productive. All the evidence was laid bare on the table for her to see. Everything she had asked her mother to snoop for.

Agent Marks escorted her to the door, but she stopped and stared at the table one more time.

"You looked at the tapes from the garage and the analytics building," she said. "You didn't see his face?"

"He never showed it," Agent Bones said.

"He knows the building pretty well," Taleah said. "I think people there would remember seeing him."

"That's a good idea," Bones said. "We'll have this investigation wrapped up in a couple of days at worst."

Taleah strode to the door and let the heartache tower within her like spires of smoke twisting skyward in the mountain dawn. She attempted to bury her emotion, to discard it, and to confront the rest of the day with renewed energy. When she got in the car, she pushed her head against the steering wheel and listened for the sound of her horn. The dark was treacherous, and even one step could spell doom.

20
Eclipse

"I love you too, sweetie," Reggie said softly, attempting to plaster his face with a false grin that Rebekah would see right through. Taleah had explained everything from what the cops had found to what she now understood. Fear danced at the corners of her voice like a ballerina skirting the shadows, but there was something else, too—an untold determination. He could hear it in her voice and the imagined look in her eye would mirror the expression she displayed when she was about to hit a home run or strike out trying.

Rebekah, already clad in her pajamas, entered the bedroom ahead of Reggie, walking slowly enough to look seductive. He'd show her the proper appreciation if it weren't for the damn wheelchair, which kept getting stuck at corners and getting its wheels jammed up with lint or whatever else the vacuum couldn't manage to attract.

"You know, come to think of it..." she started, pushing open the bedroom door.

"Thinking of it can be dangerous," Reggie replied. That was another inherited 'Willisism.' The man had always fancied himself as some sort of amateur philosopher, but with a truly unique sense of humor. What did he call it, *diabolical?*

Rebekah playfully patted him on the head. "Taleah could be just looking to get out of the house for a while."

"Woof," Reggie said. "You don't really think that's true. You're playing devil's advocate for the sake of reasoning, which doesn't always work in times like these. At some point, you just have to stop and do it, because trying to assign it logic is a waste of time,"

"I'm not sure Christine would see it that way," she argued. "Not in her DNA."

"Which the cops can't be using," Reggie said, lunging for the light switch and peering out the front window, where the streetlight illuminated the rear third of the police cruiser he was already growing tired of looking at. "Marks is a veteran, though, so probably there isn't any DNA. Meanwhile, this guy is making all the right mistakes. If you're going to screw up, do it right."

Rebekah sighed coolly, pushed a dresser drawer closed, pulled back the comforter, and lay down. She waited for Reggie to struggle from the wheelchair to the bed without rolling over or offering any further words of wisdom. Rebekah knew when not to speak and how to avoid further agitation of the flames. When the time was right, she'd roll over, wrap her arm around him, gently kiss him on the lips, and listen to his breathing. Whatever the reason for that ritual, he never admitted that it worked. But it got him thinking about other things. She could be manipulative in the right ways, which was what Reggie had fallen in love with all those years ago.

"Or do you think I'm being too dramatic?" Reggie asked.

"Of course not. Just a different way of processing events."

Reggie nodded in frustration, sighed, and rested his head on the pillow. Tomorrow, he'd push the wheelchair out the front door, watch it roll into the street and get run over by a van. And when the hospital asked him what happened, he'd claim the cat did it.

"That's always been *your* strong suit," Rebekah said. "But I guess you know her better than I could ever hope to. How do you think she's going to react?"

"She's going to try to be a hero," Reggie coughed. "She's always been independent, even to a fault. And she knows what she has in common with Mindy Caldwell."

"She's going to do the same thing you did? And you didn't try to talk her out of it."

"It was a hard day for her. Last thing she probably needed was her old man acting like an old man and chiding her for it. She'll carve her own path no matter which direction I try to steer her."

"You don't have to steer her at all," Rebekah said. "Just give her the map and she'll decide on the best route."

"Willis'd say the same," Reggie snorted. Speaking of which, how was the old bastard? He was probably in a souped-up version of the same model of wheelchair Reggie drove around the house, while Melissa cheered him on and fed him grapes, if she wasn't gearing up for the next weekend hunting trip.

The silence between them stretched as the darkness seemed to flex its muscles. Going to bed at eleven o'clock felt like an abomination. It was either so early that the day was only half spent, or too late, so that half of tomorrow would feel wasted. Contradictions, Reggie understood, were little facts of life. If he could appreciate them for their beauty, time would become more meaningful. When that detail was lost, it would be lost forever until he saw the world only in shades of gray, where subtleties pixelated on the page of consciousness.

Rebekah curled her fingers and pushed her hand up his chest. Her eyes had fallen closed, but she hadn't begun to show signs of sleep. Instead of propelling the thoughts further, he rested his eyelids, slackened his arm muscles, and tried to will himself to sleep.

Minutes passed, and then a bump sounded from the direction of the back yard. He wedged his eyes open. The silence resumed for at least another twenty seconds before a shuffling sound of paws on plastic jabbed at the night.

"Damn it," Reggie breathed. "Is that the neighbor's dog again? I'll have them put a leash on that beast."

Rebekah sighed. "Stay in bed. I'll go check it out."

"They're probably out back smoking right now, anyway," Reggie said.

"I didn't see their patio lights on."

Rebekah pushed the covers away, stood up, and quietly exited the room. Reggie breathed deeper, turned his eyes toward the front window, and gazed at the back end of the police car. A car on the street passed, pushing a sweeping yellow light through the bedroom. He thought about calling Taleah again just to make sure she was all right, but swallowed and bit his lip. She could make it on her own.

A loud thump came from the kitchen, like a boot on the tile floor. He jerked his feet free of the blanket at the exact second that a screech echoed from the kitchen. Glass shattered. It wasn't the dog. He struggled to work himself free, planted his feet on the floor, and pushed himself up. The screaming continued as panic filled his veins.

"*Nooo!*"

Staggering toward the door with adrenaline shooting through his fingers, he tripped on the wheelchair's foot tray, regained his balance, and limped toward the hall. Glass smashed against the floor amid bouts of heavy breathing and fierce grunts. Reggie growled as he bounded into the hallway. The screams grew louder with every step and descended into cold whimpers just as he rounded the bend into the kitchen.

Rebekah lay on the floor with blood in her hair and on her cheek. Desperation clung to her face like the photographic remains of a parade of doom. Perplexed with shock and horror, she clung to life just as he looked up.

"Reggie," she whispered.

He stood there over her like a shadow, lurking over the tundra of a high mountain meadow in the twilight as darkness encroached.

"Son of a bitch!" Reggie screamed, lunging at him.

The madman dodged his attack, sending him face-first into the drying rack, which was still loaded with dishes. Pain flashed across his scalp as the glass broke. Scraping across the floor with a labored heave, the attacker pushed his advantage.

Reggie didn't have time to react before fists pummeled his back. Reggie kicked at his shins, haphazardly spun around, and spit into the grisly shadow.

"St. Clair," it roared. "You were always going to die."

Reggie swore at him and lunged forward, just as the madman countered. Their bodies collided, but the attacker's mass threw him off balance. Reggie slipped on a shard of plate, hit the floor, and groaned in pain. He attempted to turn himself over as the glint of white light on steel flashed before his eyes.

He kicked himself free and managed to scoot himself around the island. The toaster's cord dangled at the other side. Thinking he'd use it to pull himself up, he grasped at the wire, which pulled the appliance onto the floor with a loud *crash*.

Out of sight, Rebekah moaned in agony.

"You hear that sound? Beautiful, isn't it?"

"Fuck off," Reggie shouted. The assaulter bore down on him with effortless fury, stabbing the knife into the counter and the floor tile, and missed with two more swipes. Reggie grasped the toaster with both hands, heaved it over his head, and launched it at the attacker.

The madman stumbled, kicked it away, and lurched forward just as Reggie struggled to pull himself up. The energy of the collision sent him straight at the table's legs. Reggie wrestled with the chair, pushed it toward the stranger, and formed fists.

Shadow enveloped the madman. Every stroke of the knife wrought more venom. He landed two quick blows at Reggie's midsection. Pain sliced at his abdomen as the swell of warm blood scattered across his skin. He moaned in horror as the attacker lunged again.

The knife grazed his shoulder as he pushed himself into a sitting position. The miss left the man exposed for a half-second too long, a window which Reggie exploited. He curled his neck into a defensive posture and shielded his face from the blow of the attacker's knees.

Tumbling over his head and roaring with a shade of enraged pleasure, the shadow attempted to right himself. The hesitation allowed Reggie to climb back to his feet. Pain rocked at his back as the wounds of shrapnel imbibed his sweat. His heart beat faster when the sounds of Rebekah struggling pushed into his eardrums.

Nothing could help her, he decided, unless he put all his energy into the attack. He timed his lunge, thinking he'd slide the madman's head into the French door with enough force to shatter it, sending a cascade of glass down onto his neck.

The attacker seemed to anticipate the move. Quicker than seemed possible, he launched himself to his feet, squared his shoulders and cocked his arm as Reggie barreled into him with enough force to expel the air from his lungs.

Agony ripped through him as the attacker slammed him into the floor and pummeled him with repeated blows to his back and shoulders.

Reggie screamed something, as he helplessly scurried to a sitting position. The front door burst open, sending a square of light into the kitchen, which illuminated the half of Rebekah's face that he could see. The gun was raised, but no order to drop the knife came.

Reggie looked up as the attacker swung open the back door and sprinted across the yard. Horror gripped him as he witnessed the entrant's petrified face and her short, blond hair reflecting the porch light.

Taleah sprinted into the kitchen as if she were stealing third base, sliding on her knees at Rebekah's motionless body.

Excruciating pain blinded him, pulling his eyes closed in a wince that felt like sandpaper dragging tears across raw flesh. He could not bear to open his eyes, but instinct forced his eyelids open. Taleah knelt near her, clutching her head and moaning just as two police officers flooded through the open front door. Blood coalesced on Rebekah's lips. Her breathing was labored, but steady. Terror had congealed into a soup of emotion and trauma on her face as agony surely raged through her nerves.

W ith terror clenching in her bones, Taleah bounced onto the porch and with a single motion, spun the key in the lock and kicked the door open. The trauma seemed to strip her bones to powder as the scene unfolded in front of her. Fear scoured her heart as figures appeared in the dark, directly ahead in the kitchen. Rebekah lay on her back, her head rolled toward the two silhouettes engaged in battle next to the glass door. She screamed something as her father peered at her. The figure hunched over him, pounding him with repeated blows until Taleah sprinted toward them.

The attacker sprung to his feet and bolted out the back door as Taleah shoved the gun into the waist of her jeans before sliding to Rebekah's side on her knees. The venom coursed through her as Reggie looked over his wife, who was breathing normally, but in pain so deep that Taleah could scarcely imagine it.

"You should have shot him," Reggie scolded, but Taleah didn't listen.

Sirens wailed in the distance as the cops vaulted through the door with their weapons drawn. One of them radioed for help while the other bounded through the back door in search of the burglar, who had already disappeared into the void of darkness.

Swallowing hard, Taleah stared into Rebekah's eyes, wishing she could speak with reason and solace rather than dread. She glanced up at her with her expression absorbing the heartache and torture. Her head tilted sideways again, and she watched her husband as the seconds ticked away into the vacuum of infinity.

Taleah attempted to relax her while she reached for one of the deep wounds near her chest. She pushed against it with as much force as she dared until the blood immersed her fingers.

The sirens blared louder with every moment. From Taleah's vantage point, Rebekah had suffered the brunt of the attack and could scarcely defend herself. But even in his own home, Reggie had succumbed to defeat, much like he had done in his confrontation with Art years ago. Memory flushed into her mind.

The rain fell that night, turning the mountainside into a soup of matted underbrush and viscous mud. Thumps and grunts had volleyed back and forth as Reggie and Art exchanged ever more furious blows until Art emerged victorious. He was going to murder Reggie in front of Taleah's eyes, but then Willis showed up and put a bullet through Art's head.

"Should have killed him," Reggie said again.

Why she failed to do that didn't enter her mind until that moment. Had rationality really given up the fight that quickly to be replaced by emotional instinct? Then again, thinking clearly at a moment like this seemed a physical impossibility. She rocked back and forth and clutched Rebekah's hand. Reggie grimaced as he attempted to peel himself off the floor. Her first instinct was to tend to Rebekah, because in her split-second decision, Rebekah appeared to be in more imminent danger. She could catch up with the criminal later but helping her stepmother presented itself as more prudent.

"I thought that was your job," she said.

"Don't move, Mr. St. Clair," Officer Donovan said. "Paramedics are *en route.*"

"You're going to get him," Reggie whispered after Donovan knelt at Rebekah's side.

"No sign of the suspect," the voice of the other cop called from the backyard. "MPD, alert all units. Suspect at large, consider armed. Set a perimeter of four blocks. Knock on every door, over."

Officer Lawrence strolled across the wooden deck to assist Donovan. From a kneeling position, he spoke softly to Taleah. "That showed real bravery, Ms. St. Clair. But you're lucky."

"I knew what was going on in here before you did. And you were supposed to be watching. Fine job."

"You don't strike me as a firearm-wielding kind of young lady," Lawrence said. "Whose gun is it?"

"Mine, for now," Taleah said coolly, before adding more lip. "And I remember you, officer. You were the one who told my dad repeatedly not to come after me. At least you're consistent."

"The situation was different," he defended. "And I was hardly the only one advising that. The FBI seemed explicit, too."

"You all were," she shot. She sneered, bit her lip, and allowed her eyes to fall on her father as the ambulances pulled up in front of the house. "Don't do anything. Just let us botch it, as usual."

Rebekah groaned as her blood seeped between Taleah's fingers. Her eyes contorted into slits as her brows gathered into a tide of wrinkles on her forehead. "Taleah," she whimpered. "Stop."

"No," Taleah said. The tears surfaced in her eyes before she could say another word. When the team of paramedics sprinted through the front door, she surrendered and scooted backward against the kitchen cabinets.

Her knee pulsed in pain as she watched it all unfold. Defeat and torment spread through her heart like wildfire ripping through stands of dry timber. Without concern for the blood on her hands, she buried her face and sobbed. Her shoulders lurched as she unleashed waves of tears. Failure eroded her senses until there was nothing left but the consequences.

"Don't cry," Reggie croaked, as the paramedics fitted his abdomen and shoulders with temporary bandages.

Being told not to cry felt so juvenile that it only bludgeoned her with deeper pain. Her tears blinded her as she clutched at her knee, which had begun to bleed through a ragged slit in the denim where the glass had cut through.

Though the fires of pain consumed her, one reality still existed. When she thought of it, the tears ceased, and her trembling became tremors of rage. She bit down on her lip, swallowed, and brought herself to her feet. The killer was still out there, and Taleah was going to bring the ire to him, whether Officer Lawrence would have encouraged it or not.

There was no approval. Everyone would scoff, including Christine, but Taleah understood her motives and the potential pitfalls of her endeavor. The 'era' was going to be over soon, and nothing could stop her.

21

Equinox

THE paramedics hauled in the stretchers in an oddly ordered fashion. The eerie calm in their demeanor and movement somehow sparked deeper anger for Taleah. She huddled against the cabinet as they first fitted Rebekah to the stretcher and strapped her down. Taleah's body trembled and her hands shook. She pushed a tear away with her cleaner hand, wiped the other on her jeans, and pushed away from the cabinet.

Officer Lawrence assisted the paramedics in strapping Reggie to the other stretcher and Taleah rose to her feet to follow them out the door. The other officer stayed behind as police cruisers, flashing blue and red strobes, flooded the neighborhood.

The more time that passed, the more it began to take on an otherworldly feel, as if lucid reality had stretched into hallucination. Taleah needled at it in thought, attempting to assess its reality. She had to be dreaming, otherwise this didn't make any sense. *Wake up.* But she could not.

Perhaps if she screamed, Christine would roll her over, shake her, and cuddle with her to absolve the demons. She croaked as she followed Officer Lawrence to the second ambulance. The paramedics lifted Reggie's stretcher and carefully wheeled him into the back of the vehicle. "You're going to be okay, buddy," one of the EMTs chirped. "We'll get you patched up."

Of course, Reggie had already been patched up. A second visit to the emergency room in a week was something that had never happened, at least as far as Taleah could remember. And not even Anna's depression during the divorce era had landed her in the hospital so frequently. Taleah herself had spent her share of time in the hospital, though not since trying to escape Art. The wounds she suffered had already begun to heal and she was admitted to the emergency room after the fact to aid in the recovery and to prevent complications or further infection.

Taleah jogged to her car, which she had parked at the end of the block. Watching the house for almost an hour before the break-in had seemed silly the longer she waited, and hiding from the cops in the bushes struck her as utterly ridiculous. But then she'd heard the noises the officers couldn't because they were in their car talking. Without thinking, she had sprinted across the street and ran in to help.

She sped behind the ambulances as they made their way to the same hospital in which Reggie had spent the better half of last week. Rage and fear constructed an alternate reality within her own mind. The conflicting, but complementary emotions brewed a poison so bitter, yet familiar, that she vocally groaned her disapproval. The hammering in her skull blasted in rhythm with her heart rate, which had grown erratic over the last several minutes as she seethed.

"Call Christine," she told herself when she hit the first light. She dug her phone out of her purse and dialed the number.

"Hi," she said. "I'm going to the hospital."

"What happened? Are you okay?"

"No. Not exactly. Can't really talk right now." Her clipped sentences chopped the conversation into tiny morsels that could be easily digested, but the stress behind her words doused it in acid.

"Taleah!"

"Come meet me if you want. I'm not hurt."

"Taleah?"

She hung up the phone, pushed it into her purse, and then accelerated with the ambulances. They pulled into the emergency lane and Taleah meandered through the parking lot to find the nearest spot. When she parked the car, she pulled out her phone, dialed her mother's number, and started to jog toward the emergency room.

"It's me," she said. "Dad's in trouble. We're in the ER."

Anna didn't speak for what felt like a full minute. Sleep had probably prevented her from assigning cause or alarm to the situation, but the delay flushed a new flurry of discord through Taleah's bones. "Are you... are you okay?"

"No, mom, not even close. Please come."

"Is Christine going to be there?"

Taleah swallowed hard when she darted across a narrow drive in front of a slow-moving car. The driver lightly pressed on the horn, which sent a surge of adrenaline through her veins and caused her to run faster. Stress butchered her next sentence into wasted fragments. "What? Don't even. Just come, for God's sakes. The homophobia... I can't take it anymore."

"I'm sorry," Anna pouted. "I'll be there as soon as I can."

She hung up the phone just before she burst through the emergency room door, checked in with the staffer, and waited to be escorted to the area where they were tending to Rebekah and Reggie. "Jesus Christ," she whispered.

Come to me.

The speed with which her instincts popped into her brain told her everything she needed to know, and even as their pace slowed, she acknowledged their presence and studied them as though they were complex thoughts riddled with emotional insight. Christine, of course, would advise against such a strategy. "Always question your instincts," she had once said. And when Taleah protested that as an indictment of making quick decisions, Christine had produced numerous studies that showed positive proof that instincts didn't always deserve ultimate trust. Sometimes, situations warranted serious reaction no matter the consequences. And she still believed that in times like those, instinct always won out.

After almost five minutes, a nurse entered the waiting area, called her by name, and whisked her through a double door where an army of nurses and doctors rushed through the open area between curtained stalls, in which victims pleaded for recovery.

"No, it doesn't hurt," she heard a young woman saying, as if the nurse was trying to convince her that the pain was catastrophic.

"Settle down," one doctor told Reggie in a foreign accent. He was in the middle of examining him when the nurse pulled back the curtain enough to let Taleah step through.

"Taleah, they're trying to kill me," Reggie said, squinting so hard that tears trickled into his stubble. "Augh."

"We're going to stitch you up," the doctor said. "You have a long night ahead and you're going to be in and out of it frequently. The anesthetic should knock you out for the duration of the procedure.

"My wife," Reggie gagged. "What about my wife?"

The doctor didn't directly respond. "We are assessing the situation. Trying to keep you in the loop if you're awake."

"Hell with that," Reggie grunted, trying to sit up. "I gotta see her."

"Mr. St. Clair, please let us help you. It's imperative that we get this started quickly."

"I saw some of the struggle," Taleah said dryly.

"Six punctures," the doctor said. "Did you tangle with the attacker?" The doctor eyed her carefully as the blood on her hands, shirt, and jeans dried into blotches of pink and crimson. "Why did he stop?"

"I had a gun," she said. "He ran before the cops came in. Otherwise, he'd be here with a dozen holes in him."

"You didn't fire?"

"It wasn't my first thought," Taleah said. "My stepmom... where is she?"

"Dr. Nelson is going to want to speak to you privately," the doctor whispered. "See her down there at the end of the hall, talking with the nurses? She's busy, of course, but talk to her. We're going to get started on your father right now and it would be best if you're not here."

Taleah reached for her father's hand, grasped it, and let go when the tears flooded his face. She didn't want to leave him, but the doctor was right. She stared at him for so long that she could feel herself growing into him with every second. Threads of pain and worry worked their way into her heart, creating a monolithic barrier that separated light thoughts with blackened chaos.

Dr. Nelson stepped away from the nurses and approached a nurse who was in the process of administering some medication to another patient. Taleah approached her quickly and waited for her to speak.

The doctor had her graying hair pulled into a tight ponytail. Her face looked younger than her hair indicated, though still managed to show some signs of age. Her white coat fluttered around her knees when she spun to address Taleah.

"How can I help you?"

"You're working with Rebekah St. Clair," she said, attempting to vanquish the frustration in her voice.

"I'd like a word. Care to chat in the hallway?"

Taleah shrugged and followed her out a double door and around a corner. Dr. Nelson wore a sorrowful look that suggested trouble, but she adjusted well enough to speak concisely.

"Is she your mother?"

"Stepmom," Taleah corrected.

"Are you close to her?"

"As close as I am to my real mom," Taleah said, swallowing back the urge to cry. Swallowing every few seconds probably made her look nervous and shocked, but appearances didn't matter much. Instead of letting the confrontation get to her, she attempted to bury the emotion. "She's always been there for me since she married my dad. Yes, close."

"Does she have any other family?"

"Just her ex, whom I've never met."

"I'm really concerned here," The doctor said. "We've rushed her into emergency surgery, and the severity of her wounds is—I don't want to say cataclysmic, but it doesn't look great. Even if we'd gotten to her earlier…"

"Is she going to die?" Asking that question so casually sent a lump down her throat and brought a tear to her eye.

"We're not giving up," she said severely. "I wanted to make sure you know that. We have the best surgeons in the city."

"God," Taleah said through gritted teeth.

"Can I do anything for you?" Dr. Nelson asked, pausing momentarily to glance at the blood on her hands and clothes. "Are you hurt in any way?"

Taleah shook her head, furrowed her eyebrows, and held a hand to her lips as the sudden urge to vomit rocketed up her throat. She attempted to suppress it, but the splatter splashed onto her shoes. "Sorry," she choked.

"No worries. Would you like to wait outside the OR?"

"My girlfriend and my mom are coming," she said after swallowing and wiping tears from her eyes. "I'll wait for them."

"Good," Dr. Nelson said. "Emotional support is a good thing. As long as you aren't alone. If you change your mind, she's in OR-3 on the second floor. Take the elevator up and the receptionist will take you there. I'll check in here in an hour or so."

Taleah staggered to the end of the hall, collapsed onto a chair about ten feet from a Latina woman and her three children, who all looked ashen. Hiding her face from them in shame, she waited, bit her lip, and swallowed.

The tears blinded her almost the moment Anna walked through the door. Defeat and anger pulsed through her, but the torment cleansed it all away, scouring it from her heart so completely that she wondered if she'd ever be able to use them again.

Anna sat next to her, pulled her into a tight embrace, and didn't speak for several minutes while Taleah surrendered to the blistering agony. Waves of tears pushed through her eyes until there was nothing left but dry, itchy flesh and smeared mascara. If she cared about her looks at all, she'd be horrified, but vanity was the last thing on her mind.

Christine galloped through the front door, skidded to a stop next to her, sat down, and flung her arms around her. She bit her lip, bowed her head, and let them gently console her until the shards of torture ran out.

When she looked up, Christine was the first to speak. "What happened?"

Taleah's recount was so fragmented that it left gaping holes. She didn't explain how she got there or why she ran into the house, or that she saw her father fighting with the intruder. She didn't even mention holding the gun up ready to fire and then dropping it the second she witnessed Rebekah lying on her back in a pool of blood.

"Oh my God."

"How is he doing?" Anna asked, her voice cool and calm.

"They're in there sewing him up, I guess," she said. "He got him six times, in the shoulders, abdomen, arms... but you know dad. He wants to see Rebekah."

"He got Rebekah, too?"

"Her first," Taleah said. "So many times. I can't believe she's alive."

"Maybe it's a miracle," Anna suggested.

"Dr. Nelson said it didn't look good," Taleah choked. "Then I puked on her shoes, which I guess sort of comes with the territory of being an ER doctor."

"Do you want to see her?" Christine asked.

Taleah shook her head. "I want a plan. He's out there and I have to stop him."

"You don't think he got what he wanted? Like he's going to wait it out this time just in case you father makes it and then decides to try it again?"

"He knows the cops are going to catch him," Taleah said. "I think he's going to leave the city." She stared at her mother for ten seconds before her voice steadied itself. "I want you to find out where he's going. Dig up everything, listen in on Sergeant Bones, even though he's onto you. You can do it."

"I don't know," Anna said, shrugging. "It seems like I'm not going to find anything."

"Damn it, mom! Don't say you don't know, just do it. I'm not waiting anymore. I have to end this before he kills Mindy."

Christine audibly gasped. When Taleah had confided in her the secrets of her past, she'd mentioned Mindy and Christine knew how much she thought of her. Though she never displayed trust issues, mention of her name always brought a reaction.

"And what are you going to do, run off and confront him alone?"

"No," Taleah said. "Emmanuel is coming with me. I might have to kidnap him to get him to go along, but he's already in enough trouble."

"I'm going, too," Christine said, sitting up straight.

"No you're not," Taleah shot. "I'm not going to let you. He's not going to have a problem with killing you just because you got in the way."

"I feel the same way," Christine snapped. "You're not alone."

"I love you," Taleah said, squeezing out a lone tear. "You're my every-thing. But I have to do this."

Christine sighed, brushed her feet across the tile floor, and stared toward the end of the hall, where a nurse was explaining something to an old man who looked disgusted and appalled. "I love you too."

For the first time, Christine was the one shedding tears. Taleah pulled her closer, put her arm around her back and squeezed. It was like breaking up, but it had to be done. If emotion could drown her, there was enough to fill Lake Michigan with some left over. The spasms of pain, frustration, and rage swept across her once again.

Anna studied her and altered her expression slowly until she looked terminally horrified. Taleah darted her eyes back and forth across the room. The Latina and her family shuffled off to the end of the hall, possibly headed for a vending machine or the cafeteria, leaving Taleah alone with the two women she trusted most, apart from Rebekah.

For now, there was nothing she could do. Helplessness consumed her, tearing her apart from within with tides of acid. She buried her face on Christine's shoulder, closed her eyes, and drifted into a broken sleep.

22
Solstice

NIGHT stretched on like the throes of an epic dream sent scurrying into oblivion by the sound of shuffling. The first thing she felt was Christine's hand on her shoulder and her own face absorbing the heat from Christine's body through her shirt. It would have been a cozy moment, but mountains of regret and pain loomed just out of reach. Perhaps she could delay their impact by refusing to open her eyes, but Christine had already realized she was awakening.

"Nice nap?"

She didn't open her eyes, but the shuffling paused, commenced, and intensified somewhere just behind her where her mother had been sitting. Her voice cracked as she spoke. "What time is it?"

"Almost two-thirty. You slept a good two hours."

She allowed her eyes to pop open, but kept them narrow so the light wouldn't cause her headache to explode. Her knee ached when she pushed her foot across the floor. The pain caused her eyebrows to furrow and her arm muscles to clench. The blood covering her jeans and her shirt had dried, effectively ruining the clothes she'd changed into after work. "I wouldn't call it good," Taleah responded.

Christine's voice squeaked as she squeezed Taleah's shoulder tighter. "I'm sorry. About all of this."

Taleah whispered back. "I know."

The shuffling continued for several more seconds and then ceased. The sound of paper being flipped over snapped through the air, followed by a low grunt that sounded like some kind of realization of a mistake. Taleah lifted her head, unwilling to commit to being awake just yet, but then stretched her arms, straightened her back, and rubbed her eyes.

"Damn it," Anna whispered as she read what was written on the sheet of paper.

Christine spoke up. "She's been at it more than an hour, ignoring me, of course, just looking at stuff, checking things like she's catching up on her bills or something. Seems like a strange place for it."

Taleah didn't comment. Of course, there was a time and a place for everything. Anna didn't follow the same rules of time as most normal people. When some problem she was capable of solving got stuck in her mind, she'd devote all her energy to it no matter where she was or what she was doing.

"I know there was a cab ride," Anna said in monotone. "After the incident at the garage because he wouldn't have been able to escape on foot. So I've been trying to figure out what the fare might be for a two-mile trip. Assuming he paid for the ride in cash."

"Why two miles?" Taleah asked, rubbing her forehead.

"Just a guess," her mother noted. "Not a good one, from the looks of it..."

"Have you tried calling the cab companies?"

She sighed. "Not at this time of night. The police might have more evidence on this than I do. And I checked that out, too. Sergeant Bones seems like he wants to be hacked. Everything is unsecured, including his personal phone. You know what he texted to Officer Ramirez an hour and a half ago?"

Taleah rubbed her eyelids, and then winced when she moved the leg she'd cut on the broken glass.

"Cabbie's late. Alvarez tip him off?"

Her eyes widened the instant she heard the name. After stretching her back, she sat up straight, eyed the blood on her jeans, and waited for more.

"Does that name mean something to you?" Anna said without glancing up from the paper, as if Taleah's reaction had already answered the question.

"They were talking about Jesse Alvarez yesterday morning when they asked me to meet them, but I was under the impression that they had him in custody."

"They might, but doesn't it seem odd that he would have anything to do with the cab driver who just happened to pick the bad guy up from the garage? I guess a phone call is in the cards."

Taleah shrugged and leaned back without saying anything. Anna stood up and started punching numbers into her phone while a woman in a white coat strolled toward her in the hall. Taleah scanned her face from afar, hoping for signs of good news, but the doctor's expression wasn't telling. Watching her approach and waiting for what she had to say was like torture. Finally, after Anna had stepped out the glass door onto the sidewalk, Dr. Nelson sat down and clasped her hands in her lap.

"Just thought I would bring you an update. Surgery went well and we've transferred her to ICU. Still critical, but the surgeons did a great job. She's sleeping now, and probably will be for the next six hours when the medication wears off. We'll have more then. You can always check on her when you want. Have you heard how your father is doing?"

Taleah didn't have the nerve to feel relieved, but at least she wasn't delivering bad news.

"I sort of fell asleep," Taleah said, resting her hand on Christine's knee.

Dr. Nelson recognized the affection for what it was and tried to smile. "I'm headed back in there now to check some things, make the rounds before Dr. Whistler takes over. I can check in on your dad if you'd like. And you should probably get that knee looked at."

Taleah raised her eyebrows and lifted her head before deciding. "It's just a little cut, but I would like it if you checked on him."

"I'll see if they can bandage it for you." Dr. Nelson stood up and straightened her jacket before smiling at Christine. Taleah watched her disappear through the double doors and then glanced sideways to the glass front doors of the ER. Anna waved her hand around as though she were in a heated discussion and then lowered her palm to rest it on her forehead.

"She's like a dog with a bone," Christine said.

"I yelled at her about her attitude toward you," Taleah said. She thought about grasping Christine's hand but the dried blood made her feel uncomfortable. With every moment, she became more and more conscious of how she looked and how she smelled. A shower, she thought, would at least temporarily ease the pain and relax her nerves, but she had no desire to return home.

Through the window, Anna raised her hand, furrowed her brows and pushed her head forward as she spoke. She was giving Sergeant Bones an earful, and it served him right. How he'd been considered smart enough to lead an investigation made her head hurt, but then again, he brought skills and experience to the table. And he was related by marriage to the former chief, who had unsuccessfully run for county Sheriff a few years ago.

After glancing to the small windows on the ER doors, she lowered her eyes to her lap and touched at the tatters where her jeans had torn on the glass. The sore ached when she dabbed at it. A bandage would do her good to ward off an infection.

"Does it hurt?" Christine asked.

She nodded and wrinkled her forehead.

"We should get you home and cleaned up."

"I'm not going home," Taleah said.

"You need rest and you need a shower." Christine watched her move her leg and frowned. "Good thing the doctor's going to take care of that."

"It's not deep," she said. "Besides, I had other things on my mind."

"Right."

The doctor emerged through the door looking relieved. She unzipped her coat and approached them with a curious bounce in her step, though Taleah could sense the weariness in the doctor's eyes.

"He's being moved into observation," Dr. Nelson said. "They've got him on painkillers, but he's aware enough for now. He says he wants to talk to you for a moment before you go home."

Taleah nodded and stood up. Her knees ached as her muscles stretched. Sleeping on a metal-framed chair, no matter how padded, did a number on her back, which only a thorough massage could alleviate.

Dr. Nelson greeted her and walked toward the glass doors quickly. Taleah swung open the double doors to the ER with Christine at her heels. In the moment when both the ER doors and the glass front doors were open, the sound of harsh yells filled her ears. It shouldn't have given her pleasure that her mother was berating a police sergeant over the phone, but it offered a strange thrill and a gentle dose of adrenaline.

The din of doctors and nurses shuffling through the room had taken a downward pitch over the last several hours, and patient complaints seemed few and far between. Taleah navigated the narrow walkway between curtains, some of which had been pulled open. An elderly man sat upright on the bed opposite her father's partition. He frowned at her and picked at something on his forearm while he ostensibly waited for the doctor to give him the update he needed.

Taleah peeled back the curtain to witness her father's body sprawled out on the narrow bed with his head propped up. He glanced at the old man first, then studied Taleah with a look of entrenched sorrow carving canyons in his face.

"God, you look awful," she said.

Christine hardly had the nerve to look at him. The beeps and the lights were probably invoking waves of misery. She allowed her arms to slacken by her sides and pretended to stare at something interesting on the floor.

"You should look in the mirror," Reggie said. "But they won't let me have one. And even with all this, they're asking for my insurance information. I asked them if they had some sort of frequent customer discount, but guess what? This month's special is they charge you *more* on your second visit."

"Dad."

"Really."

"Have they told you anything about Rebekah?"

Reggie squirmed. "Won't let me see her, but yeah. It's good news. Listen. I don't know what you're planning on or why your mother won't come in here to see me, but you need to get home and get some rest. Those newspaper articles aren't going to edit themselves."

Taleah considered telling him she wasn't going in to work. In reality the thought had never crossed her mind, but now that she thought about Jalene, she understood that Jalene wouldn't want her there at all anyway after the ordeal of the last night. Instead, she bit her lip and tried to ignore the scars and the fresh stitches, some of which were covered by the gown he wore.

"They're going to put me on some meds, which will probably knock me out. The best thing you can do for anyone right now is to get home and rest. You'll feel better in the morning. Don't worry too much about Rebekah and me. I have some experience with the staff here and they won't let me sneeze without checking me out for seizures."

"Okay," she whispered.

The doctor with the accent returned after a few moments carrying a clipboard with a few sheets of paper tucked neatly together. He looked as though he came from some region of India, though his accent seemed to indicate he'd been adept at English for most of his career. He glanced at her knee and then into her eyes. "Dr. Nelson says that we should bandage your wound. Did this happen while your father was being hurt?"

Taleah looked to the floor and nodded sheepishly.

The doctor looked closer at the sore through the hole in her jeans. "Why don't you change into a gown and I will be back in a few minutes."

After removing her jeans and draping the gown over her shoulders, she stared into Christine's eyes as she waited for the doctor returned with the bandages.

"You are not allergic to any medications, are you?" the doctor said without so much as glancing at her.

She shook her head and waited for him to treat her wound. "Doesn't look bad," he said. "This will not be waterproof, but a quick shower won't take it off. Wait at least thirty minutes so the gel can do its job. You will be feeling better soon."

He quickly applied the bandages and disappeared so that Taleah could get dressed. Being indecent in front of her father felt awkward and unnerving, but Reggie didn't watch.

After the doctor disappeared through the dividing curtain, Reggie motioned for her to lean in closer, grasped her arm, and held it firmly for several seconds. "Thanks for coming. You saved her life and mine."

The tears quickly formed at the corner of her eyes, and seeing this, Reggie altered the tempo and pitch of his voice to something more fervent, yet serene.

"I have faith in you. You're going to do the right thing. And you're going to make that son of a bitch pay."

Taleah shrugged as if she didn't know what he was talking about. Such a line of defense usually warranted her a few points of grace, she'd decided, but the misery of the words and the pain under which he uttered them fueled the fire in her heart. He was usually right, and doing what he said, regardless of what instinct dictated presented itself as the correct choice.

"Go," he said. "And remember what happened last time."

This injury was like a mild itch compared to what she'd experienced seven years ago in Art's custody. Everything from the pain to the recovery crushed her spirit with blinding pain. For now, she hardly even felt her leg unless she touched the scar. A weary nod was the only reaction she could muster without spilling more tears onto his gown.

She released his hand, stepped backward toward the old man, and stared back into the eyes of her father. The pain in his eyes seemed to expand every second. She could offer nothing other than the three words she seldom gave him. "I love you."

More tears spilled on her cheek a she stepped away with Christine beside her. There would be more use for those words, she thought, if she returned from dealing with the killer, whose identity remained shrouded in mystery.

Anna waited for her in in the waiting room, pacing back and forth with a look of stoic victory icing her face. She waited until Taleah arrived at her side to share the news.

"Sergeant Bones is being relieved of command and the FBI is taking over. I'd like to think that had something to do with me, because of his security issues and that I got him to tell me some important things they've learned in just the last few hours."

"Tell me about it at home," Taleah said. I think I need a shower and to rest. Do you mind if I crash there?"

Christine frowned, but understood the gravity of the situation. She said nothing, only grasped Taleah's hand and held it firmly.

"Of course," Anna said. "Good. Are you okay to drive yourself?"

Taleah nodded. She walked hand in hand with Christine until she arrived at her car, but the two didn't utter a single word to each other until they stood at the tail end of Taleah's car and stared into one another's eyes. If she could just stay here, in this moment, all the turmoil would melt away and she'd emerge a happier and more powerful version of herself at the end of it all. Christine was more than accommodating, which was perhaps a weakness in its own right, but a welcome one. The soul she showed when she looked at her communicated everything Taleah needed to know. She was never alone. The precipice was growing nearer and the veil that separated future from past offered her a tiny glimpse of what lay beyond, if she ever passed through it.

They could get married, though neither of them had ever so much as brought it up. She had no plans for now and didn't want to make plans. Christine would likely frown on that anyway without some kind of rational discussion on the benefits and pitfalls of the proposition.

They kissed goodbye and parted. Christine walked away slowly as Taleah started her car.

The drive to her mother's house would normally take nearly a half hour during daytime traffic, but the late hour would effectively shave off at least ten minutes. Twenty minutes afforded her plenty of time to think ahead, instead of remembering the pain in her father's eyes or the agonizing scene in the kitchen.

Crying felt like the only natural emotion to show at the moment, but the tears didn't come, which somehow only spread further guilt into her heart. Everything about this was foreign, but harrowingly familiar. The contradiction was maddening. It was as if life was spinning like a penny on a table next to a lamp and the speed of its rotation allowed the light to bend and reflection to shine on Lincoln's face even as his memorial faced the light. If she had time to sit down and deconstruct everything piece by piece, perhaps she could supply the logic that would explain the phenomenon. Still, the rotation could only slow as the system lost its momentum due to friction and air resistance, making the president spend longer and longer in the dark until he fell either on his face or his back.

The night lurched onward like the slowing penny.

She arrived at Anna's house around fifteen after three in the morning. Taleah checked her phone when she parked the car. Christine had sent her a text message. "Bringing you some clothes to change into. Luv U."

She fumbled with the keys and decided not to answer. Instead of talking with her mother, she stripped down, got into the shower, and felt the hot water pour over her aching flesh. When it was over, she wrapped herself in towels and slipped one of Anna's spare robes over her shoulders.

A fresh set of clothes was stacked on the arm of the couch when Taleah sat down and ran a comb through her wet hair. Anna nodded at her and showed her the screen of her laptop.

"They saw this car parked at a hotel lot near the airport, but they can't find the vehicle now. Notably, it matches the description of a car Reggie's neighbors saw the other day."

The plum and rust-colored sport utility vehicle would be recognizable from memory because a dent marred the rear quarter panel and one of its mirrors was missing. She committed it to memory and then examined her bandaged knee through the crack in the robe.

"And the cab driver also mentioned he might have seen that car. He said he paid with cash and picked up the killer, who didn't tell him his name, on Eighth in front of the escalator at the marketplace and took him out to one of those house manufacturers on Federal Way."

"When they raided that property, they found something interesting. There in the office, there was a blueprint for a new unit that had been shipped up to Atlanta for like a hunting cabin. Prints they found on the blueprints matched a set they found on the phone the killer had used to call you."

"It's going to take three days to get there," Taleah said, trying to calculate which interstates she'd need to travel.

"Or a few hours, give or take," Anna corrected.

"It's only accessible two ways, and both of them are dirt roads. You're going to want to be careful, though because of RV traffic. Lots of hunters up there."

"Georgia?"

"Idaho. The quickest route is that turn-off on the backside of Lucky Peak. That's paved halfway to the end of the lake, and then you go uphill to the next dam. The road gets narrower after the dam."

"I'll leave after I get some things together tomorrow," Taleah said. "Did Christine say anything when she dropped these clothes off?"

"Nothing important, just that she loves you." Anna paused. "I'm trying to understand it. I hope you can be patient with me. I can be friends with her."

Taleah looked down at her knee again and pressed against her scar. She sighed. "Just treat her like she's my best friend. She doesn't want to be looked at as different, just as human. I need you do to do this for us."

"Taleah, are you suggesting—"

"I'm not suggesting anything. Please."

"I'll try."

Taleah closed the gap in the robe and brushed her hands through her hair. In a pinch, she could always style her hair just by getting it wet and running her hands through it; such was one of the benefits of having short hair.

"There's something else, too you know." Anna paused. "The Kleinman family had their ranch burned in a wildfire a week ago and they've been homeless ever since. The FBI has kept an eye on them from time to time in a little motel in Emmet, but they left that motel days ago and haven't been seen since. Sounds like Agent Marks is a little worried that they're going to come in contact with the suspect and with the evidence they have, it's easy to see why."

"Mom," Taleah said. "I don't know anything about them. And I'm sure there won't be any cellular service up there in the mountains. But he has Mindy and I'm going for her, too."

"What did your father tell you?"

"I don't know if I should tell you," Taleah protested. "You're going to go berserk at him."

"What am I going to do, divorce him?"

Taleah frowned and gulped. "He told me to make the bastard pay for what he did to him and Rebekah. It's the only thing I can do."

"You're going to kill him?"

Taleah shook her head and bit her lip. Weariness crept up within her. Nothing could be as final and horrifying as what she was about to say, but there was no point in letting it fester in her heart like a sore that would never heal. "He's going to kill me."

23

Lunar

CHRISTINE'S voice woke Taleah late in the morning as she lay on her side facing the back of the couch. The best Taleah could gather, she was discussing something with her mother about being prepared. Having a brother who hunted, she claimed, made her somewhat knowledgeable regarding the wilderness. Taleah opened her eyes, rolled onto her back and stared at the ceiling as the conversation stopped and started.

"No, she's going to need that, too. My brother never goes without one. And just in case, purification drops."

"This one big enough?"

Christine seemed to grow impatient the longer it went on. "Are you expecting her to run into a pumpernickel?"

"It has a serrated—"

"Forget it," Christine sniped. "I'll get her a pocketknife."

Taleah's mind flashed to last night when she'd burst into the house and the intruder was plunging the bloody blade into her father's shoulder. She closed her eyes and groaned as a jolt of pain worked its way up her spine. She gripped her knee under the sheet and then made a halfhearted attempt to sit up.

"Are those waterproof?"

"Well..."

From the living room, she could hear Christine audibly sigh and step back. Rummaging commenced, followed by the forceful shutting of a cabinet door.

Her mother sighed and the conversation stopped for several seconds.

"They will be fine as long as she'll be able to keep the box dry. Put some cotton balls in with them to absorb the moisture."

Taleah's head ached as she began to itemize everything she might need to do. Christine would be sitting at her side lecturing her on survival skills within minutes, she guessed. Instead of waiting for it, she silently got up, grabbed her clothes, and tiptoed to the bathroom.

Christine was waiting outside the bathroom with an impatient smile when Taleah opened the door. She flung her arms around Taleah's neck, planted her lips against hers, and then led her back into the living room.

"We've got your car packed with some stuff," Christine said. "I borrowed a few things from my brother. Hopefully you don't have to use any of it, but it's better to be prepared. You'll find a spade, a change of clothes, a poncho in case it gets wet... and a good pair of shoes."

Taleah grunted "thanks" and sat down on the couch next to Anna, who had slid her laptop out from under the couch and brought up several detailed maps.

"This is Atlanta," she said, pointing to a small black dot amidst a sea of green on the screen. "You've got some forest service roads that ultimately don't lead anywhere, but it's a good idea to know where they are and where they come out. You're going to want to opt for the Arrowrock route, though it's more dangerous than going through Pine and Featherville. Less distance and better scenery."

"I'm not going for the sights," Taleah said after clearing her throat.

"There are lots of game trails. Hiking... horses. And it looks like one camping area has been closed. "The town is mostly abandoned these days, but sportsmen and backpackers frequently visit some of the cabins through November."

"Are there rangers?" Taleah asked, noting the shades of green that surrounded the dot on the map.

"A few, probably, but they're going to stay out of your way."

"My brother told me a few ways to get their attention if they are nearby," Christine said. "Shooting three times will work and they should be able to find you if you burn some green kindling and send up some smoke."

"What about flares?"

"Good way to start a forest fire even if you could get them." She scratched her neck and sat down next to her so that their hips touched. "I've also stocked you up with a couple of water bottles and one refillable. If you're going to be out walking around, you don't want to carry too much water, because it can be heavy. Your friend is going to need some, too."

Taleah eyed the map for several minutes as her mother scrolled. She wouldn't be able to memorize everything, and her GPS wouldn't work very well in that area.

"Come with me," Christine said.

They stood up and walked to Christine's car. They sat in the front seats and Christine pulled a compass out of the center console. "I stole this from my brother's gun storage." She held it level in her hand and waited for the red needle to stop moving.

"I know how to use a compass," Taleah said.

"You're going to want to find a bearing when you get somewhere you have a clear view. Take note of what the mountains look like in every direction and try to get a feel for the lay of the land. My brother said it is a good idea to make a monument when you get set up, so that you know where you've been. Sometimes in the trees it can be difficult to assess where you are going, even with a compass."

"I see."

"Does Emmanuel have any backpacking experience?"

Taleah shrugged, not wanting to think about him just yet. Christine handed her the compass, swung open her door, and walked into the driveway to open Taleah's trunk, which carried a backpack stuffed with supplies and clothes.

"Got some flashlights in there, some rope, extra bullets."

"I can't believe you," Taleah said. She hung her head low, wrapped an arm around Christine's waist, and breathed slowly.

Christine kissed her gently and reached into Taleah's jeans pocket. She pulled out a coin, which she must have placed in the pocket before delivering them to Anna's house. The coin, she claimed, had been in her family for generations. After placing it in Taleah's palm and closing her hand around it, she turned to face her and gripped her waist with both hands.

"It's for good luck. Trust me, it works. If you ever need it, just take it out, turn it in your fingers three times, and close your eyes thinking of me."

Never one to believe in inane superstitions, Taleah stared at it, trying to feign curiosity while Christine attempted to read her thoughts. Of course,

Christine already knew this about Taleah and had to invent a little more silliness to make it seem worthwhile. Whatever her motive, Taleah guessed it wouldn't work but decided to play along.

"And when you get back, you and I need to talk."

Taleah shook her head. "Um..."

"I'm not saying anything else."

"If I get back," Taleah said mournfully and with a hushed voice.

Christine slackened her posture, closed her eyes, pulled Taleah closer, and pressed her lips tightly against hers.

"Say goodbye to your mother. We'll try to text you to keep you up to date."

"We?"

"Didn't she tell you? We're best friends now."

Taleah laughed and made her way back into the house. Anna stood behind the door with tears in her eyes and rested her hands on her hips. Taleah hugged her tightly.

"This is a stupid idea," she said, "but I guess I can't stop you. You be careful."

"How is dad? And Rebekah?"

"Resting," Anna said tenuously. She shook her head and pulled away as streams of tears wet her face. "And Rebekah's still in ICU. They're monitoring her closely."

"Good," Taleah said.

Christine followed her out of the neighborhood as Taleah contemplated her next move. Agony and sadness coursed through her as she drove and each time the tears tried to form at the edge of her eyes, she summoned the anger she'd need to survive. Drawing it in with every breath could serve up danger, she surmised, but she swallowed it willfully like a medication. Its darkness would propel her. As the minutes passed, her hands and her jaw began to shake with rage.

She cooled it down by remembering Christine's kiss as soon as Taleah had turned down the boulevard that led to her office. Taleah wandered the city for several hours, stopping at a few stores to buy food and suitable knives, and then stopped to dial Emmanuel's number.

It rang four times before he picked it up. "Are you busy?" she said.

"I am going to get something to eat," he said. "Then going to the Center for a few hours. Do you want to join me?"

"I was hoping you'd help me with something," Taleah said. "And this is going to be easy to say 'no' to, but I'm desperate."

Emmanuel waited long enough to swallow, and then spoke slowly. "I will do anything you need. I hear it in your voice. Do you want to tell me?"

"I will in the car," Taleah said. "Meet me next to the Anne Frank Memorial on Eighth. Is that okay?"

She hung up her phone and parked. Twenty minutes passed before her passenger door opened and Emmanuel sat down in the seat. They exchanged small talk while they made their way to his apartment, where he would stuff a backpack full of necessities and a change of clothes. Dinner was next. The afternoon sped by so quickly that Taleah hardly had a chance to recognize the passage of time. She sped along the highway toward Lucky Peak as the sun began to inch downward. In an hour, the sun would start to set into brilliant shades of orange, blue, and gray.

They drove until the highway began to wind up a steep hill toward the top of the dam just outside the city. The canyon walls stained black with shadow as they drove, and the sun disappeared behind the foothills. Sunset in this canyon came earlier than it did at the rim because of the angle of the sun. The shadows grew longer as the evening progressed. Gradually, the sky's turquoise began to fade into darker hues. The moon rose over the lake, casting glittering reflections over the water as a half dozen boats sped across its surface. People water skied in the wake of one of the boats, which had curled into a spiral path.

Before they had a chance to take in the scenery, the road continued its ascent up the hills. Ten minutes passed before its blue waters, calmer now, appeared once again. The road pitched downward and a crowded marina hugged the foot of black cliffs. Most of the drive would take place under the cover of darkness but she could not wait. The moonlight danced on the waters as she crossed a long bridge, slowed down, and turned toward the marinas along the water's edge.

The pavement ran out by the time she made it to another marina, but dozens of boats and campers littered the roadside and sent plumes of dust into the gathering darkness. She swallowed when she saw a sign indicating that Atlanta was more than an hour away, even at highway speeds.

"You did not tell me what happened," Emmanuel asked.

Taleah watched the reflection of the moon flicker on the choppy surface of the lake, swallowed, and let a single tear form at the corner of her eye. She'd replace the emotion with anger soon enough, she decided, but letting her guard down temporarily seemed the right thing to do. After all, Emmanuel had a right to know.

"I spent hours in the ER last night. I was watching my dad's house from across the street because I was worried. And when I heard a scream, I ran in. He was attacking—trying to kill my dad and his wife. When he saw me holding the gun, he ran for it. He got away."

Emmanuel watched her closely and frowned as night enveloped them. They reached another dam, this one constructed of concrete, at the end of the lake. The road took steep switchbacks up a slope toward the top of the dam and Taleah kept the pace steady. For several minutes, Emmanuel uttered no reply. She glanced sideways at him and saw the whites of his eyes next to the moon's reflection on the water.

"Are we going to find him?"

Taleah felt her lip twitch and allowed it to flutter as she gripped the steering wheel harder. Remembering the agony, the pain, and the horror of the last night, the ambulance lights flashing, and the screaming of the sirens brought the disgust to her brain so efficiently that it surprised her. She dwelt on it for several seconds before pushing out a fake smile and accelerating to the top of the dam. Her voice shook as she answered, "He's going to hurt her, and I've got to stop him."

24
Zodiacal

THE pines pierced the darkness, cutting a jagged line across the horizon where millions of stars shimmered in a sea of dark blue above the black silhouettes of the trees. Taleah's headlights blazed through the darkness as she inched down the packed gravel road to study every building she passed. The whites of Emmanuel's eyes flicked in the darkness as she eyed a small cabin. Its windows showed no soft glow inside, though the porch light collected insects and fluttering particles of dust. Emmanuel remained silent, as though cautiously pondering.

The forest seemed eerily vacant and devoid of life from this vantage point, but of course dozens of animal species stalked the woods even in the middle of night. The headlights pushed through the trees for about two hundred yards and disappeared. Near the road, invisible lines strung between pines supported drying clothes.

Though many of the cabins were occupied, it was impossible to discern which ones were. She decided that any structure with lights on either had an owner inside or nearby. Emmanuel seemed to realize this, too, and began to ignore every such unit.

Taleah said nothing to him, reached a dead-end sign in the narrow gravel road, and stopped the car. She decided to flip on the dome light and glance at the map she'd purchased, but it was hopeless. The map didn't show enough detail to pick out every street. She'd need to back up more than a hundred yards instead of continuing because the narrow drive would not allow any kind of efficient turn around. She pushed the stick into reverse, rested her elbow on the seat, and backed up slowly to a white sign that marked the intersection of Spruce and Lodgepole Streets.

Lodgepole Street appeared to dogleg to the left after passing one house that was settled at the edge of the gravel. A drainage ditch paralleled this road and crossed through a corrugated metal culvert buried under the gravel. Taleah noted the number, which was easily readable below a single, unshielded bulb. Behind one window, a soft yellow light glowed. Most of these cabins consisted of less than five hundred square feet of living space, a shared kitchen and living room, a wooden porch with a barbecue grill, and acres of forestland.

After the dogleg, the road straightened out for what looked like maybe a half mile. It ascended a shallow incline and then flattened out. This road represented a perhaps newer addition to the 'town' of Atlanta, a fact easily assessed by noting the width of the road. It gently widened out to enough space of washboard gravel to fit two cars side-by-side and a three-point turn would suffice to backtrack if she decided it was a dead end. The extra space allowed her to speed up, though she didn't want to drive too fast because of the late hour and the noise it would produce.

When she hit the accelerator, gravel clinked off the underpinnings of the car, churned through the wheel wells, and roared like continuous thunder through the canopy.

Atlanta wasn't so much a town as it was an old mining outpost that predated the turn of the century. The only government building still in operation was the forest service post, which occupied a small, log-framed building with single windows on each side adjacent to one of the two roads in. A shuttered exchange store and a boarded-up post office marked the entrance to the town. Within the last thirty years or so, all mining had ceased and the only indication that any mining had ever taken place were the large mounds of shattered rock and bark that were scattered through the woods. The Featherville entrance to the small valley pushed through old-growth forest that was sparse enough for grass to overtake the mounds of rock. The densest clustering of buildings seemed to favor that entrance, while the Lucky Peak entrance followed a mountain stream as it curved through the denser conifers.

Taleah noted the expanse of trees as she looked straight ahead. The road seemed to disappear into a thicket of pines as it approached the statuesque shape of what seemed to be the tallest mountain in the area, a rocky spire with a flat top studded with pines.

"There isn't much here," she said.

Ahead, a driveway jutted off from the main road. It bridged the ditch with a culvert and curved back parallel to the road a few hundred feet away. The oblong shape of the building appeared like a gray rectangle behind the gently swaying trees. She stopped the car and studied it for long enough to decide it looked like a manufactured home with two-tone siding and smallish windows. She parked the car at the side of the road and swung open the car door.

"I think this is the house," Taleah said, attempting to recall how Anna had described it.

"Might be," Emmanuel said, following her lead.

She popped open the trunk and shuffled through the contents of her backpack until she grasped the barrel of the flashlight. She flipped it on, withdrew the pocketknife, and stuffed it in her jeans. The blade was a perfect four-incher made of stainless steel with a well-crafted wood casing that the blade folded into. She removed the magazine from the gun to make sure it was fully loaded and wedged it into the waistband of her jeans.

Emmanuel tested his flashlight and examined the pocketknife Taleah had bought for him. The two blades had looked promising in the store and were exact duplicates. It had been easy to admire the workmanship, although a least a dozen other hunting knifes offered more features at a similar cost.

"What do you say we look through the windows and see what's here?" Taleah stepped into the rocky ditch after she gently pushed the trunk shut. Emmanuel studied the driveway and visually concluded that jaunting through the woods would give them better cover should the cabin's owner return.

"Good idea," Emmanuel said.

The terrain was a rough construct of gravel and broken shale overlaying matted, compressed dirt, though which tufts of underbrush rose. Taleah kicked a pinecone out of the way and listened to the sound of claws scurry up a nearby tree trunk. The sudden noise caused the tiny hairs on the back of her neck to stand upright and a faint shiver to race down her spine. Emmanuel trod more carefully while he paced about five feet behind her.

"This land is beautiful," Emmanuel said. "In Jordan, we have mostly desert, and the city. One road near the border with Syria has trees and mountains. We drove there one year and enjoyed the trees. With my younger brother and family. It takes you away from the city, from everything you know. And the mystery is good for your brain."

"I've only seen it on a map," Taleah said conversationally. "And whatever footage they sometimes show on the news with the war in Syria, it looks poor."

"The cities are old," Emmanuel said. "And they do not have many trees. The streets are crowded, but some areas are more prosperous than others."

"Has your family ever been to the United States?"

Emmanuel shook his head and stepped over what appeared to be an active anthill more than a foot wide, where thousands of ants labored. "I want them to come. But I worry sometimes about the climate here with what the politicians are saying."

"Politicians are full of hot air," Taleah said. "They say whatever they think the people most likely to vote for them want to hear. They don't mean it most of the time and it doesn't have to be true. It just has to rile up those people who fear."

"That is not unique to the US," Emmanuel said. "I could tell you some things I heard about refugees from Syria before I came to university. Maybe sometimes the fear is deserved."

Taleah nodded slowly at the insinuation, but consciously wanted to doubt it was true for some reason. She swallowed when she stepped to the long side of the building. The windows were not cut low enough in the wall to see through and only darkness existed behind them anyway. She shuddered when a sudden, cold breeze sifted through the tree trunks.

The forest brought her memory to life in lucid detail. The exact shape of the mountainside, the smell of the pines, the crackle of flames as pinecones exploded into sparks, and the groan of the trunks were but fragments of a world she'd left behind. The images were severe. Blood, sweat, and tangled hair were everything she could see, while the grunts and growls of her host permeated her brain with regular torture. She would gasp and scream as her feet splashed in mud and thumped on hollow-sounding earth. Terror washed over her.

But in all the visual and aural cues, one curious emotion became obvious. The terror had taken her life apart, just as the killer seemed to by systematically deconstructing Taleah's personality. The shattered glass in the kitchen combined with the trees and the shadowy image of the intruder attempting to stab her father to death with a knife that must have been longer than the one she'd purchased from the store. That detail pulsed somewhere beneath the surface, ready to strike at just the opportune time, when she was most vulnerable to its scars. The cops couldn't even do anything, and Officer Lawrence had warned her not to go looking for him. The rage simmered somewhere in her veins, but she kept it bottled for now.

"Looks too dark," Emmanuel said. "Are you thinking of breaking in?"

"Maybe I should," Taleah said. "Poetic justice and all."

Emmanuel backtracked and made for the steps up to the front door while swirling his light along the rocky ground. He sighed when he reached the top of the stairs and Taleah stepped up behind him. "I do not understand that saying."

"Poetic justice?"

Emmanuel stared and waited for her explanation.

She sighed coolly and stammered, "Well, you know about poetry. How the words flow together to shape meanings that are not totally obvious at first until you really think about it. It's like that, but real. Like if a killer who hanged a man were sentenced to death by hanging."

He nodded slowly and stared at the darkness beyond the pie-shaped windows in the top third of the door. Taleah tried the door handle and jiggled it slowly.

"Americans have so many idioms," Emmanuel said casually. "Learning about them is fun sometimes."

"Any other ones you're wondering about?"

"Maybe some," Emmanuel said. "But not right now."

She pulled the knife out of her pocket and examined its blade. It appeared to be long and narrow enough to wedge in between the door and its frame. As long as the door wasn't dead-bolted, she could separate the seal enough to wedge the knife in and push the lock open.

Emmanuel helped her tug at the seal until she was able to insert the knife into the gap. She ran it up and down the frame until she felt metal on metal. Wedging the knife up and down, she managed to click the lock open. When Emmanuel twisted the handle and pushed on the door, it flung open and crashed into a small table holding a lamp. The lamp broke when it contacted the hardwood floor. Taleah shone her light down at its fragments for long enough to discern that it was made of two parts of antlers joined together by glue or small finish nails.

The remainder of the living room seemed to be decorated in the rustic motif, with mostly unpolished wood making up the surfaces of tables and chairs. Small pillows were tied to rocking chairs with string and cobwebs dangled from the ceiling. Taleah flipped the light in all directions. No one appeared to be there, but she walked down the narrow hall and peered into the two bedrooms just to be sure. She sighed heavily and trod back to the kitchen, where Emmanuel stood with hunched shoulders over an unpolished, unpainted wooden countertop.

He stared with wonder for several seconds until Taleah appeared next to him.

"These look like precious stones," he said.

Taleah gasped. She'd listened to her father tell his original tale of investigating the kidnappings all those years ago and remembered what he'd described as a sort of non-religious cross device with gemstones embedded in its wood. Now that she was staring at something resembling that image, horror struck her.

"What the hell?"

The countertop appeared to be carved and burnished with a wide, uneven arc traced by hand. Like a simple wheel, four spokes separated the arc into segments. At the corner point of each wedge, a wide divot appeared in the wood. Taleah grasped what she guessed was a rounded sapphire and inserted it into the one of the slots. It fit the gap with a little room to wiggle. She removed the stone and placed it back in its pile, took a yellow ruby, and tried the same technique. The stone fit one of the other holes better. As each stone was cut to a similar size, she guessed each of them fit. But there were five stones. Taleah glanced at all of them. One stone was larger than all the others. A shaded field of blue held an opalescent five-pointed star in its midst, and when she stared at it from different directions, it seemed to twinkle.

She swallowed hard and stepped away from the countertop. "I know this is the place. It feels so wrong."

"You can tell me what happened to you," Emmanuel said. "After I tell you."

She gaped at him and then retreated to the front door. Being well-adjusted to the darkness by now, she stepped outside and flicked the light off. She inserted the knife into her jeans and made her way to the approximate point where they'd first approached the cabin.

Emmanuel began his story by speaking plainly and lacing it with little emotion. "When I was young, a gang was trying to recruit me. My parents were not perfect in their practice of Islam, hardly ever prayed, but my mother always wore the hijab on her head. The gang was purist and they tried to get me to believe their point of view. I had read parts of the Quran here and there in school, but we didn't read it at home. My mother and father worked a lot, leaving me home with my brother.

"They came one day with guns, and they went through the house, taking away a lot. And they dragged me out in the street. They took off my shirt and beat me with stones until I was bruised and bloody. My father chased them out and they never came back. I learned later that they attacked and murdered a Christian woman who dared to show her face in public without a husband.

"And after that, we moved somewhere else in Amman, to be safe."

He stepped toward the car and turned around to face her. She breathed slowly, stepped forward, and tiptoed into the ditch. Pain and nervousness coursed through her veins. Her fingers vibrated around the flashlight handle. They stood there at the edge of the forest for almost a full minute before she could summon the nerve to speak.

Talking about it sent shivers down her spine and her emotion to break her voice, though tears didn't come.

"When I was a little girl, six, I think, my dad was involved in a crime scene where several women were kidnapped. The man held them in an underground bunker, chained to the walls, where he raped and tortured them. The cops and the FBI helped my dad track and discover who this person was. And then he got in a confrontation with the man after his traps almost burned him. He was on this ridge along a ravine when the man attacked. In the confusion, my dad got a shot off and it hit him. The man slid down into the ravine, disappeared, never to be seen again... until I was seventeen.

"I was dating this dork skateboarder boy at the time and playing softball, so I was waiting for him in the park one night. A man tied me in the back of his truck, threw out my phone, and drove me into the woods. He stashed me in a cave, told me it was all about my father and getting revenge for shooting him. My dad managed to track him down and found us, even though I'd tried to escape several times. He was just bigger and stronger, and he could throw me around like I was nothing. He hurt me. When my dad and his friend found us, they fought, and eventually Willis shot him dead.

"But not before Mindy showed up." Taleah's voice cracked, but she steadied it and went on. "She was the only survivor of the kidnapping eleven years before. And we sort of became friends after that, but we didn't really get to talking about our lives that much. We have a lot in common. To think that this madman has her here somewhere, abusing her and making her relive it all is... damn it... too close to home.

"My dad said he used gemstones to signify his victims."

"You think it might be him again?"

"No," Taleah said. "I don't know. He's dead. This FBI agent, Marks... he saw the body himself and he knows, even where they buried the bastard's remains."

"Then someone knows about him," Emmanuel summarized. "That's why we are here. To confront him?"

"I have to," Taleah said, choking back the agony. Her heart beat faster as she stood there shaking, feeling like the darkness and the pain were causing her to wilt into nothing. Emmanuel could perhaps try to reassemble the pieces, but without a picture of the whole, or what it was supposed to look like before Art tore it apart, he had nothing but his own predisposed opinion, which would never be enough.

She'd heard stories about Islam from people who claimed that it was a religion of violence, misogyny, and homophobia, but consciously doubted whether any of that were true. And here she was in the forest alone with a Muslim man, and they trusted one another.

Emmanuel was here for him when she needed him. Apart from her father, Emmanuel was turning out to be the most generous man she'd ever met.

Taleah removed the coin from her pocket and stared at it for a moment, feeling it in her fingers as though its copper were Christine's flesh. Christine couldn't have believed in all that superstition stuff, but Taleah understood her motive in telling the story. Taleah wasn't alone. She carried Christine in her heart. In her mind's eye, her image would undulate amongst the trees, giving her the emotion and energy she needed to march onward. The mad man had to be here in these woods somewhere, and Taleah was going to find him.

25

Entropy

G RAVEL sputtered and roared as Taleah inched along the old washboard road toward the mountain peak. After a rise in the road, it veered to the right, descended a gentle incline, and then twisted into a series of tight bends. The tiny rocks pelted off the insides of her wheel wells and the chassis continuously. She decided that keeping toward the center of the road where less erosion had taken place would make for a quieter and more comfortable ride, but the bumps and craters in the road made it feel as though her car were being torn apart piece by piece.

The headlights illuminated a wide swath, but the cone mostly stayed within the corridor of the road. Breaks and clearings in the trees were commonplace, offering less density for forest fires to burn and lending the area a much different feel than the Lochsa wilderness, where she'd been holed up before. The light scattered as she drove, reflecting off of tree trunks, rocks, rustic fence posts, and numerous other landmarks.

On the left side, a barbed wire fence trailed the road about a hundred feet from the valley of the narrow ditch that must have channeled storm waters to shield the road from runoff and mud. She kept the speed steady at near twenty-five miles per hour, which made the flora creep by slowly. More than fifteen minutes passed when the barbed wire seemed to have disappeared and the road veered northward. A spur cut off from the main road and quickly disappeared into the forest. At the fork, she pulled to a stop to decide which route to take.

The killer would have Mindy as isolated as possible, so it seemed stupid to lurk near what classified as a major route in this area. She flipped on the dome light and checked the compass. Trying to steady her hands and failing, she watched the needle spin around and sway wildly from side to side. She bit her lip and attempted to steady her muscles with her other hand, which only marginally helped.

When her muscles lurched, Emmanuel reached for the center console and clutched her hands. The needle centered on north, and Taleah studied the lay of the land. She'd lost sight of the mountain as it had disappeared into black. The spur route flitted off to the north while the main road swerved eastward. On the map, most of the green shading had been located due north of the dot labeled Atlanta.

"What do you think, go north?" she asked.

Emmanuel shrugged. "You decide."

Taleah groaned when shards of memory scraped at her mind. She remembered being shoved inside a camper shell in the back of the truck, gagged, and bound. A quick series of bumps had indicated a railroad crossing. She had been working at trying to loosen the ropes and thought she might have had a chance at escaping. Art, having underestimated her, had stopped to tighten her bonds, which in turn had disallowed using the broken rock to try to saw at the ropes. The ropes had burned as they sawed across her wrists and ankles as panicked tears had filled her eyes.

Then, the FBI had failed to track him down quickly enough and ended up using Reggie's trail to lead them to the group. Remembering this, Taleah's lip began to tremble. She bit at it so as to appear calm, but Emmanuel must have sensed the fires burning and altered his expression to one of compassion to counter the explosive venom filling her veins.

"You feel angry," he said matter-of-factly.

"What?" Taleah shook her head and began to navigate the narrower road more slowly than she'd sped along the main route. "That's... okay, that's true."

"I would feel the same," he noted. "But sometimes in a fight, the opposition expects you to react a certain way and base their strategy on it. You make it sound like this man knows you."

"I don't know who he is," Taleah admitted. "But you are right. What would you do?"

"If you need to be angry to fight, that is one thing. You need a plan for how to deal with when it gets you in trouble. A way of escape... a defensive approach."

Taleah swallowed and considered his wisdom. Then again, he'd never quite been in a situation like this with a man this horrifying. His first move would be to box her in so she couldn't escape and to use his raw strength to batter her senseless.

Emmanuel flashed a knowing look and proceeded to watch the forest roll by as Taleah struggled through turns on a steep grade. This route would have been a terminal forest service road, she guessed, and so unimproved that it hardly showed on any map. When a tight switchback curled toward the west, she glanced in the rearview mirror. So many stars glittered down in the dark that awe struck her fancy. In all the universe, earth was just a speck of dust in a cosmos so mind-numbingly vast that it would take eons to get from one edge to the other, even if one could theoretically travel faster than light. The sky was sparse yet teemed with tiny points of light millions of miles away. A world so unimportant in the grand design was vital to everything man knew, even down to his means of measuring time.

They didn't speak for several minutes. When the road straightened out and offered a more level stretch, she sped up. Even so, the miles faded away slowly. Ahead, what looked like a narrow game trail snaked off to the right along what appeared to be a narrow ridge. She stopped the car and shone her flashlight in the direction of its travel. The trail disappeared after crossing a shallow portion of the roadside ditch, but upon closer inspection, parallel trails existed. The trees along the ridge seemed to grow more densely at this altitude. Taleah shrugged as she worked the light back and forth until a glint of reflection caught her eye. She focused the light, adjusted her eyes and stared. The vehicle seemed to be parked behind a row of trees some three hundred yards away.

Together, they got out of the car, quietly closed the doors, and stared at each other. "It's probably a hunter," Taleah said, popping open the trunk. She uncorked the water bottle, took a sip, and then repacked it before flinging the bag over her shoulder. Emmanuel followed her lead. Even with only two bottles, the water seemed heavy on her back. She pushed her fingers into her pocket to clutch the knife and released it. Instead, she pulled the gun from her waistband and walked along the tire tracks through mud, underbrush, and dry grass. Emmanuel followed in the other tread.

Keeping the gun level was tricky with her nerves in the state they were, but she managed to steady her shoulders even against the mountain cold. According to her dashboard clock, it was a little after two in the morning. Hunters would be stupid to hunt in the middle of the night, unless this particular hunter was on an overnight trip with a sleeping bag. She surrendered to the idea until they got two thirds of the way to the parked vehicle. She looked up at it and nearly gagged. It matched the description the cops had given her mom almost perfectly.

"Oh my God," she whispered. "This is it."

They quickly erased the last hundred yards or so. With adrenaline pouring through her veins, she angled the flashlight down and examined the inside of the car. The floor mats were caked with dried mud and the seats with a haze of dust. A long knife lay on the passenger's side seat and a black plastic bag had been draped over the headrest as if it would be needed to dispose of whatever garbage needed hauled out. To her surprise, the door was unlocked. She wedged it open and peered into the bag. So far, only some rags and paper towels had been discarded, but when she focused the flashlight, her heart nearly stopped. The rags were stained with crimson blood. She sighed, closed the door, and grabbed the knife.

She slipped the knife into her jeans pocket as she continued to stare. On the floor beneath the passenger's front seat, a corner of white paper protruded into the circle of light. She grasped it with two fingers and pulled it loose. Before she managed to smooth it out, she knew what it was. The front of the page showed a photograph of Mindy Caldwell that looked as though it had been lifted from social media. She swallowed hard and flipped the paper over. On the backside of the sheet, a small dot marked the end of a hand-drawn line that zigzagged to the edge of the paper. The other end of the line forked in three directions with dots at the terminus of each. A large question mark was scrawled in the center of the page.

Without a second thought, she folded up the sheet of paper and stuffed it in her back pocket.

When she glanced up, her eyes fell on Emmanuel, who stood with his head hanging and his shoulders narrow. His flashlight was pointed to a spot at the edge of the ridge where what looked like a narrow dirt trail disappeared.

She looked in that direction and then back to his eyes. He flipped the light back and forth in sweeping arcs and swallowed. "Footprints," he mumbled.

Several different sets of prints were pressed into the mud near the car and Taleah guessed that all of them had been made near the same time. It didn't take much thought to connect the dots. The information didn't surprise her, either. She stared at the footprints for almost a full minute before silently coming to a decision on who had left them.

"Turn off the light," Taleah warned. "Or point it down. He might be able to see us up here."

Emmanuel conserved the light and watched Taleah's flashlight make circles on the ground. She left the doors to the vehicle open, approached the edge of the ridge, and then began to trek down the slope. A narrow, moon-shaped valley carved a divot in the mountains, which seemed to indicate that a water source existed at the foot of the mountain.

They paused every five minutes to drink, and then continued. Taleah kept the gun in her right hand, stepped over a fallen tree, darted between boulders, and then continued on her trajectory. Emmanuel stepped lighter and slowed the pace. Each time she noticed him falling behind, she would stop to take in the landscape, to drink, or to look at the compass. Emmanuel paused for a sip of water on the second stop, and they resumed their hike.

Checking for footprints in front of her every so often, Taleah followed the trail for perhaps as long as forty minutes. The blackness expanded when they reached the foot of the mountain. Taleah listened for the sound of running water and, hearing none, trekked onward as the footprints dug deeper into the dirt.

Taleah stopped, unscrewed the lid on her bottle and took a long drink. A few seconds later, Emmanuel moaned. He stood still and was using his hands to try to wedge his leg free from a crack between two rocks. She dropped the water and helped him wrestle it free.

"God, that looks like it hurts," she said.

"Yes... ouch!"

When his foot came out of his shoe, she reached down and crumpled the leather so that she could jar it loose. She handed the shoe to Emmanuel, but he'd leaned against the rock and groaned. She flipped the light to his ankle and found that a piece of twine was knotted around his leg.

"What the... how did that happen?"

He shook his head and looked up as Taleah flipped the knife open and cut the twine. "It is sprained, I think. I can walk."

He barely finished that short sentence when orange flames flourished out of nowhere. He screamed as the fireball licked at his feet. Instinct flung him from the rock and propelled him into a sideways run paralleling the foot of the hill. She chased him, but the flames followed, raced right past her and consumed Emmanuel's leg. He fell into a heap at her feet, moaning and slithering like a snake in the mud.

"Emmanuel, stop!"

A strand of twine had wrapped itself around his free leg, and the flames were starting to devour his pants. He screamed and rolled around until the burning twine loosened itself. Taleah withdrew the knife and carefully cut the rest of it away as the flames bit at her hands. Emmanuel groaned again and pain seared across Taleah's flesh.

She'd sacrificed her hand to the fire to get Emmanuel free. The pain seemed to boil as a new strain of anger flashed through her like a mushroom of yellow and orange flame. Taleah gulped, stepped forward, and then fell painfully to the ground. She'd tripped over a rock. Drawing in a breath of air before righting herself, she took in the unmistakable aroma of gasoline. The dry grass in front of her was soaked with it. She flung herself to her feet as Emmanuel struggled to right himself. Before she could steady herself against a tree, a spark flashed, igniting the grass. She screamed, readied herself, and sprinted through the towering flames.

Pain clawed at her legs as she ran. Emmanuel staggered behind her, limping and grimacing as he ran. In the confusion, the mass of footprints disappeared. Taleah lost her bearings and ran in the path of least resistance, which just happened to coincide with a gentle downslope.

From ahead, cries, groans, and screams penetrated the night. Taleah stopped suddenly, looked all around her and realized that she was trapped in a small valley buttressed by wooded mountains. With an injured companion, the landscape acted like a noose. The only way out of the trap was to fight it, or the madman would kill both of them.

"Taleah," Emmanuel rasped. He knelt down in the grass and looked back at the flames, which hesitated to lick at the trees. "We cannot get away."

The voices sounded again, somehow even louder. The spasm of her muscles allowed her little time to think and to react. Before her was a choice. She could try to escape and meet her own fate, or she could intervene to save Mindy and the man she was with and suffer the consequences.

Taleah gulped hard, grasped Emmanuel's hand, and pulled him to his feet. Emmanuel pulled his knife from his pocket and held it out for the imminent attack. Taleah placed the killer's knife in her pocket, withdrew the gun, and held it in both hands before they advanced into whatever hell awaited. Her hands shook, vibrating with the viscosity of adrenaline, terror, and rage. She perched an agonizing frown on her face as her lips twitched. She blinked as the smoke prodded at her eyeballs.

"You're not getting away," she screeched into the night so forcefully that it made her throat hurt. "The FBI is going to be here any minute. You're surrounded."

Muted shivers erupted from the dark behind a thick group of ponderosas. She swallowed and waited several seconds for a reply.

"Do you hear me? Come out! You son of a bitch!"

"Taleah," Emmanuel gasped.

A gargled scream reached up like a tempest in the night, clawing at the stars above with a gravelly churn that mimicked the cry of an eagle. "No! Run away! Save your... *Aauuugh*!"

Taleah's blood filled with venom. She bit her lip, steadied the gun, and began to step forward as Emmanuel limped along. Nothing could have prepared her for what happened next.

26
Gathering

PAIN encircled her ankle as she stepped closer to the source of the screams and cries. Some unknown force propelled her forward while her leg was being jerked backward violently. When her face hit the dirt, the rope dragged her away from the trees into a clearing. The impact jarred the gun from her hands. When her backward momentum stopped, she reached for the knife with precious few seconds to spare.

Anger surged within her, stirred with alarm and terror. With her fingers trembling, Taleah gripped the knife and cut the rope from her ankle. The shredding sound of screams pierced the night, spreading icy terror through every chamber of her body. Emmanuel had disappeared from sight, but she knew the screams were his.

By the time she released her ankle, fire formed a barrier between her and the spot where she'd been standing before the trap dragged her away. The flames towered overhead, licking and tearing at the stars above, which seemed to cower in the orange glow. Taleah's first motive was to find the gun.

She forced herself to her feet, swallowed, and sprinted through the curtain of flame as a new batch of hurt seared at her arms and waist. The glint of flame reflected on polished steel caught her attention immediately, but a shadow that moved across the ground got to it first. Taleah witnessed only the limb of a silhouette reach for its handle.

In order to protect herself, she widened her trajectory to loop around the stranger. At that instant, Emmanuel yelped in pain. "Take it!"

She slowed, grabbed the pistol, and sprinted for the trees as the adrenaline surged through her veins. She spread a frown across her face as she ran. Her footsteps jaunted over uneven ground, and she nearly tripped on a protruding root, which planted just enough surprise to make her look down. That was a big mistake.

Her chest collided with low-hanging branches, and she hit the ground on the recoil, dropping the gun again. The muted breathing and whimpering of several victims in agony wisped into her ears like vapors rising off a pot of boiling water. She scrambled on the ground for the gun, oblivious to the scene that unfolded around her. When she struggled to her knees, horror enveloped her.

Within the trees, a cool, yellow flame cast morphing shadows on the tree trunks. It was only bright enough to illuminate basic shapes and the faces of those present if they lay close enough to the source of light.

Several bodies writhed on the ground, bound by ropes. Her heart sank when her eyes fell on a pair of girls, naked and covered in blood. A bound woman lay next to them, her eyes flooded with tears and terror. The madman stood over a lanky figure, whose face was mostly obscured by a burlap sack. He grunted in horror as the killer huddled over him, holding a gallon of water directly over the man's head. The water glugged out of the container, fell onto his face, and filled his mouth. He gargled and screamed between horrific gasps.

The three figures that lay next to him whimpered and groaned. Before she could decide what to do, she made the mistake of looking at the rest of them. The woman lay halfway on her side, facing the girls as they cried. A gauze of blood covered her scalp and large portions of her hair looked as though it had been ripped from her head. Taleah recoiled and stared at the two girls.

Each of them was tied to the ground via long wooden stakes and sturdy rope. One of them, a teenager, screamed when she saw Taleah. Her voice shredded the atmosphere like a team of raging sirens. Taleah looked away and groaned. Their bodies were covered in mud and blood. Their wrists stained purple as the ropes burned across their skin. Neither of them could so much as plead for help.

The water jug hit the ground with a giant slosh, and Taleah spun the gun toward the killer as he lunged at her. She squeezed the trigger and fired two quick shots at his chest, but her hands were shaking so badly that both bullets missed their target.

The man lowered his shoulder and plowed into her headfirst, landing on top of her. She howled as he hit her in the face repeatedly. The gun bounced out of her hand as he battered her. The agony slammed her face and skull with the weight of boulders. Taleah winced and balled her fists so tight that blood squeezed through her fingers. She spun her neck, kicked at him, and managed to get him to back off enough that she could slash his face with two easy blows.

They didn't faze him. He attacked with vicious zeal as one fist collided with a tree. He growled into the darkness as his long, curly hair slashed against her face. At this instant, realization crowded her mind. Art was not dead. He was pummeling her. His fist struck twin blows into her abdomen. She shrunk from the attacks, curled her legs up and withstood several brutal hits to her back.

Emmanuel's scream penetrated her ears just as Art's attacks ceased. Emmanuel threw the knife wildly. It grazed Art's shoulder, ripping a fresh hole in his tee shirt and sparking an expanding spot of blood. He spun around in place and absorbed Emmanuel's staggering charge. With his stance offering the perfect leverage, he easily lifted Emmanuel high above his head. Emmanuel grunted as his back struck the bark. He fell to a heap and emitted a low groan just as quickly as he'd run to attack.

As Art turned his focus back to her, Taleah recoiled, backing against the tree, and managed to kick out her foot just in time. Art's knee collided with her foot. He winced as he regained his balance. In her split-second window, she dove for where the gun must have lay, but missed. Art pounced on her back with a fury she could only imagine in her most brutal nightmares. He tore at her clothes. She felt the fabric of her shirt gradually give way, spun herself to her back, and formed a hard angle with her knee. He pounced on her again, but her knee struck his groin with just enough force to cause his entire body to tremor with pain.

A look of surprise trailed across his face as she struggled back to her feet. Her fist closed around the knife as she regained balance. While he bent over, she feigned another kick to his knees, and instead plunged the knife into his shoulder. He rolled away and howled in pain as Taleah darted toward him.

Her attack didn't strike with enough speed or force to avoid being countered. In a naturally defensive posture, he reached out his hands, grasped her clothes, and absorbed a weak swipe at his back. She felt his blood in her hands as he flung her upward, over his shoulder, just as the knife jarred loose. Her momentum somersaulted her onto the younger girl, who yelped in pain upon impact. The girl shrieked as the knife clawed at her naked skin. Taleah rolled over and struggled to her feet just as Art's fist closed around her throat.

Violently, he lifted her off the ground, spun at his waist and drove her into a tree trunk, facing the other victim. The knots and broken-off branches gnawed on her back like fangs. She winced in pain, flailing her arms and legs wildly as she screamed.

Art growled at her. "How's daddy?"

"You..." She let her voice drop an octave and felt her lip quiver as she filled every syllable with unchecked contempt. "You killed him."

"He was so weak. Weaker than you."

"I'm not weak," she rasped, glaring straight into the dark of his eyes. "You are."

The killer stared back, loosened his free hand and grazed her face with the back of his fingers, almost lovingly. "I knew you were going to come."

"Piece of *shit,*" she whispered. Her trachea felt as though it were being sealed shut. She kicked and spat at him, but he didn't so much as flinch.

"You don't know me. Let me introduce myself. I'm Art Rassine."

She nearly choked on her words. "Art Rassine is *dead!*"

He laughed mercilessly, flexed his arm muscle, and lifted her up higher, with his free hand still grazing her face.

"Foolish bravery. And everyone thinks they have the answer. That Willis character killed an imitation. What was he called? The shadow? He failed to anticipate what your pathetic father hurled at him. And it was his own rage that was his undoing. When your father shot him on that ridge... I was there, but I fled. Hiding for eighteen years does things to you. That man was a fraud. I am the real Art Rassine."

"I hate you," she rasped painfully. "You underestimated me, too." Before anything else could happen, she opened her mouth and snapped at him. His reflex kicked in fast enough for him to retract his free hand, but her teeth caught his flesh anyway. She bit down as hard as she could, swatted at his face with all her might, and unleashed a throat-scorching roar.

Art backed away, lowered her, and then turned to his right. He tripped backward and dropped her on her knees. Emmanuel was on his knees, wildly slashing the knife back and forth. One of his swipes cut across the madman's leg. He kicked Emmanuel away with enough force to send him scurrying against another tree. When Art had Emmanuel on his heels, he gave up on him, turned his attention on Taleah, and backhanded her just as she got to her feet.

His knuckles collided with her face. She ducked on instinct, spun her ankles, and dove at his feet. She formed fists and pounded at his legs and knees until her hands hurt. Art grasped her shirt, nearly ripping it clean off. He gripped her by the bra strap and flung her away from the trees. The world spun as she flipped backward and landed on her butt. She yelped as the pain dug into her backside but was not about to give up.

Rather than deal with Emmanuel, Art sprinted at her in effort to spear her again. The crown of his head spiked against her elbow as she put as much up-force as she could manage behind her parry. The position felt similar to swinging a bat. The momentum caused him to stagger. She bit at him and clawed until he was forced into retreat.

This time, she didn't relent. She crashed a fist into his eyeball, kneed his groin, and then slapped him with her other hand.

"I expected this from you," he grunted. "You're nothing like your father."

"You never fought him," Taleah gritted. Her lip twitched as the fire caught in her eyes.

Emmanuel lurched back to his feet, and screaming, half-limped at him. Art anticipated this attack quickly enough to adjust. He spun to face Emmanuel, lowered his shoulder and hoisted Emmanuel over his head. Emmanuel bit at his ear, but only managed to nip a fold of flesh. He growled as he slammed Emmanuel's head against a tree. When he collapsed, Art pummeled him with repeated blows to the head.

Emmanuel groaned, folded over, and lay still. The distraction offered Taleah enough time to scan the ground. The light from the little fire glinted off the metal of the gun. She turned and dove for it just as Art balled his fists for one final assault.

She rolled over in agony as the madman pulled at a root. He ripped it out of the ground and slung it at her. Its jagged end smashed against her scalp as her fingers grazed the cold steel of the weapon. Again and again, Art slammed the root down on her. She fought back by punching his back, with her free hand, focusing on the bleeding area to inflict maximum pain.

Art groaned as she struck at the tear in his flesh from Emmanuel's knife. She hammered it repeatedly as he landed the root on her head again. She staggered backward and grasped the handle of the gun behind her back.

Instead of paying attention to that hand, Art kept pounding on her skull until she was dizzy. The blaze of his attacks kept up until she'd managed to bring the gun all the way up to the back of his head.

He sensed it in an instant and attempted to end her life before she could react. Instead of hesitating, she angled the gun slightly away from herself, pressed it against Art's skull, and pulled the trigger. The shot roared through the canopy like thunder as the bullet whisked past her face and kicked up a cloud of dust nearby. A shower of blood spattered onto her face and Art collapsed in an instant. She stood up, hovered the gun over him, and squeezed the trigger again. The bullet ripped into his back. She raised it to fire again, but instead stood there trembling in rage as the victims stared on in shock. Emmanuel limped toward her and closed his hand around her wrist.

She twitched and trembled with agony and ire as Emmanuel coaxed her into dropping the gun. "It is okay," he said. "You got him."

Taleah collapsed in his arms and sobbed deeply and dryly. Her arms, legs and head hurt so badly that she feared passing out. If Christine had been wise enough to pack aspirin, she'd take a dose and offer one to Emmanuel as well.

Rassine's body lay motionless as she glanced at him. Together, they stood up and worked to free the captive family. Taleah didn't have to ask who they were. They were the Kleinmans. How they ended up here, she could only guess at, but there was not enough time to ask questions. They were suffering. The father was on the edge of death from torture and the girls shivered. Sympathy and rage tangled in her mind until nothing remained of either. Life could go on, but the pain confronted Taleah at the last second.

Her heart sank and her knees buckled. Mindy Caldwell was nowhere to be seen.

27

Illusion

IT should have hurt less, but somehow the anguish only grew deeper. Ending the nightmare and bringing Art Rassine to justice was like a pinprick in a void of black, but its promise flickered in the chaos and burned out, leaving only the scars of bitterness. Both literally and figuratively, she had blood on her hands, and killing the killer could never cleanse them.

She shook uncontrollably for nearly a full minute while Emmanuel, struggling to stand on his own, propped her up and offered the cooling effect of his embrace. She could not bring herself to glance at the body. If she could somehow vaporize his image from her mind, she thought, she would do it in the blink of an eye.

Emmanuel seemed to teeter and shiver in the cold, but Taleah couldn't see his face. When she opened her eyes, she found herself peering into the terror emblazoned on the girls' expressions. She at last wedged herself free from Emmanuel's grip, staggered, and approached the younger girl. She knelt down and placed a hand on her forehead, which had gathered crimson specks and a narrow stream of blood, which had begun to congeal. A ring of purple encircled her neck, touched with red skin. Above her left breast, a ragged puncture oozed blood. Not knowing what to do, Taleah pressed her hand against the wound as the blood leaked between her fingers.

"Are you okay? What's your name?" Though she meant to gently whisper her questions, they came out like dry rasps. Art had damaged Taleah's throat so badly that speaking meant turmoil and pain.

"Chloe Kleinman." Her voice broke into a tortured cry. Tears spilled onto her cheek, and she writhed against the cold. As if on instinct, she attempted to cover her breasts with her arms in the presence of the strangers.

"You're cold," she said. "Where are your clothes?"

She glanced upward, rolling her eyes backward as if to indicate that her clothing had been discarded somewhere behind her. Emmanuel limped in that direction, disappearing behind trees, and then returned empty-handed. He shrugged and searched Taleah for cues.

"She can have mine," Chloe's mother said slowly, with a hushed voice. She struggled against the ropes and fell still.

Still clutching the knife, Emmanuel limped to her and began to saw at the ropes. "You're Chloe's mother. What is your name?"

"And Melissa's," she amended. "It's Kendall. This is my husband, Chuck."

"You help my daughters first," Chuck coughed.

Chloe had let her head roll back. She breathed heavily, struggling to get every breath out. The younger of the two daughters, she had received the worst of Art's wrath. Taleah studied her face, where a dozen strands of hair appeared to be uprooted and matted against her face. Confusion and torment doused her eyes. Taleah turned to her and asked her how to help, but Chloe could not utter a reply. Instead, she coughed, turned her head, and stared blankly into the eyes of her mother.

The light seemed to fade from her eyes as Taleah watched, horrified. She had landed on Chloe moments ago, she understood. Chloe reached across the dirt and the mud for her mother's hand, touched her fingers and issued one last breath.

In panic, Taleah pulled back Chloe's hair, cleared her lips of blood, and attempted to give her mouth-to-mouth. Pressing on the girl's bare chest, she heaved and cried and ached. *Please don't go,* she pleaded.

But Kendall Kleinman had already conceded to the most brutal truth. There was no saving her. Taleah pressed on for more than two minutes, unsuccessfully. The injuries were too much for her. Taleah guessed that Chloe was about twelve years old. So many experiences remained for her to live, but nothing could stop her from releasing her soul into the wild and retreating to that mystical place in the sky where all was love and peace.

Taleah once again collapsed next to Chloe, pried her eyes open, and stared at Kendall's partially pulverized face. "I'm so sorry," she rasped.

Kendall could only nod.

"God," Chuck coughed. He bent at the knees and attempted to roll toward his wife, whom Emmanuel was just getting loose.

When she was free from her bindings, Kendall started to pull her arms out of her long sleeves so that Melissa could be comforted.

An idea came to Taleah's mind as she shook her head at Kendall. She looked at Emmanuel and grunted something only half audible. "Stay and keep an eye on them. I'm going to find my bag. I have a change of clothes that might fit Melissa."

"Let me go instead," Emmanuel pleaded.

She shook her head and stared at his legs. She suspected that the sprain that slowed him was severe enough that he should refrain from moving it. Letting him walk seemed like a foolish proposition.

Taleah turned away and jogged to where she'd left the bag when the fire nearly burned her. A hundred yards had seemed to go by much faster when approaching the danger, but now that she fled, every step seemed to linger on the doorstep of infinity.

The flames danced above her backpack as she approached it. Her head pounded when she slung the bag over her shoulder. Returning to the thicket of trees, she pulled the clothing out piece by piece and sized them up. The pants would be a squeeze, as Melissa appeared to be fuller in the hips and longer than Taleah. Emmanuel had already cut her free.

Taleah pushed the ropes away, knelt down, and began pushing the girl's legs into the jeans. The jeans were a little too tight for Melissa to snap them. Emmanuel helped her lift her arms and torso so that Taleah could help pull the shirt over her head. Melissa sat on her own, knelt over her sister, and moaned.

More tears splashed onto Taleah's cheek. Finally, she felt ready to ask the question that had tiptoed at the edge of her mind for the last few minutes. "Did you see another woman? A little taller than me?"

Melissa nodded and pointed. "I think… I think she got away? The… he chased after her."

By the direction Melissa indicated, Taleah guessed that the trail was about fifteen degrees off the one on which she and Emmanuel had arrived.

She shuddered and looked in that direction. There, the trees swayed denser against the night. A sense of foreboding punctured her. She silently wondered what time it was, hoping that the sun would come up soon. Weariness had begun to massage her legs and her head so forcefully that she felt as though she were going to pass out. Using clipped sentences, she instructed Emmanuel to stay with the family.

If Taleah guessed right, Mindy couldn't be far. She would have seen the fire, heard the screams, and come running. Excitement at first bit at her heels and then faded as a dark reality dawned on her. She fought the tears for as long as she could. Frantic, she called for her.

"Mindy! It's me, Taleah."

The darkness flushed through her mind as the trees issued their coded replies. They held a secret that Taleah could only uncover by traversing deeper into the canopy. Her trajectory grew wild. The slope of the land told her that she was approaching the bottom reaches of the ridge, but by now she trod through forest more than two football fields from where she and Emmanuel had originally descended.

Nearly a half hour passed. The pain grew bleaker with every step.

She shrieked when she heard the howl of a wolf far away. Spinning as the chill raced down her spine, she tripped on a protruding root and hit the ground. Her knee collided with a rock, and she clutched at it, groaning.

The root she tripped on appeared in her peripheral vision, but its image began to blur and morph into the shape of a human hand. The soil around the fingers was soft and unstable. Taleah clawed at it with her fingers until she'd revealed more of the wrist. When she pulled, the limb came loose. She dug at the earth until she hit what felt like a torso.

Working at the dirt feverishly, she ignored the pain. When she rolled over the corpse and cleared the dirt off the face, she nearly swallowed her heart. The face was easily recognizable as that of Mindy Caldwell.

The tears came freely as she hunched over Mindy's lifeless body until her image blurred into a field of tan. She moaned as she pulled Christine's coin from her pocket. The arm that was still attached to Mindy's shoulder lay flat against the ground. She pried her fingers open, placed the coin in her palm, and then closed it. Bending down further, she let her tears wet Mindy's soil-covered flesh, kissed the dirt on the back of her hand, and rasped three words that dug deeper into her soul than any sentence she ever thought she'd utter. "For good luck."

She glanced back several times as she cleared her eyes, making her way down the slope and into the pocket of trees where the Kleinman family mourned the loss of their beloved Chloe.

By the time she reached them, she concluded that the bright star she'd witnessed near the top of the mountain was actually an aircraft of some kind. The flames from the traps still licked at the sky. Taleah watched as the light attempted to settle on the horizon before disappearing behind the trees near the funneled end of the small valley.

She breathed deeply, pressed against her head, and found Emmanuel sitting on the ground. Kendall and Chuck were examining his ankle and prodding at the bones.

Taleah didn't say anything, but Chuck looked up and swallowed, then coughed. "Brave young man. I had a horse that wouldn't walk for three days after a sprain. This is precautionary just in case it's fractured."

"Can you find me a branch or a stick?" Kendall said without looking up.

Taleah disappeared behind the trees, her mind and heart racing. A long stick lay on the ground near a giant ponderosa trunk. Taleah gripped it, snapped it in half, and carried both ends back into the grove.

Kendall wound part of a rope around one hand as Chuck held Emmanuel's leg steady. He winced as she fit the stick to his ankle and then began lashing the stick to his ankle.

Taleah shrugged when Emmanuel looked up, his eyes searching.

Melissa asked the question that Emmanuel seemed to be considering. "Did you find who you were looking for?"

Taleah nodded slowly and knelt down in the dirt near where the bullet had left Art's skull and plunged into the ground. His body lay motionless like a boulder four feet away from Emmanuel. She glared at Art's body and let the rage course through her until she shook with fury.

She writhed closer on the ground, pushing until she was inches from the huge wound on the back of his head. "I hope it hurt, you son of a *bitch!* I hope the bullet lit your skull on fire as inched its way through your cranium. Piece of SHIT!"

Mellissa appeared at her side, wrapped a bloody, sweaty arm around her shoulder, and stared at him. She took several moments to form a sentence and spoke clearly as the weariness crept into her eyes. "He isn't worth it anymore," she said. "Let go."

Taleah cowered in the shadow, buried her face in her palms and sobbed. Even in victory the bitter taste of defeat plagued her senses and pressed poison into her heart. Few of them talked for what felt like a half an hour. At long last, Chuck and Emmanuel looked up toward the horizon. Voices clamored through the wilderness, approaching fast. And then, somewhere behind the visitors, the sound of ATV motors drifted amongst them.

Taleah lowered her face and waited.

Paramedics, police, and FBI officials began appearing. The nightmare was at its breaking point. She instructed them to load Chloe and Emmanuel onto the vehicle first. If there was enough room, Chuck and Kendall could ride along. Taleah needed to stay behind. She insisted upon it until a familiar voice brought a fleeting sense of warmth.

She halfway looked up when Agent Marks knelt beside her. She wasn't interested in talking to him yet, but it would be a necessity. Should she really confront him for his failure? The desire to rip into him touched at the base of her brain until it faded away into the dark. She sat there until the horizon began to glow with a faint blue.

Agent Marks clutched her shoulder, offered her a sip of water, and then stared at the changing skyline, where the wash of twinkling stars faded into rising sun.

28
Realism

O NE paramedic and a small team of police officers stayed behind. The officers communicated in short, clipped sentences while photographing and collecting evidence from the scene, while the paramedic performed a quick examination on Taleah. He shone a light in her eyes and asked her at least a half-dozen questions about her pain level. But the pain didn't matter anymore, she decided.

"You need to get to the emergency room," the paramedic said. "Bruises can heal, but twisted ankles, burns, concussions... those are too serious to ignore."

"I'm not done with her yet," Agent Marks protested. "Stay here and give her a ride in the helicopter when we're done."

Rather than argue, the paramedic stuffed his instruments into his bag and, issuing a gruff *humpf,* began to examine the scene, where the team of investigators congregated.

Marks stood, sighed at Taleah, and offered a hand to help her up. Her head ached as she stood and in the ten minutes since she'd sat against the tree, the soreness had begun to creep into her legs and arms. She winced as Marks led her by the arm away from the scene. He retreated deeper into forest, until the lights from the investigating team offered little more than a haze that seemed to linger on thin air.

Breathing in and out deeply, she swallowed hard, as if to remove the anger from her throat so that she could talk. Instead of speaking in her normal voice, what came out was alien and dismal, a rasp that felt as though it could have shredded her larynx.

"You're going to chide me for coming out here and finding him while your investigation missed its chance to catch him."

He shook his head and sat down on a fallen log that rested about a foot off the ground, offering a high bench. She hoisted herself onto the tree trunk next to him and looked into his pale face. The expression surprised her in that it looked so meek, but he was good at faking emotion to great effect and she wasn't going to let it work on her.

"No. You were right."

"What?" She was mocking him. "For once in his life, the great Agent Torrance Marks admits he's not infallible. That'll be on the eleven o'clock news."

"My mistake was not taking the reins from BPD sooner. Without Sergeant Bones, you wouldn't even be here."

Taleah almost choked. His sincerity seemed all at once muted, revealing the true Agent Marks, a calculating conman willing to play mind games to get what he wanted. "You... bastard," she breathed.

Again, he nodded. He tapped his toe and kicked a pinecone as he built up his next sentence. "Really good work, by the way. Beating us up here. But he could have killed you."

"Me? It's all about me? You don't know anything about me. I saved lives last night. He was going to pick them off one by one."

"It was all about you from the beginning," Marks said. "You know it."

"Was it? That says something about you. Should have retired when your partner did. At least he knew what he was doing." She cut her sentences brutally short, but she didn't care. The pain in her head ebbed and then reemerged before she could establish a resilient emotion that didn't vanish after everything Marks said. Whatever game he was playing, he excelled at it enough to coax even unwilling participants into the mix.

He sighed, breathed heavily, and continued. "He knew about you. He knew about your history with him. How to exploit it. If I were a betting man, I'd say he never truly wanted you, but he wanted your father so badly that getting you in the process wouldn't have been a negative. Appears as though his miscalculation was his undoing."

"He didn't miscalculate... anything," she said through gritted teeth. She was able to amend her statement before Agent Marks started to speak. "Funny thing is, he said I wouldn't recognize him. That we'd never met. Maybe *that's* your biggest mistake."

"Tell me what else he said."

She shrugged and looked off into the darkness, where the morning dew had begun to glisten on the leaves of undergrowth from the blue light, which began to sharpen the edges of the nightmare to construct an even uglier landscape. "That he was Art Rassine... The real Art Rassine."

"That's interesting."

"Interesting?" She raised her voice so loud that it startled the wildlife. She balled her fists and slammed one of them into the log at her side. "It's not *interesting* when people die. Your malfeasance is the reason. They should fire you before you find another set of dead bodies and call it interesting."

"Taleah, please calm down."

"You can go to hell! Incompetent and sophomoric. Just get out, and take your *interesting* investigation with you. I don't care what you have to say."

He seemed to snarl, but his voice remained flat. "Maybe, then, you should just let me talk."

She watched him rub his eyes and curled her lips. The fire in her eyes intensified as the anger washed deeper into her chest, rumbling like heavy boulders slumping at a hillside. "You look tired," she said, feigning concern.

"I haven't slept," he admitted. "It has been a long night."

"Poor you," Taleah mocked. "Driving all night, almost getting killed, finding your friends buried in the woods... not the same thing at all."

"I know you're angry," he said.

His voice seemed cold, but if she wanted to, she could exploit the crack and explode into a tirade that would make a normal man feel tiny. Instead, she used it as a kind of salve to her wounded psyche. If she reacted reasonably, he would allow his lack of candor to fester inside him until it began to decay his soul. She'd never see the spoils of such a tactic, she knew, but the imagination would more than suffice.

"Tell me about it then," she said. "How?"

"How did the real Art Rassine happen to know about you?" He cleared his throat, straightened his back, and continued. "He was already onto Reggie before Reggie even knew what he was dealing with. See, Art Rassine had a crime of opportunity when he witnessed a car accident where a young woman had been spooked by wildlife. In her attempt to avoid crashing with it, she went off the road. She survived, of course, but he decided he would take her to the Harrison ranch and patch her up. But moving her alone would have been enough to kill her. But he liked the sensation of being in charge so much, he decided to kidnap more women. And then he turned it into a game, basically daring Adams County to try to piece the clues together. Turns out, they needed Reggie. He didn't plan on Coles and me."

She wiped something wet from her head, thinking that a tree had dropped dew into her hair. When she examined her hand, the scent of diluted blood filled her nostrils. That would have been Art's brain matter, she guessed.

"But he started to look at Reggie almost like a worthy opponent. And he outwitted him with his traps and clever planning in that clearing where he fought your father for the first time, and nearly killed Willis.

"What your father... what we didn't understand, is that there was another person in the forest that night. Big brother and little brother. The little brother always emulated what the big brother did, which irritated big brother. Little brother thought he was helping, but big brother had a plan to let him escape and hunt him down later. Instead, little brother caught up with him on the ridge where your father shot him.

"And then little brother wanted revenge. Took him years of planning. Even did business with some seedy people to get what he needed. And what better way of getting revenge than taking Reggie's only daughter and torturing her?"

"So you let the whole thing get out of control over mistaken identity. I thought the FBI had resources that no other law enforcement agency could ever dream of."

"Everything was identical because they were twins," he explained.

"I've seen that explanation on TV," she said shortly. "How many times do you people have to be fooled by it before you expect it?"

"It actually doesn't happen that often," he said. "Television shows are looking for unique angles and they know what sells. Real police work is not so easily fooled."

"And yet, here we are," Taleah jabbed.

He nodded, rested his hands on his lap, and slumped his shoulders. Understanding seemed to push forth into his expression by the second, which caused Taleah to squirm. Instead of letting the notion get to her head, however, she planted a frown on her face, gulped, and listened to him continue to drone on.

"Rassine, of course, had a foil when he learned that his brother was planning something. But that all changed when Willis killed the little brother. Now, all of a sudden, he's exposed, and there are loose ends to wrap up. Even though everyone assumed the case was closed, he knew something would come to light soon. And it did. The Kleinman family had found a key piece of evidence on their property after James McAwan befriended them. McAwan was already in contact with Art Rassine. And Jesse Alvarez confirmed it.

"Alvarez, then, was playing both sides, because he knew you. He gave Rassine info on you, and then turned around and attempted to obstruct Rassine, which also turned out to help him, when Alvarez called you.

"If Rassine had figured that out, he would have killed Alvarez, too."

"That's all... *interesting,*" she said, coughing. "Then how did Mindy get involved?

"Mindy Caldwell was one of Rassine's targets from the beginning. Turns out that Mindy wasn't really dating the second murder victim. They were wingmen, so to speak. Ms. Caldwell helped him meet men, while she met some people, too. A manager said she saw Ms. Caldwell flirting with at least one woman and two men on separate occasions."

"When McAwan alerted Rassine to that," it made finding her easier. "But it just so happened that the second victim already knew about his bomb plot, which was an attempt to kill both Reggie and Willis. He became another loose end."

She breathed out and watched the sky tinge yellow on the horizon through the trees. "Is that all?"

"McAwan and Alvarez are both going to prison, possibly for the rest of their lives. Since you killed Art Rassine, the deals they wished to make are no longer necessary."

"Don't you want to know where Mindy's body is?" Hearing herself say those words somehow felt hollow, so devoid of emotion that her brain would have to fill in the cracks. The resultant chill raced up and down her spine until she shivered. Even after years, she really didn't know much about

Mindy's life after she helped Reggie confront the fake Art Rassine. Her apparent preferences didn't really surprise her.

"Can you lead me to her?"

"Yes," Taleah said. "I think your agents will want a closer look with forensics. I don't want to see her face again, but I can lead you to her. I guess I do owe you that."

"Or you could be charged with obstruction," Marks said.

Taleah wanted to laugh, but her head hurt and sorrow enveloped her soul. "Don't make threats you aren't prepared to back up," Taleah shot.

"Knowing when to make threats is an innate tool in an investigation," he said. "It's like playing poker. If you can get a subject to believe you hold cards that you don't really have, you can bait him into making mistakes."

"Do you normally use it on witnesses?"

"Only when the witness is a possible suspect, too," Marks admitted. "But it's not really different than how the press treats witnesses. You play to their emotions, too. The sympathy. And unconvinced masses eat it up, because you are also appealing to their innate biases."

She shrugged. "You have it wrong. Reporters report the truth, even if it makes some people uncomfortable."

"Not interested in arguing with you," he said.

"I'm not *interesting?* That's funny coming from you."

"Lead me to Ms. Caldwell," he said. "Please."

She stood up, stretched her back, and gingerly stepped away from the log. Their trek would take about twenty minutes, she guessed, and her muscles already ached vigorously enough to make the journey exert excruciating pain. Marks grasped her shoulder from time to time to prevent her collapsing.

Her bones ached and her head hurt, making the walking more difficult. Once or twice, she nearly collapsed under her own weight. She retreated against a tree and leaned over panting and groaning before continuing.

He navigated the rocks, the downed trees, and the mud with surprising skill. Almost twenty minutes later, Taleah was able to recall the lay of the forest from memory. She stopped about a hundred feet short of the loose dirt where she'd dug up Mindy Caldwell's body. Agent Marks disappeared into the thicket to examine it and take pictures, allowing her mind to rest. She sat down on a fragment of a broken pine trunk, buried her face in her hands and gave up the burden to emotion. It all swirled within her so viciously that she needed an avenue to release it. The rage had reached a boiling point. Frustrated tears spilled onto her cheeks as she writhed. She screamed into the crook of her elbow to muffle the sound, balled her fists, and pummeled the nearest tree so hard that it made her knuckles bleed.

Agent Marks would probably hear her and note the soreness of her hands but it didn't matter anymore. Suddenly, her father and Rebekah occupied an entirely different plane of reality that only intersected the one she'd wandered onto. She didn't know how or when she'd make it back to a normal world, but the entire concept by now seemed so foreign that normalcy would have been a hallucinogenic drug. For now, she didn't want to think about anything but Christine. Maybe she'd save her reality from caving in on itself, to prop her up over a circling abyss. She'd need it, but she also needed to speak with Emmanuel, to at least thank him for helping.

Emmanuel was the unlucky one. She had dragged him into the mud with her thinking that he'd be a lifeline, but his life would now be altered beyond recognition. She could agree with him for not wanting to see her, but he also knew what he was getting into. His motivation remained a mystery to her, other than the fact that his coworker had been killed and he wanted closure. If his idea was dating, she would have to push him away because Christine meant everything to her.

The introspection on Christine made her remember the coin. All she had to do was turn it three times for good luck, but the luck came not from the coin, but from remembering her. It gave her hope and something else to fight for. If Agent Marks were examining Mindy's body, he'd certainly find the coin and think of it as another clue. But the clue would only lead him to further understanding about Taleah, and Taleah wasn't even interesting. Still, she wanted the coin to end up with Mindy. She would tell Christine how she lost it in the chaos... anything but the truth.

But then again, long-lasting relationships were built on truth. She would spill it sooner or later and honesty would be the best medicine for a wounded heart. Mindy Caldwell may not have been related to Christine, but she was a worthy recipient.

At this realization, her heart failed her, and she succumbed to tears of grief. When Agent Marks emerged once again, he returned empty-handed.

"The ME and forensics crew are going to determine cause of death. That you apparently moved the body will be easy to see."

"If I didn't trip on her arm, no one would have ever found her," Taleah said, wiping the tears away.

Agent Marks held out his hand to help her up. As the pain in her leg and head began to throb harder, he wrapped his arm around her shoulder and assisted her back to the setting where the family had been tied up. The paramedic waited there with an ATV and silently loaded her into its padded back seat.

Before the paramedic drove away, Agent Marks approached her side and frowned. His expression seemed to indicate an unspoken remorse or some deeper meaning, but whatever it was, he managed to hide his intention long enough to engage her with conversation. Taleah massaged her temples even as he stretched out his hand to shake.

"I didn't get to thank you for your help," he said. "Maybe someday you'll be able to forgive me."

Taleah said nothing. She exerted no pressure when she shook his hand. The sooner he was out of her life for good, the better. She promised herself not to think about him.

"And send Reggie and Willis my greetings. I'm getting on a plane back to Salt Lake. Taking a day or two off while the forensics team pieces it all together. And then I'll look at all the evidence and close the case."

As the paramedic steadily accelerated away, Agent Marks only stood and watched until he was out of sight. The thought of seeing her father again built a lump in her throat. His joy in for her survival would mute the blank sensation that came from finality. Reggie knew an end when he saw it, he always said. She wanted to present the case to him, tell him the truth about what had happened, and leave out nothing. She owed it to him. Not for saving her life or to finally put the history of Art Rassine to rest. Not for accepting her truth with Christine, and not for anything but being her father.

29
Black

SAINT Abigail's Hospital stood tall, clad in red brick and white concrete, amidst the historic buildings of downtown's east side. The neighborhood retained its stately charm, even as the hospital complex claimed more and more territory. Some considered it 'Exhibit A' on the need for strict comprehensive planning due to the small residential blocks being gobbled up by auxiliary buildings and garages. One street had been dead ended to make way for the emergency entrance, while a garage allowed another street to cut underneath it.

It was nearly midday by the time the hospital released her. The haze of the nightmare had drawn black curtains over her soul, but the daylight seemed to erase the memory and replace it with a dull throb in her temples. Her mother and Christine had come to visit while she was under the influence of painkillers. Christine's kiss had been sweet, but Taleah wished she could forget Anna's sobs, which stabbed at her gut with such raw power that, rather than pity, only afforded her matching tears. When the CAT scan had indicated no signs of concussion or other major damage, Taleah felt surprised.

The elevator ride to where Emmanuel rested was short. When she got off, she passed an ice dispenser, a snack machine, and the nurses' station. Taleah knocked before entering the room. The walls were clad in some kind of beige, patterned wallpaper and trimmed with wooden chair rails and a thin crown moulding, part of which had been removed. Emmanuel's eyes widened when she entered. He adjusted his bed so that he was sitting up and waited for her to speak.

"I thought I should drop by now that the ER let me go. After I showed Agent Marks... the rest of the scene, he escorted me to my car. Christine showed up. This is our first stop in town, but we both thought it would be better if I come up alone."

"How are you?" he asked. He winced slightly as he reached for a drink on the table, and then sat back. His body language and her hospital stay had somehow worked to cool her emotions and allow rationality to prevail.

"In a lot of pain," she said. "But still standing."

"Have never been in an American hospital," he said, glancing at the cabinets and the sink. He laced his fingers across his stomach.

"Is it what you expected?"

"Everyone always complains about how it is so bad here," he commented. "I do not understand. It is better than I imagined. Always compare to Jordan. But there is no comparison."

Taleah leaned her head, considered a response, and stretched her back. "It's good to see you in one piece. What did the doctor say?"

"The ankle is only a bad sprain. The x-ray machine did not show fractures. They put me in the CAT scanner because they worried about concussion symptoms. And they gave me drugs. They will not let me go home until they are satisfied."

"It was so stupid of me to expect you to come with me," she said somberly. "I don't even want to ask why you did. I would probably have told you 'no.' And then I got you hurt, which I'm mad at myself about."

He shook his head and slightly wrinkled his nose. "I do not have any true friends here. Except you. In university, you were nice. I felt that day when you needed help with your newspaper assignment was the day I knew."

"What did you know?"

"You were different. I studied your eyes."

She flashed a faint smile and relaxed her shoulders, thinking back to that day where, with Jalene next to her, she'd broken one of the rules and got personal with an interviewee. It was a necessary move, of course, but she hadn't quite realized how deeply he'd looked, and she didn't want to know what she'd found. "You do that a lot."

"A person cannot lie through his eyes," he said. "And you have never lied to me with your tongue. I saw you needed help. Then the killer murdered a good man, who helped me on a lot of projects. I had responsibility to help."

"Still, though," she said, "I got you hurt."

"You didn't," he said quickly. "He did. But it was worth it. I do not think any of that family would have survived if you did not take me."

"He would have killed me, too," Taleah said, allowing her eyes to narrow. Her voice had grown mellow and somewhat distant, stretching her intended inflection into a haze that obscured what she really meant. "He wouldn't have had to stop when he was choking me or"—a tear squeezed out of her eye—"or smashing my head with that branch. If you hadn't taken him on, even though your ankle had to hurt like hell."

"I am not a good fighter," he said. "I did what I had to."

She stepped toward him, bent at the waist, and wrapped her arms around him. "Anyway... thank you. And if you want to hang out some-time—"

"I would enjoy that," he said. "But your girlfriend?"

"She'll love to get to know you, too," she said. "Unless it makes you uncomfortable."

He shook his head and Taleah straightened her back to smile at him. Smiling felt so uncommon that it immediately gave her a rush of adrenaline. The air was cool to her lips, as if she were wearing a minty lip balm. The motion of her muscles seemed to lift up her heart, letting the pain and anger drip out the bottom.

"I'll call you," she said.

Christine waited in the main lobby, leaning against a red brick-clad column at the top of a wide, tiled stairway. Now that her muscles could move freely, the aches started to ebb. When they got into Christine's car, which she'd parked on the bottom level of the underground garage, Christine perched sunglasses on her face and smiled.

"I guess we're going to a hotel. "Your dad is out already but wasn't ready to go back home yet."

Taleah's eyes squeezed shut. She pried them open, rested her palm on Christine's, and waited for Christine to start the car. She wound through the traffic, past the hospital Reggie had been admitted to, and into a four-story hotel building adjacent to the city's biggest and oldest shopping mall.

Christine guided her to his room. Taleah knew something was wrong the instant she closed the door behind her. The room was so dark that she could barely see him. He sat on the edge of the bed with a box of tissues on the nightstand next to the lamp. No lights and no television brightened the room. The shades were drawn. She stepped forward, sat next to him on the bed, and sighed painfully.

Reggie's shoulders convulsed. He rubbed his eyes. For a long time, she didn't know what to say. The silence seemed to last forever, but it was not insistent on conversation. Instead of saying anything, she rested her palm on his knee and glanced at Christine.

"You tell me you got him," Reggie grunted.

"I did," Taleah said. "He's dead, but... Chloe Kleinman. She didn't make it. And I found her. Mindy."

"I remember her," he said. "What did she say?"

Taleah frowned, lowered her eyes to her lap, and drifted toward sleep. When he moved, she opened her eyes and, realizing that she didn't answer his question, stammered. "I mean... It's..."

"You've had a long night," he croaked in the darkness. "I understand you were friends."

"I was too late," she whispered.

"You were not," Reggie said, his voice gruff and cracking. "I got a call from Agent Marks, explaining all that happened. You should feel lucky to be alive."

"I don't," Taleah said. "It hurts. Everything hurts. It's like every time I open my eyes, every time I look back—there he is, standing in the dark in the rain. The shine in his hair from the grease. And his voice. It's shit. It's torture. And killing him didn't make it feel better."

"It's not supposed to," he said. "But you know it's over now. At least you have closure so you can start to reassemble the pieces. Me, I'm not so lucky."

"Dad." The tears flushed her eyes before she even felt them coming. They seemed to sting on her cheeks like some kind of hot acid that could eat away her skin, leaving only mush and bones. She sniffed, leaned against his shoulder, and groaned, "Goddammit."

Come to me.

He stroked her hair impatiently, without regard for the dried blood. With every second, his touch grew tenderer. Moments later, his shoulders lurched. He reached for the tissue and attempted to steady himself.

"Rebekah's gone," he whispered. "When your mom and I divorced, that was different. I can't take this."

The agony within her heart spiked. Where it had felt elevated, it sank to a new low, to the darkest of black, where only one kind of light could react with it. Every flaw and blemish magnified. If she could truly break, she thought, her heart would be shattered into a million pieces, each carrying the tiniest speck of pure white.

Her father's sobs began to fade. As the tears on her face dried, she drifted to sleep. Buried deep in the conifers, her heart rumbled. She was no longer running. Her legs strained and stiffened and her head ached. He stood before her, a hulking shadow against the dark backdrop of the forest. Moonlight highlighted the greasy, curled ends of his long hair. In his hand, he carried what looked like a staff, a long, stretched shadow with a pointed end. If he flexed his muscles, he could snap it in two and hurl the fragments into her soul. There he waited, menacing, but never moving to attack. The world drifted into ultimate dark before she opened her eyes.

Christine sat next to her patiently, waiting for the waves of endless guilt to pull away. She rested a palm on her shoulder and her eyes, tinged with sorrow, seemed to sparkle as they burrowed deep into her heart. "I love you," she said.

30

Ethereal

THE keyboard lit afire as her fingers conducted a symphony on white. Her heart poured from her chest onto the pages as she pounded away at the keys for more than four hours, long after Christine had gotten into bed. It wasn't the time, she promised herself. It was the experience. The first words and sentences were stubborn and forcing them out felt like ripping out her entrails, but once those sentences faded from memory, the blood flowed more smoothly.

The passion, the energy, and the agony spilled out of her as she typed, unaware of time's passage. When she slammed the period onto the last sentence, she rubbed her eyes, looked up at the clock, and wiped a tear from her cheek.

Jalene had told her to write, to not let anything get in the way, and just put words on the page. She'd promised that if she began the journey, the words and emotion would come easier.

The result didn't read like a diary entry any more than the Bible resembled a medical glossary, but the words jumbled together in cohesion better than she imagined. It would take hours, even days to rewrite the whole into something worthy of print.

The four thousand words reminisced on the history of Art Rassine before digging into the numbness prescribed by violence. Taleah took two days to fully recover. Jalene implored her to take as much time as she needed, so she wrote at home, knowing that Monday morning, her experiences would become known to thousands of avid readers. Sharing that bit of her felt like exposure, but the story needed to be told, and Jalene knew that only one person could tell it.

Rebekah's funeral would be Saturday morning and by that afternoon, her energy would be spent. She grappled with the concept of death as she faded into dreams. What did it feel like? Did a white light shimmer and expand from the tiniest pin prick until it overwhelmed her with nothing but white? Was it like an empty room where the walls were merely a canvas on which to paint her soul? And in the midst of it all, how would she view the survivors? Would she be forced to stand in line with Mindy, Chloe Kleinman, and Art Rassine himself?

When the hours bit into the morning, Taleah awoke on the couch with a headache. The day spelled pain and misery. It was something inescapable for now, but there was always something sweet that lingered somewhere beyond that veil and tasting it meant stepping forward.

The mourners filled nearly every pew in the chapel. The tears cascaded down her cheeks even before the first words were spoken. Christine volunteered to follow the hearse to the cemetery. Taleah skipped most of the makeup and decided on wearing just a splash of black. She waited for almost everyone to leave, except for her father and Christine before she stepped forward and knelt before the casket. She frowned, clasped her hands together and spoke softly.

"I'm sorry. You were always there for me in everything I needed. I never expected you to be my mother, or even a close confidant, but somehow, even those words feel insignificant now. I never meant for any of this to happen. Please forgive me."

Christine gripped her shoulder and helped her to her feet. Reggie stood behind her, clutching his heart with both hands as if to shield it from the most powerful emotions. His face gleamed as tears trickled from his eyes.

"You are not responsible," he choked.

She said nothing, only nodded and looked to her feet as she slowly turned away from the casket. She didn't blame herself. But the burden was so severe that she needed someplace to deposit the weight, if only for a few moments.

Drained from giving up, from fighting the torment, and from the glare of the sun, Taleah collapsed into bed in the early afternoon. Nightfall draped over the city quickly as she awoke. Christine sat beside her, kissed her forehead gently, and massaged her shoulders.

Monday sped away quickly as she worked to edit some of the stories about Rassine and the case of the bombing. Jalene greeted her with a hug instead of her customary handshake. And later that night, Christine suggested a trip.

Taleah rolled her eyes when the destination formed on Christine's lips. "Table Rock."

"God," Taleah said. "If I see one more cross…"

Christine wobbled slightly at the sarcasm but remained firm. She closed her eyes, nodded, and spoke kindly. "I don't remember seeing any crosses. It was the most unchristian Christian service I've ever seen."

In that, Christine had a point. Taleah finally relented. They departed for the mountain before sunset. The clouds glowed with orange as the sun sank toward the flats beyond Lake Lowell, obscured by the haze of pollution. On clear days, the mountains in Oregon would be visible from this height, but the air didn't allow circulation, which caused the smog to settle in. When the orange faded into a cool blue that grew darker as the minutes rolled by, Christine clutched Taleah's shoulders tighter as they reclined in the backseat. She mouthed something to herself and then waited for Taleah's breath to settle.

"Beautiful night," she said.

Taleah grasped her hand and kissed her cheek. "Only because I'm sitting here with you. You never told me last week what you wanted to talk about."

"I had to wait," Christine said. "You don't ask for a raise the same day you buy a car."

Taleah opened her eyes and smiled, before issuing her a sideways glance. "Why is that? Does your need for transportation depend on your paycheck? Or does the salesman inherently know he can target you for a higher price?"

"You know what I mean," Christine said.

"Oh." She pursed her lips and gazed out at the city lights, which seemed to sparkle all the way to the horizon, shooting up orange, yellow and blue spikes into the sky, where the different colors mixed in a splendor of lucid light that seemed to dance like the aurora. Up here, the darkness and light down below offered peace and serenity. The cool white glow of the cross overhead highlighted Christine's face so naturally that it took her breath away. "Oh."

"So I'm asking for a raise," Christine said. "I think we deserve it."

"I mean…" Taleah stammered. "Wait. I'm not good with this kind of stuff. You know me, the ultimate literalist."

"You see the nuance in things better than anyone I've ever met," Christine protested.

Taleah shrugged. "Maybe you'll have to ask me nicely, like when I asked you out."

"I remember that night," Christine said, creasing her lips. Her heart rate seemed to ratchet up every second.

"I'm sorry," Taleah recited. "I seem to have misplaced my pen. Do you want to have coffee with me?"

"Of course," Christine explained, "I didn't know what you were really asking, or I would have giggled and sprinted into the hallway like some sixteen-year-old prom queen after the football captain made a fool of himself."

"Sure," Taleah said.

"But you already knew, which is why you were interested in the first place. I made the connection during my class later that evening, when someone said something about you."

"That was awkward," Taleah said softly.

"Not as awkward as this," Christine said. She struggled against Taleah's body and Taleah pulled away just enough to allow her to move. In the waning seconds, she stared out into the dusk and took in the glow of the sky, allowing it to touch her soul with that same graceful light.

When Taleah looked down, the sparkle caught her eye. Christine said nothing as she held the tiny black box in her outstretched palms, which hovered over Taleah's lap. The diamond reflected back the white light from the cross, which sparked Christine's eyes with the miracle of true love. Taleah forced the box closed in Christine's palms, leaned over, sealed her eyes and kissed her.

Only one thing could make this night more perfect, she told herself, and Christine was strict when it came to alcohol. After Christine drove home, they sat in the candlelight on the couch, sipped on the wine and talked until bedtime.

The end of the era should have filled her with expanding emptiness as time faded away. This time, only one emotion reigned, and it was the most important one of all.

Acknowledgements

Dear loyal reader,

This book has been a long time in the making. I would like to take this space to explain how it came about and to thank those involved in the process for their assistance.

When I wrote *Era Sinistra*, I didn't know there was going to be a sequel, let alone two of them. This idea came to me separately and sprouted from an image of a tank farm in chaos and two people being injured in the blast. This was going to be a standalone story until Taleah emerged as the main character. She references her traumatic experiences often, and it became clear soon after that this was, in fact, going to be a second sequel to the series.

My characters surprise me often, even those I have been writing about for years. They tell me who they are along the way, and older characters tell me how they have changed.

This novel has been a joy to write, and I hope that joy extends to you, the reader. It was not always easy. Some people tend to think of thriller writers as heartless monsters to inflict so much pain upon their characters. This isn't really true, however. Writing the ending of this story pushed me to the limit and nearly devastated my spirit.

I feel that this story should not be so controversial. The divisions in our society are hard to witness right now and these are conversations we should be having if we as a people ever hope to heal the gulf between 'sides.' This story humanizes the discussion. I believe in treating all people as people, equal and one, not as 'them' or this group, that race, or this religion.

I would like to thank you, the loyal reader for your patience and for your eagerness to read these stories.

Second, my thanks go to Jeanine Henning, who continues to develop stunning covers for my books. She is an incredibly talented artist and illustrator. A book's cover is as important as any other aspect.

Third, I would like to once again mention Elayne Morgan at Serenity Editing Services. She does a thankless job, a job which is better unseen, digging into the tiniest details to ensure consistency and voice. Having a second set of eyes is invaluable and Elayne finds issues that authors' eyes cannot see.

Finally, I would like to give a shout out to my wife and my daughter. For emotional support, matters of believability and relatability, and for simply giving me the time to put in the work, my gratitude has no equal.

Now that all of that is finished, allow me to share some exciting news with you. The original *Era Sinistra* has been on my mind since I finished writing the sequel. It was probably the most necessary installment in the series, and writing the second and third books have opened my eyes to what could have been. And now that that first book is out of print, I have decided to rerelease it. This isn't simply a rerelease. The entire book is getting a makeover. Major rewriting is underway, and when that is complete, the novel with get a brand-new cover and a new title. Look for *Era Sinistra-Nova* at some point in the future, when I get down to re-envisioning the concept.

More rerealeases of older books are in the works and I'm excited to share them with you.

I hope you have enjoyed this book. More exciting projects are in the pipeline, so stay tuned!

-bm

About the Author

Brad Mathews bends genre rules by creating dynamic, unorthodox characters thrust into criminal investigations.

He is known to use abstract imagery to construct striking realities that build into suspenseful mystery tales.

Mathews is Certified in Plumbing design, and his extensive Building Information Modeling experience gives him a unique ability to detail mechanical and industrial settings in his novels.

Mathews resides in Boise, Idaho with his family.

Also By Brad Mathews

Things Wrapped in Plastic
Vacancy
Rain Dance
Where the Nightmares Rehearse

Thousand Branches Series
The Thousand Branches
The Venom Storm
The Satyr of Fulton Manor
Tomb of the Phoenix

Era Sinistra Trilogy
Era Sinistra
Era Sinistra-The Shadow
Era Sinistra-Skyglow

Decay
The Girl From South Track
Revelation